FOR SPACIOUS SKIES

Johny Sundstrom

FOR SPACIOUS SKIES

Land of Promise – Book I

Johnny Sundstrom

Also by same author:
Dawn's Early Light
(available from Xlibris)

To order additional copies of this book, contact:
Xlibris
844-714-8691
www.Xlibris.com
Orders@Xlibris.com
552387

This story takes place during a migration from western Virginia to southern Oregon following the War between the States.

dedicated to

Boyd Upchurch
(1919-2013)
Mentor and Friend:

a fine writer and a southern gentleman whose grandfather's finger was shot off at Appomattox in one of the last battles of that War.

Acknowledgements

*I would like to honor and thank
my parents, Lee and Phyllis, who
taught me the Bible and its stories*

*Special thanks and admiration for
Felisa Rogers, author and blogger,
who proof-read this novel, and provided
significant assistance in correcting and
editing language and time-lines.
She has been a tremendous help*

*I am also grateful to Lisa Shultz Tucker
who proof-read and provided valuable
comments on the first complete draft.*

*Cover photo by Rosemary Pazdral
Author photo by Maximilian Länge*

Author contact: <siwash@pioneer.net>

"Now the Lord said unto Abram,
Get thee out of thy country,
and from thy kindred,
and from thy father's house,
unto a land I will shew thee . . ."

Genesis 12:1

Part I

Virginia

April 1865-November 1866

CHAPTER ONE

Aftermath

Abe Saunders was wounded on the morning of General Lee's surrender at Appomattox, during the final battle of the Army of Northern Virginia. He'd been sent west from Danville, where President Davis and remnants of his cabinet had stopped on their flight from the fallen capital of Richmond. His instructions were to find Lee and deliver a message from the President to the General. Saunders didn't know the exact contents of the message, but from conversations overheard at headquarters, he surmised it contained instructions for terms of an armistice, should it occur.

Making his way on horseback by way of back roads, and not knowing the countryside, he was fortunate to meet a local farmer. The man was fleeing with his family and possessions loaded on a large hay wagon, and he told Saunders he'd heard Lee's army was in full retreat, stopping only to make delaying moves against the Union forces, and that the battlefront was probably some twenty miles ahead. The lieutenant rode hard all night as best he could, until he heard the sounds of small arms fire directly ahead of him.

At daybreak he left the country, galloping his horse overland across numerous fields. He was headed in the direction of some smoke he could barely see rising in the early morning April mist. As he picked his way through a stand of timber, he was suddenly confronted by a patrol of troops in tattered blue uniforms. He wheeled his horse around and fled, only to be shot in the elbow, knocked off balance by the impact, barely able to stay on his horse. He ripped the scarf from around his neck and, racing back the way he'd come, he managed to wrap it around the bleeding arm and its torn sleeve. With the sun now rising, he pushed the horse forward until he found a rutted wagon road stretching in front of him. He turned onto it, swung back toward the west, and rode as fast as he could.

He arrived at Appomattox Courthouse, a small village and local government seat, and was deeply relieved to see gray uniforms ranked across the road near a large, proper house and grounds. As he pulled his horse to a stop and slid from its back, two young soldiers approached. Awkwardly saluting with the hand he'd been using to cradle the wounded arm, Saunders staggered forward until the men caught him and half carried him toward the gate of the house.

"I need Lee—" he said, gasping for breath through clenched teeth, "—message from the president."

"Here, sit down, here on this bench." One of the soldiers steadied him as the other ran off toward the nearest band of officers, gathered near carriages lined out along the muddy roadway. In a matter of minutes, two officers headed toward the wounded man. Saunders was having trouble focusing his vision and staying conscious, but still he attempted to stand and salute the two men. The soldier beside him held him down.

"He just rode in here from that road by the church, says he's got a message for the general, message from the president."

"I'm Colonel Ridgestone. Can you tell me your name and assignment?"

"Lieutenant Abraham Saunders, 3rd Cavalry, attaché to President Davis, his assistant chief of staff. I have a message from the president . . ." He lost focus and fell backward, nearly off the bench and out of the grasp of his supporter.

"The message, written or spoken?"

"Written, in here." He brushed his good hand against the front of his coat.

The colonel reached inside the coat and withdrew an envelope. He turned to his companion.

"Get this man medical attention, quickly."

The sky was clearing directly overhead, and there was the sound of many horses arriving at once. Saunders lost consciousness and crumpled back against the soldier now standing behind him. A medic ran up and began cutting the scarf and sleeve away from the wound. The colonel with the message had run to the front stairs of the house and was escorted inside just as General Grant and his large party arrived, dismounting or climbing out of carriages. The sounds of gunfire from the east had died away.

Six days later, the news of Lincoln's assassination reached the straggling remnants of the Army of Northern Virginia. By this time, Abe had regained some of his strength and was using his good arm again. He'd been assigned to help drive one of several wagons carrying other more seriously wounded soldiers. They were moving south and west, away from the scenes of skirmishes and continued hostilities, away from the troops who had either not heard of the surrender, or ignored it. Every hour brought more rumors of what was going on behind them and what lay up ahead. The small caravan was headed to the town of Big Lick, and for this six-wagon convoy of the wounded, there was nothing to do but keep moving, hoping they'd be left alone.

"What's your name, soldier?" asked the doctor who was riding with Abe on the seat of the wagon. "We haven't been introduced, except in surgery."

Abe was about to answer with his name and rank, as was the usual formality, but he hesitated long enough for the doctor to prod him again. "Your name, soldier, and don't worry, we'll all have new and different names before this is over, so you might as well use up the one you were given." He laughed loudly and his teeth nearly lost hold of the shredded cigar held tightly between them.

"You're right, I was thinking about my name," the young man said. "But, all right, I'm Lieutenant Abraham Saunders."

"Well, I'm Doctor James, and that's either my first name or my last—can't recall." He gave out another burst of laughter. "And you're from the president's staff, or were. You talked about it in your delirium while I was trying to decide whether or not to saw off that arm of yours." He laughed again, quietly this time. In the wagon behind, men moaned as they bounced over a particularly rough stretch of road.

Their wagons each carried a staff with a white flag attached behind the seat. It was hoped this would be enough to allow free passage through this area where Union troops were still engaged in mopping up operations and securing the countryside. Abe remained weak from loss of blood and had to hold on to the seat for security. His wounded arm, the left one, was heavily bound and immobilized, with what remained of his coat sleeve pinned up to his collar to act as a sling. The jarring of the wagon on the worn-out road kept his teeth clenched tight as he struggled to suppress the sounds of his pain. Off in the distance they could see what they hoped was the smoke from hearth fires in the town of Big Lick, and not just more burning and pillage.

A little over a week ago he'd received a letter from his home in Middleburg, North Carolina, informing him of bad news. The sadness of losing both his father and uncle to the enemy was hard to take. He only hoped that his mother was still alive and safe. The beautiful young woman he was engaged to, Irene Ruth Foley, was supposedly out of harm's way and awaiting some word from him. All of this news had come in the last bag of dispatches to reach Davis and his staff, just before they rushed to begin their final retreat. Irene . . . Irene Ruth . . . Irene, Irene, Irene . . . if only he had one of those new photographs to carry with him next to his heart, to hold up to his lonesome eyes for comfort and consolation . . .

"What're you thinking about, young fella?" It was the doctor.

"Nothing much."

"A girl. Ten cents to a dollar it's a girl. You left her behind. And have you heard how she is? Irene, I think you said her name was while you were thrashing about on my operating table."

"Yes sir. I won't deny it."

"Well, how is she, where is she?" He spit the soggy cigar butt from his mouth and began searching his coat for another.

"She's all right, sir, or she was when she wrote this message to me." He pulled a worn sheet of paper from his inside pocket. "What is most critical for her situation is whether or not she will be trapped between Sherman's troops and her home in Carolina."

The doctor succeeded in finding and lighting a new cigar, which he immediately began chomping into a facsimile of the previous victim of his front teeth. "Well, son . . . God bless her and her family. Hopefully Sherman and his boys are hell bent on getting back home to their own sweethearts now that this mess is wrapping up."

Suddenly the lead wagon stopped short in the road ahead. A small group of horsemen emerged from the woods; the men waving rifles and shouting at the driver.

"Well, hell, I reckon it's time to plead for mercy," the doctor said as he handed the reins to Abe and climbed down to the ground. He walked forward along the line of wagons and shouted to the horsemen, "Medical transport. Guaranteed safe passage here, there, and everywhere."

"Union men or Confederate mules?" a man shouted back. His three comrades had their rifles shouldered and aimed at two of the drivers and at the doctor.

"I'd say we're neither anymore, now this whole terrible mistake has ended." The doctor was now standing next to the spokesman of the group. "Cigars?" He held four of them up as an offering to the ambushers.

The man leaned down and grabbed for them, and the doctor jerked them back out of reach. "We're a medical caravan. Let us pass."

Now he held out the cigars again and this time he didn't do anything to prevent the mounted man from taking them out of his grip.

"We don't give a damn about you bastards. Have you got any foodstuffs?"

"Almost nothing, but you're welcome to share in what we've got. In the third wagon you'll find salt pork and moldy bread. Have at it, sir." And with that the doctor turned on his heel and walked back to rejoin Abe on the wagon.

The horsemen surrounded the third wagon and one jumped down to rummage around in the bed. Just as he lifted out a sealed crock that looked to contain brine and meat, one of the wounded lying in the wagon's bed with the supplies jerked upright and twisted his crippled body so he could aim his pistol straight at the face of the Union raider.

The wounded man spoke slowly and loud enough for the group to hear. "This here War's over and if's you take our stuff, you're no more than a common thief."

"Whoa, boy. You might live a little longer if you ain't stupid. Gimme that pistol."

There was silence except for the loud click of the hammer being cocked. The doctor shouted at the wounded man, "Drop that gun, soldier, or you'll get us all killed."

A shot rang out as one of the mounted riflemen fired into the wagon, and then another as the pistol discharged as it dropped from the dead man's hand.

"Now, who wants to be next?" one of the Union men said, climbing into the driving seat of the wagon with the supplies and the now dead man in its bed. One other wounded soldier lay in the wagon. The soldier in tatters of blue pushed him out, leaving the dead man alone. "Take my horse, kid," he said to one of the mounted men, "and let's get out of here before we have to kill the rest of these bastards." He slapped the reins on the butts of the emaciated horses and got the wagon moving.

The doctor stepped out in front of it. "You'd be doing me a favor if you leave us the foolish one. I'm held responsible to deliver every one of 'em to the hospital up ahead."

"Suit yourself," the driver said.

"Abe, climb down and help me roll him out of that wagon." Then he shouted at the rest of the convoy, "and don't anybody else do anything foolish while these blue-coats take their leave."

Abe slid down off the wagon seat and struggled to get into a position where he could help the doctor unload the fresh corpse. With only one working arm he didn't see how he could be much help, but he did manage to assist in lowering the tailgate.

The doctor mumbled to him, "See if you can slip that pistol into your dressings there. It's the only one we've got."

Abe thought he might be selected as the next fool himself, but it was an order. He could die following an order, but then many men had. That's what war was all about, following orders and dying. Irene Ruth, he thought, forgive me if I'm wrong about this. Then as they jostled the bleeding body out the back end of the wagon, Abe slipped the man's gun into the snug place where his pinned-up sleeve held his arm tight to his side. The raiders were laughing at something one of them had said, and then yelling for Abe and the doctor to hurry up.

The body slid into the mud of the road and the driver whupped the horses into a bit of a trot as the whole bunch hurried off with the wagon and its foodstuffs.

"Ain't going to be over for a long time yet," the doctor said. "Give me that pistol, son, you wouldn't be able to hold it steady enough to aim if we needed it."

Abe slipped the gun free of his sleeve and handed it over.

"I didn't even know he had this. Now, let's get back on the road. You boys that's able get down here and throw these two into that there other wagon. Getting late."

It was near dark when they pulled up in front of a partially damaged brick building with a torn hand-painted banner that spelled out, Big Lick Free Hospital. Although the place looked abandoned from the outside, they could hear the muffled sounds of screaming from within.

"All right, boys," the doctor yelled out. "Get 'em down off the wagons and those that can walk, head inside." He turned to Abe, saying, "You go in, and see if there's stretchers and folks to help carry in the rest of this lot." Just then they heard a commotion up the street from where they had parked the wagons. The rumble of gun carriages and shouting filled the air. Galloping horses came charging along the muddy avenue, followed by artillery and cannons of several types pulled by more wide-eyed horses and driven by men on their backs or riding the guns like charioteers. The doctor grabbed a bystander and yelled a question about what the hell was going on.

"Possible attack down by the river," the man said, and then pulled away and ran off.

"All right, Abe, don't just stand there, got to get these men inside. Hurry in and find us some help."

Although there was hardly any room inside the hospital and no empty beds, they were able to get the fifteen wounded men inside the building and laid out in a long hallway. The dead body was left in one of the wagons. Abe was exhausted from the chaos, and feeling the weakness all over his body from his recovery. He tried to remain standing, waiting for whatever was next, but found himself slumped against the wall and sliding down to the floor, unable to remain conscious.

When he awoke, it was dark outside, as could be seen through a few high windows at the front of the building. He had no idea how many hours had passed, but it was pain in his arm that awakened him. Fresh blood was seeping through the bandage. The whole previous day had been too much and now that it was nighttime there was no sign of any activity other than the occasional sound of screams and yelling from deeper within the building. He looked around for the bodies of the wounded men they'd brought in earlier, but saw none of them. He pushed himself up on his knees and was struggling to stand when Dr. James appeared in the shadowy gloom of the hallway.

"All right, son. Let's take a look at you now. The rest of them are gonna either die or are being taken care of. We made it just in time for a few of those boys." He helped Abe to his feet and led him into a small room lit by a dimly burning lamp.

"I'm all right, sir, I'm sure there's others who need you more."

"That may be true, son, but I need you more."

The doctor unpinned the empty sleeve and removed Abe's coat. He could see spots of freshly coagulated blood where the soggy bandages had been pressed against the wound.

"Haven't got a new coat for you, so I think we'll just have to turn this one inside out when we put it back on. Lay your arm up on this desk. No, don't try to straighten it."

The doctor gently turned the arm so the soggy bandage was in the lantern light. He worked quickly to remove the cloth, suddenly ripping the shirt sleeve away. Abe fought against the pain and the need to scream, but he couldn't stop the moans that escaped his clenched jaws.

"It's alright boy, let it out. You're hurt and you got a right to sing like the rest of these canaries in here." The Doctor swabbed as gently as he could with the clean portions of the rags, trying not to disturb the wound and start up the bleeding again. "Talk to me about anything, your home, where you came from, whilst I wrap this thing up again. Hold it still, this is gonna hurt. This here salve has to go deep."

"I come from North Carolina." He let out a loud yell, biting his lip to shut it off.

"Good, that part's done. Nice country, North Carolina. Did you live by a river?"

"Yes, sir." His jaws clenched almost too tight for any talk now.

"And did you go fishing much?" The doctor tied one knot, and then another.

"Yes, sir, fishing."

"That'll do, soldier. Now let me slip the rest of that coat off and . . ." He turned the coat inside out and helped Abe back into it, expertly fastening what was left of the sleeve into a sling once again. "Now what say we get something to eat? You can walk, can't you?"

They found a meal being served at a church a ways down the street from the hospital. When the smell of food filled his nose, Abe was amazed at how hungry he was. Bowls of stew were dished up for them, with bread on the side. A young woman carried Abe's bowl to one of the tables. She had her head down and her auburn hair kept him from seeing her face.

"Can I get you some hot water to drink?" she said. "I'm sorry but it's all we have."

"Thank you, yes."

As soon as they were seated and served the water, an older gentleman sat down next to the doctor. "You're the doctor, just arrived. Am I right?"

"Yep, that's me."

"Pleased to make your acquaintance. I am also a doctor, but a doctor of divinity, Reverend Doctor Randall, pastor of this church."

The doctor offered his hand and they shook. The reverend just brushed his hand over Abe's shoulder and smiled at him.

"You men must be exhausted. You're welcome to stay here. There's a room with cots behind the sanctuary. You'll never be able to sleep at that infirmary. And then perhaps in the morning we could have a talk. There are some issues I need help with, issues concerning the immediate future of my ministry, of my congregation. The young woman who served you will show you to the room. Bless you, and may you get some sleep, you both look like you need it very much." He stood and bowed slightly, and then moved away to talk with other diners.

That night Abe was restless from the renewed hurt brought on by the re-dressing of his wound, but each time he was awakened by the pain, he was exhausted enough to fall back into a fitful sleep. Each time Abe awoke, he could hear the doctor, breathing deeply and moaning softly. Abe had the thought that this man must be able to sleep through almost anything, having spent so much time at the front lines, and also behind them, in makeshift hospital camps and the like.

When daylight came, he was sleeping deeply, and this time he was awakened by the sound of singing coming from the church sanctuary, the sound of a choir of voices. He pulled himself to a sitting position on the side of the cot and noted that the doctor was already gone. He started to stretch and realized he couldn't, no matter how much he wanted to. So he settled for raising his good arm and rolling his head back and forth. A window high up in the wall showed blue sky above, so different from the drizzly and damp days of the past week. He was able to struggle into his boots using his one good hand, and he stood up, ready to face the unknown of this new day.

He found a toilet room, relieved himself, splashed water on his face and hair with one hand, and then looked around for some kind of towel or rag. There was none, so he brushed the drips from his face, smoothed his hair and wiped his hand on the front of his coat. He realized that this was the first time in months that he'd used running water from a faucet. He smiled at the simplicity and pleasure of plumbing. When he was somewhat cleaned up, he found his way to the back of the sanctuary where he could sit alone in a pew and listen to the singers as they practiced their hymns.

He found himself drifting into a kind of prayerful state brought on by the singing, and the dimly-lit sanctuary, its vaulted ceiling, and the stained-glass windows at either end. It was the kind of place that made you want to quiet yourself and your thoughts and open your heart, but this morning, looking up at the bright colored light coming through the large windows, he couldn't help thinking back to the time he was left all alone in his father's shop. His father and brothers were in the business of fabricating this very type of windows for churches throughout the South. On that particular day, one he would never forget, he'd been reprimanded by his father for speaking rudely to his mother and knew very well he would be punished.

"You have disgraced your mother with your sinful tongue. The boy Jesus would never have spoken to his mother in such a way. You'll be left here at home while the rest of the family goes to the river to fish and have a meal in the outdoors. Perhaps being left behind will help you to gain more respect for your parents. And the next time this happens, you'll be given a session with the Lord's strap. I'm giving you fair warning."

Abe lived in fear of that strap of old harness leather, but not in enough fear to be able to control his sometimes rebellious thoughts and the voice that gave words to those thoughts. He never wanted to speak out to his mother, but sometimes it just seemed that she had no idea how hard it was for a boy to always be on his best behavior. After all, she was, or had been, a girl. And he knew that she often kept his outbursts to herself, not telling his father, and rebuking him with the same words his father would use, but without the same harshness. There were times, however, when she did feel it necessary to report these instances to her husband in her own cautious way, knowing that the punishment would be swift and severe. It was, after all, her duty as a mother to fulfill the charge laid upon all parents by the Good Book, and she was an obedient mother and wife.

That bygone afternoon, when everyone else had left, he wandered through the shop picking up pieces of cut colored glass and looking through all the different partially completed projects. He grew more and more upset at the thought of what he was missing with the family, and how unfair it all was. It was completely unjust that he should be compared to the Son of God whose time on earth was spent as an unnatural human being, born unable to sin while everyone else was a descendant of Adam and Eve and condemned to be a sinner, each and every one. The boy got angrier and angrier as he stomped about among the painted drawings and half-formed images of Jesus the Shepherd, Jesus the King, Jesus on the Cross. Then in a fit of rage at the sight of Jesus the boy helping his carpenter father, Abe lashed out first with his fist and then with his boot, smashing the lower section of the glasswork and jumping back to avoid the dislodged pieces falling from above his head.

Now he was frightened, really frightened. How could he have done such a thing, and what would happen to him now? He knew he would be found if he lied. There was no more severe punishment than the one that came with that sin. Cleaning up the broken shards of color would do no good either because there was no way the securely held frame and its picture could have fallen and broken by accident. He had to get away. He thought of hiding the strap, but that would only increase his father's anger and there were plenty of other instruments of punishment available. No, he just had to get away, but to where?

He ran to the house and grabbed a blanket and a heavy coat, two apples, a chunk of cheese and part of a loaf of bread. Then he fled to the forested land behind the shop, going further into its depths than he'd ever been, until he was above and behind the small town itself, climbing the ridge in a floundering run.

At that moment, the dreadfulness of his reverie was interrupted by a hand on his shoulder. He looked up into the kindly face of Doctor Randall, the church's pastor. The man eased himself slowly into the pew next to Abe and spoke softly.

"I trust you were able to sleep well enough?"

"Yes sir, thank you for the place to rest."

"Did the singing awaken you?"

"I don't sleep very deeply with this," he brushed the arm in its sling.

"Of course. They're almost finished, and then we can talk."

The singing was, in fact, reaching a sort of a crescendo as a woman's voice soloed into the great ceiling of the sanctuary and seemed to vibrate the very air of the space. Then with the fullness of all the voices of the choir, it was done. The singers hugged one another, gathered up their songbooks, and disappeared out the door at the back of their loft.

"We're very pleased with our choir here at Saint Paul's Episcopal Church. They are a dedicated and talented group, making a 'joyful noise unto the Lord.' Wouldn't you agree, my young friend?"

"Yes, they're excellent, sir."

"Before all this destruction descended on our lovely town I used to take walks at this time of day, joining with the rest of life and nature, becoming one with each new day. Now it's been either too dangerous or too chaotic to refresh oneself with the clean air, muted glory and the fresh start of each day's work and reward . . . But what say we walk around this tabernacle of ours and let me show off one of God's homes on earth."

"That would be fine," Abe stood up stiffly and waited.

"And then we'll retreat to the parsonage to break our fast. I'm sure you're feeling some hunger, what with all you've been through."

They slipped out of the pew and Abe followed Doctor Randall down the aisle to the platform and its twin pulpits at the front of the church nave. Abe still couldn't get the broken glasswork out of his mind as he gazed up at the large window depicting the resurrection of Christ in the wall above the choir loft.

As if he knew what the young man was thinking about, Doctor Randall said, "There are certain times of the year when the rising sun actually shines through the image of the sun in this window. It's very early in the morning and I'm usually the only one who sees it, but I have a wish to someday hold a service at that time. If only it happened on Easter morning, don't you think?"

Abe smiled agreement and thought how close to idolatry these things came. It wasn't an original thought, nor was it the first time it had crossed his mind. As a matter of fact, when he'd finally showed up back at home after hiding out in the forest for three days and nights, it was exactly what he'd told his father as his excuse for breaking the glass images in the shop. That they were false images and God prohibited people from worshipping false images. His father held the harness strap tightly in his hands, tugging it back and forth across his thigh.

"I'll think about that, boy. I'll think about that, but only after you've paid the price of your sinful act of wreckage and sacrilege . . . Bend down . . . I'll think about it!"

And then, swinging the strap with full force, he struck. Abe was knocked to the floor of the barn, his face smashed into the loose hay. He bit his teeth together as hard as he could to keep from crying out.

"Get up, boy, get up," his father yelled. Abe slowly pushed himself up on his knees, his body shaking from the deep sobs he fought to keep trapped down inside his lungs. "Now, get yourself up into the loft and don't come down until someone comes to get you." With that, his father turned and stomped out of the building. The boy crawled his way up the ladder to the loft where he lay down and let the choking sounds of his pain spill out into the hay. He couldn't believe his legs weren't broken from the power of the blow against them. He had never been hit so hard, but why only once?

"Are you all right?" Doctor Randall interrupted his memory and he nodded yes quickly. "I thought perhaps you were lost in prayer,' the man said gently, "but it seemed more like you were asleep on your feet. I'm sure you're still in shock from the difficulties of your trip, and of course, from your wound. We can look around more, later. I think now we should get a bite to eat, don't you?"

They left the main church building and walked quickly through a shower of rain to the Reverend's home, which was not far from the much larger building. Within minutes they were being served a fresh, hot breakfast and steaming cups of sassafras tea. Doctor Randall bowed his head and offered grace for the meal and gave thanks for the health and safety of his young guest.

"Go to it, son."

"Doctor Randall, do you know where the Doctor, uh, the other doctor has gone?"

"Ahh, my doctor twin, Doctor James. Yes, I saw him early this morning. He was on his way back to the infirmary. He asked me to take care of you and said he wouldn't need your help today."

"I don't know where he gets his stamina. I've hardly seen him rest since I've been in his care."

They ate in silence for a few minutes. The servant refilled their cups with hot tea, and took away the plates they were finished with.

"Thank you, Mattie. Well, young man, how does that feel to you now?"

"So good. It seems I've been much hungrier since I started healing from this."

Doctor Randall studied him as he sipped his tea. Abe felt a little nervous. He was, after all, a stranger, and he thought that perhaps he was even a fugitive by now.

"Are you a member of any church back when you come from?"

"Yes, I grew up in the Methodist church where we lived."

"Well, that's fine. My goodness, I just realized I don't know your name, or at least I don't know the name you're using," he smiled and went on, "Doctor James told me not to pry, that things are very dangerous right now. But I would like to be able to call you something."

"Yes, sir." Abe was glad he'd already thought about this and was able to provide an answer. "Lester Greene, sir."

"Really, I knew a family by that name down in Georgia. Would that be Greene with an 'e' at the end of it?"

"Yes, sir." He thought quickly. "But I've never been to Georgia."

"Of course, I just thought you might want to have heard of them in case someone else asks. Quite a well-known family from the War of the Colonies. Moved south when it was over."

"I don't think we're related, sir."

"Probably not. So tell me—you've been raised in the faith, a Christian—how has your faith survived this horrible conflict, this terrible War between brothers and states?"

Abe looked down into his cup and took a deep breath. This was not a good question for him to have to answer. For months he had been battling within himself about how he could give acknowledgement to a God who was allowing this carnage and bloodshed to go on and on. He'd even begun thinking to have a look into the history of his family and see what it meant to be a Quaker, as some of his mother's people had been. He glanced up and saw that Dr. Randall was waiting for his answer.

"Well, sir. It certainly gives one a test, it certainly does . . ."

"And what good is faith if it can't be tested? Our Lord had his greatest test the night before he died."

"Yes, sir.

"But war gives a man a different perspective on the Creator's plans, I would say."

Abe wanted to reply, but thought better of it. He'd so often felt that God had turned his back on the whole country, on both sides in the War, but he didn't feel it would be appropriate to suggest that to Doctor Randall, so he remained quiet, hoping it wouldn't be taken as rudeness.

"Well, Lester, I've been thinking a lot about this War and the ways of God, and I'm oft-times despairing of any way to heal this terrible wound we've inflicted on one another in this conflict. Precisely because it's a wound of both the body and the soul of our nation and of our people, no matter which side they've taken. How can God allow for such pain and suffering, such destruction and treachery if He truly cares for all of His children? I have been praying over this matter for the past several years now, and I am still unable to reach any understanding of some of these things."

Abe nodded politely while his thoughts raced to understand how this man of God could speak such apparent sacrilege. It was what he himself would say if he had the opportunity and the courage.

Just then there was a knock at the doorway of the dining room, and a female voice asked softly, "Father, may I interrupt? I'm sorry, but I need to ask you something before I leave."

"Of course, my dear, come in, come in."

The source of the voice entered the room and Abe saw the young woman who'd served them the night before. She was barely full grown, a young woman of startling beauty and brilliant blue eyes. He looked away quickly to avoid staring.

"Sarah Beth, meet my guest, Lester Greene. Lester, this is my daughter."

"Pleased to meet you, Miss Sarah." He'd spoken with his voice, but his eyes said much more about the confusion he felt as he tried to compose himself in the face of such bright and fascinating good looks.

She smiled at him and with a laughing tone said, "Pleased to meet you as well, sir." Abe couldn't tell if she was mimicking him or speaking as herself. She continued, addressing her father now, "I must go to the infirmary. I have promised to be there for most of this day. But I wanted to see if you needed anything before I leave."

"No, dear, I'll be fine. I have this visitor and then I have my studies to keep me busy."

Abe wasn't sure whether he should speak, but he cleared his throat and when they both looked at him, he said. "I must also be going to the infirmary. I'm sure Doctor James can use my assistance, limited as it might be."

"Well, he did tell me to make sure that you were rested. He said he doesn't want a relapse on your part."

"I'm feeling well enough now. Sleep and this delightful meal have done a lot for me." He wiped his one exposed hand with the napkin from his lap and made as if to stand. "I would be pleased to accompany you, Miss Sarah, if that were convenient."

"Miss Sarah Beth to you, Mister Greene. Well, I suppose you might get lost if you try to find it on your own, being a stranger in town and all," she tossed her long auburn hair and turned to go, "I'll be ready to leave in ten minutes."

Doctor Randall gave Abe an amused look when she was gone. "That there is one headstrong girl. Been that way all along. Her mother passed away a few years ago, and Sarah Beth has been in charge of things here ever since, at least in her own mind." He paused and folded his hands across his chest. "Now, let's talk about you. It is my assumption that you may not be able to freely return to your home, either because it has been captured or destroyed, or even because you may have a price on your head. The other doctor told me you had served on President Davis's staff."

A somewhat alarmed expression crossed Abe's face before he could hide it.

"Don't worry," his host continued, "your past is safe with me. In the chaos of these days, I doubt there's much interest here in our town in looking very deeply into anyone's history. We really need all the folks we can get to keep on going here," he paused. "We've lost so many, especially our young men."

"Seems to be true everywhere," Abe said softly.

"Yes, it is. Now, let's talk frankly before the young lady returns to take you away. I spoke with the other doctor about your situation, at least as it is at the present time, and he assured me that you are bright, capable, helpful and also quite courageous when the need presents itself. I am willing to offer you a temporary place to stay with us here, at least while you go through your initial stages of healing, and then we'll see," Doctor Randall said. "What do you think?"

Abe's immediate thought was that he had no plans at all, nowhere to go, and that the minister was correct in suggesting that for him, travel at this time might be risky.

"Yes, sir. I think you're right about my situation, but I am not looking for charity, nor can I accept it without some opportunity to compensate. So, thank you, I'm sure I'll be all right."

"But I need a young man, even one with a wounded wing. I need help around the grounds and buildings of this establishment. Of course more about that when you've got your strength back, but I also need some clerical assistance, just the kind an assistant chief of staff might have the experience for. Are you right handed?"

"Yes, sir."

"Then I presume you'll be able to write soon and do minor recording chores. So, enough said—you think about it. Come back here this evening and we'll discuss it further over supper and perhaps a glass of sherry. Now, get yourself ready. She's never on time, but she never waits for anyone else."

"Thank you, Doctor Randall, you've been most kind. I'll see what the other doctor needs from me and I shall try to return this evening, or send word with your daughter if I cannot. Thank you again, for everything."

He left the room quickly, seeking the door to the outside. The pain had become nearly unbearable over the past few minutes. He wasn't sure what he'd done to cause it. Nothing that he could remember. His teeth were grinding as he crossed the yard. He would have to unfasten the sleeve, loosen the arm and try to move it into a different position. He tried to smile when the sudden thought raced through his mind that his heart must have started beating faster and pumping harder when he saw Miss Sarah Beth for the first time, and blood is a part of swelling.

He found his way to the room where he and the Doctor spent the night, gathered up his cape and few belongings, shoved them into his kit bag. He undid the pins of the sleeve and was able to very slowly drop the arm and extend his fingers. He flexed his thumb and the pain shot up from his wrist to his shoulder, but it was lessening now. If he could get to the infirmary, there would be something for the pain, hopefully, if they hadn't run out. He re-slung the arm just as he heard the young woman's voice calling him, "Lessss-terrrr."

He stabbed the pins into the sleeve and hurried into the sanctuary where she was waiting, a coy smile on her face, and an umbrella folded under her arm.

"I'm sorry if I kept you waiting," he said, "I had to get my things, and . . ."

"No excuses are necessary, Mister Lester Greene. Come." She led the way out of a side door and into the daylight. They passed through the grounds of the church and onto the road. Just then they heard the sound of artillery fire coming from down along the river. Lester quickly moved to the other side of the young woman so that his good arm was nearest her.

"Has this been happening often?"

"The cannons?" she asked.

"Yes."

"Only since the War began," she smiled. "Come along, can you walk any faster?"

"Of course." He picked up his pace to match hers.

Just then a boy with an armful of newspapers came trotting toward them yelling out the headlines, "Union soldiers searching for Davis . . . Union troops . . . searching for President Davis."

Lester motioned him to come closer and he tried to reach into his pocket for a coin, but it was too awkward, as he had to reach across himself to the opposite pocket on his wounded side.

"Here, Jeremy, give me one of those. I'll pay you later." The boy handed a paper to her and mumbled, "Yes'm."

She tucked the paper under her arm to protect it from the drizzle that had started up again. "You can have it when we get there," she said to him. "Now Mister Greene, tell me how old you are, if you don't mind my asking."

They walked around a large puddle and crossed over to the more protected side of the brick street.

"Twenty-four, ma'am."

"Well, I guess you're too young for me then, I'm looking for a mature man to court me, someone of means and with a great deal of experience in the world."

"Yes ma'am."

"And stop ma'aming me. Stand up for yourself. Tell me you're way more than enough experienced for a stay-at-home girl like me, or tell me I'm just a child, or something that shows your backbone, Mister Greene."

"All right," he replied, "how young are you?"

"That's better, and I'm seventeen, almost, and I've been to Richmond and to Petersburg and just about everywhere in Virginia that matters."

"Well, you're far too young to have been many places, but you've made a start."

"My, my, Mister Greene can get a bit snappish now, can't he?"

He stumbled, caught himself and almost reached out for her arm as a sharp groan escaped his sealed lips. She instantly took hold of his good arm and steadied him.

"Are you all right? Are you in pain? Let me help you." She took hold of him and eased him a couple of steps to where he could lean against a building. "Just take your time. I've helped many men walk down the hallway at the hospital. I can certainly help you."

He didn't want to let her know how much pain he was in from the jarring his elbow took when he'd stumbled. "I'll be all right. Thank you."

"You'll be all right someday, but right now you must be more careful and get some good rest. Here, put your good arm over my shoulders and we'll walk slowly. I think you'll be better off at the infirmary."

He did as he was told, trying not to put any weight on her seemingly slight shoulders as they moved slowly down the edge of the roadway. He could see their destination not too far away. Although his head was throbbing, he now felt like he would make it with no more problems. He tried to make light of the situation in his mind and thought about how close he was to her and how strong she seemed to be under his good arm.

A woman caught up with them from behind, calling out the girl's name, "Sarah Beth, I must talk with you."

They stopped and Sarah Beth turned to face the voice. "Why, Mrs. Barton, good day." She slipped out from under Abe's arm, but still supported him.

"And who may I ask is this fine young man?" Mrs. Barton asked.

"Mrs. Barton, this is Lester Greene. He stayed at the church as father's guest last night and I'm helping him back to the infirmary. He was wounded in battle."

"Oh, my dear young man. I must thank you then, we all owe you for your courage and sacrifice. Have you heard they're hunting for the president, Mr. Davis?"

"Yes, we just got the newspaper from Jeremy," Sarah Beth said quickly.

"Well, I really must speak with you. It's about something . . . personal," the woman said.

Abe spoke softly, "I'm quite sure I can make it that far." He glanced toward the medical facility and separated his good arm from Sarah Beth's grasp.

"Are you sure now, Mister Greene?" She lowered her eyes and gave him what he thought was a quick mischievous smile to go with her show of excellent public behavior.

"Yes, thank you. Will I see you later on?"

"Of course."

"Pleased to meet you, ma'am," he said to Mrs. Barton as he moved away, intending to take a couple of strong steps to show Sarah Beth that he was all right, but she reached out, stopped him and stuck the newspaper in the coat pocket under his good arm.

As soon as he was inside the building he looked for a chair or a cot to settle onto before dizziness overcame him and caused him to fall. He found a bench and quickly reclined back with his head on its arm. He twisted so his good hand could remove the newspaper from his coat pocket and used that hand to unfold it. The headline read, "HUNTING for DAVIS." Its dateline was two days prior.

Abe's eyes scanned the text beneath an old photo of the president. The Provisional Union Government of Virginia had issued warrants for the arrest of the Confederate president and some of his officers and staff for conspiracy to murder the president of the United States. He loosened the pages to read what came after that part where it was continued to the next page. There were no other names attached to the article. The text went on to say that evidence of a plot to kill Lincoln had turned up, placing suspicion on the Confederate embassy in Canada, and that it implicated Davis and many of his supporters. It then went on to describe Lincoln's wounds and the grief of his widow and the national days of mourning that had been declared by the Congress. But still no names of any other indicted individuals.

He lay back, closed his eyes and tried to shut out the sounds of screaming and moaning coming from down the hallway. Just then a young soldier stopped in front of him and asked his business.

"I arrived with Doctor James and some wagons of wounded. If he is here, I would like to see him," Abe answered.

"Your name?"

"Please, just inform him that his lieutenant is here, the soldier who accompanied him from Appomattox," he pointed at his injured arm, "with the elbow wound." The orderly saluted and moved off down the hallway.

The doctor wouldn't recognize his new name even if he gave it, and from now on he was going to be careful to whom he revealed his actual identity. He settled back on the bench to wait as comfortably as he could.

CHAPTER TWO

Patrols

After a couple of restful weeks, Abe settled into the role of Reverend Randall's clerical assistant, and also found ways to assist in light work around the church grounds and buildings. It felt good to be using his body, at least in a limited way, after the enforced inaction of recovery. He was getting used to being Lester Greene. Although he'd been unable to find any information linking a Lieutenant Saunders to the Lincoln assassination, he was not about to reveal his true identity in his recently adopted home territory. It had now been six weeks since the wound and Doctor James's repairs seemed to be working. The skin over the joint had healed well, even though it was a bit tight; he couldn't quite move the joint to flex his muscles or newly-healed skin.

The War had ended and the amount of devastation was finally being reckoned up. It was staggering to the South as a whole but especially to the minds of the citizens of Virginia. Since their state had been the site of so many of the battles of the War, the amount of acreage damaged by fire, traffic, shelling and other impacts was nearly incalculable. Great numbers of people were living in camps. For the summer months that would prove adequate, but with the change of seasons and the oncoming winter, a crisis was in the making. Most of the small towns and villages overrun during the War were already looted or stripped of usable items, and very little re-building had gone on. Charitable and church organizations were strapped to their limits and the need for services was rapidly increasing.

The hospital, where Abe had been treated and was now helping out, was one of the busiest places in town, with its convalescing veterans and community volunteers constantly coming and going.

Over the past few months, many of the permanently disabled had been transferred to Fort Lewis on the west of town for temporary holding, but with an unknown future. Abe was glad his injury was not serious enough to make him a long-term physical or mental cripple. As it was, he would accompany Reverend Randall on regular visits to the more seriously wounded at the hospital, and sometimes he carried out visits on his own. The hospital was also the most convenient place for him to spend a few casual minutes with Sarah Beth, away from the church, and where they both had the excuse of duties that called on them. He continued to find her fascinatingly beautiful, and a bit of a mystery by virtue of her uncanny ability to read his mind and make fun of him without any of it seeming mean or cruel. He actually enjoyed her perceptions of his personality and quirks, though with any other near-stranger, he might have found such intimacy offensive.

Sarah Beth was rather proud to be known as the young man's helper when he was making his visits. She was not quite a nurse, but competently helped him in his work as he assisted her father and kept track of these visits and their content. Some of the neighbors and citizens, such as Mrs. Barton, had been quick to whisper that Sarah Beth had eyes for the new fellow staying at the church. However, she had publicly demonstrated such a familiar and even brash way with him that the wagging tongues were by this time more likely to account for the two of them by referring to him as the brother she never had.

She did enjoy his company, but was still unable to get him to talk about himself. As the summer slowly passed, her curiosity grew more urgent every time he avoided a question about his past, where he came from, or what he thought he would do with his life once he was healed. She knew it was rude to press someone the way she did, but he could at least give her some kind of answers. After all, in her mind, she really was his only friend now.

One day while they were strolling back to the church from their afternoon at the hospital, she took hold of his good elbow, steered him into the cemetery adjacent to the church, and quite forcefully sat him down on a bench.

"Now, see here, Mister Greene. You did not start out life in the army in the middle of a War. You act like God himself set you down on this earth, full-grown and ready to fight, but I know and you know that you came from somewhere before that, and you were even once somebody's baby."

He looked up at her flashing eyes and resisted the urge to smile at her outburst. "I guess you're right," he said. "I just don't remember being someone's baby. Do you remember being anyone's?"

She didn't answer as she stamped her foot and walked a short ways away. It was one of those mid-September afternoons, slowly easing its way into the long dusk of a fall evening, with the first hints of a breeze and a slight chill in the air. The leaves on the oaks of the graveyard fluttered and whispered, casting flickering light and shadows on the grassy areas between the graves. In any other situation, it might have seemed like a time for a calm and quiet meditative conversation, respecting the dead who surrounded them, welcoming the end of the humid days of summer. But no, Sarah Beth whipped her bonnet off her head, shook out her long wavy hair and nearly screamed at him.

"No, I don't remember anything. I'm just like you. I came from nowhere and I'm going nowhere, and I'm beginning to very much dislike you Mister Lester Greene!"

He smiled and dared to say, "And I'm beginning to very much like you Miss Sarah Beth Randall."

"Oh you, you're just horrible." She turned on her heel and stomped away down the pathway.

Just then a young soldier came running toward them, waving. He ran right past Sarah Beth and came to a stop in front of Abe. "Sir," he was nearly out of breath, "sir, I beg your attention. I've just come from the fort and the Major wishes to speak with you, right away, sir."

Abe had met the major in charge of the fort located just outside of the nearby Salem township. It had been home to a military operation during the years of the War, the base for protection of the western border of the state. Since surrender, it was used as a home and hospice for the wounded, and as a supply depot for distributing foodstuffs. Under terms of the surrender, these two functions were still allowed and the Union permitted a small contingent of troops, previously Confederate but now under the occupation's jurisdiction, to remain in those quarters as a kind of police force in case of civil disturbances.

"Have you any idea what it's about?" Abe asked.

"No sir, only that the Major told me to tell you he seriously needed someone like you with combat experience."

"But the War is over, and we're not allowed to fight. Not anymore."

"I am only sent to request your presence. He said post-haste."

Sarah Beth had stopped leaving and had been listening. She came closer. "You mustn't go, Lester. It sounds as if there will be danger, and you are in no condition for any such thing."

"Miss Sarah Beth, I can't say no. Even if we're no longer at war, I am still not released from my obligations. Who do you think has provided for my medical care?"

"Well, the army, but whose army? And who is this major?"

"Please go on home and inform your father that I shall be along as soon as I can. He'll understand. I'm sure." He stepped closer to her, and now turned her around and gently pushed her in the direction of the Church. Then he said to the young man, "Come, take me there."

The Major wore the insignias of his rank on a medical uniform jacket. He held out his hand, shook with Lester, and then let his fingers graze the bulge of the still reinforced elbow. "Healing all right, lieutenant?"

"Yes sir, quite well I think.'

"Well, now that Doctor James has left the area, I may want to take a look at it myself, just so we're assured that it is healing as well as can be expected. By the way, I'm Major Callahan, ex-commanding officer of this post, and still in place since no one has replaced me or ordered me to stand down. We are now becoming almost exclusively a medical installation, as I'm sure you know. Come with me to my office where we can talk."

The space was small and filled with medical paraphernalia, military clothing and books.

"And you are Lieutenant Lester Greene, I've heard tell."

"Yes sir."

"Well, I don't really care what name you use son, but I need you for your rank and for your experience."

Abe felt a slight shiver of doubt about the situation in response to the major's allusion to his name. He was apprehensive Doctor James may have revealed his real name in a professional exchange with the major. "I really don't have any medical experience, sir, except for the little I've gained helping out at the infirmary, over the past few weeks."

"Not talking about medical experience, son. I need an officer with a bit of combat expertise, training and background, you know."

"But the War's over."

"Wars don't end just because generals put ink to paper. We have a different kind of battle going on now, son. We've got roving bands of marauding veterans from both sides raiding and pillaging the already stripped and ruined countryside. Winter is coming and these men have no homes, no jobs, and their only skills seem to be what they've acquired in these violent campaigns of the past few years. Have you heard much about these incidents?"

"Only rumors and a few accounts from some of the patients in town."

"Well, they're not just rumors. They're a serious threat to our public safety, and to any chance we may have of recovering from the devastation of this War. There are reports that some of these groups are coming closer to our area, and there is no protection being provided by the Union forces, and the Army of Virginia has been disbanded. We must make ready to defend ourselves, our wounded and convalescents, from this outlawry. There's a small armory here at the fort. There are men who have recovered sufficiently to function physically, but most of these men have nowhere to go, or, if they do, no way to get there. I am asking you to take charge of training and mobilizing a self-defense corps for the fort and for the neighboring communities. How soon can you start?"

"Sir, I'm not sure about this. I have a position with the church, the Episcopal church in town. I am still not very able, and my combat experience was limited to serving as an attaché in two battles. Even then I was then mostly serving in administrative work. I'm afraid I am not really who you need."

"Well, I'm afraid you're all we've got, young man. I'll expect you to report for duty tomorrow at noon. That should give you time to arrange your affairs. You may tell your Doctor Randall that you will still be able to serve his needs on a part-time basis, and to live where you will. Hopefully this won't last very long as an assignment. I'm sure you can find some good men to take over in your place once you have the training program up and running. That will be all, Lieutenant."

Abe stared at the floor, and then looked back up at the Major, who was now counting out some kind of pills and placing them in envelopes. "Yes, sir," he said, as he saluted and turned on his heel to leave the room.

When he neared the church grounds, he found himself realizing that this name issue was getting more and more complicated. And yet, as far as he knew, the danger for members of President Davis's staff had not yet passed, so he would have to live with it. Unfortunately, the false name caused multiple problems; he'd just recently realized that Irene Ruth had no way of getting in touch with him. There may have been letters addressed to Abe Saunders that were returned or had simply disappeared in the post-war chaos. He decided he would write to her the next day, and somehow communicate that he could be reached in care of one Lester Greene, perhaps even at the fort . . .

Doctor Randall and Sarah Beth had waited supper for him, and both of them were curious as to his business with the Major. Sarah Beth had obviously rushed home with the news and shared it with her father. Abe tried to minimize the situation. He didn't want to alarm them with the news of the marauders, and he wasn't sure how they'd feel about his returning to a role in continuing the conflict. When he'd explained as little as he could while still providing answers their questions, it was clear how they thought about the situation.

Doctor Randall listened carefully, but, as Abe answered his questions, it was an effort to keep Sarah Beth from interrupting. After a pause during which she stayed silent, the pastor said, "Well, I would have to say that, as far as I can tell, you are under no obligation. The Army of Virginia no longer exists, and there is as yet no Union presence hereabouts. We are living in a vacuum where the only authority seems to be our old local government and a volunteer hospital. I hope you didn't make a commitment until you've had time to think this through."

"Father, he can't do this. He's still a wounded man, he's working for us now, and he's already said he's finished with war. I heard him say so myself."

"Sarah Beth, my dear, the young man will have to make up his own mind; and he is not so much working for me as he is providing valuable service in exchange for a place to stay and recuperate. This is his decision to make, and it is not up to us."

"Sir, the Major did take my commitment to you into account and said that this new role would be of short duration and not be full-time every day."

"Perhaps we can have a few minutes to discuss this in the morning. When must you give him an answer?"

"I need to go back to the fort for further conversation with the Major tomorrow, sir."

Sarah Beth stood up quickly and shook her head back and forth, "Oh yes, we'll have the men decide in private. Just like they decided to have this horrible War. I won't allow this, and I am the *woman* of this house now. That should count for something." She tossed her hair again and left the dining room.

Doctor Randall settled back in his chair and began filling the after-meal pipe he allowed himself, saying, "Another delicious supper. I don't know what I'll do if Mattie decides to leave now that she's a freed woman."

"I hadn't realized she was actually a slave."

"Owned by one of the families in our church. They moved here not long before the war started."

"Has she spoken of leaving?"

The Reverend blew some smoke toward the ceiling, "Not a single word, but I can't help thinking it's on her mind."

"Well, sir, if you'll excuse me, I have some letters to write."

"Of course. Sleep well and we'll have our little talk in the morning." He smiled and said, "Men's talk."

Abe was perplexed as to how to notify Irene Ruth that he that he was OK and that for now there was no way he would be able to independently arrange to return home. He surely didn't want to mention the possibility that he could be wanted for anything in connection with the assassination, but didn't know how to explain why he couldn't receive a letter from her in his own name. Finally he just wrote that he was staying with a fellow soldier, named Lester Greene, in Salem, Virginia, and that mail was so disrupted that nothing would get to him unless it was sent to someone with a long-time residence in the area. He then went on to describe his wound and the progress it was making, healing rapidly and causing much less pain now. And he did mention the kindness of the local Episcopal minister who had given him some small amount of work so he could earn his keep.

He nearly drifted off to sleep, but wanted very much to have this done with and posted the next day. Who knew what had happened to mail service between here and their home ground? If service existed at all, it could be slow. He also wanted to be honest with her about the lack of prospects for a young man with only one good arm in the aftermath of the War and its destruction. He forced himself to pay attention to the script as it filled the first page and then another, but it was so difficult to address someone he hadn't seen for two years. He had no idea what she was doing or how she was feeling. She may even have almost forgotten him by now. He counted on the depth of his own feelings to serve as a measure of hers in their similar situations. With that thought in his mind, he finished the letter with a tender and simple salutation of "undying affection, Abe," and he planned to post it on his way to the fort next day.

In the morning, Sarah Beth was absent from the daily breakfast, and her father was late. As Abe sat in the dining area alone, his attention was drawn to the pretty dishes affixed to one of the walls. Each plate carried both flower images and text, and he had been told they were the collection of Sarah Beth's mother. Although his two hosts referred to her frequently, neither the girl nor her father had seen fit to provide Abe with any details concerning the woman's death. He only knew that it had been a few years ago and was possibly some kind of breathing or lung disorder.

Doctor Randall entered the room and took his place at the table. "So sorry, young man. There was a misunderstanding about choir practice this morning and I found myself standing in for the secondary school principal, our lead tenor. I'm sure they'll all be glad when he returns from his business in Richmond."

"So travel to Richmond has opened up again?" Abe asked.

"It appears that officials of our towns and institutions have an exemption on the travel bans from the Union highway guards."

Mattie brought in plates of steaming food and placed them on the table. She made a soft sound and stood still, not leaving abruptly as she usually did.

"Yes, Mattie, what is it?" The Doctor said.

"How am I supposed to put good food before you, Doctor Randall, if I have to keep it warm for half an hour after it's ready to serve?"

He took a bite and chewed slowly, "Tastes fine to me, excellent even."

She shook her finger at him and quickly backed out of the room.

"Oh Mattie, Mattie," he said softly. "She's a bit of a perfectionist, have you noticed?"

"Yes sir."

"And also a bit of a tale-bearer, I've heard, so it's best we save our conversation until we're in my den."

They finished the meal in silence, and the doctor exclaimed quite loudly over his shoulder, "Excellent, just excellent." He was answered by silence.

The two men were soon sitting quietly in the minister's den, a room they both used for work and for times of quiet contemplation. The shelves of books that lined the walls had titles and authors from all walks of life, and Doctor Randall had pointed out that he arranged them more by time periods when they were written than by the alphabetical surnames of their authors. He said it gave him a chance to stumble across the unexpected when he was searching for any particular title.

Then the minister cleared his throat and spoke quietly, "And your feelings about fighting and killing these days, have they changed since you were in the War?"

Abe was silent, taken off guard by the abrupt question. He realized he wasn't sure of an answer.

The doctor spoke up again, "Well, let's wait on that for a bit. Perhaps it's better to start with the larger view. I will tell you that, as a so-called Man of God, I have had great difficulty throughout this War because of the absolute surety with which both sides, Confederate and Union, claimed the guidance and support of the Divine Creator of all men. Right and wrong seemed to disappear under the burden of this belief held in common by both sides and by all parties to the conflict. And what did God really have to do with any of this, with either side or with the futility of men trying to see whose side could kill, maim or banish more of the other side? And yet, every Sunday, I was expected to pray for victory for our side."

Abe looked down at his hands and decided to risk saying what he was feeling at this moment, "And did you?"

"No, I prayed for peace, and for the safety of our family members in the horrible situation we found ourselves in, for an escape from the intolerance and hatred that led men into the tragedy of such conflict . . ." he paused, turning to look out the window, "and there came a time when I was rebuked by some of our congregation . . ."

"Rebuked?"

"Literally chastised for not calling on the Lord to give our side the victory . . . Dora, my wife, was one of those who demanded that I use my powers as the shepherd of our flock, her words exactly, to call down defeat on our enemies so we could get this thing over and done with as quickly as possible."

"What did you do?"

"With the congregation or with my wife?"

"Well, I guess either, or both."

"It was difficult . . . I think any man of conscience will have a difficult time in periods of crisis, such as our recent War. I did not take it as any sort of exceptional prejudice against either myself or my thinking, I simply tried to find ways of satisfying those who refused to understand that thinking, and I accepted that there would be those who would never understand me. Dora was a different case altogether. She was just as devoutly impatient with the foolishness of all the killing and devastation as I was, but her solution was to win the War quickly rather than find a way to avoid it. And her faith was such that she thought God could be prevailed upon to assist in that effort." He paused and reached into a drawer of his desk for a framed photograph. He handed it to his young assistant. "As you can see, she has the same look of determination we often see in her daughter's expressions."

Abe took the picture and held it carefully in the light from the window.

"There is a definite resemblance. And both of them are very beautiful."

"Yes. And both of them are beautiful and confident in their looks and their thoughts. I tried quite unsuccessfully to convince Dora that God might very well be above the futilities of man's wars, but she came back with scripture from the Old Testament that clearly showed God taking the side of the Hebrews in many of their battles . . . But this is really not what we need to be discussing today."

"May I ask, with your permission, what happened with your wife?"

"Pneumonia that wouldn't be cured. She died from the blood in her lungs. Three years ago. There were no competent doctors of medicine left behind for the citizens, or she might well have been saved."

Abe handed back the photo and the woman's husband replaced it in the drawer.

"Now, about you, young man. What will you do, and, more importantly, why?"

"Sir, I think we need to determine if this threat is real. Are there truly armed veterans forming groups for the purpose of taking what belongs to others? Then it is a legal issue and the civil authorities should exercise the right to deputize citizens. In the meantime, if it is true, then the remnants of military authority are obligated to respond."

"Spoken like a staff officer to a President. Be cautious with your language skills. Sounding legally adept may not be in our Lester Greene's best interests."

"Yes sir. I assumed we were speaking to one another in confidence."

"Of course."

"So, you ask why. Why would I help now? And maybe just as important, could I even be of help now," he said as he fingered and smoothed the sleeve of a newer coat that was also pinned to his jacket.

"What would be your duties? I believe you mentioned training?"

"Yes sir, the Major is asking for a short term commitment to train some of the patients, and perhaps some others among the locals."

"Let me speak from the position of a naysayer for a moment. You have no duty to this town or its residents. There is no formal military authority in place, and both my daughter and I have heard you say, with some feeling I might add, that you want no more to do with warfare. And then there is, of course, the role of God's will in your life."

There was a long silence and the older man knew that he was applying rather an undue amount of pressure on the younger man, knew this, but could hardly help himself. He had taken quite a liking to this Lester, and was beginning to rely on him for assistance with the more challenging aspects of his ministry, even with some of the content of the messages he prepared and delivered to those who sometimes doubted his worth even as they depended on him.

"Your questions are fair and prudent," Abe replied. "The answers are much less clear or even available to me at this moment. My obligation to this town and its citizens is simply my obligation to any part of humanity that might find itself victimized by unusual circumstances beyond its control. The question of authority and whether we serve either a military or civilian authority seems to be a practical matter, depending on what is in place at the time. Since my arrival, I have seen very little evidence of any civil authority besides the fire protection units. And although, given that the fort is primarily a medical facility, it is also a garrison with a small armory with a chain of some command, largely based in the person of the major . . ."

"And God?"

"And God . . . Sir, with no disrespect, my experience of God's guidance in my own life is somewhat limited. I have neither felt His hand pushing me forward or holding me back. At times, I must admit that I have felt His absence more than His presence. This War and my part in it have done nothing to change that. I'm sorry."

"Don't be sorry, son. You have every right to depend on your own experience. You are in a very similar position regarding your faith as I was placed in by the challenge to pray for the victory of one side over another. But the Major needs an answer, so I think you must deal with that, and we should plan on continuing this discussion of ours, no matter what you decide . . . and I want you to know this, young man. I will support you in whatever you decide, based simply on an intuition I have that while none of us is particularly chosen by God, some of us are more relevant to his plans than others, and you appear to be one of those. Go forth, and do whatever it is you must do, with my blessing."

Abe stood and nodded his head in heartfelt deference to the older man's empathy and concern. He had a sudden memory of his own father and the lack of trust that characterized much of their time together. No, he thought, that comparison is unfair, and this is a unique blessing and opportunity that has nothing to do with anything else.

"Thank you, sir."

A few days later, he was in the woods above the church grounds, quite a ways away, practicing with a revolver he had secured from the armory. He missed the accuracy of a rifle, but his elbow wouldn't cooperate with the weight of a heavier weapon. He had always been a fairly good shot, learning on squirrels in his youth, and then excelling during military training. However, the truth was he'd only fired a few shots in actual combat.

The woods were a calming and lovely retreat from the bustle of the town. He hadn't realized how much he missed casting about for pathways and noticing small details in the vegetation and life of a forest. It had been years since he'd just wandered for a time in his own company and the surroundings of the natural world. It felt good and he was pleased with the rapid re-acquaintance he'd made with the weapon in his hand. Hopefully he would not have to use it, but the comfort it gave him was essential to the new role he'd so recently accepted.

Just then he heard his name being called out, at least the name he was now using. "Lester, Lester."

Sarah Beth's voice, with something of a singing quality to it, filtered through the trees and blended with birdsongs and the other sounds of a living woodland. At first he was tempted to conceal himself, since he had no place on his person to hide the gun, but then he realized that he wasn't really a secret from her, at least not in his current activities, and she'd probably heard his shots. Her silent treatment following his announcement that he was assisting the Major had only lasted one day before she was plying him with questions about the training course he was designing.

"I'm over here," he hollered. He caught sight of her brightly colored dress and coat, and watched as she picked out a path toward him. He thought how she really was part girl and part woman, and that someday soon that would change once and for all.

She stopped about twenty feet away from him and leaned back against a fallen tree. "You've been shooting," she declared with a scowl.

"Yes, I guess I have."

"If you're not going to be fighting, why do you need to be shooting? Tell me that." Now she took a couple of steps toward him and held out her hand. "Give me that gun, Mister Greene. Don't worry. I'll give it back to you. I just want to see what kind it is."

He stepped closer to her, wondering quite how to respond. As he started to hold out the gun to her, she darted forward and seized its barrel in her hand. "It's still loaded," he said.

She pulled it away from him, saying, "Good. I'll just shoot at the center of the stump over there, about half way up, in the middle."

She took aim and fired. Rotten wood fell to the ground leaving a hole exactly where she said it would be. "I guess if I can't stop you from forming a militia, I might as well join you."

"Where did you learn to shoot?" he asked.

"When mother was dying I spent time in the woods, I couldn't stand to be around her illness and all of the visitors. Father told me not to wander up here, that there could be all manner of strange people passing through our woods, even Union troops. I refused to give up my time alone and asked him for a gun to protect myself. He was reluctant, but I was able to convince him that it was for my safety. Father listens to common sense more often than not."

She handed the pistol back to him and went back to sit against the fallen tree. Abe tucked the gun into his pinned up sleeve and squatted down on a rock. A soft spatter of raindrops rustled in the leaves above them. 'It might rain," he said.

"Oh yes, let's talk about the weather," she said. "That'll avoid the real subject . . . I want to know who you are, where you come from, and where you're going. I want to know if you plan to be one of the fighting men of your militia or if you will give it up when the training is complete. I want to know who you think I am and why you think I'm so easy to ignore and to play stupid with. I want . . . oh well, that's probably enough."

"May I ask what your interest is, Miss Sarah Beth?"

"All right that's fair. You are the first man, besides my father, that I've ever lived in the same house with and you are the most stubborn and secretive person I know. It is my intention to either find out who you really are or to judge all men by your example of dissembling and hiding behind a persona of shyness and mystery, none of which I really believe or want to put up with."

"Well, I'm beginning to think you may have a great future in the courts of law, interrogating witnesses and formulating judgments."

"You know they don't allow women in courts of law; so just answer and stop avoiding my questions." The raindrops were coming faster.

"Perhaps we should be walking toward your home while we talk further. It may turn into a serious shower."

She just stared at him for a long moment and then came toward him and hooked her hand into his good elbow. "All right then, let's walk, and you talk."

They took several steps in silence and then Sarah Beth pulled Abe to a stop and turned him toward her. "Lester, please don't think poorly of me. I am rude and impatient, but I do mean well, and there are things about me that you don't know."

"Such as?" The rain was letting up a bit now.

"I have very few friends, really none, and I want you to be my friend and I don't know how to do that."

"Why don't you have any friends? You're a wonderful girl."

"It's not easy to explain . . . during the War many people turned against father because one of his sermons was about 'Blessed are the peacemakers' and he said that God was weeping because of the fighting and killing that his children were going through . . ."

"He told me something like that, but not so clearly. What did people say, or do?"

"The next Sunday, my mother and I were the only people in the church for the morning service. No one else came. It was awful."

Now he took hold of her arm and gently pushed her forward toward home, "And then what happened?"

"Father went ahead as if nothing unusual had happened and gave a sermon just to Mother and me but he didn't use any of his notes, so I knew he had changed what he'd been going to say. He talked about how Christ had taught that we should 'love our neighbor' and always be ready for his return. Mother stood up then, and said to him that he was in danger of becoming a 'false prophet' and left the sanctuary. She tried to take me with her, but I wouldn't go. I didn't know what to do. I was crying and Father got down on his knees and prayed for God's love for all his children. The next week is when Mother started getting sick . . ."

Now there were tears on her cheeks and she pulled away from Abe and wiped at her face, then went on, "My friends from the school no longer wanted to be my friends and wouldn't talk to me. Mother even told me that I would have to choose between Our Lord and his armies, and my father and his traitorous beliefs. And that's the real reason I started running away to these woods and hiding from everything that was going wrong."

Abe took a handkerchief from the inside pocket of his coat and tried to wipe at her tears with it. She took it from his hand, blew her nose and wiped her face, then handed it back. "So," she said, "now you know why I want to know all about you . . . I'm just so lonely and there's no one else."

He wanted to reach out with his good arm and pull her close to comfort her, but that wouldn't be proper. He wanted to speak, but didn't know what to say. He cleared his throat and took her hand and started leading her forward, avoiding the fallen branches in the way.

"I don't know what to say, I don't know what to tell you. About me? I've been in the Army since I was twenty years old. I grew up in North Carolina. The only news I've had from my family is that my father and uncle were both killed defending our town against Sherman and his army at the end of the War. I don't know what's happened to my mother."

They could see the outline of the church's steeple ahead. Sarah Beth took her hand from his and straightened her coat and hair.

"Father said he didn't know if you would be able to return to your home."

"It might not be there."

"Yes. But Lester, what will you do? What is before us now in these terrible days? I am so frightened. Father told me why you're training these men. They say the War is over, but that it will still go on a long time, what will become of us when the Union comes in?"

"I don't know. We'll just have to trust God and be as prepared as we can be. The first problem will be foodstuffs for this coming winter. The Major is already talking about rationing the supplies at the fort and he'll have none to spare for the townspeople."

"You seem to think about everything, Mr. Greene. I really do wonder what you were doing in the War. I think you were very special."

"Not special at all, just fortunate to be a survivor."

"A survivor with a damaged elbow."

"It's not damaged, at least not permanently. Every day it's getting a little better." He opened the gate in the fence surrounding the church grounds for her. "Now, here, you're home, and in good time too, the rain is coming now, look at the darkness of those clouds."

"Yes, and thank you for trying to put up with me. I didn't mean to intrude on your privacy, but I told you why. I feel better now that we've talked."

As she turned to leave his side he stopped her with a low voice, "Sarah Beth, I must ask you for your confidentiality."

"Why Mr. Greene, that's the first time you've ever dropped the Miss before my name. And what confidentiality?"

"The Major doesn't want the reasons for what I'm doing with some of the men to become public knowledge. He doesn't want to cause alarm among the townspeople. You know how rumors and panic spread these days."

"All right, you have my promise, but in exchange you'll have to keep me informed of the situation and of your part in it. Agreed?"

"Yes, what I can tell you, I will."

She spun on her heel and walked quickly away, turning only to look back and say, "Good evening, Lester."

By the end of the first week of training the new militia, Abe was feeling fairly satisfied with their progress. Most of the twenty or so men had plenty of experience with guns and shooting, both from before the War and during. Due to various wounds, such as missing fingers and eyes, some had to relearn their skills and acquire new techniques, but mostly they were very glad to have something to do besides the enforced inactivity of hospital life. Marching was out of the question for those missing parts of their feet and legs, but it was surprising how quickly they found ways to move around on innovative inventions of crutches and canes. One soldier created a plug for the long-barrel of his rifle that allowed him to use it as a crutch, and then quickly remove it to make ready to shoot. Another was using a Y-shaped stick as a cane so he could kneel and steady the gun in the crotch of the branch, since he had lost both a foot and an arm in an artillery blast.

Abe encouraged the men as much as he could, telling them that although they were a volunteer force with no legal standing, the people of the area would be very grateful once they found out about this protection. In the meantime, he passed on to them the word from the Major that this mission was still to be kept secret due to their fears of citizen panic and rumors. One afternoon, one of the men spoke up and said that he'd heard a story of two gangs of marauders across the line in North Carolina that had gotten into a shooting battle over a herd of cattle they'd encountered at the same time, both groups claiming that they'd found it first. When Abe asked the man how he'd heard this, he said that some mail had just arrived at the fort the day before.

When the training session was over, Abe headed over to the commissary to inquire if there were any letters for him. The clerk asked, "Name, soldier?"

"Lester Greene."

"Yes sir, Lieutenant, letter right here for you, came in yesterday."

Abe took the envelope and was relieved to see the return address was from Middleburg, NC, in the handwriting he knew so well. Since his duties for the day were finished, he headed down the road toward the town and the church. Along the way he stopped at a bridge that crossed the creek branch. He climbed down the bank and found a boulder to sit on. For a few moments, he listened to the water flowing by and could almost imagine hearing voices in the sound of the current as it sloshed through the rocks of its bed. He held the letter carefully in his good hand and used his teeth to make a small rip in the covering. He drew out the single piece of stationary and unfolded it on one leg.

The script was perfectly written in a cursive style that was rather new at that time, characterized by a gentle slant and more ornate capitals. It was clearly from Irene Ruth:

Dearest Abraham,

It has been so long since I'd heard from you. I was most fearful that something terrible had happened, not that having your poor arm wounded isn't a bad thing, it's just that I am so relieved to find out that you are still with us. So many lives have been lost forever. I was so sad to hear about your father and you uncle. They perished with honor defending our community against the horrors of General Sherman and his rabid troops. Your home was destroyed, leaving only the chimneys of the house standing. They are calling these charred chimneys Sherman's Candles and so many fine homes have been destroyed in this way. Your mother seems to have been able to escape, but I'm not sure where she is.

He stopped reading to let the feeling of loss settle into his heart, again listening to the rippling water and its voices. Where would his mother have gone? How could he find her now? He was still unsure if it was safe for him to travel eastward, and, even if he were not wanted for the conspiracy affair, there was significant danger in any travel these days. And what of Irene Ruth and her family? He returned to his reading.

Father says we can no longer stay here. There is very little food as the storehouses were raided and emptied and the new crops of last spring were burned over. I had never imagined such destruction. Father has a cousin in Philadelphia up in Pennsylvania who has offered to us, as his "most unfortunate southern relatives," sanctuary in a home and with some employment should we be able to find our way north. Our family is in complete agreement that this is a terrible thing to have to face, but it seems we have no choice. It will be a very long time until things have settled hereabouts to where folks can make their livelihood again and we have lost everything. It has been suggested that I will be able to contribute to our family's needs by giving

*lessons as a teacher of piano that you know I have
always studied and been able to play.*

*I am hoping that this letter will find you, but have no
assurance. I don't know when or how we will ever see
one another again. It is all so terrible, and so painful.
I don't even know the location of my father's relatives.
I don't know how or if we will ever see one another
again. Please don't forget about me. I promise to
always remember you.*

Yours in His Love, Irene Ruth

He folded the letter with his hand and tried to slip it back into its
envelope. It was almost as if she knew they would never meet again.
But was it so impossible? Perhaps heading north would be best for
him as well, but how would he find her? He'd heard Philadelphia was
a large city and she hadn't even given him their relative's name. Again,
he was suddenly aware of the sounds of the water streaming by just
below his feet, sounding now like a very sad song. And his mother,
would she have found a way to reach her sisters in Wilmington? But
that was even farther from where he was now, and without being able
to ride horseback himself, it would be a treacherous and unpredictable
journey by stage or any other type of wagon. The trains, even if there
were one, weren't able to travel any distances yet, as there were so
many damaged bridges and trestles to be repaired. He decided to
write to his aunts and see if by chance they could tell him where his
mother was. This letter had found him easily enough under the name
of Greene, so he would try that again.

He placed the letter in the pocket on the inside of his coat and
stood up. He tried to picture Irene Ruth's beauty in his mind, closed
his eyes and was still unable to see her in his imagination. As he
slowly opened his eyes, he felt the moisture of tears building up and
then a few drops slid down his cheeks. He was more alone now than
he had ever been in his life, even in battle. He knew that compared
to so many, he was a fortunate young man, but at this moment that
was no consolation. He was in a strange landscape with no family, cut
off from his past and from the only place he'd ever called home, and
now he was also feeling more and more cut off from a future. Without

Irene Ruth, the plans they'd made were useless, and his dreams of a family of his own were lost as well.

He picked his way slowly up the bank to the road and crossed the bridge. Just as he got to the other side, he heard a clatter of hooves behind him and a lone horseman pulled to a stop. He looked up into the face of an older man still wearing the hat and coat of the Army of Virginia. The man peered down at him from above.

"I say, young fellow, can you tell me of an accommodation worth paying for, just for tonight?"

"Yes sir, I believe the Blackstone Inn would be satisfactory. It's only a short way ahead at a turn-off where you see their sign."

"Appreciate it. But say, wait, haven't I seen you before? Weren't you the young fellow attached to our dear president? I believe you were. I reported to him on occasion"

"No sir. Never was." He lowered his head, frightened by the intensity of the man's gaze.

"Well, I guess when you get my age; all the young men look more or less alike. Good day, then. And take care of that arm." He slapped his horse with the end of the reins and galloped off.

Abe let out his breath and tried to calm his thoughts. It was as if he had asked the question out loud whether or not it would be safe for him to travel back through Virginia and then south to his home. Would he be recognized? Asked it aloud and was then given all the answer he needed at this time. Now, more than ever, what he really needed now was a way to find out if there was still any real danger in being Abraham Saunders.

CHAPTER THREE

Skirmish

A month passed with training and rumors, but no incidents in the Roanoke River valley. Since receiving Irene Ruth's letter, Abe tried hard to find out more about the investigation into Lincoln's death, without raising suspicions as to the reason for his inquiry. The only possibly reliable information came from a newspaper reporter who visited the fort while working on a series of articles about convalescing veterans. Abe happened to be waiting to talk with the Major when he overheard the reporter telling the fort's commander that new and more reliable reports indicated that the Canadian office of the Confederacy was suspected of organizing the assassination.

Abe knew that office had served as a sort of embassy for the Southern states in their attempts to gain foreign and Canadian support for their cause. Although he'd had very little to do with that effort, he was aware that those officers and representatives were especially dedicated, and had a reputation for willingness to take many risks in their attempts to build a second front to attack the North from its rear. They had even attempted to recruit and train Canadians to fight for that plan. Although nothing ever came of it, their strident words and attitudes were often commented on by battle-weary officers in the army of Virginia, who were quick to point out that it was easy to be patriotic and militant a thousand miles from the battles.

Since being recognized by the officer on the bridge that day, Abe had allowed his beard to grow, and was more often than not seen wearing a floppy-brimmed horseman's hat that would usually keep most of his face in shadow. None of the men in the militia were outfitted with full uniforms, but many of them wore some piece or other to identify themselves: a cap or a shirt or army-issue boots. Abe was pleased with their apparent commitment, but was unsure how they would react to a real test if they were called upon to perform in a disciplined and courageous manner. He'd been unable to find anyone who had the leadership to take his place, and he was still training and leading the men, in spite of Sarah Beth's constant reminders of his promise to step out of that role.

Once he was sure he could attest to the Major that the band of men had reached an adequate level of performance in drills and marksmanship, he and the officer met to decide how to proceed. Rumors of marauders had become more commonplace, and citizens of the area were spreading frightful tales among themselves. There was very little verified information, but what had come to light was enough to bring the town's governing council to the fort for a meeting. The Major informed the men of the town that he had been preparing for just such an eventuality, and that, with the professional assistance of Lieutenant Lester Greene, a troop of trained men was prepared to defend against threats from any such riff-raff. He then asked Lieutenant Greene to say a few words about the new contingent.

"Well, Major, sir, and gentlemen, as you know there is no formal presence of a military detachment bivouacked at the fort or anywhere else nearby. Recognizing this potential weakness of our defensive capabilities, the Major requested that I train the most able-bodied men hospitalized here at the fort. We now have twenty such men organized and somewhat trained to act as an initial response to any report or untoward approach by outsiders bearing ill-intent for this community." He sat back down next to the Major at the front table of the small meeting room.

"Any questions?" the Major asked.

"Yes sir," the town's councilor general spoke up. "We are very pleased to hear of these preparations of yours. What are your plans for deploying these men?"

"Well, sir, we were reluctant to have them appear in any public way, as it might cause unnecessary fears among the population by showing that we too are concerned."

"However, sir," the townsman replied, "those fears now exist, whether founded or unfounded, and I would suggest, nay urge, that this special force be charged with patrolling various of the roads that surround and enter our communities. This would alert those enemies of our people to these preparations and to your men's existence and readiness, and it would give some amount of comfort to the local populace." There were signs of agreement among his fellow councilmen.

"Well, your Honor, we shall take that suggestion under advisement and begin at once to develop a few strategic opportunities for just such an opportunity to do that. In exchange, I would ask that this eminent body of the town's leadership take it upon yourselves to spread the word that this is exactly what will be happening, so that it will be seen as coming from a legitimate source. We don't want to encourage any vigilantism. For the time being, you may refer to this initiative as the Fort Lewis Patrol and Home Guard."

After a few more points of discussion, regarding routes and locations where the patrol might appear and the methods by which they could identify themselves to the citizenry, the meeting was adjourned. The Major and Abe talked briefly about this rather surprising turn of events, and planned to meet together the next day to map out a few more detailed plans.

As he was preparing to leave for the evening, the Major held out his hand and took his lieutenant's good hand in his own. "Now, you must remain in charge. I can't have such an important responsibility left in the hands of men with no leadership experience. Also, I intend to approach this council with a request for financial support for the patrol, and some of that would hopefully be allocated as a stipend for yourself. Now, get some rest, son, we have quite a challenge ahead of us."

Abe saluted and slowly turned and went to the door; then he turned back and said, "Sir, my experience is mainly in administrative affairs, and not in this kind of thing. I hope you will remember that when the time comes to deal with any of my shortcomings."

"Of course, of course. Besides, as I've told you, who else have we got?"

"Yes sir."

As he walked away from the fort and toward the town, he was surprised to find himself thinking of Sarah Beth's likely response to this new responsibility of his. It certainly wouldn't be calm and reasonable, that much he was sure of, but then what else could he do? She would have to be made to see that he really had no choice. These thoughts then led to further questions in his mind as to just why this young lady had such influence over him and his thoughts.

The next morning, before Abe was to leave for the fort and his planning session with the Major, Doctor Randall called him into the study and asked for a few minutes of his time.

"Sit down, son. It's been too long since we've had a chance to have a heart-to-heart conversation, and there's no way I couldn't have noticed the time your other responsibilities are taking, and taking you away from my work for you here. Now, that is of no real consequence, as I was getting along well enough before you arrived. Not nearly so well, let me say, but getting along. But I am concerned about what you're getting yourself into here."

"Yes, sir. I was meaning to talk with you, and then some things changed and I have not yet been able to see how it will affect what we can do about it."

"And what has changed?"

Abe went ahead and described the essence of the meeting with the council and the requests they'd made. He felt that he could reveal some of the planning that would be taking place, but also admit that he had no way of knowing what was going to happen in reality now that his training group was, in effect, being mobilized to counter real or imagined threats to the town and its inhabitants.

"I am not sold on this strategy, Doctor Randall. I am not sure if calling attention to ourselves will serve as a deterrent or simply make us a target for this apparent rash of small roving bands of desperate men."

The doctor leaned back in his chair and studied the young man in front of him. He had taken quite a liking to the refreshing and honest demeanor of his new assistant, and he was beginning to wish that there was some way to retain his services now and into the future. The congregation's loss of faith in their pastor, as demonstrated by their leaders and others, was a severe blow to his idea of himself and just what it is to be God's servant among men in a time of war and chaos. He was hoping that this young man might, in due time, take on some of the responsibilities of meeting with members of the church and helping them to understand that the ways of God are both clear and murky, depending on a given situation and its precedents. To deal with the lack of qualified ministers as a consequence of the War, a training program was now being re-started at a certain nearby seminary; Dr. Randall had been considering trying to find some way to afford to send the young man away for short periods of time to be educated in elements of the ministry. Now this came up, another new development at the Fort, which seemed to almost set the stage for a kind of competition between himself and the Major for the young man's time and commitment.

"And how are you feeling about this direction, not as a strategy, but as an investment of your own time and abilities? Before you answer, I understand that this is an opportunity to further develop your aptitude for leadership, but I would have you remember that there is no formal element to this rather unilateral activity, and that it has no sanction or backing from any truly legitimate source. It is, in reality, governance without government."

"Yes sir, I am aware of this and have been giving it some serious thought. I really don't know what to do, except that you yourself said in a sermon a few weeks ago, that the Ways and Will of God often show themselves in the opening up of opportunity, but you also said that such openings can be a form of temptation. So what would you say I'm to conclude from all of this, and from this apparent need for my services?"

"You have learned well, my boy. Anyone who seriously attempts to understand the Will of God, in their own life or in the larger affairs of men, will be greatly challenged by the confusion caused by what can only be called His divine and mysterious purposes. I have always taught that the way of honor and compliance with God's ways is to be accessible, without trying to shape the future to ourselves or ourselves to that future. For me, it sometimes works and sometimes leaves me grasping for guidance in a world that seems filled with silence when my heart is crying out for a Voice with answers."

At this point, Abe was tempted to reveal to the doctor the rest of his dilemma, his assumed identity and its causes, and to share the constant level or doubt and fear that this caused him. But what good would it do? The man already knew of this, but, in his own words, there were no obvious answers to the questions that surrounded Abe and pulled him this way and that.

"Sir," he said, "I want to assure you that I am truly grateful for what you've done for me, taking me in, supporting me and offering your kind words when I most needed them. I certainly don't want to appear to abandon you, nor can I in good conscience abandon these brave men who have volunteered their broken bodies and wounded spirits in the service of a town and community that is not even home to most of them. I feel I must see this through to a point when I am no longer needed, and then when I am able, to move ahead with my own life."

"Son, I welcome your honesty and acknowledge your burden. Know that you are welcome here for as long and for as much as you need from us. The real challenge you must face now is with our own dear Sarah Beth. I wouldn't want to be in your boots when she finds out that you are continuing to proceed down a road with the potential for more fighting and more of this growing responsibility."

"Doctor, believe me, I have been thinking much on this, and," he gave a quick nod, "I was hoping I could ask you to intervene with her on my behalf."

The Doctor gave a sudden sharp laugh and leaned forward. "I think I would rather lead your men into combat than face the wrath of our young lady . . . But I will do what I can to prepare the way for you, short of sacrificing myself on that altar."

He stood up, came around the desk and as Abe also stood, he embraced the young man and gave a heartfelt blessing in a soft voice, asking for God's guidance and protection of this young man, a young man who was becoming more and more like the son he'd never had. Then the older man turned quickly away, drew out a handkerchief, blew his nose loudly, and said, "Go now, you have your work to do, and I have mine."

By the beginning of the third week of patrols, they had done the maneuvers four times, two times in each of the first two weeks. They had gone out the north Post road twice since that was the area closest to any rumored intruder presence, out the south road along the river, and down the main road east. They had seen nothing of importance to their mission, but local citizens, particularly those living more isolated outside the town limits, had been extremely welcoming and some had even waved Confederate flags as the lieutenant and his contingent passed by their properties, or when they were sighted at the intersections with other by-roads.

Abe was feeling quite pleased with the relative discipline of the men, as those on horseback were able to hold some semblance of a formation. They were assigned to guard in front and behind the two wagons carrying the more severely and permanently wounded

members. The Major let Abe know that the town fathers were very
pleased with the appearance of the patrol, and that there was a sense
of relief among the merchants of the town who had been fearing some
kind of cut-off of their meager shipments of supplies from the outside
world.

Abe had even seen some leadership potential in a young man
who'd been an artillery squad sergeant during the last year of the War.
This soldier, Byron Matthews by name, had lost one leg when one of
the guns he was overseeing blew up and killed three of its soldiers
and took Byron's leg with them. He was ready and willing to help out
in any way he could and seemed most afraid of being left out or left
behind due to his handicap. Abe placed Byron in charge of the second
wagon while he himself rode in the first one.

For their fifth foray, first one of the third week, they headed
south again into a more remote area of the territory that had been
allocated for their patrols. Suddenly, they heard gunfire from the left
side of the road and up a rise in a small stand of woods. As they had
been trained to do, the men in the wagons hunkered down behind
chest-high reinforced walls, and the horsemen moved around to the
side of the wagons opposite the source of the shots. One of the most
important things Abe had done was to have any men he could find
with carpentry skills add strength to the wagons in such a way that
they could be used as a mobile barricade, a kind of facsimile trench
for the men to take shelter within. The horsebacks also positioned
themselves so the wagons were between them and any assault. The
only men left exposed were the two who had to stand with the teams
of draught horses to keep them from bolting or tangling in their
harnesses. Abe had instructed these men to make sure they kept the
horses between themselves and an attack.

Abe gave the order to return fire if another shot came from the
woods. The men talked quietly among themselves, the riders trying to
calm their horses, and the men on the ground with the teams likewise.
Suddenly a single horseman burst from the cover of the trees firing
his pistol at them. He turned sharply and galloped down the road away
from them. Two patrol men stood up in the wagons and fired after the
man. Abe shouted for them to get back down. An eerie silence settled
over them.

"Should we go after him, Lieutenant?" one of his horsemen yelled.

Abe hesitated, not wanting to divide his troops without knowing what else was in the woods or ahead. "No. You won't catch him now." Just then a horse whinnied from upslope in the trees. Another shot rang out.

Some of his men fired back. "Hold your fire," he called out. "No sense wasting it if we can't see them."

One of his horsemen called to him in a low voice and volunteered to ride back toward town and then circle back above the skirmishers in the woods, to find how many enemy were up there. Abe realized that they'd be pinned down in this spot if they didn't either try to retreat or flush out the attackers, but he had no desire to sacrifice any of his men.

He nodded and gave the volunteer permission, adding, "But take another man with you, Private Spencer. And make sure you've gone that way far enough they think you've gone for help before you circle and come back this way."

The two men galloped back the way they'd come. More shots were fired from above, one hitting the side of one of the wagons. Two of his men fired back in the direction of the shots. Then it was quiet again.

Abe yelled as loud as he could, "In the woods. Who are you? What do you want?"

There was no answer. They heard the sounds of several horses thrashing through the underbrush, headed in the same direction as the first horseman had gone earlier. They were staying out of sight. The sound of thunder came from beyond the low mountains to the west. It was going to rain. Three of his horsebacks whirled their horses around the wagon and stopped in front of Abe.

"We want to go after them," one man said. "At least to see where they're headed."

"Wait," Abe said. "We'll see what Higgins and Spencer have to say."

"But they'll get away."

"I'm quite sure they'll get away anyway," Abe said.

Just then Higgins and Spencer came pounding out of the trees, pulling up just in front of the first wagon.

"They're gone, sir. No one there. Just a burnt out campfire."

"All right, let's move ahead. You three," he said to the other eager riders, "head after them but don't engage in any way. Turn back the minute they stop, or when you reach the settlement road by the bridge. That's an order."

The men rode off quickly, leaving the two wagons with their passengers and the rest of the mounted men. Abe gave the order to push forward and they moved out.

The next hour passed without incident or contact with any of the band of riders they'd flushed out of the woods. A farmer driving a two-wheeled cart came toward them at the intersection of two roads where their own four riders were waiting. The man hollered for them to stop and talk to him.

"They was six of 'em," he yelled, "riding like hell. Most nearly ran me off the road, that way." He pointed back the way he'd come.

"Ever seen any of them before?" Abe asked.

"No sir, but they weren't carryin' nothin', no supplies. Nothin'."

Abe heard thunder and felt the first splatter of raindrops.

"We'd best start back," he shouted. "Be dark by the time we're back at the Fort."

Sarah Beth had come home from her shift at the infirmary at her regular time, just before supper. When she found that Lester wasn't back yet, she became concerned. Although he'd been late before, he was most often on time for their late evening meals, and she suggested to her father that they give him a few more minutes before they started eating.

"Well, you'll have to tell Mattie, then. You know how she gets," he replied.

After she informed Mattie of the delay, she went out to the porch and sat in the large swing. Lightning flashed to the west, with the muffled sound of its thunder. Rain was on its way; the air had that smell. And here she was, trying not to worry about Lester Greene. He'd assured her that the duties he was performing were to be short-lived and that there was no real danger. She tried to believe him, but the infirmary was a hotbed of rumors, all the way from stories of Union army detachments on the march to occupy their town, to tales of marauders torching farmhouses and molesting women. In some ways, it made sense to her what Lester was doing. But it was also dangerous or there wouldn't be a need for it. Over the past couple of weeks, since the patrols had started, he had seemed more willing to talk with her, but she still had no idea of who and what he had been before the War or before he'd come to their town. She pestered her father for more information, but he'd only said that in these times a man had a right to his privacy.

What she really wondered about was his status as a man. Was he single, or betrothed, or even married to someone back where he'd come from? She told herself she didn't want to care about that, didn't want to care because it wouldn't make any difference. He clearly considered her just a girl and not the woman she knew she was becoming. The way he looked at her with kind of a secretive smile when she was upset with his silence and with his continual refusal to tell her about himself . . . Well, that smile could easily be a sign that he thought she was a bit childish and silly. It all made her promise herself that she was going to somehow show him that she was worth his friendship and trust, no matter how many years separated them.

Mattie called to her from inside just as a torrent of rain unleashed itself upon the trees and buildings of the church grounds. "I'm coming," she called back.

The lightning flashed across the tops of the mountains and the thunder rumbled in her ears. He was out there somewhere, on foot, getting soaked. Why wasn't he home, why didn't he feel that this was his home? She promised herself she would try something new, something softer, less challenging. She needed for him to think of her as a woman, if only to prove to herself that she really was.

Mattie served their plates of food already dished up, leaving Lester's empty. Doctor Randall complimented her on the wonderful smell of the steaming food and the woman smiled and said, "Wait 'till you eat it before you get all carried away."

Just then they heard stomping by the side door entrance to the rear of the kitchen.

"Must be him," the doctor said.

"I've been so worried," his daughter replied.

"Well. We'll see that there's nothing wrong and then we can say grace together and have this delicious smelling food. I didn't think I was hungry until this was in front of me."

Sarah Beth could hardly wait for Lester to come in, but he was taking his time, probably drying off and trying to make himself presentable following his outdoor activity in the downpour of the afternoon. Finally he came into the room and apologized for being late.

"Something must have happened," the girl said quickly.

"Not really," he said as Mattie served him his plate, with what looked like an extra-sized portion. "Thank you, Mattie."

"You going come in here looking like a drowned cat, you must be hungry, so eat up. There's more where that come from," the woman said sternly.

"Are things well with you, young man?" the doctor asked.

"Yes sir, everyone is all right, fine. Bit of a cloudburst out there now. We saw it coming while we were on patrol and hurried back to the fort. Got there just in time."

"But you had to walk home through it all," Sarah Beth said. "Poor Lester."

He was relieved she seemed distracted by the storm. He wanted to be able to talk about the day's events, but only in private with the doctor, and this made it easier.

Sarah Beth looked over at him and then addressed her father, "Don't you think he looks very distinguished in his wet hair and rumpled collar?"

"Yes, of course," her father answered.

"I don't think he looks like a drowned cat at all, more like a heroic soldier putting up with all kinds of weather and misfortune."

Abe looked at her with a question in his eyes. And then said, "That's one of the nicest things you've ever said to me, even if it isn't true."

"Oh, it's true, and there are many other nice things I could say if I wanted to."

Abe smiled and said, "Well, don't use them up all at once."

Doctor Randall interrupted their dialogue, saying, "I had someone come into the church today, to speak with me. He said there'd been strangers out south of town. Said they'd raided a farmhouse, killed a couple of pigs and made off with the farmer's last bag of seed corn. This man laughed, and said, wait until they try to eat any of that corn. It'll break their teeth even if they soak it a week . . . Have you heard anything about that?"

Abe glanced at Sarah Beth, and then looked to the Doctor, "No sir, I hadn't. But then the fort was pretty well closed down for supper and I didn't see the Major or anyone who might have heard something like that." Thinking to himself, this was important and he needed to find out more as quickly as possible.

"Perhaps I could help you with those sermon notes after we finish here. I'm not sure but I may be rather busy most of the day tomorrow."

"That would be fine with me. Sooner it's done the better."

"But what about me? You two always go off together and I was going to play the latest songs I've learned on the piano with Mrs. Balcolm."

Doctor Randall looked kindly in her direction and said, "We won't be all that long. Maybe you can practice a little and then we'll be right along."

She started to complain and then remembered her promise to herself, and simply shook her head saying, "Oh, I'll be all right. You need to talk, and I need the practice anyway." And with that, she gave a quick curtsey, excused herself and was gone. The two men looked at each other with a kind of bafflement. This was someone different than they were used to.

When the two men were alone together in the doctor's study, neither spoke at first, each waiting for the other, and then they both spoke at once.

Doctor Randall repeated himself, "You go ahead, what's been going on?"

"I'm really more interested in your news. You see, we had a bit of a run-in with a small group south of town. A few shots were fired, and they rode off. We didn't try to follow with the wagons and riders I have at my disposal. How far out was that farm you heard about? And is everyone all right?"

"It was about twelve miles, near as I can tell from what he told me. A few miles past where the road to the Wallow settlement takes off from the Post Road."

"That's about where we got to before coming back. Did he have anything else to say?"

"He said the farmer told him these strangers were well-armed and joking about taking on the Yankees at the fort here. When I told him there weren't any Union forces hereabouts, at least not yet, he was surprised. Maybe that bunch thought you were Union when they fired at you. Anyone hurt?"

"No sir. Seems they had a small campfire in the woods above the road when we came along. They fired at us and one of them rode pell-mell out of the woods and off down the road. I sent a few riders to try and circle up and see what it was, and then the rest of the bunch took off through the woods. We think they went toward that settlement. A farmer in a cart told us he saw them going that way."

The doctor was silent for a few long moments, and then said, "So now it begins again. Such a short time of near peacefulness."

"It may not be such a problem if we can reach them before they cause more damage. If they're Confederate, it might be enough for them to find out that our patrol and the fort is still, for all practical purposes, held in Southern hands."

"Perhaps, if they're not too afraid of any and all authorities." The sound of the piano could be heard through the thick door and the doctor stood up and patted his companion on the shoulder. "Best go listen to Sarah Beth before she forgets herself and gets ornery again. We'll get to those sermon notes another time."

Over the next few days the story of the skirmish got out and grew to exaggerated proportions by word of mouth, and there was no official statement forthcoming to counter the rumors. In a conversation, the Major had informed Abe that his patrol operation had no official sanction, any more than the Fort's hospital did. What Lieutenant Greene was leading could be viewed as a 'paramilitary force' with the approval of the town council and an ad hoc chain of command for which the Major would take responsibility. When it came right down to it, the whole business was without legal footing. They discussed the post-war chaos and its effect on the population, but since neither of them were in communication with any Union leadership, it was all speculation. They admitted to each other that what they were doing was based solely on their own desire to get things done in any way possible.

After further discussions over the next couple of days, it was decided that the Fort Lewis-based patrols would hereafter be called the Salem Town Protection Force and be chartered by the council in much the same manner as the Volunteer Fire Department. The council hurriedly met and approved the action, and named the Major and Lieutenant Greene as "peace officers of the town" with responsibilities for public safety outside the town's formal boundaries, and throughout the countryside up to the limits of any other neighboring towns. A front page notice was published in the weekly newspaper and hard-paper posters of it were put up at various main road intersections. While there was no mention of the organization's Confederate roots and personnel, it was assumed that the signature of the council chairman and his title of "Interim post-Confederate Magistrate" would somewhat assure those who feared some kind of imminent Union takeover of the area.

It had been three days since the skirmish with no mention from Sarah Beth concerning it or its impact on the citizenry. Abe had been away from the home and church most of each of those days, but was still at meals and close enough to have been interrogated by the girl, if she so desired. He was somewhat perplexed by her silence and polite smile whenever he and the Doctor asked for some private time away from her; he hadn't asked her about it directly, so there hadn't been an opening for such a conversation between them.

Then on an evening following an uneventful patrol to the north of the town, he found her waiting for him on the porch of the house. In the quiet of the evening, a pink glow highlighted the silhouettes of the western mountains, and the seasons of summer and fall seemed to hover at the edge of their changeover, momentarily sharing this twilight of the day. She was working on a project with yarn that spilled from her lap. As he came up the stairs, he knelt and began to collect the tangle of colored string. She smiled down at him and laughed gently.

"Why, Mr. Greene, I believe you're on your knees. Perhaps you have some apology to make, or perhaps you're just very tired from your hard day at the Fort."

"Neither, I'm gathering up someone's spilled yarn. Any idea who it belongs to?"

"Well, I couldn't say. But I'd be happy to have you untangle some of it and help me make it into a ball, if you please."

"I could do that.'

She patted the seat on the swinging chair beside her. "Lovely evening, don't you think?"

"Yes it is . . . Like this?" He held out his hands and shuffled the skein of yarn in the way his mother taught him when she'd needed his help.

"Why, yes. You must have done this before."

"Only a little," he said, concentrating on the motions of her hands as they rolled the yarn into its ball, favoring one of his own but pleased that there was no pain from this activity.

She patted that hand to show him where a few strands had tangled, and said, "So I've been wondering if you'd ever want to tell me about that battle you and your men fought a few days back. People are saying you're quite the leader of your men."

"No, not at all. And it was a hardly a battle, more like a little skirmish over an accidental meeting of two groups who weren't expecting each other."

"Well, that's not what I've heard," she went on quickly, "I've heard that you and your men were attacked from ambush and chased those outlaws away from here. They're saying they'd already raided a farm and set it on fire after stealing whatever they could carry and making off with it. They say you and your men chased them out of the country to help make us all safe again. We should be very grateful to you, lieutenant."

He didn't know how to reply. He, too, had heard these reports and couldn't help thinking that some of his men had been bragging a bit more than they should have. But he was curious about some of the things she'd said, so he asked, "How badly did folks say the farm was burned? Completely, buildings and all?"

"I really don't know, but we must all just hope and pray that those outlaws have the fear of God and your protection force to keep them on the run." They were quiet for a few moments as the last of the yarn in his hands was taken into the ball. She looked directly at him, making him uncomfortable enough to look away and then back again.

"Lester, I want to remind you that you made me a promise. You said you would not be going anywhere near any fighting, that you would stop all this when the training was finished. Is this the way I'm supposed to trust your promises?

"Sarah Beth, I can see how you might be upset, but I really had no choice. The training is not finished, yet the town's council pressed us into active service for the protection of the citizens. And I must say . . . I had no idea there would be encounters of any kind. I promise you it was totally unexpected . . ."

She interrupted, "Another promise, Lester?"

"Please listen. What happened was above and beyond the duties that had been assigned or considered for this exercise. And besides, there never was any real danger, just a few random shots exchanged, and then they fled."

She looked down at her project and the ball of yarn in hand. "Lester, I can't help being so terribly proud of you, even as I am also terrified of what you've gotten yourself into. I just wish we could run away from all this war. It just hasn't ended . . ."

A small sob escaped her throat and he looked over at her, now with a different feeling than the defensiveness he'd just been going through. She was still so young, and her fear seemed real, but at the same time he could see the way she was struggling to express all of the conflicting feelings this created inside of her. He remembered how she'd sounded just like this when she told him about losing her friends and then her mother. He wanted to put his arm around her shoulders and pull her close for whatever comfort he could bring into her life, but he held back because she was already enough of a woman that it wouldn't be proper; besides she might even be offended. Just then she turned to him with her eyes full of tears and leaned her face into his shoulder, the one with the good arm.

"What is going to happen to us? Is there no hope?" she cried.

"There, there, we'll find a way. Things can only get better from now on."

Mattie called them in to supper.

"Oh, I must wash my face . . . Lester, please don't leave us, don't leave us here alone. We need you. Father and I need you." She jumped up and ran into the house, leaving the ball of yarn rolling across the floor and her project on the floor as well. Abe gathered it all up and carefully straightened it out. Then he too went inside, taking one final look at the first stars beginning to fill the darkening sky.

When the first snowstorm of winter came, it brought a temporary end to the patrols. It also brought refugees to the fort. Although there had, as yet, been no official notification of an assumption of power by the Union, the Major and his medical services at the fort continued to perform the function of a convalescent center for wounded who had no other place to go. Foodstuffs had been put up, and, after many requests for aid from churches and charities as far away as Richmond, several wagons full of staples and supplies had shown up. Doctor Randall was instrumental in sending out these pleas for assistance. Now many members of the church seemed willing to forget their resentment of some of his war-time sermons, and they joined in providing help.

These new refugees consisted mainly of veterans from the Army of Virginia who had been eking out their survival by living off the land, occasional thefts, and some charity. They were extremely suspicious of the reluctant welcome they received when they approached the fort in groups of two or three. The Major and his helpers assigned them to stay in one wing of the facility and they were provided with two meals a day. They were also encouraged to hunt for meat in the hills west of town, but warned against harming or taking any livestock owned by local farmers. By the second storm of what was turning into an early winter, a few families began straggling into the fort, asking for shelter and sustenance. They brought with them remnants of their poor harvests and offered their work in exchange for shelter.

Major Callahan called in his lieutenant for a conference on the increasing need for both supplying and policing the new arrivals. "I can't just throw open the gates of the fort to any and all who might be down on their luck. I just can't do it. We're military, not angels of mercy. Help me out with this. If I close the fort we'll have worse problems in the countryside, if I open it up we'll be overrun. What do you say?" Abe didn't answer right away. "Well, say something."

"Sir, since our first minor skirmishes, we've had no further incidents involving the patrols."

"True enough. Seems to have worked."

"Perhaps there's a way we can use these men to do some other kind of work, hauling and guarding supplies for our merchants. Earning a share of the foodstuffs, if there are any."

"Possible. And some of these newcomers might be able to work off their keep, but dammit, lieutenant, there's got to be a limit, we can't just open our gates to every hard-pressed man or family in the countryside. We go under ourselves if we don't draw some kind of a line."

"Sir, have you heard of any other situations like ours, and what they might be doing in similar circumstances?"

"No, I haven't, but if I had a good messenger I could trust, I might be willing to send him for word east of here. In the meantime, see what if any, more help your preacher friend can come up with. You're dismissed."

As the days went by and more families showed up in the town and at the fort seeking assistance, a Ladies' Assistance Society was formed and charitable activities were organized to benefit the wayward and the homeless. Sarah Beth was recruited by the women of this new group, based on her experience with the hospital, and her connection with her father's church. A few of the older women even went so far as to confide in her that they held nothing against her for the disagreements which had taken place over her father's ministry. And more than one expressed sympathy over her mother's passing. Still, as far as she was concerned, it was the work that was appealing, and she wasn't inclined to accept the company of these women, many of whom had backed their husbands in standing so staunchly against her father.

Sarah Beth was assigned to serve at the fort as an aide, caring for sick children and helping their mothers. At times, her schedule and Abe's coincided and they could spend time together walking to or from their work. The cold wind of the winter weather was often almost too much to tolerate, but they encouraged one another to bear up and be strong, their voices muffled by the heavy knitted scarves she'd made for both of them.

On one especially bitter cold day, the previous day's melting snow had frozen solid on the walkways and in the streets. Their days had been exhaustingly long as they were both trying to keep things running somewhat smoothly in the absence of necessary supplies, and to cope with the desperation of the people they were trying to provide for. It was quite dark and as the two of them went to cross a side street on their way home, Abe lost his footing on the invisible ice and went down hard, on the side of his wound. He was unable to withhold a sharp scream of pain, but immediately tried to get back to his feet.

Sarah Beth pushed him back down, saying, "Stay right where you are until we know how badly you're hurt."

"I'm all right," he said. "I just fell down. And maybe you could try helping me up instead of pushing me down."

"Your arm? Did you fall on your arm?"

"No, I don't think so."

She was kneeling beside him. He found himself a little more shaken than he'd thought and he had to lie back, turning onto his good side. She was kneeling, and took his head and shoulders in her lap.

"There, there. Just catch your breath and try to be still. In a minute we'll see how badly you're hurt, but right now you have to catch your breath and calm yourself."

They stayed like that for a few moments, her gloved hand gently stroking his forehead and her voice softly lilting in a soothing kind of singing without words.

"It's too cold to be lying in the street," he said. "I'd like it if you'd help me to my feet." He pushed himself into a sitting position, as she moved to support him from behind. She eased around to his front side so to help pull him all the way up. When they'd struggled together to stand, she stood very still with her arms around him, steadying and still humming softly. He leaned on her and slightly twisted the wounded arm inside his coat, checking to see if it had been impacted. It hurt, but seemed to be all right. He was fortunate it hadn't been any worse.

They stood that way for a few more long moments until both of them seemed to realize at the same time that they were locked in what could look like a long embrace, and that although there was no one else nearby, they were in a public place.

Abe removed one of her arms from around himself, and said, "Thanks. We should get going. I think I'll be fine now."

She took his good arm in her grasp and began leading him forward. He was aware that it was her strength that was supporting him as one of his legs was still trembling from the shock of the fall, and he needed all the help he could get from leaning on her.

"We'll be home very soon. But let me know when you need to stop and rest," she said loudly through the muffling of her scarf.

Abe had been paying careful attention to the random and sporadic news items he could collect from local sources concerning the capture and imprisonment of the ex-president, Jefferson Davis. He kept a file in the desk he used in Doctor Randall's study, and added to it whenever he could. The most interesting document, and the one that frightened him the most, was the declaration issued by President Andrew Johnson very soon after he took over from Lincoln, following the assassination and just before Davis's capture. The new president, in the form of a proclamation issued in early May, 1865, stated:

> *Whereas, it appears from evidence obtained by the Bureau of Military Justice, that the atrocious murder of our late President Abraham Lincoln . . . conspired, incited, and procured by and between Jefferson Davis, late of Richmond, Virginia, and other rebels and traitors against the United States, we do hereby offer and promise the following rewards: one hundred thousand for Jefferson Davis . . . and suitable rewards for the arrest of all persons named in this proclamation.*

Unfortunately for Abe, the newspaper article he'd obtained did not list or name the others mentioned in the proclamation for who those rewards were offered. And since the capture of Davis on May 10, 1865, there had been no other mention of these individuals in any of the coverage he'd found.

Davis had since been confined in a military prison at Fortress Monroe, near Norfolk, and very little more was being said about him or developments in the case against him. According to the few articles that referred to the former president, long delays were expected in bringing him to trial, delays caused both by difficulties in re-establishing courts following the War and by the question of whether Davis was a prisoner of the military who had captured him or of the civil courts who might possibly claim jurisdiction.

Taking all this into account, there was very little Abe could do to change his situation, or to give up the false identity that gave him some small sense of security. The fact that he had not healed up enough to become self-reliant in terms of riding horseback or even for wagon travel was also keeping him where he was. He was quite certain that Doctor Randall knew enough to be aware of his predicament when expressing solidarity about the risks to both of them if he were found out. The minister would certainly be implicated in harboring him, that is, if he truly were a fugitive.

As to what the Major at the fort knew, it seemed he didn't or wouldn't care as long as he was able to depend on his young lieutenant as both an assistant in those affairs of a quasi-military nature, and as a confidant to complain to about the ongoing chaos of the fort and its diverse and changing populace.

The closest Abe had come to being discovered was when one of the soldier patients, recovering from a severe head wound, seemed to recognize Abe as one who helped transport him to the town from Appomattox. He'd sat up in his bed one day when Abe was passing through the ward he was confined to, and suddenly he spoke out with, "I know you, you drove the wagon with the doctor I came on. I know you. Who are you?"

Abe vaguely recognized the man from the bandage that still covered the top half of his head, but since there hadn't been any other contact between the two of them since that time, he wasn't sure. However, the incident was enough to cause him some serious concern.

He spoke quietly to the man, saying, "Perhaps you're right, perhaps we did come here together. I myself was wounded and was being transported just as you were. But I was no driver, couldn't have been." He gestured at his still sleeveless left arm.

"What's your name," the man asked abruptly.

"Lester, Lester Greene."

"No, it's not. Don't remember what it is, but ain't Lester Greene. That don't sound right."

"Well, it's my name, and I hope you keep on getting better." He quickly left the foot of the man's bed and kept walking away, determined not to chance coming into this ward again.

The man shouted after him, "I'm thinking on it. I'll be thinking on it!"

Abe left the hospital wing of the fort and found a quiet place to calm himself and think this through. Should it come up again, the obvious way to deal with this man was to point out that the head injury most likely addled the man's thinking, and that, while they may have arrived together, there was some mistake in the man's memory of who Abe was or had been.

CHAPTER FOUR

Changes

One year after the official end of the War, spring was late, but it came quickly when it did come, with a flourish of colorful flowers and noisy songbirds. The green buds and leaves leapt forth from their winter hiding places and the sky was more often than not filled with puffy white clouds hurrying somewhere else. The affairs of both the medical and the refugee services of the fort's quasi-official operations achieved some kind of routine orderliness now that the food shortages of the winter had abated and the roads were more passable. Sarah Beth and Abe continued to attend to their various responsibilities, frequently sharing the time walking back and forth together. The young woman had maintained her more cordial behavior toward this new friend of hers, and they often found something to laugh about or to point out to one another in the scenery or along the paths they took between the fort and home. Abe was now able to lift his arm up to the level of his shoulder. He was able to practice using it to hold up the front end of a light rifle while pulling on the trigger with his good hand. He'd spent many hours over the past year exercising and working the slow-healing limb, and was now able to put it in a sleeve and perform various simple functions. His elbow was still stiff and he despaired of ever regaining anything like real flexibility, but just being able to walk down the street swinging his arm in rhythm with his legs was a new and welcome joy.

He received one more letter from Irene Ruth, addressed to Lt. Lester Greene at the fort. It was very brief and simply announced that they had been living in the city of Philadelphia through a "horrid winter" and that the family had no plans to return to Virginia. She closed with the words, *"I hope you will find your own happiness now, even as I am seeking mine."* Although he couldn't be positive about her meaning, those words certainly seemed to imply that she had no further plans to see him or continue pursuing any of their mutual plans or dreams. In a way, it seemed quite clear to him that this was the natural outcome of their circumstances, and he needed to recognize within himself that his own memory of her was dimming and less important to him as time moved on. On the other hand, there were still leftover feelings that she should have waited longer for him to be able to resolve his difficulties, and it should still be important that they had in fact been betrothed. All of this came along with his realization that for whatever reason, he had never discussed Miss Irene Ruth with Sarah Beth, and probably never would now that all that was apparently over.

In the middle of May, news came that the case against ex-President Davis was transferred from the military authorities to the civil courts of Virginia, although he remained in custody at the federal prison of Fortress Monroe. To Abe, this seemed like a hopeful sign—the civilian court was more likely to handle the case based on Davis's actions as President of the Confederacy, rather than as leader of a conspiracy to assassinate Lincoln.

Doctor Randall continued to avail himself to as much help as he could get from his young assistant, and even attempted to get Abe to serve in the church as a lay-minister, visiting the sick and consoling the bereaved. This would have presented a clear challenge to Abe's rather vague assessment of his own faith in the doctrines and teachings he would have been dispensing to members of the congregation. He was able to avoid the offer by depicting the coming summer months as probably requiring a renewed and increased workload for the patrols. Every week they heard more reports of armed gangs of displaced veterans and outbreaks of theft, along with news regarding the increasing numbers of free but homeless slaves. Other groups like his were being formed to protect their small towns from vagrant attackers, and the climate of violence was increasing with the warming of the weather.

The one antidote to all this social displacement and unrest was the number of jobs now available, jobs re-building blown-up bridges and the tracks of the many rail lines that had once crisscrossed Virginia and its neighbor states. The newly united government was pouring material and financial resources into rebuilding the economic foundation of the defeated South, and the new vision seemed to include a lot more manufacturing than had ever been seen in that region. Whether or not agriculture would eventually resume its leading role was a subject widely debated as the changes brought about by the loss of slave labor were still becoming known, and were not yet fully understood or calculated.

The local school for young women had reopened following the Christmas and New Year holidays, and Sarah Beth resumed an interrupted education. Her studies were largely designed to create the perfect mistress of a home she would someday manage with grace and all of her charm and skills. She also was allowed to take up a class in mathematics with an emphasis on financial accounting for household income and expenditures. None of this interested her very much and she often complained to Abe about the irrelevance of the curriculum.

"I will not let my life simply be wasted within the walls of a house and serving only the needs of one family," she told him one day as they were walking from the fort to the church. "I've seen too much of life and misfortune to think only of myself and my close kin. There are so many who need so much, and I have been so fortunate."

"What would you do about it?" he asked.

"I'm not sure yet. Maybe I'll become a medical doctor."

He looked at her set mouth and intense gaze, and knew it wasn't a time to argue or make jokes. "I don't know where you can get that training."

"Because I'm a girl?"

"Because you're a woman," he said, wary of her proven ability to trap him into saying things he didn't necessarily mean.

"Yes, I know. But the first medical college for women opened in Philadelphia, in 1850, and there must be others by now. Father's looking into it."

"Well, that's good. Your experience these past few years will be useful." He was distracted by the thoughts of her and Philadelphia and Irene Ruth all coming together in his mind at the same time.

"I just want to do something in my life. Something that isn't based on war. That's all there's been since I was little."

"You're fortunate not to have had the fighting come here."

She looked at him and her expression softened. "It came close, but you're right. We escaped the worst of it. But you've seen it. You've been in it."

"Very little. Only a couple of battles, and after the first one I wasn't on the front lines, I was with the generals and officers."

"You must have been important. Here," she pulled him to their favorite bench and sat down. "Tell me what you really did.'

He realized that he'd let out something new for her to question him about. "Not much. I mean, I was just a boy myself, and they needed young fellows to run errands and take messages back and forth."

She looked at him even more intently than usual. "Father told me not to ask you about your time in the army. He said sometimes it's better not to know everything, and we have to be careful in these times when we don't even know who's got the power around here anymore."

He tried to shake her off. "Well, it's nothing important. I didn't do anything wrong, if that's what you're worried about."

"I'm not worried about what you might have done. I'm worried about what might happen to you from now on."

"Let's talk about you instead. All right?" He leaned over and picked a stray flower that was growing out of the grass at the end of the bench. "Here. For you and for your success in whatever you decide to do."

She took the flower and held it gently between her two hands, touching them to each other as if in prayer. "Lester, have you ever been in love?"

He didn't answer right away and she was looking down at the ground. If he said yes, what would that do to her curiosity? If he said no and she somehow found out later, it would be another deception, and already she'd more than once been upset and hurt by his inability to keep a promise.

"When I was younger, I might have thought I was," he said.

"I don't care about your stories. I don't want to know about your past in that way. I just want to know what it feels like. I want someone to tell me what it's like."

"Well, I'm not sure I'd be the one. I really don't know much about it, and, even if I did, I don't think I could put it in words."

"Yes, I know. Mattie said the same thing when I asked her. She said it doesn't go into words very well. But I want to know—so when it happens to me, I'll know what it is. If my mother were still alive I could ask her, but I don't have anyone."

He stood and took one of her hands to help her up. "I'm sure you'll know when it comes to you . . . now let's get home before Mattie's angry with us."

She held onto his hand and looked up into his eyes and then away, saying, "I think about it all the time. That and what I'm going to do with my life. Sometimes they seem the same."

He let go of her hand and smiled down at her. "You have almost your whole life ahead of you. You don't have to hurry."

As the summer passed, Abe was surprised to discover that Sarah Beth had participated in the delivery of three babies born at the fort to women of families who'd lost their homes. It wasn't unusual for him not to know this. Men, especially young, single men, were hardly ever included in discussions of pregnancy or birth. But he was suddenly very curious about how it had been for her. When asked, she simply informed him that she'd told him about wanting to be a doctor and that working with the midwives was probably the best way she could get herself started on that path.

Doctor Randall was visiting the fort more. A small congregation had cropped up among the convalescent soldiers and refugees who were staying on while waiting for some kind of help to get resettled on a piece of land or in a job. There were times when he urged Abe to fill in for him when he couldn't meet all of his obligations, but Abe was reluctant, and let the minister know that he felt unqualified. He also said he was having a hard enough time fulfilling his duties as the clergyman's assistant, and as the de facto military leader on the local scene.

The War finally seemed to have truly ended and its immediacy was slowly receding from the forefront of everyone's minds. The issues of economic recovery and social adjustment to new governing structures involved many of the citizens in a wide-ranging search for blame for the events of the recent past. Politicians, bureaucrats and all manner of interlopers from the North were being sent into Southern states, and both Union government officials and the opportunists referred to as "carpet baggers" were showing up in many places. Elections were scheduled and candidates chosen from among newcomers as well as long-time residents. The quest for votes and fairness at the ballot-box were both topics of heated conversations and sometimes fighting. Once again Doctor Randall was pressured to take sides from the pulpit, and while it was a risk in light of what had gone before, he once again pledged himself to a kind of sacramental neutrality as far as his own messages from the pulpit were concerned. While this pleased no one, it did keep him from being targeted by any one of the many factions that were forming in the chaos of the post-war times.

He and his young assistant continued to have occasional discussions about history and current events relating to God's place in the affairs of men. One day, while working together on the notes for an upcoming sermon, the Doctor asked Abe if he'd ever thought of moving west.

"Not really. Oh, I guess perhaps a bit now and then."

"Well, it seems to me that that's where the opportunity lies for a young fellow like yourself, especially one with a possibly problematic past. I understand that once you get past St. Louis, there are no questions asked and a man is taken at his word as long as he doesn't get caught lying or cheating in his dealings with all the others much like himself."

"I guess I've not given much thought to all that. I was just hoping that someday soon I could safely find my way back to where I grew up, find my mother, and perhaps reclaim some of the family property and business."

"Is your mother still alive? Have you heard from her?"

"She was somewhat ill, but still living when I last heard from my cousin Flora. As far as I know, Mother's been staying with her sister, that's Flora's mother."

"Well son, from what I've heard, we're a lot better off out here than they are back where you came from, and you know as well as I do that we're not all that well off. Things could turn bad very quickly. I'm reminded of the days of the prophets when they warned their people of God's wrath and the need to cleanse themselves of wayward and selfish thinking. More and more I see man's desperation pitting one against another, and the enmity that remains from the War is beginning to creep into everything we do and say. Why, just the other day, there was a meeting of some of this church's elders to consider breaking away from the sister churches in the North because they were considering ordaining colored men as ministers of a few congregations. Can you imagine a colored man in our pulpit?"

"No sir, can't say as I can. Where would they get the divinity training? Where would they get the authority?"

"Well, Lester Greene," the doctor gave a quick smile as he said that name, "here's my dilemma. I have already seen that day coming, and the authority to be God's shepherd here on earth does not come from men, but from God Himself. At our meeting, I opposed this spirit of dissension and division, and cautioned against taking a political stand in matters of the Church. After all, both the Union and the Confederacy gave at least lip service to the historic separation of church and state. And we should do likewise . . . But our board wasn't satisfied with what I had to say. We'll see where it leads, but I must say I am concerned."

There were no incidents for the patrols during the summer months and Abe was beginning to worry about the morale of the men, whose grumbling sometimes reached his ears. The problem was that reports of what were now being called "marauders" were coming in from further west, as far away as Missouri and Kansas, and some of the men wanted to leave Fort Lewis and strike out for more action and possibly more rewards. He couldn't blame them, but his position was such that he needed to remind them of the hardships of such a journey for men whose convalescence had been successful, but whose disabilities were, like his own, permanent.

Because of the lull in any apparent need for the services of the patrols, and therefore for his own role, he had twice approached the Major to request time away from his responsibilities. Both times he had been informed that it was only because the patrols were so effective that there hadn't been more incidents requiring their active response. Sarah Beth continued to occasionally remind him of his "promise" that he would remove himself from these duties as soon as the training phase had been completed. His only honest reply was that he was trying to be relieved of this small command, and would keep on trying until such time as he was released.

Meanwhile, the young woman had assisted at three more births and was now qualified to deliver on her own if the need arose. Abe often saw her with one or more of the infants she had helped to bring into the world. She and their mothers would take them out into the central courtyard of the fort to give them some fresh air and sunshine. The oldest of them were even allowed to try to crawl a bit on the hard-packed ground of the old parade grounds.

Once, on one of their walks home at the end of a day's work, he asked her if she would be leaving soon, headed for medical school somewhere. She laughed at him and replied, "You know that's impossible. Those places have waiting lists a mile long and they're all in the North where a Southern girl will always find herself at the bottom." She paused, looking straight ahead. "I think I'll just wait and see what you do."

Once again, autumn was beginning to transform the countryside, and although the area's crops had been more successful this summer than last, the continuing lack of transportation and the number of abandoned farms did not bode well for the coming winter. Many of the homeless who'd taken sanctuary at the fort were fortunate to have found some kind of work and a place to stay, either with relatives or working for others. But now the Major was receiving more and more inquiries concerning his plans for returnees whose employment and accommodations had only been temporary. And once again rumors were being spread about armed gangs who had moved west, but were returning to Virginia's relatively civilized and more bountiful resources.

One afternoon when Abe was putting final arrangements together to have the patrols double as hunting parties that could supply wild game to the kitchens of the fort, he was summoned by the Major. "You've got a letter here, son. And before you read it, I need you to speak your mind on the subject of allowing Negroes to come into the fort. There are an increasing number of ex-slaves with no visible means of sustenance and some of the charities in town are asking what I'm going to do about it." He handed the letter across the desk. It was addressed to Lt. Lester Greene in a small, neat and feminine script. The name on the back of the envelope was Flora Cavanaugh. There was no address for this sender, but it was clear it was from his cousin.

"I'm sure you're curious, no matter whether it's from an admiring lady or a relative, so I won't keep you long. But this issue is going to require some serious decision making. First of all, there is still, in fact, no government out here in these parts. Oh, I know the local bunch consider themselves to be functional, but do they collect any taxes? And the fire department has been fortunate not to have any serious burns they couldn't handle with their scarce volunteers and old equipment. Myself, I'm much more concerned about civil law and order. If we start taking in the colored refugees as well, we run the risk of being attacked both politically and even physically by angry citizens and who knows who all else. In addition, we also take on the burden of possible conflict between those staying here inside the fort. So, Lieutenant, what would you do?"

Abe looked down into his hands and turned the letter over a couple of times. He really had nothing to say, at least not right at the moment.

"All right, son. I didn't expect an answer right away. But I do think you'll have to help me figure out how to turn your patrol into some kind of an organized police force for the preservation of order here on our grounds, and maybe even helping out in the town."

"Sir?" Abe finally spoke up, "I'm not at all sure I'm the one for you to be consulting on this. I have no experience and I'm too young to exercise any authority whatsoever. These men listen to me and follow my lead only because they've got nothing better to do. And we are only just beginning to implement your request for us to become a hunting party to provide fresh meat for the people, and now this . . ."

"Don't worry, boy. If all this goes ahead, you'll be given all the authority you'd need. We'll back you all the way, with the combined influence of the town's council and the state's administrators in Alexandria, who are surrogates for the Yankee government. It's them that have told me I'll have to have police protection for the fort if it's to continue to receive any further financial or material support. I don't think you know how critical that support is. We wouldn't last a month without it, and now they've asked us to earn it in this additional way. You're the man to do it. Think it over. I'll be gone briefly, but when I return, day after tomorrow, we'll start working on the details and organizational matters. For now, start getting used to being called both lieutenant and chief of police."

He stood up and extended his hand. Abe took it and shook with him. He'd been thrown into a complete state of confusion and didn't trust himself to speak, so he just nodded his head and turned to leave.

"Son, I hope that letter's good news."

"Thank you, sir."

Abe was anxious to read the letter, but he wanted to be done with his duties and have a private time and place for it. He returned to the small armory building the patrols used as their headquarters and made sure that all of the guns were clean and stacked away. He finished the inventory of ammunition he'd started earlier that day, and made sure that all the cabinets were closed and secured. It wasn't a big change in mission to focus on hunting rather than aimless patrolling over the same roads, week after week, but it was a morale benefit for the men, who seemed to respond with a new sense of purpose and excitement, not unlike when the patrols first began. Becoming a police force, however, was something quite different, and he wasn't sure how they'd respond.

He locked the building, gathered up his coat and gloves, and set off walking home. It was still a little strange for him to call the church and its grounds "home," but he found himself using that term more often than not. Of course, as he frequently reminded himself, all of this was only temporary and the time was coming when he would have to make some decisions and moves that addressed the future and whatever he intended to make of himself. His elbow was still improving slightly and slowly, but the chances of recovering full flexibility seemed to be less and less. His ability to compensate for its limitations was becoming the habit of his life and movements. At this point, the one thing he hadn't yet been able to do, and was very much looking forward to, was riding horseback on his own once again.

The late afternoon was turning into one of those fall evenings when the soft sunset blue of the sky fades away ever so slowly. The song of the local birds increased in what seemed like an attempt to hold back the night. He reached the bridge and considered climbing down to the water's edge, but instead he continued on to a bench that faced the stream on the other side.

He sat still and quietly gathered his thoughts. Once again the Major was putting him in a no-choice situation where he would have to go along with a request that was more like an order. Or he'd have to stand up to the man with a refusal that would most likely be interpreted as ingratitude for how he'd been provided for. The only solution that would make his refusal acceptable would be his need to leave the area, but he could think of no likely reason for that. He took the letter out of his pocket and thought about it. Perhaps there was an answer sealed in its contents. He used a small pocketknife to slice the envelope along its top edge, and drew out the thin, textured sheet of paper. He unfolded it and began to read:

My dear Cousin Abraham,

It has been such a long time since we have seen you, so much has happened to you and to us. Times are very hard and we are wondering if you will ever return this way again. Your Aunt Caroline, my Mother, thinks you will. I am not so sure, especially now that your Mother has passed on to her reward. Yes Abe, I know of no other way to tell you this except to be very straightforward. The doctors are not sure of the cause of her demise, but to me it is clear that she was lonely and her grief for your Father took her away to join him once again in the better life beyond. Mother and I are so sorry and offer you our deepest sympathy and care.

He stopped reading and looked up into the sky above him with almost no feeling at all. It was as if he'd known this was coming, that it had to happen and that there was nothing that could be explained or taken personally. Of course his mother would fail to go on, would give up and pass away. She had given everything to her family and to her neighbors, and suddenly she'd been more alone than ever in her life. He felt his own emptiness, but knew this was not yet mourning, which would come later, if at all. He shook his head and rubbed his face with his good hand, realizing that it was now he who was alone with no family, with no one out ahead on the path in front of him. Those who'd always been there were gone now, and he would have to make that path his own, on his own, or he would become lost. He went back to reading:

We have heard nothing from or about Irene Ruth and her family since they left for Philadelphia. I assume that you had heard that. I hope you are not saddened by this turn of events, although I know you loved her in your heart. I, myself, was never partial to her, and would wish you the best in moving ahead with your own life, free of those obligations that might well have taken your own life away from you in service to her family's needs. I suppose I shouldn't write like this to you now, but I'm not even sure if this letter will reach you, and have little hope for any further opportunities to reach you in the future.

The other news of importance to you is that my brother and your cousin, Louis, has decided to seek his fortune in the West and will be travelling your way rather sooner than later. I beg you to take him in, and even provide him with your advice as he describes to you what he is about. It is enough to say that he is somewhat bitter at having been too young for the War and equally upset by the absence of any exciting opportunities for a young man in the midst of the destruction and waste that surrounds us at this time. If he reaches your location, I am sure he will fill your ears concerning his ideas and fantastical plans for a life on what is called the Frontier. I am very worried for him, but cannot convince him to think otherwise and I tender him into your hands if you can find a way to convince him otherwise.

We love you, Abraham, you were always like a brother to me, and I will miss you with all my heart until I see you again, either in this life or the next.

Your loving cousin, Flora

Abe re-read the letter slowly, folded it carefully and held it loosely in his hands. The sound of the water seemed to have grown louder and his thoughts were muddled and empty of any idea of what this meant for him as next steps in his life. His mother was gone, so now it was finished, the family that had at one time been his entire world. He wasn't sure how he should react. Should he send a letter of his own to his aunts, expressing gratitude for their taking in his mother toward the end? Should he just respond to Flora and have her give messages to her own mother and their aunt? And, above all, was there now any point in even considering a return to the land of his childhood and younger days?

As he pondered these things, the voice of his cousin seemed to echo in his mind with her curt dismissal of Irene Ruth: "never partial to her." And now Louis might arrive unannounced at any time, hopefully looking for Lester Greene rather than someone named Abraham. Abe rechecked the address on the envelope and it was indeed sent to Lt. Lester Greene. There was hopefully, at least a chance that Lewis would ask for a Lieutenant Greene, rather than his cousin, Abe Saunders, when he arrived.

Louis was six years younger than himself, and Abe remembered him as a wild kind of youngster, often gone into the woods outside of town for a few days at a time, playing at or really being what he called a frontiersman, alone and hunting, fishing and roaming the hilly countryside. They often had fun together as children, but Abe remembered spending more time with Flora than with his youngest cousin. He wondered what . . . Just then he heard Sarah Beth's voice from the bridge, interrupting his thoughts.

"What are you doing there?"

He pushed the letter into his pocket and stood quickly. "Enjoying the quiet," he said, starting to move toward her.

"Stay there. I want some quiet, too." She crossed the bridge. "I have had such a day." She came right up next to him and took his hand in hers. "I am so tired from walking and walking these crying babies."

"Why you?" he asked.

"One of the new mothers lost a lot of blood during her birthing, that was yesterday, and she's almost too weak to do anything, can barely nurse her baby. And another one is just exhausted from having had almost no sleep for a week because her baby has the colic and cries all the time. So, I'm the walker, and the rocker. Wears me out." She sat down on the bench and pulled him back down next to her. "You look sad, are you all right, and don't tell me nothing's wrong like you usually do."

"I guess I'm all right." He paused and then decided to go on. "I just got word that my mother passed away."

"Oh, Lester, I'm so sorry. When? How?"

"I don't know any of the details. My cousin wrote to me. She thinks it was grief for my father and her being mostly alone now."

"She was staying with her sisters, you'd said."

"Yes, but that wasn't enough, I'm sure. Perhaps if I'd been there, I could have helped, could have made it different."

"Lester, you can't blame yourself. And there was no way you could have returned. Father says . . . oh-oh, I'm not saying that."

"Father says what?"

"Nothing, just that it might not be safe for you to return home, or something like that. I don't remember now."

"Of course." He looked at her closely, "I almost believe you."

"Was there other news?"

"Not really, just that life is very difficult, people are leaving, and some are even heading out west."

"Lester, Lester, I'm so sorry," she said as she placed her arm around his shoulders. He suddenly looked up to the bridge, aware that they were close together and could be seen. He eased away from her arm and stood slowly.

"Let's go home. I'll be all right."

She looked up into his eyes and gave him a small smile that was so filled with soft concern that he could feel tears forming in the corners of his eyes. He shook his head and turned away, pulling her back toward the road. It would be better to mourn when he was alone.

The next day when Abe arrived at the fort, there was a strange covered buggy tied to the railing in front of the Major's office building. He walked past it toward the armory where he'd arranged for some of the men to gather this morning, but was interrupted by his name called from the Major's doorway.

"Lieutenant, Major wants you to come in for a minute."

He walked toward the voice and passed inside. In the anteroom, three men in long coats were standing with the Major.

"Gentlemen, this is Lieutenant Greene, my most able assistant and the organizing commander of the patrol you asked about. Lester, these gentlemen are Union government marshals. They've come from west of here to warn us of what may be coming our way."

He turned back to the men and asked if they wanted a place to sit and any kind of refreshment.

"No sir, that won't be necessary. We've got to be moving along, need to make it to Richmond as quickly as possible. Lieutenant, we've heard about your organized corps of wounded veterans. We admire your initiative in these perilous times. As we were telling the Major here, things are breaking down the further west you go, and some of this chaos may be coming your way. Missouri may seem like a long ways away, but when men are on the run they can travel pretty fast. How many men do you have that can handle their weapons? And how many can ride unassisted?"

The Major spoke up, "I'll answer those questions sir, if you don't mind. We have lost some of our volunteer troops due to their recovery and subsequent return home. Others have no home to return to, but are becoming fully capable. All in all, what we've got is more like a volunteer force of irregulars that can hardly be expected to perform as a regular combat unit. That being said, the twenty or so men under Lieutenant Greene's command are more seasoned than many of the troops who fought in the War, and are quite eager to serve when needed. What we lack are the financial resources to assure that they will be given enough of compensation that they'll remain here. I'm sure you understand that we have no authority for forced conscription in this activity."

"We understand," the spokesman said, "and will make this known at the highest levels in the state's government. As far as holding out any hope of success for your request, there's no way to say what's possible and what's not, but it is certainly a most legitimate request. In addition, we will recommend that an officer and squad of own regulars be assigned to support this activity. You are truly the guardians of the gateway between the lawless lands to the west and the civilized territory from here to the east, and you shouldn't have to do it alone." The spokesman saluted and the three men turned on their heels and left the building. Within moments the sounds of their horses and buggy were heard leaving.

"Well, it's finally come. We've lost our independence. From now on, from now on . . . I just don't know what will happen." The Major beckoned his lieutenant into his office.

"So you think this will change things, sir."

"Oh yes, we've been found, discovered, and we're not a problem for them, rather we seem to be a solution to one of the Union government's problems, God save us now. So, young man, I believe you may have a short-lived period as a hunting party, but I do urge you to go ahead on it as quickly as possible. Then we'll just have to see what happens when this so-called small squad of Union soldiers and their commander show up. It will be most interesting for me to be taking orders from someone again, especially a Yankee."

"Then, I best go ahead as we planned?"

"Yes, hell, who knows if any of this will happen. As far as I've heard, the Union Army's no better off than ours. Winning isn't always everything it's blown up to be. I'm sure you can imagine what I mean."

"Yes sir. I guess we'll just have to wait to see what comes of it all. Do you think there's truth to their warning about more renegades coming this way?"

"I don't believe it any more or less than any other rumor we hear on a daily basis. Besides, the more fear you can spread around, the more power you have, and right now everybody on both sides is scrambling for whatever little bit of power they can get their hands on. Son, I believe we've seen the last of this country's time in the forefront of history. Don't see how we'll ever recover from this whole sorry mess. But then it's not our problem, is it?"

"No sir. I'll be going then, if we're done here. Men waiting."

"Go, go, get on with it. And in case I don't ever tell you enough, I'm very grateful for all your help and counsel. Don't think any of it has gone unnoticed."

As Abe walked across the grounds of the fort to where some of his men were waiting, he couldn't help thinking about the change he'd just seen come over the Major. First time he'd ever talked about the effects of the War, first time he'd thanked his Lieutenant. Maybe he was looking ahead to his own loss of power. After all, he'd pretty much had full control of the fort and its affairs for some time, and he'd done a pretty good job of it, as far as Abe could judge.

Several nights later, Doctor Randall invited Abe into his study for another one of their man-to-man talks. Of course Sarah Beth was curious, and beginning to agitate, but her father quieted her objections in short order.

"My dear girl, there are times when things call for a conversation between two and only two people. I'm sure you'll find this true enough once you're married."

She seemed to blush slightly and quickly left the dining area.

"I say, has that girl of mine ever let on how she feels about you?" He spoke softly.

Abe was suddenly tongue-tied, but mumbled out a few words, "I don't think so."

"Well, she's got no one besides the two of us to give her affection to and a young girl will naturally have affection to give. I'm her father, and you, you're the fascinating young stranger from who knows where . . . Why don't we adjourn to the study?"

They sat quietly for awhile, sipping a pleasant, after-meal sherry. Then the Doctor drew out of his desk a small, bound booklet.

"This is the Constitution and Governing Rules of Conduct for our Church and its fellow congregations throughout these now once again 'United States.' People have been sending me citations and quotations from this document for several months now, more and more lately. It seems that the clamor for secession has not subsided all that much, in spite of the War and its terrible consequences. Now, it is the Church which is being driven asunder by factions and fractions of unholy competition over matters which have no place in our Houses of Worship, or amongst the Men of God . . . Lester, I must unburden my heart to you once again, for I fear we may have to make some fairly major changes in our lives, at least Sarah Beth and myself."

"Are you all right, sir?" Abe asked, remembering that the man had been to see a medical specialist recently, but never talked about it.

"Am I all right? I suppose so, in mind and body, I suppose so. It is my soul that is upset at this time, in these continuing days of pain and lost hope. The board of deacons and their various supporters have finally announced to me that they are considering joining, with many other Southern congregations, in a move to separate from our brethren and sisters in the North. To dissolve the bonds of holy union, even as our political realm reunites its own. And the issue is somewhat the same. The rights of autonomy and self-determination for each congregation, and the restrictions placed on the ordination of our ministers and clergy. Why, it's as if we are going to fight the War over again, only this time without cannons and rifles, using instead slanders and slurs against one another's failures in holiness and devotion to the One God who is above us all. I am sick at heart, young man, truly sick at heart. I thought it was bad enough to be chastised for praying for peace in the midst of a war, but now I am being rebuked for standing against the belief that God made the black man ineligible for the study of His Words and most incapable of interpreting them to His flock."

He paused to pour himself another half-glass and offered some to Abe who politely refused.

"Let me get to the point, son. Simply this. I am convinced I will be removed from my position in this church by its leaders and its congregation if I don't subscribe to the Articles of Disassociation being promulgated by many of our churches here in the South, all because three black men have been ordained ministers of the Lord in Philadelphia, New York and Boston. And I say unto you, may the Lord have mercy."

He sank back into his chair and covered his face with his hands. Abe sat quietly not knowing what to say, or if he should even try to speak. After some time, Doctor Randall sat up abruptly and slapped his hand on the desk.

"But I have forgotten myself," he said. "How rude of me, going on about my problems when you have lost your mother. Sarah Beth informed me this morning. Said she was waiting for you to tell me, but thought I should know if you were holding it inside, keeping it back from me. I am so sorry to hear this."

"Yes, sir. I did receive the news a few days ago, but hadn't the chance to bring it up to you. I was aware of some of this turmoil you're going through and felt it better not to concern you with something that can neither be changed nor helped now."

"Well, thank you, I appreciate your concern for me, but I want you to know that both my daughter and I have come to consider you as almost a part of our small family, and if there's anything we can do, you must let us know and help. Do you have plans now? Would you ever try to return to your previous home now?"

"No, sir. That would be impossible, and it would serve no purpose. Whatever has been done for her has already been done, and I would only add to the burden of the rest of my mother's people if I were to arrive there."

"Well, I'm sure you know what is best, in this case. For the time being, please rest assured that we will continue to be grateful for your presence in our home and wish you to be assured that the invitation continues. Now, if there's nothing else, I must begin composing an answer to the upstart wardens and vestry, defending myself and my opinions in these matters of faith and their lack thereof. I have no doubt they have already contacted the bishop himself."

Abe stood to leave, and then leaned forward with his good hand on the desk, "Sir, there is one other thing. In the same letter I was informed that a young man, my first cousin, may be headed this way on his journey to the western country. If he arrives, I'd need to accept him as a visitor and a relative. Is there any chance that he could have a few days of accommodation in the quarters that I first used here, the addition behind the sanctuary?"

"Of course, Lester, family is family."

"Thank you and good night, sir. I do hope that your reasonable approach to these religious matters will be understood and heeded by others. I know I agree with you. Good night, sir." He turned and left the room, closing the door behind him.

As he walked down the long hallway to the front of the house, Sarah Beth stepped out of a small room and stopped him with a touch on his arm. She whispered, "I want to talk with you, on the porch please."

She led him around the large veranda to the swinging settee, in the near-dark of the still pleasant evening. They sat together, swaying gently for a few long moments.

"I told father that your mother had passed away. I thought you would have informed him, but since you hadn't I took it on myself. He was very upset, for you, and for us, because now he's afraid you will leave. He is going through a difficult time now with the Church and its backward and mutinous leaders."

"Yes, I know, we just talked a little of this."

"Well, I don't know what's going to happen, but it can't be good for him, or for us. He didn't back down last time, and he won't this time. Father always places his principles and his faith above the wishes of people, no matter who they may be."

"I'd think that's an admirable quality in a rector of a church."

"When the petty and the blind lead the blind, I don't know. I know I should not talk like that, but they're so mean-spirited and father is the most sensitive man alive, even though he tries hard not to show it . . . Lester, what will happen to us?" She clutched at his arm, forgetting it was the damaged elbow. He gently removed her hand and flexed his arm.

"Oh no," she said, "your arm. I'm so sorry."

"It's all right, doesn't hurt anymore. I think it's healed as well as it's going to, and there's not really any pain anymore." He took her hand and placed it back on his arm. "It was just a reflex, honestly."

"If you're sure."

"And to answer your question, I don't know what's going to happen. I don't think anyone does these days. Things are changing out at the fort and I'm not sure I want to stay on with what's coming. I just don't know. There have been Union men there talking about sending in some of their troops to help us out. And they didn't ask us if we needed help. The Major's a bit worried . . . but don't talk about this with anyone."

"Oh no, I won't. I promise. But you must also promise me that you won't leave us, not while things are so upsetting, please Lester."

"Of course, I'll stay as long as I'm needed. Now we should go in, or you'll get chilled."

"Wait. One other thing. Remember when I asked if you'd ever felt love?"

"Yes."

"Well, I think I have now."

He tried to see into her face in the darkness. "Really? Is it someone I know?"

"I can't talk about it. I just think I know more about it now than I did."

Surprise was his first feeling, followed by curiosity and then concern, "Well, I do hope you know what you're doing," he said.

"Lester, I think one of the things about love is that you don't know what you're doing. I read that in a book called *Thoughts for Living*."

"I suppose that's right, then. But we should go in. It's getting late." He stood and helped her to her feet. Lamplight from within the house shone briefly on her face and he could see a shine in her eyes that could be either tears of sadness or happiness. "Come now," he said, and led her around the corner of the house to the doorway, and then inside. Suddenly she pulled away and was gone, rapidly climbing the stairs to her room. She turned back once and said only, "Goodnight, Lester."

Tensions were growing within the fort among those who'd come for refuge. Some of those who had been there the longest resented the arrival of additional newcomers, fearing that there wouldn't be enough for everyone as winter came on. This was especially apparent between some of the whites and coloreds. The Major called Abe into his office for a conference concerning the situation and ordered him to give strict instructions to the men of the patrol that it was their job to maintain the peace, and that they were specifically forbidden to engage in any of this potential competition. Abe was also instructed to assure everyone within the fort that help and supplies were on the way and that there would be no tolerance whatsoever for any outbreaks of conflict among the residents. Punishment for causing such problems would be immediate expulsion with no questions asked or excuses considered.

Abe tried to frame this message as best he could without causing defensive and blaming reactions among those he would be telling. He soon abandoned the personal delivery of this message in his own voice and had notices printed and posted in many prominent places throughout the Fort. He got the Major to sign it and he himself co-signed. A few of the men of the patrol tried to engage him in discussions about the issue, but he said simply that the message was clear and there was no reason for not following its directives.

In spite of these precautions, the tensions continued and harsh words were sometimes exchanged between individuals. Abe instituted inspection tours of the fort's grounds and premise. The tours were random and unscheduled and seemed to instill a bit of caution among the residents. While this appeared to be somewhat of a solution, he was soon made aware that a new danger existed as a result of empowering certain members of the patrol with police-like duties. Some of his men seemed to take their limited power of overseeing the behavior of others as justification for becoming more aggressive, and there were even a few accusations of favoritism in the enforcement against arguments and conflict. Sides were occasionally being taken, against Abe's orders, and he was now unwillingly drawn into the role of a mediator or even an informal judge.

As the autumn weeks turned colder, and the first snow flurries fell, dusting the western hillsides with a white outline, Abe found himself more and more frustrated with his duties and more and more anxious to leave all of it behind. If only he had some choice or alternative. He was in this restless frame of mind when he heard one of the men calling to him from the gateway into the fort.

He walked briskly across the open space of the former military parade ground, hoping that this was not an emergency or any untoward event in the making. He caught sight of his patrolman and another man standing just inside the open gates. The bright red hair of the stranger looked instantly familiar. As he drew closer he could see that it was indeed his young cousin, Louis, and that there was a horse standing just behind him.

"Lieutenant Greene, this man says he's here to see you about finding someone you're supposed to know."

"Thanks Albert," Abe said, and when the man turned his head back to the stranger for a moment, Abe put his finger to his lips in a sign for silence from his cousin. "I'll take care of this. You're dismissed from this post for a few minutes. Come back in a half hour."

The patrolman took his cane from where it was propped against the gatepost and shuffled away.

"Abe? Abe? What the hell is going on?"

"Louis. Don't use that name around me, not here. I'll explain when I have the chance. I am Lieutenant Lester Greene, assistant to the commander of this fort, and in charge of its small security force." He lowered his voice to a whisper, "Lester Greene, have you got that?"

"Well sure, Abe, I mean Lester, long as you let me in on what this is all about."

"I will, as soon as we can get some privacy. Now, your horse looks hungry. You can tie him out on that patch of grass along the wall there. If you're hungry as well, we'll find you something to eat. If not, you'll have to wait with your horse until I can get away to take you to where I'm staying, to where I can put you up, for a few days at least."

"I've got some food in my saddle-pack. Might as well use it up before it goes bad." He held out his hand and Abe took it in a long handshake.

"Glad you made it here all right, Louis, very glad . . . Oh, it might be better if you put that pistol you're wearing in your saddle pack. I don't think you'll need it here." Then he turned and walked back to the building where he'd been before all this.

Part II

Missouri

November 1866-May 1868

CHAPTER FIVE

Decisions

Louis stayed with Abe for several days before they got the opportunity for a private conversation that wouldn't be interrupted. They took rifles and went into the woods some ways above the town and practiced with a small supply of ammunition Abe requisitioned from the fort for use in recovering his own skills. Louis brought his handgun and gave Abe a chance to shoot it. His previous experience with a pistol had been with a two-hand grip and sideways stance, but he found that once he got control of the recoil he was proficient one handed. With more practice, Louis assured him, he would get quite accurate.

As the Saturday afternoon wore on, they stopped to share swallows of whiskey from a flask that Louis produced from within his jacket. "I don't hardly drink much," he said as he handed the container to Abe, "but there's some times that call for a bit of celebration, don't you think?"

With the exception of wine when Doctor Randall and Sarah Beth invited guests for supper, and the sherry he and the minister sometimes shared during their evening talks, Abe had taken almost no alcohol since before his injury. He carefully sipped on the flask and felt the burn spread through his chest. He hoped he could believe Louis; he'd seen many a young man let the bottle get hold of him.

Louis took a full swallow and then, screwing the cap back on the flask, looked intently at his cousin. "So, Cousin, why the new name? It's real hard for me to keep from using Abe since I've known you all my life. I think it's easier for me to just call you Cuz than to remember now you're this Lester fellow."

"Cuz would be fine, especially if it helps keep you from slipping up and calling me by my old name. The explanation is both simple and complicated." Louis offered him another drink. He turned it down, and the younger man put the flask back inside his coat. "As you must have found out, I served on President Davis's staff as an attaché for the last year or more of the War. When it ended for us and Lincoln was shot, accusations were made that the assassination was the result of conspiracy on the part of our president and some of his staff. As far as I know this was the fabrication of angry men looking to blame Southerners for more than just the War itself. In any case, to this day, I have not been able to find out what is going on with all of that, except that Jefferson Davis is still imprisoned and the trial has not yet been held."

"Wow, you really were right up there then. Must have been exciting for you. I'm still angry I missed it all, being too young."

"Most of what I had to do was no more than glorified clerical work, transcribing and sending orders out to commanders, making records and lists of supplies and the debts that were incurred, and so on."

A large gray squirrel screamed at them from a tree some twenty yards away. Louis drew and fired almost instantly, and missed. "I'm out of practice," he mumbled. "How'd you get hurt? Bet that wasn't in an office."

Abe told his cousin about the ride to Appomattox and Lee's surrender, the wound and the ride across Virginia with the wagons of injured, most of them worse off than himself. And he went on to tell of the very wonderful hospitality of Doctor Randall and his daughter.

"That Sarah Beth is something of a wildcat," Louis said softly. "Wouldn't want to have to try and tame her."

Abe thought about this, recalling a couple of incidents when Sarah Beth and his cousin had already exchanged sharp looks at something one or the other had said or done, mostly involving himself. "She's not so bad," he said, "just had it hard since her mother passed away. And there's been some troubles for her father within the Church. Hopefully they'll go away, but it seems that some of his beliefs and those of the more unenlightened of this congregation's leaders just don't fit very well. We'll most likely see how that turns out sooner than later."

"Abe, I mean Cuz, I'm headed west, way west. I want you to know that. Hey, I'd even like you to come with me. We'd make a great pair.

We'll be frontiersmen, like Kit Carson and those others. There's still time out there for killing Indians and fighting outlaws."

"Now, Louis," Abe said quietly, "it's probably not all that exciting. Mostly I'd wager it's a hard life with low chances of success or even survival."

"No worse than war, Cuz, and since I missed that, I've got to make up for it. I've read everything I can get my hands on about life out there. I not going to miss out this time, and there's a fortune to be made if you get the right chances. Think about it. Besides what can you be doing here?"

"Well, I have been thinking about my next move, but we'll just have to see. Doctor Randall has explained to me that God's directions don't always come in a Voice we can hear, but more often in the way our opportunities and our needs line up. We'll just have to see about all that. Anyway, this day's getting on and we should head for the supper table. Isn't that Mattie quite a cook?"

"One of the best, but she gets away with saying things I've never heard a colored woman say before."

"Well, that probably has a lot to do with our reverend's beliefs that God made everyone equal. That's one of the causes of his troubles that I told you about. Hey, I'll race you to the creek at the bottom of the hill."

They both took off running and jumping down the hill through low-lying brush, bumping off of trees and nearly falling every step of the way. It was the first time since his injury that Abe had felt confident enough to try anything so foolish. When they reached the small creek, he tried to catch his breath and wondered if it was the small amount of alcohol that stimulated him to such foolhardiness. Probably not, he thought, probably just the time of day and the memory of all the games and fun and competition with his cousins when they were growing up.

Abe was granted permission from the Major to involve his cousin in the work of the patrol. As one of the few able-bodied members, Louis was useful in the hunting forays the group was undertaking. The supply of meat was increasing, but the men now had to go further afield to assure themselves of a decent return for their efforts. The women of the fort and volunteers from the town, including Sarah Beth, were busy drying, smoking, salting, canning and corning the meat they stripped from the bones. As the fall weather began to turn cold, stockpiles of venison, bear and even raccoon meat quickly accumulated and added to the urgency of preparing and storing the produce of the gardens and all the other food gathered for the coming winter season.

One evening as they finished supper, Doctor Randall asked Abe to join him in the study. It had been some time since the two of them had a session together. Abe was still keeping up with much of the minister's correspondence and turning his sermon notes into pages of neat script, but they were very seldom together in the study at the same time.

Sarah Beth quietly stated, "You both had better not expect me to entertain Louis here while you have your special men's talk."

"Why Sarah Beth, what's wrong?" her father spoke up seriously.

"I just don't like the feeling of you two running off as if we're the children and you have to leave us out of things."

Louis smiled and seemed to be enjoying the exchange.

Abe stood and excused himself, saying, "I have something to attend to, and then I'll be right with you, sir."

"It won't take us long this time, dear" the doctor was now smiling as he watched his daughter shake her head and put an exaggerated scowl on her face. "We wouldn't abandon our young adults, would we?"

When Abe entered the study and closed the door behind him, he could tell this was going to be a bit more serious than their usual conversations. The doctor was holding a small book that Abe recognized as the church's denominational constitution. The minister's large desk copy of the Bible was open in front of him.

"Sit down, Lester. What I have feared has come to pass, and I'll need your help.

The committee established by the leaders of the congregation has recommended a full and complete separation from the Northern Church and an alliance with what was now being called the Church South, an emerging association of both Church of England congregations and some from the Methodist organization as well. Two days hence there will be a meeting of those who are interested in this debate, its conclusions and direction. It will be held in the sanctuary at five o'clock in the evening. I would request that you attend, as a witness and as a note-taker for me. I cannot avoid thinking that this has taken on the elements of a trial of my person and my beliefs, in that it is well known that I oppose this movement as both divisive and in violation of the Word of God and His teachings."

"Yes, sir, I had no idea this was happening so fast."

"Neither did I, young man, but hysteria and action seem to go hand in hand, especially when they are based on overturning the recent feelings of defeat in the War and are based on a misguided and futile attempt to restore pride and power through another secession. I would also ask you for a few hours, either tomorrow or on the day of this meeting, for consultation and some assistance in the preparation of my statement and a defense of my position. I will not back down this time, nor will I ask any man's forgiveness for resisting this unholy path with all of my being. God's will be done."

They sat in silence for a long moment as Abe turned these developments over in his mind, and his mentor thumbed through the constitution.

"Just let me know if and when you're available, son. Now, you'd best get back to those 'children'."

"Yes, sir. I'll try to be back here mid-afternoon tomorrow. And sir, I'm sorry to hear about this. It doesn't seem right to me, and not just because it involves you."

"Fine. We'll talk further. Now, if you will, please leave me to my prayers."

As Abe let himself out of the study, he could hear the notes of the piano in the parlor. It was Sarah Beth and the melody was slow and somber. It was an old hymn that he could not remember the name of, but was lodged in his memory along with other churchly echoes of his childhood.

As he neared the closed door of the parlor, he looked around for Louis, thinking the younger man might be out on the porch or seated in the reading room. No one was about. He opened the door slowly, and quietly moved into the room. Sarah Beth's back was toward him as she bent over the keys. He could hear her humming along with the tune's melancholy chords.

After a moment, she stopped playing and turned toward him as if she'd known he was there. "How is Father?" she asked.

Abe had no way of knowing how much or what she knew, but it wouldn't have made much sense to avoid her question. "He's not doing so well."

"I know all about it, Lester. I know it's breaking his heart and challenging his faith. That's why I was playing this hymn of grief. Do you know it? Listen, "The storm has passed and we are now alone . . . Pray children, pray for your souls and for your salvation . . . lest the storm return, lest the storm return"

"I heard it as a child and recognized the sound of it, but had no memory of the words . . . Sarah Beth, he will need you now, more than ever."

"And you as well, the son he never had." She stood and came toward him, her hands held out, upturned. "We both need you. Oh, how we need you now. Please, please don't run off with your cousin," her words seemed to tumble out in a rush. "Please Lester. I've heard him paint his tales of the West. I've listened to his dreams and I am so afraid that he will sweep you up in those plans, and then what will happen to us?"

She placed her hands on his shoulder and drew him closer. He responded with an arm around her waist.

"I'll be here as long as I can be. I promise you that."

She buried her face against his chest and he felt the gentle sobbing that had begun inside of her. "Sarah, Sarah Beth. You must be strong now. Your father has no one else."

"He has you," she whispered.

The next morning, on his arrival at the fort, the Major summoned Abe to the old staff headquarters. Overnight, word had come from the recently instituted headquarters of Military District Number One, the most effective arm of the provisional Union government of post-War Virginia. A telegram had been delivered announcing the creation of the Western District of Virginia under the command of the state's military administration and to be directed from their own Fort Lewis.

"They say they're going to put forty troops here, charged with protecting the civil government of both the Roanoke Valley and our neighbors across the state line," the Major informed Abe as soon as he arrived. "No telling what's to happen with the families we have here now, and as far as you and me, I'd say we're probably both out of a job."

"When's this supposed to happen, sir?"

"A field visit by a squad accompanied by an assessment team intends to arrive next week. I've been ordered to cooperate fully with them. They act as if I'm in their army now. But I suppose that's better than being hanged or thrown in prison."

"What will you do, sir, once they've taken command?"

"I won't know what my options are right away. And I sure as hell don't want to join this leftover Union Army. They're looking for people to give ruined plantations to, down south of here and in the Carolinas, badly damaged lands, but land all the same. Perhaps it's time for me to go back to farming. I grew up that way and got away from it as soon as I was old enough to join the army. Frankly, Lieutenant, I don't know what else I can do. What about you?"

"Well, I don't know either, but it sounds like it might be time for me to move on, sir, or at least find a different occupation. You met my young cousin and he's all set on heading west, says he'll make his fortune out there. Can't say as I think it'd be all that easy, but it might be worth taking a look. So I guess I don't know either."

"Well, one thing's for sure, young man. This place is not going to be what it has been, and I doubt anyone will need our services here for much longer. I want you to know how much I've appreciated being able to depend on your assistance, your advice, and your ability to take on important responsibilities. And don't think I didn't recognize how reluctant you were all through this. One of the hard parts of my job here has been to convince you to have the confidence to help me get through what's been almost two long years."

The Major stood up from behind his desk, came around it and extended his arm in a handshake. Just as Abe went to take his grip, the major switched hands and grabbed Abe's left hand, the wounded side. He took that hand and shook it gently, gripping Abe's other shoulder with his free hand.

"You've made a strong recovery, young Abraham, and you'll be fine from now on, no matter where your life leads. If you ever need a reference, try to find me. I'd be proud the stand up for you. Now go and get things ready for that damn Yankee victory party that's coming to town. By the way, they warned me that a few of the soldiers may be coloreds. They've been recruiting."

Abe thanked the Major for his kind words and backed out the door, still stunned by the Major's use of his real name. He wondered how long the man had known. Maybe all along. Probably the doctor had told him. Well, he thought, a friend is a friend, and an officer can also be a friend, as it turned out. And now there would be colored troops.

Abe rounded up some of his patrol men and informed them of the coming changes. He offered them his own support in what came next for them, and, following the major's example, said he'd be pleased to compose letters of reference if they so desired. In the meantime, it was their duty to straighten up, sort out and prepare everything they'd accumulated as a patrol. Get it into good enough shape to hand over to the fort's new administration.

The men were unanimously unsettled by the news, but each one of them vowed he'd never serve the Yankees, no matter what. Abe simply smiled and said, "I know exactly how you feel, but things have a way of changing and one never knows about never."

Within a couple of hours he had the men and supplies in good enough order that he could leave for his appointment with his other mentor, the beleaguered Doctor Randall. Just as he was leaving the fort gates, he heard screaming and shouting from behind the barracks that housed refugees. He ran to see what was causing the outcry. Rounding the corner of the building, he saw a small crowd of Negroes surrounding one of his patrol soldiers. It was Big Thomas, a giant of a man who'd lost one of his arms.

"Corporal Thomas," he shouted, "stand down!" The man lowered his raised fist and backed up against the building. Relief showed in his face.

"Sir, I didn't do nothing," he said loudly. "It's a mistake."

"All right, all right," Abe yelled with all of the authority he could muster. "Quiet, quiet now, all of you."

He noticed that two women held another, who was shaking and sobbing. Two of the men were still locked in a pose of physical readiness for a potential attack against the Corporal. Guarding his sidearm with his good hand, Abe stepped in between Big Thomas and the two men.

"Now, what's this all about?"

One of the Negroes spat on the ground and said, "He made a move on my woman, sir. I seen him and I heard him. He didn't know I was behind him."

The other Negro spoke up, "Seem like he done forgot you-all lost the War."

"Enough." Abe turned to the corporal. "What do you say?"

"I wouldn't never do that, sir. I wouldn't. I was just trying to help. She was carrying that whole load of laundry and stumbled when she passed me by, and I said to her, 'Can I help you, Miss?' All of a sudden these boys tried to jump me."

"Ain't true," the first man said, "I heard him say to my woman here, 'Can I have a kiss?' I swear on the Bible that's what he said. Why else would she be crying so?"

Abe glanced over at the group of women, and then down at the huge pile of clothing on the ground. The woman had stopped her crying and was looking at him intently. "Ma'am," he said, "can you say what happened here?"

She shook her head no, once, twice, and then again.

"Well, it certainly would help if we could hear what you heard."

She was looking with fear at the man who claimed her. Abe got the sense that if she contradicted him, she would be in a hard and possibly dangerous position the next time they were alone together. At the same time, her words of recollection seemed like they would be the only solution in the situation.

Abe looked back at Big Thomas and saw the concern and even fear in the man's eyes. Abe suddenly recalled that the night before, this man, along with several others, had told him they would be leaving the fort because of the Yankees coming. They swore they'd never work for the Union Army, and they informed him that they had a place to work with one of the men's fathers over near Richmond.

Abe was in doubt as to whether to involve the Major in this dispute. He knew that if he could work it out, it was best to reduce the tension as quickly as possible and separate all the parties. Prolonging things with an investigation would leave it all boiling away. Then he hit a on a possible solution that seemed like it could work.

"Corporal Thomas, in the absence of any impartial testimony, and in sympathy with the difficulty that has brought these people here for refuge, I will ask and order all parties to cease and desist in perpetuating this conflict. I hereby order you, Corporal Thomas Chambers, to gather your personal items together and to leave this fort by tomorrow morning, not to return until such time as you are ordered or requested to do such by the proper authorities." He turned to the group of Negroes, saying, "And, as for the rest of you, return to your quarters and have nothing more to do with this man, either in conversation or in any kind of fighting, or you too will be banished from the grounds of this military base. Come with me, Corporal."

He started to turn away and caught a glimpse of the supposedly affronted woman's face as she nodded and clasped her hands together, almost as if she were thanking him. At least, he thought, he could take it that way if he wanted to.

He and the corporal strode quickly from the scene, and when they were some distance away from it, the corporal asked, "Why you kicking me out? I'm telling you I didn't do nothing wrong."

"Corporal, you told me yesterday you were leaving anyway. Let them think of it as a punishment and they will be satisfied. You and I will know it's simply a ruse to calm things down and restore some order. That incident by itself could have exploded and spread to the whole place. We're fortunate it didn't."

"Well, you're right about me leaving. Yes sir, I see what you're saying, but I sure just meant to help her out. I sure didn't mean to make no problem or fighting."

"Well, Thomas, next time you ask a miss for a kiss, make sure you speak more clearly." He gave the big man a friendly shove, and the man chuckled and pushed him back. "And be sure to see me tomorrow before you leave. I'd like to have a goodbye with you. You've been a good man, and a good soldier."

The big man smiled and turned away, headed for his barracks.

Once again Abe left the fort on his way back to the church grounds. Now that he was calming down from the challenge of that upsetting incident, his mind returned to the Major calling him by his real name. And to all the choices it seemed he was facing all at once. Walking along, he couldn't help turning over in his mind the good reverend doctor's words concerning God's method of showing us our own pathway. About how life, in a sometimes seemingly random fashion, creates the coming together of both need and opportunity. Just now, he'd seen it work in settling this potentially dangerous dispute. He thought about what the minister had told him in some of their talks, how the Voice of God begins to sound an awful lot like our own inner voice as we try to understand the shaping and shifting of our own destinies here among the complications of our lives. Finally, his thinking centered on his promise to Sarah Beth, and his growing awareness that it wouldn't feel right to leave her and her father behind at this time, no matter what his future turned out to be.

The delay caused by the uproar at the fort made him late for his appointment with Doctor Randall, but the man accepted his apology with a wave of his hand and plunged right into the issues. He'd looked up all of the statutes of church governance that allowed for the separation of a congregation from the denominational authority, as well as those rules governing when the denomination itself could suspend a congregation. He referred to several of the clauses to help explain to Abe why this church and the others it would join in a breakaway move had no grounds for such action. Then he read from the letter he'd received, being circulated among those now calling themselves the Southern Methodist Episcopal Church:

> *"Let it be known that the actions of certain congregations, specifically those in Philadelphia, New York and Boston, in their unilateral and unauthorized manner have jeopardized the unity of the Denomination, and have thereby given us (the undersigned) both the right and the necessity to dissolve those bonds which have heretofore united us together in the work of our Lord Jesus Christ and for our Heavenly Father.*
>
> *These actions include but are not limited to: the induction and granting of authority as Rectors and/ or Vicars to those whose qualifications can be neither proven nor evaluated; special consideration and untoward exceptions to the rigorous and time-honored training required by any and all applicants for such responsibilities as are identified in the Constitution of our Church; the failure to seek a consensual referendum on such appointments to positions of ecclesiastical authority and ministry; and engaging in structural changes to the procedures and processes which have long been exercised in both traditional and statutory codes of conduct and discipline among members and their leaders in our Church.*

"Lester, it's nothing but a thinly disguised attack on the inclusion of Negro clergy ever, in any way, shape or form. And it flies in the face of the new reality that even here in our beloved South there are already Negroes running for election to the legally constituted houses of the legislatures, Negroes being appointed to the benches of our courts. It is illegal, and, dare I say, immoral to proceed in the manner they outline, and I, for one, will not condone or participate in this action . . . Now how do I say that without getting my head blown off?"

"Isn't there some scripture that could help you out?"

"I'd start with 'Blessed are the meek for they shall inherit the earth.' And then I'd go to God's words to the children of Israel as they fled Egypt, 'One law shall be to him that is homeborn, and unto the stranger that sojourneth among you.' But why should I bother? They won't listen; their minds are made up."

"And what will you do if they refuse to listen, if they take formal steps against you? I don't believe they'll allow you to continue your service if you oppose their decisions."

"Lester, it simply may well be time for me to move on from here. Like the Israelites themselves, leaving the land of their slavery and fleeing the judgment of Pharaoh. Fleeing into the wilderness, or at least the next best thing, heading west into the new lands. What do you think? Would you come with us?"

"Sir, I'll admit that I have been having similar thoughts myself. My cousin is completely dedicated to the west and the adventures he thinks he will have, not to mention the fortune he believes is out there. Those considerations aside, I have nothing left to return to where I was born and raised, and I am fearful of what is coming in the next few years with all this racial struggle."

"I believe you're right. I think this conflict within our own church is only a beginning. Perhaps I should just resign and leave them to their own devices."

"Doctor Randall, I wouldn't have mentioned it, but today at the fort I was barely able to avert violence between some of the Negroes and one of my patrol soldiers, all over an apparent misunderstanding."

"Lester, tonight pray for me, and pray for yourself and Sarah Beth, that we may hear the Voice of God within our hearts and minds, that we may see our direction more clearly, and that we may walk in His ways. Thank you for your company and commiseration. You may leave me now, and let's not discuss any of this at supper or until we have entered into the fiery furnace of judgment waiting for us at tomorrow's formal inquiry, or whatever they're calling it."

The church fathers voted unanimously to separate from the Northern churches and to accept Doctor Randall's seemingly spontaneous resignation. They gave him four months to remain in his living quarters and to carry out day-to-day oversight of church affairs, but they also announced that they would be inviting guests to the pulpit; in this way they could find the man who was the best fit for ministering to their needs and upholding their principles.

Abe resigned from his duties at the fort, and began working as a guard at the town's small jail and as an advisor to the chief of police. He was able to collect a small stipend for assisting the chief in dealing with certain incidents of theft and assault that were becoming more and more frequent as the post-war economic trials worsened. Although he did not take an active role in the physical side of law enforcement, he was useful in preparing papers for the courts against those charged with infractions. Sarah Beth continued to serve as a midwife's assistant and nurse at the fort, but her heart was obviously no longer in it and she never again talked with Abe about becoming a student of medicine. She was somewhat forlorn at the possibility of leaving behind the only home she'd ever known, but with Abe as her only friend, as she put it, her connection to the place was much weaker than it had been before these troubles with the Church had so beset her father and taken their toll on her as well.

Louis was the only one in the small household who seemed completely happy. He soon left on a train to St. Louis, via the route that had just been reopened. He said that his 'namesake city' was calling to him, but he promised to return and help them all move west once he'd scouted the lay of the land, as he put it. Before he left, he revealed to Abe that he'd brought a small bag of gold coins that Abe's mother had left behind when she passed away. It wasn't much, just what Abe's father had when the War began. Louis said that Abe's mother hoped it would be enough to get her son started on the next period of his life. At first Abe was upset by the seeming deception with which his younger cousin had concealed this, but he listened to his cousin's explanation, finding it interesting even if it did not exonerate Louis completely.

"As she was dying she told my sister that she wanted the best for you, always had, and that this was to help you gain a new start in life because the old life was gone now. Since it was apparent to me that you weren't ready for your new start yet, when I arrived here to seek that new life, I decided to wait until her wishes could be fulfilled."

"And what if I didn't go along with your wild schemes for this new life of mine?" Abe asked, still somewhat perturbed.

"Abe or Lester, whoever you are, I had faith in your insight into the strangeness of the circumstances of these times. To put it in Doctor Randall's words, I knew that you would hear the Voice of God calling you west. So I waited, and I was right. No? Yes?"

"I'll let you get by, if only because of how it turned out. None of us knows when we are being used by God in realizing His plans in this life. And you yourself may be more His instrument than you think. But you still were out of line in making this decision on your own."

The winter passed in a strange and inertia-filled kind of way. Abe even remarked to himself that it was like those drills where the troops stand and march in place. His work for the town was not challenging and the small stipend it afforded was barely sufficient for his needs. However, he found it quite interesting to be assisting Doctor Randall in sorting through, discarding and packing, the fruits of the man's ministry over the past couple of decades.

He enjoyed the work because it gave him insights into what the man wanted to keep and was of value to him, and that which he was willing to discard as having outlived its relevance or usefulness. Many were the hours during the short days of winter that were spent in reminiscences and reviews of significant events and passages of the life and times the man had lived through and interpreted for his flock. In addition, Abe found himself more and more enjoying the company of Sarah Beth, and this sorting activity was perfect for that, as both were needed helping out with the project.

She had matured since he'd first met her, and he wondered if he too had changed as much. Certainly the War had been a strong dose of reality for him and he wasn't allowed to remain the youth who'd joined the army at age eighteen. As he thought about it, he felt that he had been changed more by outside events and circumstances than by any inner processes or realizations. It also seemed to him now that his response to the chaos and uncertainty of the past few years gave him a kind of confidence he hadn't had growing up. The responsibilities that had been thrust on him had required a new sense of decisiveness he'd never felt before. The unexpected role of assisting a major leader such as President Davis, or even one such as Doctor Randall, gave him an awareness of what it took to overcome doubt, even when a man had no certainty to go on. The ability to evaluate conditions and then make a decision, right or wrong, was what made a leader, and it was something that he'd been challenged to learn and adopt as a part of his responsibilities with the patrol. Of course, the second thing that made a good leader was the ability to recover from a poor decision, whether it had been based on the lack of good information or whether it was just a mistake in judgment.

Abe remembered hearing about one day in particular that was very hard on the president, had in fact sent him into days of despondency and a need for solitude that excluded all but the necessary communication with his subordinates. Abe had been assigned to the president's headquarters shortly after those events which led up to the defeat of Lee's army at Gettysburg. Before the battle, the president received a messenger from General Stuart asking for permission to circle the Union Army and attack from the rear in the area of southern Pennsylvania. With no way to consult with Lee on this matter, the president gave the OK, and when Stuart's cavalry failed to arrive in time to provide logistical and intelligence support to Lee's army, the Battle of Gettysburg was joined and the Confederate troops suffered extremely grave casualties and were forced to retreat back into Virginia. Abe arrived to fulfill his assignment at the headquarters almost immediately following this terrible defeat, and was witness to much of the soul-searching and recriminations that followed the events. He was able to see the tremendous personal effort it took for Davis to accept responsibility and pull himself together in the face of such a defeat and the harsh outcry of the Southern press.

The memory of that period of time, when he was such a young soldier, was one of those things that Abe thought he would never forget or get over. At the same time, he was somewhat grateful for those opportunities to be close enough to see and experience the impact of defeat, and the resilience that he had come to identify as one of the principle characteristics of a strong leader. Since he'd learned of the congregation's treatment of Doctor Randall when he prayed for peace rather than victory during the War, and since he'd seen for himself the treatment the man was subjected to in this recent episode, he was convinced that a man's ability to hold to his principles and beliefs in the face of disastrous events was what gave him the character to withstand being reviled by lesser men. These examples fostered in him the desire to develop the strength and commitment to go on in the face of hardship, and to rededicate himself to whatever role life placed upon him.

On the other hand, it seemed somewhat the opposite with Sarah Beth and what he observed in her growing up and becoming more of a distinguished young woman. She appeared to be one who was affecting the things around herself more so than being affected by them. She seemed to have inside herself a natural strength that was less affected by what went on around her, and more that it was she herself who was affecting those things. Abe tried to understand what it was about her that gave him this feeling, and could only come up with the idea that it was more the way she went out and found something to do, as in the work at the hospital and with the midwifery, and then shaped those activities to what she had to offer. He admired this developing characteristic as it was shown in the changes to the girl he'd encountered when he first arrived, but he was still able to be surprised by her frequent lapses into what could only be described as childishness, such as her tiffs with Louis or her dramatic pouting at being excluded from things by her father, and himself as well.

One day, while they'd been sorting through sermons from before the War, her father excused himself and left the study, saying he'd return shortly, and then would like the privacy to discuss some things with Abe. As soon as he'd left and the front door of the house was heard to close shut, Sarah Beth turned on Abe with her eyes flashing and literally hissed at him.

"What?" he said.

"What? You don't know? Before you came father always discussed everything with me. I was his only favorite. Now I can see that he always wanted a son and when you came along, you became the one he depends on. I simply can't abide it anymore."

He had no words for a reply, but the short silence that followed her outburst was agonizing for him, and he had to say something. "Sarah Beth, it just isn't true. He often tells me how much he values your help, and your love for him. He says that he could never get along without you."

"All right, Mister Greene, you want to bring up my love? I'll tell you something about my love. You can't have it, much as I want to give it to you, you can't have it because you don't understand that I am now a woman and I know what love is. I know what love is because I don't have it and when I see other girls with their beaus and their happiness, it just shows me how wrong I've been about you." She stood up and turned toward the door.

"Wait," he said, "what is this? I've no idea what you're talking about."

"Of course you don't. You don't have any idea what goes on in a woman's heart. And I'm tired of waiting for you to grow up enough to find out."

Her shoulders began shaking and she took hold of the door's handle. Abe stood and stepped toward her, reaching out and placing his good hand on her shoulder. He tried to ease her around to face him.

"Oh you," she said through her tears, "you just don't know, do you?" And then she spun toward him, kissed him suddenly, and pulled away, struggling with the door he was holding closed. His hand went to his mouth and then he reached around her shoulders and pulled her close to him.

"I'm sorry," he said. "I didn't know."

She pushed him away and nearly threw herself out the door. He heard her running up the stairs. Now what, he thought, and that was all he could think at that moment, now what?

More than a month went by before Abe ever saw Sarah Beth alone again. A month in which she always seemed to be with her father or Mattie or out of the house on some kind of errand, a month in which Abe found himself thinking about her more than he ever had before, thinking about the young girl who'd asked him if he'd ever been in love because she wanted to know what it was like, thinking about his answers and how he hadn't really answered her. Now he wondered if what he'd felt for Irene Ruth really was love or just some partial version of it. And what was he feeling now, now that Sarah Beth had startled him with her admission and her challenge to his feelings or lack thereof?

It was during that month that a letter came from Louis out in Missouri. One Saturday a Union soldier from the fort came to the parsonage looking for Lieutenant Lester Greene. When Mattie told him someone was at the door to see him, his first reaction was to deny that he knew the person, or to have Mattie say he was no longer thereabouts. Then, looking out from behind a curtain, he saw the envelope in the man's hands and convinced himself that he'd best admit who he was and take the letter if it was truly for him.

The return address in the corner of the thick paper of the envelope showed that it was from Louis Cavanaugh, and it was postmarked from Independence, Missouri. Abe accepted the letter and thanked the soldier, quickly closing the door and walking into the vacant study where he sat in the chair he was most used to.

Louis's script was a scrawling, large-lettered style that seemed to slide downhill on the page. Perhaps he'd been writing with the paper on his knees. There was no date.

> *Dear Cuz,*
>
> *I've made it here and we're in luck. I've signed on with a freight wagon train that will be leaving St. Joseph in the later part of May. There's room for both of us and some of the men are taking their families with them. The other trains, the ones made up of emigrants leaving for the west are not nearly so interesting and one has to pay the wagon master and his backers to join. With this job we get paid for driving and we don't even have to have our own wagon. I don't know how it could be better.*
>
> *The caravan leaves for a destination of the Great Salt Lake carrying supplies for them Mormons that live out there. The word is that they are all right people if you don't cross them or criticize their ways. There will be a returning trip carrying hides and furs from the Colorado mountains if we don't want to stay there or go further.*
>
> *Cuz, I have met Buff Belmet, one of the most famous of the freight masters and he is hardly much older than you. He is a powerful young man with more know how than any other two fellas I've met out here. He will be in charge of our train until he splits off to head for New Mexico. Then we will be led by Silas Murdoch, a Southern man from back near our home country.*

*Write me and tell me when you will arrive. I can meet
you somewhere and I expect you will take the train, at
least as far as St. Louis, which I am sure you know is
named after me. Ha! Can't wait to see you and tell you
all about everything else. Hurry!*

Louis

Abe re-read the letter and then carefully folded it and placed it the pocket inside his coat, an action that somehow reminded him of that final letter from Irene Ruth. He was glad to hear from Louis, and to hear that the young man was doing all right for himself. It was a little unnerving the way his cousin seemed to take all of this for granted, and his thinking that Abe himself didn't really have much else to look forward to. But what Louis didn't know was the difference that had come about in Abe's connection with Sarah Beth and her father, and how his own fate now seemed mostly tied to theirs, at least until it became clear what their direction turned out to be.

He didn't have long to wait. Two days later Doctor Randall, waving his own letter in the air, called him into the study. "It's come," he said, "the news I've been waiting for. Lester, the Lord has His own way of working, but sometimes it seems downright surprising to someone whose faith is being tested and whose hopes have been crushed by the weight of some of his fellow man's folly. Sit down, son, and hear what this is."

Abe sat quickly and leaned forward. The older man continued to wave the paper in the air without even glancing at it. "Two months ago I wrote to the Church fathers out West. I no longer had the stomach or the patience for my fellow Southerners that once carried me along. In the hours of my prayer following the judgment of this congregation and its errant leaders, I kept seeing the setting sun as if it were beckoning to me. So I wrote a letter of inquiry and this is the answer." He now read from the single page in his hands, "We have received your inquiry with both respect and sadness. As you know the Church here in Missouri has taken no such actions to separate ourselves or to divide the denomination over the actions of some of our Northern brethren. We took neither side during the War and now that God has seen fit to restore peace to the land, we are ready and willing to begin the process of healing that is of such pressing necessity. We have investigated you and your record, and are pleased with what we have found. You truly seem to be a man of God, struggling to live His truth in these days. We hereby offer you the position of Rector of the Vicarage of St. Joseph. Please advise of your willingness to accept, and the timing of your potential arrival to meet with the bishop here in Jefferson, Missouri."

He lay the paper down on his desk and smoothed it out while bowing his head, "Oh Great Father in heaven, blessed be Your will and Your ways of working in the hearts and lives of men. Thank you, Father, in the Name of your Son, our most holy Jesus Christ. Amen . . . Well, young man, what do you think of that?"

"I think that if it's what you want, and it seems like it is, then you are to be congratulated. And recognized for your admirable faith that all things have their purpose."

"Yes, you're right, if ever in my life a need has been met with its reciprocal opportunity, this must be it. I am grateful, but I am not going to allow myself to become joyous until I cross that Mississippi River on the road to my New Jerusalem. Praise the Lord."

Abe had seen the older man happy several times before, not so much lately, but never quite like this. As for the doubts surrounding his own strange concerns with whether or not Louis and his plans fit the path he himself should be on or not, they were almost banished in the similarity between Doctor Randall's new direction and the need for him to respond in like manner to opportunity in a time of need. If this wasn't the still, quiet voice of God providing these possibilities, then he would have to be asking for a louder voice to negate them.

"Sir," he said cautiously, not wanting to distract the man from his moments of gladness and praise, but feeling also the need to present his own situation. He had waited several days since the arrival of Louis's letter to speak on that, but perhaps this was the time he'd been waiting for. "Sir," he continued, "I too have been visited by an apparent indication of what and where I may be heading next."

"Well, speak, son. What is it? That was going to be my next question, what of you? What will happen to you in all of this upheaval? Believe me, you are welcome to stay the course with me. I have become very attached to your assistance and consultation, but at the same time I recognize that a young man needs to find his own way."

"I know you remember Louis. I've heard from him now, just in the past week. He too has found what he considers to be the next big step, for both of us, and beyond all imagining, at least on my part. He is located right now, even as we speak, somewhere very close to your new destination. He is in Independence, Missouri."

"Not far, not far at all, I've been looking at some maps and Independence is very close to Saint Joseph. What is he doing there, if I might ask?"

"Well, sir, you heard him describe at great length his dreams to make his way to the farthest reaches of the west, to seek his fortune and the adventures of a lifetime. I believe that's how he put it."

"Yes, yes, he was very excited by all of that. The day of the frontier may already be ending, but he seemed certain that he could find what was left of it before it was gone."

"True enough, and, for better or for worse, I believe he's found his own opportunity. Apparently, he's signed both of us on as drivers of a freight wagon in a caravan headed for the Great Salt Lake country. Sight unseen and without much of a background in freight hauling, he sounds like he's convinced himself that this is the best thing that ever happened to him and he's counting on me to make the journey with him . . . I haven't even had time to think it through. As you know, I've been spending my free time trying to get back on a horse and re-learn what I once knew. I actually was able to completely saddle up for the first time the other day, even with this." He held his wounded arm straight out and shook it vigorously. "No pain, and strength is returning every day. I believe that as long as the horse cooperates, I'll be on my own again, mounted and mobile. That will please me."

"Of course, what a triumph, when you have spent such a long time without it, without what was once so much a part of you. I commend you for your patience and your persistence. Best of luck with that . . . Now, if I may interrupt, there is one other matter you and I must address before we get too far ahead of ourselves down these apparently parallel roads. We will each of us have to let Sarah Beth know what this is all about. And believe me, it will be very difficult to present any of it in such a way that she is persuaded we did not conspire to exclude her from our discussions and our discoveries. Actually, I imagine that she will be quite furious. I just wish there was some way we could let her think that it was all her idea." He paused, and then went on, "Of course, that's impossible, but I do think we should take a little time, although it sounds as though we have very little time before we must get ourselves in motion, we should take a little time to come up with a way of making her feel that it's as much in her interest as it is in ours."

They were both quiet for a moment. The Reverend took his bottle of sherry from the drawer beside him, and the two small glasses which he partly filled. He handed one of them to Abe, and said, "Here's to our futures, together and separate, as God wills." They sipped quietly until the glasses were empty and Abe said, "We'll just have to continue what we're doing and let it turn into packing up for a real move, not just sorting things into boxes."

Doctor Randall went on with that thought. "We don't even know if she'll come along or simply refuse to leave these parts. Not necessarily this town, but at least the comforts of civilization as she's known them . . . But I see you're right, let's begin making preparations in ways that simply seem to be continuing with the packing we're already engaged in. And Abe, from what I've seen of her moods lately, she won't take kindly to either one of us thinking we can leave her behind, no matter what we do, or where we go."

"Yes, sir, I'm sure you're right about that."

CHAPTER SIX

Next Stage

Another month passed between Doctor Randall's acceptance of his new ministry in St. Joseph and the planned date of departure. The flurry of activity, packing the things to take with them and piling things to give away or leave behind, went on day after day. Sarah Beth had been remarkably amenable to the proposition that they would all be moving together in a westward direction. Although she said she had no idea where St. Joseph or even Missouri was located, she was sure it would be better than staying in a town filled with the stiff-necked and cruel people who'd expelled her father.

She and Abe had been carefully avoiding being alone together for so long that it came as a surprise to both of them the day that they found themselves together on the front seat of a buggy hauling extra dinnerware and paintings to a local trading store. There these items would be sold and the money forwarded to them after they'd moved west. Sarah Beth seemed particularly cheerful and not at all bashful, as she had been most of the times they'd encountered one another since that particularly awkward night. Abe was still feeling the discomfort of that exchange, but was pleased that she was friendly again. He had no desire to travel by rail through hundreds of miles with someone whose attitude toward himself would seem, at the least, somewhat spiteful.

"Look, you're holding the reins with both hands," she said, laughing. "Here, let me try." She snatched them from his hands and shook them across the horse's back. The horse gave a slight buck and a kick and then settled back into its trotting gait.

"You seem quite pleased with all that's going on," he said cautiously.

"Oh yes. Of course, Father told me you were worried that I might resent your conspiracy to make these decisions without consulting me, but since I agree with it, what's the point of being antagonistic? Besides," she said, giving him a sideways look and a smile, "it makes all the difference in the world that you're coming with us."

She slapped the reins at the horse, but this time the horse just stopped and looked around backward at her. Abe gently took the reins back into his hands and gently urged the horse on. "It seems like a fortunate coincidence," he said, "and I'm pleased with it as well."

"Father would say that it's God's will. Myself, I don't worry about those things. God is good and a blessing is a blessing." She slipped her hand into the stiffened angle of his elbow and waved to someone at the edge of the road. Abe realized how much he was looking forward to holding his head up again. Here he was always looking out for the suspicions of others. Once they'd gotten far enough away from Virginia, maybe he could even tell Sarah Beth his real name.

They shipped their luggage and other goods by freight wagon to Harper's Ferry, where they would board a train. If all went well, the train would connect them to the Pittsburg, Cincinnati and St. Louis line, which had just reopened following the repairs necessary to correct the damages of War and its aftermath. Although that rail line was located west of the major conflicts, there had been some sabotage by the Union side to prevent its use by the Confederates, and by other Southerners. Now it was described as a journey with many delays but with the likely outcome of reaching the route's end in St. Louis. They hoped to reach that outpost within a week of their departure.

The night before they were to travel by stage to meet the train, Mattie prepared a large and delicious supper for them. Sarah Beth was brimming with excitement, and even the two men could hardly maintain their usual reserve. As soon as the food was served, Sarah Beth asked about the extra setting at the table.

Her father cleared his throat and then said, in a rather strange tone of voice, "I've asked Mattie to join us in our last meal here tonight. It seems only right after all the meals she's prepared and served over these past years . . . Mattie," he spoke up, "please come in and join us now."

Mattie had removed her apron and the kitchen bonnet she always wore. She was looking special, much as they'd often seen her when she was dressed up and leaving for her church on a Sunday morning. She gave a quick bow to all of them and then sat at the empty place.

"I've asked Mattie to join us for a couple of reasons. First of all, in gratitude for all of her years of service to our family. But secondly, and most importantly, I've asked Mattie to accompany us on our journey west. She has assured me that she has no other pressing obligations or opportunities, and that she really doesn't know what would become of her if she were to stay behind. For my part, I realized that I couldn't imagine moving to a new location and living there without her help. She will not be in the same role as she has been here. After all, slavery and all of that are over now, and we're headed for a part of the country which, though it was considered a border state, was very much anti-slavery. No, Mattie will be a member of our household, and while she will continue to oversee and manage its domestic affairs, I anticipate that the rest of us must be much more involved in the day-to-day chores of making and maintaining our home, and not leaving it all on her. Now what does anyone think?"

All through his speech, Mattie was staring down at her hands clasped in her lap. She seemed to be waiting for something, perhaps some kind of permission to pick up a fork and take a bite of food for the first time at the family's table.

Sarah Beth suddenly let out a small shriek and jumped up, moving quickly to stand behind the woman and lean over, hugging her, laughing in obvious happiness. "Yes, yes, that's perfect. I have been so dreading the good-bye. Last night," she stopped for breath, "last night, I could hardly sleep, not for the excitement of it all, but for the sadness of leaving Mattie behind. She is the only person I care about in this town and I couldn't stand the thought of leaving her behind . . ." She kissed the top of the woman's head, which seemed to embarrass Mattie even more. "Aren't you happy too, Mattie?"

"Yes, Missy, I am. I am very grateful to your father for allowing this, I . . ." she stopped and wiped at her eyes with the corner of a napkin.

Doctor Randall spoke, saying, "Sarah Beth, it would be best if you take your seat. We all must eat of this wonderful meal, and then I'm sure each of us still has many things to do tonight before we leave in the early morning. Lester, our little family is growing again."

"Yes sir, and I think it's a very good thing. Mattie has helped me much more than I could ever have expected." Abe was pleased with the plan, although it crossed his mind what Sarah Beth must feel like when she realized she was left out of another decision. He could imagine that there would be some adjustments that had to be made during their travels, but, all in all, he could see that it definitely was for the best.

Later that evening, as he was making one last inspection of the house itself and the porches where he could have left some article or other, he encountered Sarah Beth. She was standing quietly at the foot of the stairway to the upper floor where he still had never been. Silently she stepped toward him and took his hand to lead him into the room with the piano. She sat down and began to play. It was a beautiful waltz-type selection that Abe didn't think he'd ever heard before.

"Do you like it?" she asked, as she paused in her playing. "I've just been learning it."

"It's beautiful. Too bad we can't take your piano with us."

"I had the same thought myself, but I'm sure there are pianos where we're going. Father said there are more pianos in this whole country than any other instrument. I thought it must be violins, but I didn't argue with him. Did you ever play?"

"Only a little. I wasn't very good at music."

"And where was that, where were you a little boy? You still haven't told me."

"No, I haven't, but I will. I promise I will tell you much more once we've left these parts. Now, please play some more of that piece before we must get back to our work."

She played for a little while longer, and then shut the lid over the keys. "That's it," she patted the piano. "Good-bye, my dear, true friend." Then she turned, stood and placed her arms around Abe's neck and shoulders. "And hello, my dear, true friend. I can't wait to hear all about you." She looked up into his eyes and for probably the first time since they'd met, he didn't look away. Then she lowered her face into his shoulder, whispering just loud enough for him to hear, "I think I do love you, Mister, whoever you are."

Abe came close to answering her with the same words.

The wagon ride was uneventful except for some high water when they had to take a ferry across a swollen river. They stayed most of that first night in the small railway station and found the benches too uncomfortable for any real sleep. Their train arrived in a cloud of steam and smoke soon after daybreak, and in no time they were on their way to Cincinnati.

Over the next two days, there were frequent stops along the way to allow for repair crews to get out of the way, or to restore the temporary rails that were in use while the damage was repaired from the sabotage and neglect incurred during the War. Cincinnati was not a large city, but it was the biggest town that Sarah Beth ever remembered seeing, and her eyes went wide with the wonder of so many smoke stacks and roadways. Her father smiled with enjoyment at her enthusiasm, while Abe tried to act as if all this was not unusual. Although many racial restrictions had been rescinded, Mattie continued to be seated in a different coach as was the custom of the times.

Their train to St. Louis would not leave until the middle of the day after their arrival, so they took rooms at a rather comfortable hotel. Mattie and Sarah Beth took a room together as mistress and servant, while Doctor Randall and Abe also secured a double occupancy room. Supper was a wonderful experience, except that once again Mattie was left out. Abe overheard the minister telling her that all that would soon change once they got to their new home in Missouri. Mattie didn't seem to mind, as she found the company of a couple of older colored women and they were served supper in a back dining room set aside by the hotel management for servants and others.

The following morning found them walking along the mighty Ohio River and admiring the commerce evidenced by the crowd of barges and boats being loaded and unloaded from docks piled high with goods and equipment. Abe happened across a particular dock stacked with hides and skins roped together in huge bundles. He asked one of the dockhands where they'd come from and the man replied that they were "all the way from the Great Plains where there's so many buffalo you can't see the ground in some places." Abe wondered if this was what Louis was talking about, the kinds of shipments that freight wagons brought with them on their return trips in the spring.

Once they'd boarded the train to St. Louis, Mattie was allowed to sit in the same car with the rest of them. She'd done some shopping and been able to put together enough food for this stage of their journey. They all settled into their seats for the long haul to the Mississippi River and then south to its big city. A group of traveling theatre people sat together at the front of their car and were quite loud, laughing a lot as they attempted to rehearse their lines from some show or other. At the back of their car was a group of six army men, obviously travelling together. Once again Abe felt himself lowering his eyes and sinking into his coat collar at the sight of their Yankee uniforms. He'd purchased and outfitted himself in what he thought was customary for a young traveling man seeking business opportunities in the west, but he didn't feel quite sure of himself in being able to play this role as if it were natural to him

After a few hours of the monotonous sound of the rails and the constant swaying and bouncing of the car, one of the soldiers came forward, sat in the empty seat across the aisle from Abe, and struck up a conversation.

"Where you bound for?" he asked.

"St. Louis," Abe mumbled just loud enough to be heard.

"Good thing, I'd say, since that's where this train's headed." He reached out his hand and Abe extended his right hand across the aisle to shake with the fellow. "My name's Thomas. Tommy's OK though," the young man continued. "We're bound for the west. Going to kill some Indians that have been attacking army supply wagons. Say, is that your wife or your sister there? Saw you talking with her. Mighty pretty. I have a sister back home, but she's still a girl. Well, hey, what'd you say your name is?"

"Lester."

"What'd you do in the War? I just missed it. Too young at the beginning and then had to stay on the farm and take care of Ma and the grandfolks, run the dairy, all that. Sure wish I hadn't missed out. That's why I'm going west, to get my licks in on those Indians . . . Well, nice talking with you. Come on back with us boys if you need some company." He stood up just as the train swayed suddenly around the corner, causing him to lose his balance. Abe reached out his stiff arm to help support him.

Then this Tommy straightened himself up and said, "Bet you got that there bum elbow in the War, huh? Sure sorry I missed it." And then he lurched back down the aisle toward his friends as the train did its best to topple him.

Sarah Beth turned around from the seat in front of him and said, "New friend, I see. I didn't hear what you said when he asked if I was your wife or your sister."

"I guess I just didn't answer." He smiled and looked away out the window.

When they arrived in St. Louis, Doctor Randall was expected to attend some meetings with the leadership of the Missouri branch of the denomination. They all arranged lodgings and spent a couple of exciting days shopping to replace some of the things they'd left behind, enjoying themselves as they wandered around in the chaos that was now known as St. Louis, Gateway to the West.

The minister was pleased with his meetings and told Abe and Sarah Beth that the leaders of the Church out here were more curious about his ideas for energizing his rather new congregation than in his reasons for leaving his previous assignment. As those conversations went along, however, the contradictions between him and the leaders of the church back home became more apparent, and he told them he wasn't going to hide any of it.

"I said to myself that if I wasn't completely truthful, it would probably come out at a later time and be worse for me then than if I told the truth now. I was rewarded by a very strong endorsement of my beliefs regarding God's role in War, and even concerning the possibility of Negroes being ordained. They did, however, inform me that this new church is at the edge of the frontier, and there is no telling who all might be coming through the door. And they went on to say that I would have their backing so long as I stayed true to the teachings of Christ and could explain myself to them if there occurred what they referred to as a 'potentially awkward situation.' I must say that I am very relieved at this point in time," he paused. "Now, how long shall we plan on staying here in St. Louis? They did allow as to how they thought the sooner I could present myself to this new congregation, the better it would be for all parties."

"Father," Sarah Beth chimed in immediately, "this city is almost too much for me to take any more of. It's dirty and smoky and crowded. I'd just as soon go where we're going and see if it isn't much better for us."

"Lester?"

"I should be moving along as well. I am supposed to have already met up with Louis."

"And you, Mattie, have we everything you need to replenish our household?"

"Yes sir, we've been busy while you were having your meetings, sir."

"Mattie, I think you ought to drop the 'sir' from now on. It may give others the wrong impression that you are still indentured or otherwise bound to us, and I don't want that anymore. We are more like a family than anything else, at least for the time being."

"Yes, sir," she said, and they all laughed.

"So, how shall we celebrate?"

They asked the landlady of their boarding house for a dining recommendation, and she told them of a small eating establishment located just a few streets away. They had a wonderful supper and then retired early in order to be rested for the next stage of their journey.

In the morning, they hired space on a freight wagon headed for Independence and then going on to St. Joseph. Their crates and trunks were located at the rail station and waiting on its loading platform, and their newly acquired goods were already at the freight depot. They decided to go on by passenger stage, carrying along only enough to take them through the rest of their trip. This arrangement would put them in Independence a day or more before the freight wagon, but it would be less physically tiring for all of them.

"By the way," Doctor Randall informed them as they boarded the stage, "our new house is waiting for us and all we have to do is move right into it. They told me it is a wonderful and very new building with running water, and for you, young man, there's a small stable waiting for a horse."

"That sounds good, although I'm not sure I'll be there if I accept my cousin's offer."

Sarah Beth nudged him with her elbow, and whispered loud enough for all of them to hear, "Don't be in such a hurry."

In short order, they then boarded the stage and were off to the western part of the state and what was to become a beginning and a new home.

Upon their arrival in Independence, Abe immediately began looking for his cousin by asking after the freighting wagon trains. He was informed that while one or two of the caravans had already left, most were still forming up down by the river a few miles west of the town. He tried to find out more before making the trip out to the camps, and asked a clerk at a mercantile store whether he knew anything about a caravan headed up by someone named Belmet. The man replied that they'd been the first to leave, headed for the New Mexico Territory. Most of the rest of them wouldn't be leaving for another couple of weeks.

"How is it they could leave so much earlier?" he asked.

"They're taking the southern route where the floods have already happened and they're the biggest train of them all with 150 wagons and the meanest bunch of drivers on any trail. The Indians will most likely leave them alone, plus they have a small bunch of army riding along with them as far as the cut-off to Texas."

"Well, thank you, thank you for that," Abe said, not knowing whether to be glad or sad as this turn of events seemed like it could be one more example of God's direction in his life. It certainly made it appear that he was supposed to stay with the Randalls, at least for the time being. As he was leaving the cavernous store, he turned back and asked, "And when would they be returning?"

"They'll wait for the hides that come down out of the mountains and across the plains soon as snow melts. Trappers and Indians bring'em in to the trading posts, and then they'll haul 'em back to here. Probably be back next June. Just in time to make a quick turn around and make one more trip west for the year. But who can say, never works out if you make too many plans. Used to drive wagon myself. Good money, but bad weather and dangerous conditions. Better off for me selling to'em than being one of'em."

"Can a letter be sent with one of the other trains?"

"Sure. No tellin' it'll get there, but you can give it a try."

"I'll need writing paper, an envelope and a pen."

"One dollar, all in all, and I'll send it out with someone I think I can trust."

"Thanks."

Abe wrote a short letter to his cousin explaining what had happened, inserted it in the thick envelope, wrote Louis's name and Belmet Wagon Train on the outside and then handed it over. He left the store and hurried back to where the others were waiting for him.

When he got there, he found Sarah Beth crying on the wide porch that fronted the rooming-house. She was alone and he went up the stairs to her. He placed his arm around her as he sat on the bench beside her.

"What is it? What"

"Oh, you wouldn't believe it, Mattie and I were walking along with a bag of food we just bought from that street market and a man pushed Mattie down, grabbed the bag and ran off."

"Is she all right?"

"I think so," she continued sobbing as he handed her a clean handkerchief from his jacket pocket. "She's with father, and she's scared, but I don't think she's hurt. Lester, we need to get out of here. I hate it here and I just pray it's not like this in St. Joseph."

"No, I've heard that St, Joe, as they call it here, is a small, quiet town, nothing like this place filled with all its travelers from the West or going there."

"Oh, I hope so, everything was going so well. Did you find anything about Louis?"

"It appears that the caravan he was with has already gone, first to go."

"What will you do?"

"I don't know. I can ride again, at least passably, but I'm not feeling confident to ride after the wagons where I've never been before, and there's no other way to try to catch him."

She wiped her face and blew her nose and looked into his eyes, "You'll just have to stay here with us." She gave a quick smile, "I am glad you're not going away."

"I don't know Sarah Beth, I feel badly for Louis. He was counting on me to be his partner in this and it feels a little like I've let him down."

"He'll be all right. If I know him, he's probably forgotten all about us."

"Possible, but not likely. Now, if you think you're all right, we should go in and see how Mattie's doing."

"Yes, you're right." She stood up quickly, saying, "Don't mind me, I just don't know what we'll do without you."

Mattie was all right, shaken but not injured. Abe volunteered to go back to the market and get food to replace what was stolen. Mattie told him what they needed and said that since they were the only people staying in the rooming-house, the hostess told her she would be allowed to use the kitchen to prepare that evening's supper. The next day they made arrangements for travelling the rest of the way to St. Joseph.

As the stage they were riding neared the edge of the town, they could look down from the bluff and see the Missouri River as it made a huge bend along which the buildings of the town were scattered like drifted remnants of a major flood. As they came closer, they could see that several of the buildings were of more than one story and made of brick. Most of the streets were lined with trees that must have been left from before the town was founded. They drove through a commercial area and then down along the docks where barges and ferries whistled to the accompaniment of an incredible bustle of loading and unloading.

"I thought you said it was a quiet town," Sarah Beth said to Abe.

"Maybe it is once you get away from the river."

Their driver agreed to take them to the location of their new home once he unloaded everything, except for their belongings. He pointed back up on the bluff to where they would he going. A bit later, when they arrived at the new house, Abe was right about it being quiet. It was situated at the corner of two roads, among other clean and well-tended homes and yards, and behind it was the beautiful and very new-looking church building.

"Here you be," the driver said as he pulled the horses to a stop.

It took only a couple of minutes for them to carry their things to the porch. Doctor Randall paid the driver and joined the others as all stood silently in the yard taking in the sight and feeling of this new home.

"Let us pray," the minister said. "Dear Blessed Lord, we give thanks to you for the safety of our journey, for having one another and for this new home and the beginning of a new life. We ask your blessing and give unto you the love in our hearts and the thankfulness in our souls, Amen." Then he smiled and, gently urging the two women forward, said, "Ladies first."

They found that the house had two bedrooms at the back of the first floor, one on either side of the kitchen, and four rooms upstairs. At one front corner was a study and library type room; the other corner was a large drawing room. Sarah Beth scampered up the stairs and back down and all through the rooms on the first floor and then came to a stop in front of the others.

"It's perfect," she said, "just perfect."

It was quickly decided that she and her father would take two of the rooms upstairs and that Mattie and Abe would have the rooms separated by the hallway to the kitchen. One of the other rooms upstairs could be set up and reserved for guests, and perhaps the fourth room would serve for sewing and other practical needs. With all of that decided so quickly, they immediately set about moving in and filling the space with plans. Their comments and questions echoed through the empty rooms that seemed to be just waiting to be home to their personal belongings. There were already beds, kitchen and dining room tables, but not much else. But it was enough, and they all greatly enjoyed these first moments and the happiness they each hoped would continue to accompany them into this new stage of their lives.

Several days and then a week passed as the small group settled into their new home. They received and unpacked the freight that had been delivered from the railroad terminal in St. Louis, and purchased or were given furnishings necessary to complete their household needs. The new congregation was still being led and preached to by a panel of visiting church officials, but the first Sunday of May was scheduled to be the inaugural service and sermon to be delivered by Doctor Randall.

Abe found himself with plenty to do, helping the Doctor unpack his papers and settle into the new study, but the minister informed him that there might be difficulty providing much beyond room and board for his services, since the family would be dependent on pledges from the congregation and a share of the offerings collected during services. This made the decision to stay a little more difficult for Abe, but after wandering through a couple of freight caravan camps on the banks of the Missouri, he came to the conclusion that it wouldn't be a good idea for him to sign on for that kind of work without a partner like Louis.

Fewer wagon trains were leaving now from St. Joe, and these were mostly headed more northerly than those leaving Independence. Several of these trains were destined to travel what was called the Mormon Trail, aiming to reach the Great Salt Lake country in time to turn around and make their return trip before the next winter. It was these trains that he visited and watched as they got organized. He was impressed by the arrangements and the need for both freight and emigrants to be joined up in the same caravan because, he gathered from comments he overheard, that the number of wagons of either type weren't always enough to guarantee safety for the trip. There were also fewer military installations along the northern route, and therefore fewer supplies being hauled to the forts and not as many soldiers to guard them.

At one point, while observing preparations for departure in one of the camps, he saw, across the crowded area, the young soldier he'd met on the train. He shouted the man's name, but the din of the oxen in their pens, the clatter of wagon wheels, and shouting men drowned out his voice. He had no horse under him to ride after the young man, so quickly gave up any hope of a renewed encounter. Later that same morning, he was witness to and almost involved in a terrible fight between two men whose apparent hatred of one another nearly led to death. A circle of other men gathered around the fighters, cheering on their favorite and keeping anyone else from interfering. When the two fighters collapsed to the ground thoroughly bloodied, the crowd cheered loudly and then dispersed. Abe lingered for a bit and was surprised to see after awhile that the two men struggled to their feet and, rather than renew their hostilities, actually helped one another on their stumbling way back toward town.

A few days later, Abe found himself in the town newspaper's office, more out of curiosity than on purpose, but he did ask to see the past few months' editions if that were a possibility. The man covered in the most ink seemed to be in charge of the small number of people working there, and he showed Abe to a small desk in a corner of the large room near the presses. Abe had decided that looking through several past issues of the local paper was probably the best way to find out what this town was all about and what might lead him to some kind of occupation to tide him over until it became clear what was going to happen next.

He started with the most recent editions and leafed backwards through several months of the weeklies without finding anything of much interest or importance. Then a headline from the last week in May grabbed his full attention: "Jeff Davis Charges Dismissed." He quickly read the background information at the beginning of the front page article where it said that Davis's conspiracy charges had been dropped; he'd been turned over to civilian authorities and almost immediately released on bail. This all seemed to be the result of the prosecution's case cited in the Lincoln assassination trial, which failed to establish any connection between Davis or his staff and the crime. The article went on to say that the government was now considering treason charges against the former Confederate president, and that he publicly welcomed this development because he was sure he could prove that the secession of the States had been constitutionally legal.

Abe sat quietly amid the clamor of the large press and the shouts of the printers. He could hardly believe what he'd just read, so he read it over again, then folded the newspaper and put it back in the box he'd taken it from. He felt a tremendous sense of freedom flow through him, realizing he'd never allowed himself to fully account for how much a burden all of that had been for him. And now it was lifted. He got up and made his way toward the front entrance where he noticed a young man about his own age standing near the door, but looking much like he belonged where he was. Abe felt a new kind of confidence that he'd been lacking for a long time as he approached the fellow.

"Excuse me," he said, "do you work here?"

"Well, I sure do," was the reply.

"Any jobs open here?"

"For you?"

"Yes, I guess so."

"Go knock on that door in the back and tell the editor what's on your mind. Might be something, might not. I do know we're real busy these days."

Abe picked his way back toward the rear office door, knocked and was hollered at to come in. After a few minutes of conversation with the editor, a Mister Wolcott, he was hired to review dispatches and stories coming in from the west, and to put together versions of them for the paper. As Mr. Wolcott said, "Our future is the West, and we'd all best be paying attention. You've got two weeks to prove yourself. Now get along and report here tomorrow bright and early, and we'll see what good you are."

As Abe walked slowly back toward the neighborhood on the bluff, he thought about what had just happened. The good news about Davis, as well as what it meant for him, and now this possible job. He'd forgotten to ask about the pay, but right now that didn't matter, so long as it was something. And right then and there, he again recognized the hand of God demonstrated in the coming together of his needs and his opportunities. He recognized that when God wants something to happen, we have to do something about it ourselves, or it might well not happen. He found himself walking faster and faster in his eagerness to tell Sarah Beth all of it: the news about Davis, as well as the opportunity and the assurance that now he would be able to stay here with them, for awhile at least, and under his own name at last.

The choir practiced that night and Sarah Beth was needed to play the piano accompaniment, so he didn't get to talk with her that evening. He did mention at supper that he was expecting some good news, but didn't give any clues as to what it was. Of course Sarah Beth pestered him for more information, but he begged off, saying that he also had something to do that evening. What that was, he wasn't sure since he's said it just to get away. He decided to take a short walk to the town's park to look for statues that might give him more of an idea about the local history.

He informed Doctor Randall that he had some leads for possible employment, and was going down to the main town to look around and get a feeling of it. He still didn't want to reveal all of his news until he could be assured that it was all in place. It was still too much of an unexpected and important set of circumstances for him to believe it completely, and yet once again the almighty "Voice" seemed to have spoken by linking together his needs from the past and this new chance for the future in a most surprising manner.

The next morning at the newspaper office he had to keep introducing himself over and over again to the same workers, of which there were only five. They seemed to recognize him from the day before, but no one paid any attention to him when he said his name; then again, he probably was speaking quite softly because he still hadn't decided at what point he would begin using his real name again. Since none of them seemed to remember what he'd said the first few times, he decided to go ahead and introduce himself as Lester Saunders. If it came up later he could say that he was mostly known as "Abe," which he could explain as a nickname taken from his middle name to distinguish him from his father who'd also been named Lester.

The editor welcomed him back and remembered enough about their interview the day before to assign him a very small desk and set him to work, although not on anything related to the western migration. The work consisted mostly in some announcements of civic affairs that needed to be arranged and expanded on from a pile of notes that were handed to him by the youngster who seemed to be everyone's errand boy.

As good a place to start as any, he thought as he carefully printed out the date, time and place for the Garden Club's weekly meeting, the Hospital League's annual fund-raising Ball, the park committee's meeting, and so forth. When he turned the completed list in to the assistant editor, he was pleasantly surprised to hear the words, "Good job Saunders. We'll see you tomorrow." This was the first time he'd heard his real last name in several years and it felt good.

Once again with some time to spend, he wandered outside of town toward the wagon train camps. On the way he caught sight of a small encampment of Indian tipis and changed direction, so that his path would take him past them. When he was quite close to the camp, two young boys dashed out of the woods. One of them jumped as he ran past and knocked Abe's hat to the ground. When Abe stooped to pick it up he could hear the boys in the bushes nearby, laughing and jabbering in what must have been their own language. He actually thought it was rather funny himself, so he pulled himself up as tall as he could get and strutted around in a circle pounding his chest and uttering low growls. The boys laughed even harder and one of them even rolled out of the bushes and onto the path before he leaped up and both ran off.

Well, that was some fun, Abe thought, wondering if he'd done the right thing. Just then an Indian man dressed in the clothes of a frontiersman approached from the site of the camp. He and Abe both stopped, facing one another at a distance of about ten steps.

"You are a man or a bear?" the Indian said with his arms crossed over his chest.

Abe tried to think of what to say, or what would be the right thing to say, but all that came out was, "Yes."

"Yes? You are a man and a bear, then." The man laughed loudly, and then continued. "Good. I saw what those boys done to you and you are not angry? Why not?"

"I don't know," Abe said, "maybe because they're just boys."

"Maybe because this is our camp, and you were not invited here. Maybe you knew you weren't supposed to be here."

"Yes, that too." He wasn't sure where this was leading and was beginning to feel nervous and apprehensive.

"Well, now you are OK to be here. You may come back some other time and ask for me. I am Left Hand Crow, known as Lefty by your people. I will call you Big Bear Man because you are not so big as a bear, but you know how to make yourself bigger than a man. Go now, but come back when you have time to sit and eat with me; I like your way with my boys."

That evening at supper Abe told the story of his encounter with the Indians. Doctor Randall was quite admiring, saying, "Well now, young man, you're first among us to make contact with the savages. Good work."

"Well, I probably shouldn't have even been going near there, but I was curious."

"And now you'll get to find out everything, won't you? I want to go."

"Sarah Beth," her father said sternly, "I don't believe you were invited. You'll just have to curb your excitement and wait for Lester to see what happens."

Sarah Beth lowered her eyes and gave that little irritated shake of her head and hair that was so familiar to all of them.

"Lester?" It was Mattie speaking. "The man was speaking in our language and you could understand him?"

"Oh yes, he was very clear in his speech. But I would like to hear them speak in their own tongue. The boys were laughing so hard when they were talking to each other it was difficult to make out what it would sound like."

There was a silence at the table, and then Abe just couldn't keep it in any longer.

"I must tell you of something else. Please don't be upset with me when I tell you this, but I ask you to listen to my reasons. I have had to carry out a very difficult deception. I can tell you all now, and we'll see what comes about because of its recent resolution."

They were all staring at him, giving him the kind of full attention he used to get when he would tell them about the actions of the patrol, when a skirmish had occurred. "First of all," he paused due to the difficulty of speaking what he was about to say. "First of all, my name is not Lester Greene. I have been living under that name since the day I arrived in your town as one of the wounded, in Virginia."

"Why? Why? And what is your name?" It was Sarah Beth.

Her father cleared his throat and said, "Let the young man speak. I am sure he plans to answer all of our questions."

Mattie placed a hand on Sarah Beth's arm, as if to restrain her somewhat.

"My real name is Abraham Saunders, always known as 'Abe' until I became Lieutenant Abraham Saunders in the Army."

"Abe? Abe?" It was Sarah Beth again, only this time the look in her father's eyes and some slight pressure on her arm from Mattie caused her to clap her hands over her mouth and sit back in her chair.

"Yes, I am Abe."

Doctor Randall leaned forward in his chair and placed his elbows on the table. "I suppose I should tell you that I knew this. The medical doctor who brought you to us, Doctor James, told me your name on that very first night, but I knew you must have your own reasons for the subterfuge. And while I am very curious, I don't think we need you to reveal your reasons."

"Oh no, I want to. That's why I'm bringing it up. You see," and he turned to face Sarah Beth, "I was a member of President Davis's staff, and when the Union President, Mr. Lincoln, was killed, Mr. Davis and his entire staff immediately became suspects and were charged with crimes of conspiracy and assassination. It was only yesterday, when I was in the local newspaper office, that I finally found those charges against President Davis had been dropped by the United States government, and most presumably those same charges against the rest of us, if there ever were any, also dropped . . . Besides, we are now very far from the authorities in Washington."

"Congratulations, young man. Ladies, let us welcome Mr. Abraham Saunders into our midst. It must be a great relief to you, my young friend." Doctor Randall smiled broadly and nodded toward Mattie. "Could you get us the brandy and glasses so we may celebrate this especially momentous occasion?"

"Certainly, sir."

"No wait," he said abruptly, "you stay seated. I will serve us all."

He returned with the decanter and four glasses, pouring out substantial portions for Abe and himself, less for Mattie and a rather small amount for Sarah Beth. "It's a special occasion, my girl," he said. "We'll have a toast." He sat back down in his chair and held his glass up. "To this young man and his new and old names. May this help bring all of us good fortune and the fulfillment of our dreams." They sipped from their glasses and Sarah Beth couldn't help giggling at being included in the drinking.

That night she began keeping a journal of "The Life and Times of Sarah Beth Randall." Her father had given her a bound blank book a couple of birthdays ago, but she'd never used it or even had much of an idea what it was good for. But this night seemed special enough to be recorded. She wrote in her small, neat handwriting,

Dear Book,

I finally know his real name, or at least I think he's telling us the truth this time.

I have been most curious to know all there is to know about this man who has become almost as one of our family. It is the same as if he is my brother, but I would rather have him as my husband, There, now I've said it, so I must take specially good care of this book so that no one else shall ever see these words.

I can't believe he was able to keep this secret for so long. He must have been very frightened by the possibility of going to prison. I do believe him that he had nothing to do with that crime against the Union President, although I'm not sure if it was truly a crime if it happened during a War, even though the War was only just ending. It is so hard to know these kinds of things.

He told us such a funny story about his encounter with a real Indian, although he said the man was dressed like any other man in this country. I do hope he can make friends with this man Lefty and some of his people, friends enough that he could take me with him to visit . . . now if I were his wife, he would have to take me. But that is still just a dream, even though father's toast asked for our dreams to come true.

Well, dear Book, that is enough for now. It's late, but I think I am too excited to sleep. This is all so wonderful, at least I think it is.

The next day when Abe reported to the newspaper office, he was told he'd done a good job the day before, but that there was nothing for him to do on this day. He left office tempted to go back toward the river and pass by the Indian camp, but he cautioned himself against seeming impatient, and besides, the man had said to come and eat with him and it wasn't the time of day for a meal.

When he returned to the house, he found that Sarah Beth and Mattie were out shopping for curtains and other furnishings. The church had set aside a small amount of money to be used to enhance the house and they were off to spend it. Doctor Randall let him know that if he wasn't busy, there was some work for him unpacking and sorting copies of the sermons they'd brought along with them.

"Imagine," he said as they shuffled through the piles of paper, "a new congregation that hasn't heard any of these. Of course, I'll have to be careful to get a feel for these people as to what they can and want to hear, but having this bit of a backlog is certainly an advantage I hadn't thought of until this moment." He laughed and then said, "Of course you and Sarah Beth have heard them all. Too bad for you."

They worked through the afternoon and were nearly finished when Abe decided to inform the minister of his employment opportunity. He'd wanted to wait until he was sure that there would be some actual income, but if the editor was pleased with his work, he couldn't see why there wouldn't be. And he knew he'd work hard to see that the his employer was pleased.

When he heard the news, Doctor Randall seemed very satisfied and even proud of his young charge. "Sounds like you're off to a great beginning here," he said.

"Well yes, although I'll be waiting eagerly to hear what my cousin has to say about his experiences and that whole opportunity. The closer I get to the frontier, the more curious about it I become. And who knows? If this position with the newspaper works out, I may even be able to go west and send back dispatches for their use."

"Could be, young man. Could be."

That evening following supper, he invited Sarah Beth to accompany him on a walk. He wanted to tell her about his opening at the paper and see how she felt about it. He hoped the prospect would excite her as much as it did him.

They walked up the gentle hill leading away from the bluff and the river, toward the east and a rising, nearly full moon. As they reached the last of the houses, the hill began to slope down to a wooded area. Below them in the gathering dusk they could see farmland stretching away across a wide valley. The sound of a single cow calling floated in the breeze above them. A fallen log seemed to have been set there just for the likes of these two. They found their way to it and settled themselves into some comfortable hollows in the huge bole of the old tree.

"Well, Mr. Saunders," Sarah Beth said when she was comfortable. "What is it that's on your mind?"

He looked at her, noting the quick flashes of her teeth and the whites of her eyes. It would be dark soon enough, but the moon would then be their light. "I've a bit more news from these past few days." He paused, not sure how to go on.

"And . . . that is?"

"I think I have a placement at the newspaper, at the *St. Joseph Herald*. I started work yesterday."

"Oh, Les . . . Abe, that's wonderful, just wonderful. Doing what, pray tell?"

"I'm sure it's only temporary, but the editor said he needed someone to write about the west and how it's opening up and the frontier is changing. People are on the move and there are plenty of dispatches and even the new telegraph messages to go through and sort out and make them into stories for the newspaper." He paused, realizing he was almost out of breath.

"Abe Saunders, I have never heard you say so many words in one speech. You seem to be exceptionally excited . . ."

He looked down at his hands, thinking about how she was right. "Yes, I guess I am a bit stirred up by this opportunity."

She reached out and took both of his hands in hers. "Well, no guessing about it. I tell you I certainly am. This is most wonderful, and you will sign your articles in your new name, well, new to me, and you will become a famous journalist of the Wild West. Oh, Abe!"

He retrieved his hands and removed his hat, nervously smoothing back his hair. He took her hands again. "Yes, and it means I can contribute to our household while I'm here."

"While you're here. What does that mean?"

"Well, it seems like after I've spent some time writing articles about the West, I probably should go and see it for myself. When Louis returns, we'll see what his trip was like and whether or not there'll be another opportunity like that." He stopped. "There I go again. Let me stop for a minute and ask you what you really think?"

"Abe? I like calling you Abe. I think this is wonderful for you. Your dreams are growing bigger and bigger, you seem to have everything figured out and I'm glad for you, I certainly am . . ." She gently removed her hands from his grasp and turned away to hide the tiny tears that had just appeared at the corners of her eyes.

"Then what is it, my dear, what?"

"It's nothing. I just don't know what this has to do with me. Oh Abe, you're going to leave me behind, aren't you?"

There was silence except for the sound of his heels striking the big log as he swung his legs, not knowing how to say whatever it was she wanted him to say next, knowing that she truly was happy for him, even as this was making things somewhat miserable for her. He could almost feel her trying not to think of all the worst things she'd ever thought about, like if he ever left her, left her and her father. That prospect was made him sad as well, but it didn't necessarily have to be that way.

She stood up suddenly, as if to go, but he caught her hand and pulled her toward him. Now he stood slowly and wrapped his good arm around her and looked over her head, back toward the east and Virginia where they had come from, where now the moon was rapidly climbing into the darkening sky.

"Sarah Beth, I'm not sure when I realized it, but I guess I don't want to leave you behind. I want to go, but more and more I find myself wanting to be with you . . . You have your father to care for, you have your studies as a nurse to pursue . . . I just don't want my plans to spoil the life you could have for yourself."

She turned her head away from him and mumbled, "Oh yes, Abe, for myself. Why would I want a life just for myself?"

"I didn't mean that, I meant that your whole life is ahead of you, and I have no plans that make any sense, just some adventurous and probably idle dreams. What you need is a time of finding out who you are and what you want."

She pushed herself free from his arm. "And you don't think I'm grown up enough to know what I want, do you? Well, Mr. Saunders, you would be surprised."

"Here, please, sit back down and talk to me about you and about your dreams. I've been selfish, speaking only of myself, and I want to know more about you."

She sat back down, a bit away from him. She sat stiffly with her face turned toward the rising moon, the shadows of her face casting it into a mystery that was one of the most compelling sights Abe could ever remember seeing. There was in her gaze at the moon and beyond an unearthly sense of secrets, and he felt that he could almost see the past and the future in her features. He was suddenly aware that this "girl" might well know more than he did about their lives and their place in the world, and he couldn't help thinking that he wasn't quite sure who she was at this moment. Then she broke the silence with a loud whispering voice.

"Abe, you are such a fool! You don't see what's in front of your face. You say father needs me. Don't you have any idea that since my mother passed away and his grief was so truthful and heavy, that it wasn't me who he turned to for comfort, it was Mattie? Yes, Mattie. Not as a lover, but as the one friend who alone could comfort him in the depths of his despair. And then when the church turned against him, once again it was Mattie giving him the strength and encouragement to stand his ground and keep his faith. Oh, Abe, he won't always need me now, now that he is free from the burdens of those hypocritical people, and out here where people will more likely allow him his privacy. Why do you think he spoke of all of our dreams?"

He was quiet for a long moment, and then, "I had no idea."

"Of course you hadn't. Any more than you know what I've been feeling all this time, even though I've told you, and told you. Oh Abe, is it just because you're a man or is it because you're you? You told me you thought you'd been in love before. Whatever happened to Miss Irene Ruth? Yes, I found out who she was; it wasn't hard to get Louis to talk about back home. Is she the reason you have no eyes for me? Is she the reason you don't notice Father being so sweet to Mattie in ways that one would never show to a servant, ways that made it a certainty that he would bring her with us? Oh Abe, what am I going to do with you?"

The thoughts and feelings swirling through his mind and bubbling in his blood left him speechless, so he turned toward her and threw one leg over the tree, straddling it and feeling like a man on a fine high-strung horse. He edged his way closer and closer to her, until he could lean forward with his face nearly touching her hair, and then he held still for that endless moment while he waited as she slowly turned herself to him and they kissed, and kissed.

CHAPTER SEVEN

Call of the West

There were days when Abe felt the need for more action and physical work. His two occupations, working for the newspaper and for the minister, were both similar, being primarily indoors and sitting down. He found himself remembering the mostly boring rides of the patrol as a highlight of being on the move, threatened by the ever-present possibility of danger, and if nothing else, good exercise. Now, he was occasionally finding himself feeling imprisoned by a desk, with no outlet for his unused energy.

It was on one of these restless days that he took a break from the newspaper office and wandered back down along the river to where the freighters and their camps offered at least a glimpse of the world of action and the tumultuous atmosphere of men at work. When he passed close to the Indian encampment, he was a bit surprised to find that it was still there, with its temporary nomadic structures looking semi-permanent in their use of that space.

He stopped, wondering whether or not he would be welcome or chased away if he were to go any closer. After all, the man he'd met might not even be there anymore. Just then two boys, looking like the two that he'd encountered before, came shyly out from behind one of the large trees along the pathway.

One of them pushed the other one forward and said something in the boy's ear. That one spoke shyly, softly, "Lefty say if we see you, tell you he back next big moon." Then they ran off, pushing on each other in attempts to be the one in the lead.

He thought about it as he walked on down toward the river. It was apparently as close to an invitation as he was going to get, and it actually made him feel good. He wondered what would happen to the camp when winter came, and if it would still be there come springtime.

Sarah Beth found herself accepted at the town's hospital, first as a volunteer, and then as an apprentice with a small stipend. Two doctors assisted women giving birth in the hospital, and two local midwifes made home deliveries. Sarah Beth was surprised at the number of women who confided that they wished they could just settle down in St. Joe, at least until the baby was a little older, but so many of them were faced with the move west, by wagon or train when the next spring came on and before, as they'd been told, the high water brought its own crises of flooding and impassable waterways filled with melting snow from hundreds of miles away. She mentioned this curious fact to Abe and asked him what he knew about it.

"I haven't heard that, but I can certainly see about it at the newspaper. It would be a good thing to know, when and how the emigrants know to leave here on their journeys."

They were taking a short evening stroll, bundled against the wind coming up from the river. Now that winter was nearly over it was somewhat surprising that there had been no real cold or frost such as they'd been used to in Virginia. Someone in the church told the reverend that it almost never snowed in this part of the country. Sarah Beth's father was very pleased by that news, because, as he often said, "The aches and pains of growing older are a constant reminder . . ." He then would wait long enough that either his daughter or Abe asked what they were a reminder of, and he would laugh and say, "I can't remember. I must be getting old."

It had been a month since Sarah Beth and Abe had kissed, and it hadn't been repeated since. They were both a little embarrassed when the two of them were alone together. At those times, they often compared their experiences at work and mostly avoided any exchange of personal words that would have taken them further into unknown territory. Not that Sarah Beth didn't want to press for more discovery, more knowledge of one another and of each other's feelings, but as the youngest of the two, she just felt it was not her place to bring up those subjects, and that her role should be one of patient waiting for Abe as the older person and as the man. Of course, in her own mind she was quite sure he never would speak up, so she'd decided to wait for a moment when neither of them seemed to have anything to say, and then come right out and ask him about his plans for the two of them.

This particular evening brought about that circumstance several times. It seemed that neither of them was in a talkative mood, or that they had very little news to share. The silences between them grew longer and longer until Sarah Beth finally took the leap and spoke what was on her mind.

"Have you heard from Louis and not told me?"

"No, I've heard nothing except that there was a dispatch from an army fort out there. It said that his wagon train made it through all right, but was staying the winter before trying to head back here next spring."

"And so what will you do with yourself, Mr. Saunders?"

He looked sideways at her and smiled, "You're so funny when you go formal with me, Miss Randall."

She smiled back and said, "Well, from as much as you seem to have to say about what's really on your mind, we might as well be strangers who've just met."

They had reached a corner at the edge of this part of town, where two empty streets met one another. A few stars could be seen twinkling in the blue sky above, where the sun had disappeared an hour or so ago. It was growing dark. He didn't reply, but stopped and stood still, taking one of her hands in his. He could almost hear her father's voice echoing from earlier in the week when he'd asked about the younger man's intentions. Abe wasn't at all sure which intentions the minister had been referring to and only replied vaguely that he was waiting to hear from his cousin, and waiting to see what God had in mind for him. The minister had smiled and reminded Abe that one of the ways God speaks to us is when we make some decisions for ourselves and then He can show us how they will turn out.

"Abe, what is it? What are you thinking about?"

He realized he'd drifted away and ignored her during this reverie, and he almost stuttered as he tried to explain. "Sarah Beth, the more I read and report on the western migration and this movement of our nation, the more I want to be a part of it. I don't want to sit here at a desk and write about the wondrous things that others are doing and are making happen. This is probably the most exciting time anyone has ever lived in, and I don't want to miss out on any of it . . ." He paused and then went on, "But I don't want to leave you behind either. I don't want us to be parted by my foolhardy and adventurous ways."

"Abe," she said, coming closer to him, "do you mean that? You've never said anything like that before."

"Yes, I very much mean it, but I don't know how it makes anything different. I will either go my way, or I will stay here. We'll have to see. I hate to think of either choice right now, so let's just enjoy this winter and its holidays, and we'll wait and see what the New Year brings."

"Abe, listen to me. There's another choice." She paused and then went on, "I'll go with you if you'll have me. I'll go anywhere with you."

He put his arms around her, both arms now, and held her close. "I don't know. I don't know. It might not be safe. It isn't a place for a young woman. Oh, Sarah Beth, I don't know."

She kissed him quickly and then leaned back against his arms, "Mr. Saunders, you have no idea how many young women I talk to at the hospital who are going west at the next opportunity, brave women and frightened women, but all of them on their way somewhere; I want to be among them, just as you do."

Abe raised his good hand to her face and gently traced its outline in the darkness that was now keeping him from seeing her clearly. As his fingers tried to read her expression, he felt a kind of a lump in his throat and suddenly had to cough. He turned away to do so, and then came back to facing her silhouette outlined by the lights of a house some ways away.

"Are you sure of that? It will be dangerous, and it could be very difficult."

"For a woman, you mean?"

"For anyone. We don't know what it is."

"But you know you want to go, don't you?"

"Yes," he said, "I want to go."

"Then I do as well."

"What about . . ."

She quickly pressed a finger against his lips. "Shhh. We'll talk about it another time. We should go now." Then she kissed him again, with fervor and shyness mixed together in this still-new feeling. "There," she said, finally pulling away, "do you believe me now?"

As Doctor Randall became more settled, his comfort with the congregation was increasing all the time. He also had more time to spend in conversation with Abe and with others. One day when he had finished dictating his next sermon to Abe, they were relaxing together in the study, listening to Sarah Beth playing the piano in another room.

"So, my young man, I'm curious how it's going with you at the newspaper."

"Going well, very well," Abe answered.

"Do you find yourself liking the work, the reading and the writing?"

"Yes sir, it's fascinating to be receiving such a variety of stories and dispatches. My job sorting through them has given me a great opportunity to learn more and more about the West and its challenges."

"Such as?"

"Oh, everything from the construction of new towns, to livestock prices going up, to massacres by and against Indians. All of it, sir."

"And you seem to want to go there, to see it all for yourself?"

"Yes sir. Very much. It's the most important thing that can happen in my life."

"More important than the War?"

"I believe so."

"Well, for me, I think that War will be the one thing that changed everything else," Doctor Randall said, and seemed to lapse into the memories brought back by the subject. Then he spoke quickly, as if waking up from a bit of a nap. "So, may I ask what your intentions are having to do with my daughter?"

Abe was shocked at the suddenness of the question, and his mind raced through all the possible answers he could think of, but there really wasn't much he could say except for the truth of the matter, "I don't know, sir. I've been meaning to bring the matter up with you. I don't know if you're aware that we seem to have developed some new feelings for one another . . . lately."

"Bound to happen," the man said in a kind and even fatherly way. "Son, and I call you that on purpose, although from the beginning I've always felt that you were more a son than a stranger. I, myself, want to be very happy for both of you. And of course I've seen your feelings for one another blossoming over these few years. Actually, I'm almost sure I've been more aware of them than the two of you."

"Yes, sir. It's all been somewhat strange for me."

"How so?"

"Well, when I arrived to stay with you, she was a girl. Now she's very much a young woman. And I guess it took me some time to recognize that change in her. And . . ."

"Now, son," the man interrupted, leaning back in his chair, "it may very well be time to do something about it."

"Yes sir, but I'm not sure what's possible. I'm very much seeing myself as a traveler, an emigrant, and looking to the West for the next stage of my life."

"Good. A young man needs a good woman to accompany him on such an adventure. If only to keep him from getting himself into too much trouble."

"But what about you? She's very important to you. I wouldn't want . . ."

The man interrupted, a bit sharply, "I wouldn't hold the two of you back. I'm doing well, haven't been better off in years, actually. This position and this congregation have inspired me after things had occurred that caused me to think I actually might have to give up the ministry." He stood up, hands behind his back, and paced from the window to the shelves of books, and back again. "And now, my faith in both God and myself have been revived, rejuvenated, I might even say, resurrected from the darkness that covered me since the death of Sarah Beth's mother and the betrayal by my flock in Virginia. I'm a new man, son, perfectly capable of taking care of myself for the time being, and of course, there's our dear Mattie . . ."

There was a silence that lasted for quite awhile. Finally Abe spoke, "Yes sir, I have recognized the change in you as well, and it is very good for all of us to have you in this present state of mind."

"I'm sure I must have been a bit hard to put up with in my gloominess and despair."

"No sir, I didn't mean that."

"No matter. What I am trying to tell you is that Mattie and I will be perfectly all right should the two of you decide to try this western business. I'm not sure I would advise it, but I want you to know that I won't stand in the way, of either you or of progress. The times are dictating great changes and those who have enough courage to seize these changes will see great benefits. Besides, now with railroads opening their way across this continent, visiting will be more and more possible as time goes on."

"Well, thank you for that, sir. But I must tell you that Sarah Beth and I have made no plans together, so this may all be a bit premature."

"Perhaps you and she have made no plans together, as you say, but I would have to say that I believe she has made some plans that involve the both of you."

A few days later, with the full moon approaching, Abe recalled the two boys' invitation from the Indian man, Lefty, and he made up his mind to seek him out that next afternoon. As he walked the now familiar path from downtown to the river, he was encouraged by the first faint signs of the passing of winter and the coming of springtime. Short blades of grass and small fuzzy buds gave signals that the climate would change as it always does, but that it would be earlier here than he remembered it back home or in Virginia. There had been no severe or harsh weather to contend with this winter, and the passage of time had been almost pleasant in its mild nights and mostly clear days.

He soon saw the shapes of tipis between the trees, and wondered what it was like to live through even mild winter months in such thin-walled dwellings. He knew they kindled fires inside for warmth, but still it must have been uncomfortable some of the time. He wondered whether the Indians around this part of the country actually used these structures themselves. In his reading of dispatches and other reports from further west, it seemed that these lodges, as the Indians called them, were more suited to and used in the plains, not along rivers such as the Missouri. If the opportunity presented itself, he would ask. Perhaps the subject could provide the basis for an article of the kind he was now writing as an occasional series for the newspaper.

Suddenly he heard a "whoop" and spun around to catch a glimpse of one of the boys standing in the trail behind him. Then he was gone. Abe continued toward the camp, knowing that if he wasn't welcome someone would let him know, and if he was allowed then that would also become clear. As he stepped out of the shadows of the trees and into the late afternoon light at the edge of the camp, he could see many kinds of activity going on, from children playing, to women grinding flour, to a few old men smoking long pipes. The boys reappeared and came up on either side of him. They grabbed his sleeves and began leading him through the tents to the far side of a roughly spaced circle of the dwellings. Beyond the tipis, Abe could see several horses in a pen made of small diameter logs.

At a distance, he recognized the man called Lefty driving the horses in a circle round and round the inside of the pen. The boys hollered and the man stopped what he was doing, rolled his rope into a coil, and lightly vaulted himself over the fence. He was once again dressed in the clothes of a typical wagoneer.

He held out his hand and Abe took it and gave a handshake in return.

"So, Big Bear Man, you have returned. This is good. Come."

He led the way to the closest structure and slapped his hand on its hide covering, calling out some words unknown to Abe. A woman's voice answered from inside.

"She says you are early. We will have to wait for her cooking to be completed." He laughed. "She is my wife, the young one. I think she always makes me wait, just so I know how important she is. Come, sit here." He gestured to a kind of leather pillow on the ground next to the lodge. He sat down cross-legged in front of Abe.

"You are welcome here. We don't get many visitors. They just allow us to be here so they can keep their eyes on us."

"Have you been here long?" Abe asked.

"Some of us people used to appear in a show they had here in the summer. We rode around the fairgrounds trying to look frightening, and we were even paid a small amount of money for it. This camp is located on ground that was a camp of the people living around here for hundreds of years, and some of these old men moved back in here when the town was very small and made their claim to it."

"I hadn't heard that. So these people are from the groups that used to live here?"

"Some are, some aren't. I myself come from very far away, in the Oregon country, but I came here as scout on a wagon train from near the Great Salt Lake. Met my first wife here. She is one of these people. Now I go back and forth between here and there." He leaned forward and spoke very softly. "I have one wife here, and one at the other end of the trail, and one who travels with me."

The woman's voice came from inside the tipi with something that sounded to Abe like a request. Lefty called for the boys and sent them running.

"She needs water brought from the little spring. But tell me of you and your left arm. I might have called you Stiff Arm Bear if I noticed it the first time we met."

"I was wounded on the last day of the War . . . I am now here waiting for my cousin to return from the West. He left driving a freight wagon before I could get here last springtime, and I'm hoping he will return with the next trains, due back sometime in the next few months."

"If the weather and the Indians cooperate," Lefty smiled. "What will you do then; what will he do?"

"If his trip was successful and it's a good thing to do, I would go with him on the next trip and work my way west, to the frontier country."

"That's good, but I would go on the northern trail if I were going. And I may very well be going myself with a wagon train of freighters and Mormons. That route has been safer up to now, and with the railroad pushing across as well, there is less chance for trouble along the way."

"And that's the trail that goes to that Great Salt Lake country?" Abe asked.

"Yes."

The boys returned carrying a canvas bucket, laughing and spilling much of the water. Lefty yelled at them and they started walking more carefully, taking the water inside the tent.

A young Indian woman in a white woman's store-bought dress came out, carrying a deep pot of steaming food. She set it on the ground between the men and bowed slightly before going back inside. Abe saw the smile that seemed to scurry across her face as she was bent over and he saw her looking at him out of the tops of her eyes.

Lefty called her back out, saying, "This is Dawn Smiling Woman, but we call her Patsy, like a white woman, just to have fun with her. Right, Patsy?"

The woman swung her skirt at him and then retreated back into the tent, saying something to the boys, who came out and sat a ways away from the two men. Lefty pulled out a short knife and speared a piece of meat. He motioned for Abe to do the same. In a fortunate bit of foresight, Abe had strapped on a knife of his own before leaving the house that morning, not thinking of using it, but not knowing what might occur if he carried out his intended visit to this Lefty person.

They ate in silence for awhile, spearing chunks of meat and chewing on its toughness, then spearing another piece.

"What's this meat?" Abe asked.

"It's not dog if that's what you want to know. Ha! Just a bull from the wagon camps."

He had laughed at Abe's expression when he said dog, but now he was serious again.

"You don't talk like you're from around here," Lefty said as he wiped some juice from his face with his sleeve.

"I'm not. From back in Carolina. What we call the South."

"The losers, some call you. Lost that War, but put up a good fight. Were you a warrior? A soldier?"

"I was in a few battles, but mostly at the rear doing official business things."

"Enough battles to get yourself wounded." He gestured at Abe's stiff arm.

"Like I said, last day of the War. My bad luck." Abe wiped his own mouth with his bare hand and then cleaned it on the short grass. "Speaking of how I talk, where did you get your English? It's very good."

"Hah, very good for an Indian, I think you mean, but that's fine, I am an Indian. Proud to be. And I really like listening to white men when they don't know I can understand them. Very funny . . . But I learned your language from my father's second wife. She is white. He bought her from what you call a Comanche. He brought her home as slave. I was very young. She didn't stay slave long though. Soon she was running his camp. From the beginning she made me learn and talk English with her. She always said she needed somebody she could talk to, just as well be you, she said."

"Didn't she try to get away?"

"No, I don't think ever. She told me the white men were more crazy than the crazy Indians. That's how she said it. She never had no children though. Just me; she adopted me pretty much. They called her Moon Fish, because she would leave the camp and go fishing in the moonlight. Said it was best time to catch fish."

"Do you still see her?"

"Sometimes. She is getting older now, but we have a good time when I see her."

His young wife Patsy came out of the tent and stood quietly, as if waiting for something. Lefty seemed to ignore her, then gave a wave with his arm and she bent down and took the pot away with her. He made a growling sound in his throat and she tossed her long braids in his direction as she bent through the doorway.

"She thinks she's in charge just like my old mother, Moon Fish. But that's good. When I go away I don't have to worry about her and the boys. One of them is hers, the other is my other woman's. Do you have wife?"

"No I don't. Not yet."

"OK. Do you have horse?"

"No," he smiled, "not yet. I'm just now able to saddle and ride again." He held his stiff arm out in explanation.

"Do you have place to keep horse?"

"Yes. Where I stay has a small stable and there's a field behind the place. I would be allowed to use it."

"Good. I need someone to take care of a horse for me. Come."

He stood up quickly and stretched, loud cracking sounds coming from his knees and shoulders. Abe got up more slowly. They walked toward the pen behind the camp. Six or seven horses were inside and several others tethered to the pen's perimeter.

They leaned on the fence and Lefty whistled to get the horses' attention. One of them, with spots on its rear and one all-white leg, trotted over to them and nuzzled into Lefty's shirt.

"She thinks I have something for her. Maybe tobacco, huh, horse. You take her, she needs somebody to be nice to her. Name is Hummingbird because she goes quick here, quick there, but I just call her Bird." He stepped back and immediately the horse began rubbing against Abe's chest and pockets.

"See, she likes you. Take her."

"I'd have to make sure it's all right with the people I stay with and find out where I would get grain." Abe scratched the horse behind the ears and she seemed to appreciate it. He felt a small notch on one of the ears and asked, "She get bit?"

"No, the man I got her from marked her that way, like a brand. And she doesn't need grain, but she does like it. But not too much, only a little or she will get fat and mean. That's how I get when I'm in camp too long, fat and mean. You get your place ready for her, and come back. I'll even loan you a saddle."

"I should give you something in return."

"Yep, maybe bring me a dog if you find one. Then we can have a feast." He threw back his head and laughed. The horse took off galloping around the enclosure, and that was how Abe got himself a horse.

Sarah Beth wrote:

"Dear Book,

So now he has a horse and spends much of his time with her. It would be foolish for me to feel jealousy of a horse, and yet that is what these feelings for him are doing to me. If this is love, it is as hard as it is easy. I care so much, and yet I think I must also be very careful. He is sometimes like a wild creature, ready to flee at any moment. I so wish I had a woman to talk with about all of this. I am at such a loss to know how to proceed. When I suggested to him that I would go west with him if that is what he wants he almost seemed to be ready to cry. Now, some tears are of gladness, even as most may be for sadness, but I think his expression was telling me that I cause him so much confusion that he doesn't know what to feel. If only he were more experienced in these things of love, but in that case, why would he want someone like me who has none.

I would talk to Mattie, but something happened that makes that difficult as well. Yesterday morning I returned early from the hospital because I had forgotten my spare uniform and the one I'd worn became soiled during a birth, as happens so often. Instead of coming through the house, I walked around behind to take the clothing from the line, and when I came in the back porch door I saw Father and Mattie through the window to the kitchen. They were embracing. I don't know if they knew I saw them, but when I made a noise dropping my basket to let them know I was there, they jumped apart. Father quickly left the kitchen and when I entered, Mattie had busied herself with her bread-making. I almost laughed out loud when I thought how funny it would be to ask her if a colored person can blush, but I immediately thought better of it and explained why I was there and went on about my business.

Oh, dear book, who can I trust? Who can teach me the ways of love, the ways of my heart as it speeds up with anticipation and slows down with dread? I am lost and cannot find my way alone. If only Mother were still with us, but then I don't imagine I could talk with her about this either. I don't think ever she wanted me to grow up.

The horse, Bird, was a great pleasure and comfort to Abe. She was affectionate, but also aloof, and he liked that about her. She would pester him for a treat when he first appeared in her stable or paddock, but as soon as he'd given her something and said, "enough," she was ready to get to work. He brought Lefty's saddle home on her as he led her through the streets, but he found one that suited him better at a used goods shop that specialized in horse gear. After a few tries, he learned to grab it in the space behind the horn and throw it up and over Bird's back. At first she would shy away and make it hard for him by refusing to stand still for the rest of the process. But soon, with his stubbornness and her resignation, they became a team for that part of the effort. Mounting was a little more difficult because he had to reach over the saddle with a stiff arm to hold his balance, put his foot in the stirrup, and then pull himself up and over with his good arm. Once again, the process took some getting used to for both of them and he felt it was quite an accomplishment when the horse stood still for it all. This allowed him to climb aboard without having to struggle with either her restlessness or his own clumsiness.

Abe and his new horse began going on rides down the hillside to the valley behind the town and before long he was able to gallop her along country lanes that wandered through peaceful farms and the dark woods of the area. One day, when he had no obligations to either Doctor Randall or the newspaper, he packed himself some food, turning down Mattie's help, but smiling at her when she said, "Someday, Mister Abe, you'll have to let a woman help you out with some of these things. Else she won't feel needed."

"Thanks, Mattie, I'll do that. Someday," he said, taking a light coat and leaving the house.

He rode slowly down the hill and onto the valley floor. He'd never been past the far edge of the lowlands into the distant hills and he made that his destination this day. The horse was restless, but he knew he needed to save her energy for this long of a ride, as well as saving his own. Especially since galloping was still something he was just getting used to.

As they trotted along, they flushed flocks of birds from the bushy roadsides. The scent of springtime was in the air. Soon it would be time to make plans for the trip west. He could feel a new urgency and excitement as he thought about places he'd only written about becoming real to him. Lefty's recommendation for the northern trail, a version of the old Oregon Trail, had proven correct as he researched it. There'd been fewer hostile encounters in the years since the War and there were several forts along the way, now staffed with veterans whose primary role was to safeguard the emigrants along the trails, as well as the telegraph and railroad, which were finally completed after many years of strife and difficulty.

He made it through the valley and the road began to climb into the hills and what lay beyond. He stopped, loosened the saddle, and hobbled Bird, letting her graze while he found his appetite eager for what he'd brought to feed it. Once he'd eaten, he lay back in the soft dampness of new grass and the warmth of the mid-day sun. He couldn't help thinking how nice it would be to have Sarah Beth beside him, but he shook off that thought when it brought with it too many complications and mixed suggestions from his mind and his heart. His true purpose had to be the western trek, and anything that didn't contribute to that was nothing more than a distraction. He knew this, as surely as if he'd heard the Voice that Doctor Randall would have recognized as a source of the strength for his young friend's convictions. Abe had **no** doubts about the good man's comments about his daughter, and his apparent blessing for their union. Abe didn't feel nearly as confident about the possibilities and responsibility that would come along with making a life with Sarah Beth. He could imagine to himself that he loved this girl and the woman she was becoming. No one else knew and even understood him as well as she did, and even her original rude intrusions into his guarded privacy had been tempered by both of them maturing, and by the shared loneliness they each felt from lacking friendships with others of their own type or age. He wondered if it was time to take her to meet Lefty and Patsy. But then he would have to explain who she was to him, something he obviously hadn't yet explained to himself.

He shook himself to awaken from the drowsiness that overcame him as all these thoughts had receded. The warming sun was lulling him into a peacefulness that was as unfamiliar as it was comforting. He sat up slowly and felt the gentle sensation of a new and pleasant calm. It would work out, it would all work out his mind seemed to be telling him. And he found himself giving voice to that feeling, "It has to work out."

He rode to the first wide bench on the rising slopes of the hillside. He could only see a little ways ahead as the roadway narrowed and steepened. He turned the horse and stared back the way they'd come, down into the valley, and then raised his eyes to where the smoky mist of the town was rising above the river's bluffs. He could just make out the darker band of forest that separated the homes of the heights from the slope down to the valley. He told the horse it was time to head for home, and he urged her back down the road, holding back on her head to keep her upright on the steepest parts of the way down.

When they were most of the way across the lowland, he let Bird have her way with the pace and she pricked her ears forward and broke into a jarring lope, comfortable for her perhaps, but rough on him. Suddenly a rabbit darted across the road, dashing right between her feet. She gave a quick jump and then took off at a full run. Abe held on without holding her back, thinking that she was truly part of the West, born as Lefty said, in the open plains beyond rivers and mountains, in country where the low hills were covered with horses like herself and the people lived in contented harmony with one another . . . or so he'd said with a laugh and a further clarification that it was true except when they had to fight other Indians or the white men.

As the horse slowed down on their hill and they had nearly reached the little stable, Abe and Bird both heard the loud shrill neighing of another horse. He pulled Bird to a stop at the fence to her paddock and climbed down, suddenly sore and already stiffening from the day-long ride. He opened the gate and led her into the small stable building. And that was when they both saw the other horse.

The structure had two stalls, one for Bird, and one he'd been using for the saddles and other items of horse-keeping. All of that was now stacked neatly by the wall and a tall gray horse was reaching his head over the side of the stall and trying to touch noses with Bird. She backed away and stamped a foot on the wooden floor. Abe slid the saddle from her back, wiped her down and placed her in her own stall.

"Welcome home, Mr. Saunders," Sarah Beth's voice said from the doorway. Abe spun around and saw her standing in silhouette against a late afternoon sun that was just beginning to drop into the far horizon. "How was your ride?"

"Good, very good, but what's this?" He nodded toward the strange horse. "Did your father get himself a horse?"

"No."

"Well, then what's . . ."

"He's mine." She walked over to the horse, who was stretching his neck over the stall. "I thought your Bird might be lonely," she said as she turned her face to the horse's neck and buried it in his mane, mumbling to herself, "like me."

It was another week before Abe and Sarah Beth had time to spend with the horses together, and it was to be their only chance for awhile; word had come that Louis was expected back in Independence within the next week. Abe planned to travel by stage to meet him and to see what was happening with their plans. He'd also spent more time talking with Lefty and was becoming convinced that Oregon was where he wanted to go. Not only would he have some kind of connection with the Indians there through Lefty's introduction, but he was intrigued by the stories he'd come across in his research about a place called Jordan Valley in the southeast corner of the new state. If anything, it seemed that a place with a name like that must have some resemblance to a promised land, or at least a place where opportunity awaited.

Sarah Beth came out to the stable to join Abe who was already saddling his mare. When he turned around at the sound of her voice, he was startled to see her standing there in the doorway of the small building wearing pants, a pair of his own pants that had been missing for some time.

"What are you doing with those?" He gestured at her legs.

"Well, I'm not going to ride west dressed like a Southern belle, you know. I knew you weren't wearing these much anymore, so Mattie and I took them in here and there and shortened them a bit, and I think they fit me quite well. Don't you think?" She spun around and stopped to pose for him. "Well?"

"I don't know. I just don't know about you sometimes."

"You never have, have you?" She came toward him and pushed him back against his horse. "Now, are you going to help me get saddled up, or do I have to do it all myself?" She kissed him lightly on the cheek, and turned to where a new saddle was placed on a rack made for that purpose. "Do you like it?" she asked, pointing to the saddle, which was a smaller version of his, of the western style but without a horn.

"Nice, I guess."

"Well, you don't have to be so enthusiastic. I didn't get it for you, you know." She tossed her hair and then caught it up into a bun at the back of her head where she pinned it. "I'm looking forward to this, aren't you?"

Abe led Bird outside and looped her reins over a post, then came back to watch Sarah Beth lead her horse out of his stall. His full name was Break of Day, but she'd already changed it to simply Morning. He was a gelding and sold to her as a ten-year-old. She'd ridden quite a bit growing up, but the past few years had been filled with so many other activities that riding was left out of her life. She told Abe that when her mother was still healthy, the two of them would take long rides together down the same roads the patrol had traveled along. She seemed to be waiting for something and he was unsure as to whether to help her or not, so he stood quietly, watching her moves as she laid the bright new blanket on the horse's back. It was most unusual to see her in pants, and he realized that he never had. Then she lifted the saddle and pushed it up and over the horse's back. Morning was fairly tall and when she tried to position the saddle on his back it dislodged and pushed on the blanket.

Abe stepped forward and lifted the saddle up and out of the way while she straightened the blanket, then set it back in place. "It'll get easier for you," he said.

"I'm sure it will," she replied, threading the cinch through its ring and leaning back to tighten it. The horse sidestepped away from her, but she stuck with it, lifted a knee into his belly and secured the wrap when he let out his breath. "Be all right, don't you think?"

"We'll see," he smiled, pleased to see how competent she seemed around the animal and the process.

They took some adjustment turns around the small enclosure and then let themselves out to take the roadway down the hill toward the valley. The horses were restless and seemed anxious to get moving, but Abe cautioned that they needed to take it carefully down the hill, lest one of them slip on the loose rock surface. Once on the valley floor, they let the horses canter for a ways and then pulled up to try some different gaits such as the trot and a lope. Once they left the road and moved to cross open fields, the horses kept trying to stop and eat. Finally when they came to a small stream, Abe suggested they climb down and let the animals graze for a bit. He removed their bits and loosely tied long ropes to their necks so they would be easy to catch, even if they were to move a ways away. Sarah Beth unrolled a blanket she brought fastened to the back of her saddle, and spread it on the thick grass. She sat and beckoned for Abe to join her.

"So, you're going away tomorrow," she said.

"Yes, I need to find Louis and he should be back any day now."

"Will you come back here? Will I see you again?"

"Of course you will. What a strange question."

"Not so strange." She turned her face away so he couldn't see her expression of sadness and foreboding. "One of these days I fully expect you to leave and not return."

"But didn't you say earlier that you'd be riding west?"

"Oh, I'll go west, but I don't know when or with whom since you've never asked me to come along."

"Sarah Beth." He found himself loosening the bun of her hair and letting it drop across her shoulders, then stroking any tangles out of it, "I don't want to leave you, but I don't know how to . . ." They were silent.

She turned back to look into his eyes. "There's one way. I keep waiting for you to think of it on your own . . ."

"For us to go? Together?"

"Yes, for us." She turned away again.

One of the horses snorted and fluttered its lips with that horsey sound.

He got up on his knees and reached again to touch her hair. She continued to sit still, facing away. When he spoke it was barely above a whisper, "I think I know what you mean." He gently turned her face to look up into his, "Would you go as my wife?"

Suddenly she was crying, her shoulders shaking and her hands covering her face,

"Oh God, Abe, oh God, yes. Yes, yes! Don't you know that it's the only thing I want. Oh Abe." She pulled him toward her as she lay back on the blanket.

He twisted himself so he could support his weight on his good elbow and began lightly kissing the tears from her cheeks. "Please, please, don't cry. Please."

She reached for the back of his head and pulled it down on her bosom and he lay there with her, feeling her breaths as they forced their way in and out of her shuddering chest. His mind was racing with a flood of feelings, most of which were concern for this person he was with, this one he was now, yes, probably going to spend his life with. He wondered if this was what the Voice meant when it told him it would all work out. How could it possibly all work out with the complications that this would bring? But for now, there was no turning back.

She pushed him up and then sat up herself. She wiped her face and blew her nose into her sleeve. It was the most unladylike thing he'd ever seen her do but he liked it, and he had to stifle a chuckle because she might think he was making fun of her. Then she laughed out loud herself.

"I knew if I wore your pants, I'd get your attention," she laughed. "Oh Abe, I'm so happy. Please don't change your mind."

"I'm happy too," he said softly. "You were crying so hard I was afraid I'd hurt you, but you're all right, aren't you?" He took one of her hands in his, "Aren't you?"

"Oh yes, I'm all right. Yes I am."

CHAPTER EIGHT

Wedding

Abe departed St. Joseph on the early morning stage. As he left, Sarah Beth was asking whether she should be making any preparations so they could be sure to have the wedding before they left for the West. His reply was something to the effect that they hardly knew anyone in St. Joe, but she insisted that many members of the congregation would welcome a reason to celebrate, and it was going to be oh so nice to give her father the chance to officiate in front of his new congregation at his only daughter's wedding. Abe nodded and then added some positive comments, trying to express more enthusiasm than he felt so she wouldn't be discouraged or saddened while he was away. It wasn't that he doubted their choice to marry, it was more that he wasn't yet sure of the immediate next steps for himself, including whether he would be able to take her with him. That was why he had to see Louis now.

When he reached Independence he secured a room at the place he and the family stayed at on their way through the first time. He slept well, then set off early the next morning to look for the camps of the freighters. His last conversation with Sarah Beth about their likely destination had been about his preference for the more northerly route, but he hadn't mentioned the arguments in its favor. He thought saying it was comparatively safer would still be frightening to her. His research had confirmed this, and he was much impressed by the recent upsurge in use and traffic on this so-called Mormon Trail. A round-trip by freighters, leaving from Salt Lake and journeying to Missouri, was taking less than five months, accomplished using primarily oxen, which were somewhat hardier than horses. The return trips accommodated emigrants on their way west, both Mormon and non-Mormon. He was fairly certain that Louis would have heard of this route, and would probably even know some freighters who traveled it.

As he drew close to the camping area most used by freight trains, it was still more empty than not. Fresh spring grass stretched out across the large field in every direction, waiting for the herds of draft animals that would be replenishing themselves for their next trip west. One small party of wagons was parked in a circle on a rise close to the river, and he made his way there. When he got near the wagons he saw a group of men throwing horse-shoes at pipes stuck in the ground. He stood quietly, a ways off, until one of the men called him over.

"What can we do for ya?" he hollered.

"Looking for someone," Abe answered.

"And who might that be?"

"A cousin of mine," Abe said loud enough to be heard. "He's a driver with Captain Belmet's outfit."

"Buff Belmet. Well you might be in luck. Word has it they're only a day away. We passed them some days back. They're big and slow, but I reckon they'll be pullin' in soon enough."

"Thank you. Can you tell me where they'll locate when they do pull in?"

"Right over there, by that grove of cottonwood. That's Belmet's usual spot. Be unloading their hides for a few days, then I'd imagine they'll move on out into the grass over yonder there for a bit. You looking for work?"

"Not exactly, just trying to find my cousin. But I might be heading out with him when he heads back west."

"Well, good luck then, sonny. You could do worse than travel with that bunch."

One of the other men laughed and joined in with, "Course you could do better too, what with the heat, and the bugs, and running the risk of losing your scalp, and then of course there's flooded rivers . . . But hell, it's a good life, ain't it boys?"

The others joined his laughter and Abe began to feel awkward, not knowing if they were making fun of him or not.

"Don't pay him no mind," the first man commented. "He's too smart to quit, and too dumb to find anything else."

"Speak for yourself , Grandpa."

Abe thanked the men, then turned and headed back for town. Just then one of the men hollered and pointed out to the west. A cloud was forming low in the sky.

"You can bet that's Belmet's dust," he shouted. "Here they come. Watch out you ladies of Independence, there be some lusty boys comin' into town."

Abe walked away slowly, listening to the men whooping and yelling about the hot time the town was going to see in the next few days. When he tried to think of any similarity in his own experience, he remembered a time when he'd been down at a port city in Carolina. His grandparents had taken him there to show him the sights and he certainly got to see some. Three large ships had docked in the previous two days and the sailors were turning the harbor area of the town into a day and night party for all comers. When Abe and his grandparents found themselves in a big crowd of swaggering, stumbling drunk sailors, his grandmother was horrified and rushed him away from the scene. Although he'd never seen much drunkenness before, he'd heard enough about it to recognize it, and was very unhappy to have to leave the spectacle behind. From the way these wagoneers were acting, a similar scene might happen in this town.

That afternoon he went down to the office of the Independence newspaper and introduced himself to a couple of staff reporters. When Abe told them about his work on the St. Joe paper, one of the men said he remembered seeing some of the articles. He said he particularly liked the personal touch Abe gave the material when he wrote about the dream of the West and the chance to be at the beginning of something very, very big.

"Well, I believe it is, sir. I truly believe it is, and I can't wait to be a part of it."

"Are you heading there any time soon?"

"Plan to be on my way sometime this spring. Waiting for my cousin to get in here from the West. Saw the dust of his caravan today, coming this way."

The reporter introduced Abe to the assistant editor. After a short conversation they agreed that as Abe travelled west, he'd send journal-style excerpts back for use by the paper.

"We can always use new material, son, and someone with a little experience. The only thing is, we'd have to have an exclusive to your reports. Can't say as I mind taking something away from those fellows up at the St. Joe paper."

Abe replied that he'd have to see what would work out best for him and that he'd get in touch if and when his plans came together. With that he went back to his room and settled in to wait for Louis and the caravan.

Next morning, as he was strolling down to the main part of town, he heard shouts and the pounding of hooves coming up the main street. Within minutes, twenty or thirty wild looking men dashing through town, swinging their hats high over their heads and whooping it up. He was sure it must be the new arrivals, and hurried along to see where they would stop.

As he turned a corner he could see the horses milling around in the street, the men dismounting and climbing the steps to the bank. One or two at a time they disappeared inside and then quickly came back out. Abe kept walking in that direction. When he was near enough to get the attention of a couple of the riders, he called out and asked if they were from the Belmet train.

"You bet," one hollered back. "Just got in and ready for everything this town has to offer. Right, Charlie?"

Charlie nodded and spat from a mouthful of chew, wiped his face with the back of one hand and asked, "What's it to you, fella?"

"My cousin left here last summer with Captain Belmet, and I was hoping he'd be returning with the same outfit."

"What's his name?" the first man asked.

"Louis, Louis Cavanaugh."

"Southern boy, ain't he? You Southern, too?"

Abe hesitated to answer, not knowing what either yes or no would bring.

"Don't worry. It don't matter anymore. War's over and we're all on the same side now, fighting the goddamn Indians."

The second man took another chunk of tobacco off his plug and said, "Yeah, we know Louis. Rowdy sonofabitch. But hardworking when he ain't sleeping it off."

"Will he be coming here?"

"No, we're cashing drafts on the bank for our hides and the stuff we hauled. He's down watching after the unloading, best he can. Somebody's gonna get his cash for him. He don't move around so good yet."

"What happened?"

"Caught an arrow in the leg, back a ways. Good thing the Captain's half doctor. Swoll up something turrible. But he's gonna be all right now. Anyhow, 'scuse me mister. I got to get some cash for the ladies. Yeee-hah!"

Both men were quickly lost in the crowd going in and out of the bank. Abe turned and set off for the warehouses at the edge of town. Drivers were pulling huge freight wagons up to the dry-land docks that served as temporary storage for the stacks of hides and some kind of tree limbs that men were pulling out of the wagon beds, while the bony oxen stood still, looking as if they couldn't take another step. Abe caught sight of a hatless head of red hair and hollered out his cousin's name. But there was no way he could be heard above the chaos taking place in front of him. He pushed his way forward among the teams and wagons, and kept trying to get Louis's attention by yelling out his name.

Finally, when he was close enough, he saw his cousin turn in his direction, see him, and throw one hand high in the air. Now Abe could see that his other arm was supported by a single crutch and there was wrapping around his upper thigh where the pants leg would have been. Louis pushed and staggered toward him and they fell into one another's arms, slapping each other's shoulders until Louis suddenly stopped and asked about Abe's wounded elbow.

"As good as it's going to get. You're the one to worry about. You going to be all right?"

"I'm supposed to go see a sawbones here in town as soon as I can. The Captain did a good job of patching me up, but he doesn't claim if it'll heal or not. Abe, how are you? I hated to leave you behind, been thinking about that all this time, but it was now or never for the job, and I took the now . . . Hell, just wait here a couple minutes and I'll be done with my loads and we can get out of here."

He limped back into the chaos, yelling and swinging his one free arm or his crutch at the oxen and anything else in his way. The other men gave him room and smiled when he passed. Abe got the feeling he was well liked by his fellows. When Louis was finished with his immediate responsibilities, they walked a short ways away from the din and bedlam of the work-site and found a bench by the side of the road.

"I've got to keep an eye out for my partner who's gone to the bank for me. Then we can go have the biggest breakfast and dinner you've ever seen, both at once. I could eat an entire kitchen full of food that isn't cooked over some damn smoky little campfire." Abe was impressed with the way his cousin seemed to have filled out, becoming even a bit brawny compared to the last time Abe had seen him. He obviously hadn't shaved for some time, but it didn't look like there was an intentional beard being developed.

"You need to tell me all about it. I can't wait to head west myself," Abe said.

"Well, it's everything I thought it would be, and more, but it's nothing easy about any of it. Sometimes I thought I'd never make it. And sometimes I just plumb wanted to give up and quit. But here I am." He looked around. "Here I am," he said again as if it were hard to believe. "Now, you'll have to tell me everything too, about Sarah Beth and her father, and about you . . . Been awhile, hasn't it?" He looked up into the sky, and murmured again, "It has been awhile."

They were soon at the Silver Dollar Restaurant and Inn, and Louis ordered a huge breakfast that included almost everything on the one-page menu. The cook and the waitress were obviously used to the routine of these freighters coming into town off the long trail and were pleased to serve them whatever they wanted. Louis wanted it all. He told Abe that it'd been more than two months since he'd seen an egg, and even longer since he ate decent bread. Together they dug into the stacks and piles of food, foregoing conversation and relishing the variety of all that was set before them.

When they could finally slow down enough to talk, it was hard to know where to start to catch up, so they jumped right into the future. "How long are you here for?" Abe asked.

"Supposed to be a few weeks and then turn back around. I'm thinking of using my stake to buy into a wagon, we could go partners."

"Not sure about that, we'll have to see, some things have changed."

"I'll bet. You and Sarah Beth hitched up yet?"

"Nah, what makes you think that?"

Louis smiled and shook his head as if he knew something, "Just figures."

"Well we have got closer. And, matter of fact, you're right, might even be a wedding soon enough."

"It's got to be before we head out. She gonna wait here for you to make it back? I'll be your best man 'less you already have one."

"Whoa, slow down. She's talking about a wedding, I said I'd have her as my wife, but I don't think we'd want to get married and then have to split up right away. I mean for me to head out on a trip like that."

"Well, there's been a few take their women along, but it's powerful hard on'em, and hard on us all, having women around when they ain't ours."

"Louis, I been thinking about the northern route, maybe the Mormon Trail; they have whole families go on that one."

"Yeah, but it doesn't pay as much. Not so dangerous. Besides I'm real attached to Captain Belmet. Why, he might even make me a lead driver, work directly for him. You'd like him a lot. They all call him "Buff" because he shot his first buffalo when he was only fourteen years old. He took me up to Taos to meet Kit Carson. Oh, now there's a man that's something."

"I'm sure he is. I've read about how successful he's been. But I have a yearning to maybe make it to Oregon. There's a place called Jordan Valley. Has a ring to it, don't you think?"

"Settling down thinking, isn't it? Ranching, storekeeping, what would you do?"

"Probably different things. Out there they need any kind of help they can get. They're even asking for men with military experience, and I don't have a lot, but those patrols taught me something. I might be useful."

"Well I'll tell you what Cousin Lester, there's nothing like the country down there in what they call New Mexico to give a man opportunity. And there's enough settlers by now to stand up to the Indians, and that's the important thing. Takes more than patrols, no offense to you and what you done back there."

"First things first, you can call me Abe now, got all that taken care of."

"Well damn, I was just congratulating myself for remembering to call you Lester."

"Well, it's OK now. They let old Jeff Davis off his conspiracy charges to kill Lincoln. Anyway, I just feel like it'd be best for us to go that way, but let's not talk about it anymore right now. We'll have time. Tell me about your adventures. What happened to your leg?"

So Louis talked and Abe listened, and after awhile they moved over to one of the quieter of the several saloons that were filling up with the freighters. Everyone seemed to know Louis and want to shake his hand or slap him on the back. He introduced Abe when he had the chance, as they worked their way to a quiet table in the back where Louis could continue his story.

"So we come across a couple of wagons," he said when they were seated, "all burned out, but no bodies anywhere. Looked like Indian work, but why would they take the bodies, and where was the rest of the bunch? Nobody travels in that small a group." He hollered to a young woman with an empty tray, "Two whiskies," and then went on. "We found the tracks of some more wagons, and Cap Buff sent me and several others off on their trail. We caught up to them pretty quick. They were scared of their shadows when they saw us, and wouldn't none of them say a word until I could convince them that we were friendly, and not outlaws. We helped them make camp, and then they started in telling us their story, all talking at once."

Their drinks came, and Abe raised his, "Here's to you, Louis. You made it, and I can see you it was good for you."

"Yep, thanks. Then so we settled them down and got'em to talk one at a time and what happened was they'd forked off of a larger train and headed for some relative's place in Texas. Said they'd been told the Indians were gone from that route and wouldn't bother with such a small outfit anyway. Myself, I don't believe Indians will pass up anything that easy, but they were headed down that trail when they saw a band of riders who shadowed them for most all of one afternoon. Then come nightfall they were attacked; well, not attacked, but just some gunshots were fired and they tried to take shelter behind their wagons and the riders came right up to them. And they weren't Indians at all. No, they were whites, maybe just like those marauders you told me about back in Virginia. Veterans of the War most likely. Anyway, they bunched up the folks from the outfit and scrounged through all the wagons, taking anything of value they could find and carry off. Then they told everyone to get back on all but two of the wagons and haul off as fast as they could. They took the horses from those two wagons, the only ones weren't oxen-pulled, and set fire to them. Rode off to the west, whooping and hollering.

"What they left behind, and we found, was several families who were now too scared to go on their way south, but wouldn't think of coming back east with us where they come from, so we took them back up to the trail we use and told them that was as good as we could do. They'd just have to wait and hope that someone would come by heading west. Turned out a couple days later we passed a small train of only emigrants, no freight. We come across it a couple of days later and they promised to find the lost ones, as we called them on their way."

Louis downed his drink and hollered for another pair. Abe protested, but the girl brought the whiskeys anyway. He asked, "Does any of this have anything to do with your leg?"

"No, hell no, but it had to do with a pretty little woman who I made a promise to see again. Soon after that we surprised a group of Kiowa, they were on this edge of the plains. Didn't look like they wanted to fight, but some of our boys were still angry about us being attacked back at the front end of our trip so they started chasing the Indians. Buff told me to go after them boys and bring'em back. Well, I caught up with them, got in front and tried to turn them back toward the wagons. They wouldn't give up and just then one of those Indians rode back our way and got close enough to fire the arrow that hit my leg. I thought he was coming back to talk. Well, that did for our boys. They lit after that bunch and killed'em all before it was over. Then they got me back to camp and Buff started working on me. Hurt some, him pulling that damn arrow out of me, I can tell you. But I'd sure hate to have it still in there," he laughed as he slowly stretched his leg out straight. "Still works, too."

"Glad of that," Abe said. "So how soon can you get away to come up to St. Joe with me?

I know Sarah Beth and her father would like to see you, and maybe we can figure things out."

Louis was about to answer when he heard his name called out across the huge and somewhat crowded room. He pushed himself up from the table so he could see who it was. "Lou! Lou!" the voice repeated.

Lou stuck his crutch up in the air and waved it back and forth to show his whereabouts, and within moments a giant of a man pushed his way through the crowd and jerked Louis up off his feet in a smothering hug.

"You sonofabitch," the big man said. "Started drinking without me, you one-legged bastard. Who's that?" He set Louis back down and pointed at Abe.

"That's my cousin Abe. I told you about him several times. Abe, this is Mad Mountain Jace. Whatever you do, don't get him angry."

Louis fell back into his chair and roared with laughter. The man stuck out a hand that seemed to swallow Abe's when they shook, while at the same time he was softly pounding Louis on the top of his head with the other fist. Then the man turned and yelled at the bartender to bring a bottle of the good stuff. Now!

Abe was hardly ready for more drinks, even one more, and he found his refusal simply ignored while the man, Jace, filled a glass for him.

"Abe, this here is the excuse I have for a partner. Neither one of us could get anyone else to team up so we're stuck with each other."

"Damn right," the man mumbled while swallowing half a glassful of the whiskey.

"I told you we might go in on a wagon and team. That way we could contract to the brokers who ship with Belmet. We'd still go with the train, but we'd be on our own for the costs and profit."

"Isn't that kind of risky?" Abe asked.

"Hell, it's risky," Jace chimed in, "especially when you've got a sniveling snake like this one for a partner. Haha. Right, Snake-eyes?" He gently punched Louis's shoulder.

Louis pushed the fist away and leaned forward, pretending to talk only to Abe. "Way I got it figured is when we're attacked by Indians, I'll just get this one to lie down and I'll hide out behind him. Better'n a dead horse."

"I better be sound asleep if you try it, and watch out I don't roll on you either."

Louis stopped laughing and looked somewhat serious as he said, "Cousin Abe here has a hankering for the northern trail. Wants to head for Oregon country. Tell him it's all taken. Those emigrants from before the War got it all claimed out, don't they?"

"Depends," Jace said, looking thoughtful. "Once you get in that empty land between Colorado and Oregon, ain't much out there but Mormons and Indians. Now me, I wouldn't want either one of 'em for neighbors."

Just then a chair flew across the room and landed within a few feet of them. Jace slid his chair back, grabbed the other with one hand and sent it back where it came from. By then it was clear that there was a fight going on at the far end of the bar, and tables and chairs seemed to be the weapons of choice.

Louis laughed and said loud enough to be heard over the ruckus, "Lay down, Jace, give us something to hide behind."

The man poured himself another half-glass, downed it in one large gulp and then stood and waded through the men between him and the fighters. He grabbed both of them by the back of their shirts and banged their heads together. "Now boys," he said, "don't go spoiling our welcome. We only just got in and you're acting more stupid then you have for the last twelve hundred miles." He lifted the two men off the floor, then dropped them and came back to the table.

"Fools," he mumbled as he sat down and poured another drink. He turned to Abe as if the commotion needed an explanation. "They been best friends ever since Santa Fe, must of just got tired of each other. Now tell me why you want to go north."

Abe thought for a moment, covered his glass with his hand when the man tried to refill it, and said, "Well, I've been studying on it and it seems a bit safer, and I'm about to marry a girl who says she's coming with me."

"Might be safe, might not be. Railroad made some enemies out that way, and then they found all that gold in the Indian Hills. But then, nowhere's safe is it? Hell, I'd think of going with you myself, if I wasn't signed, sealed and delivered to old Buff." He raised his glass and shouted for quiet. "Here's to Old Buff. Got us through one more time."

There was a cheer from the crowd, most of whom were freighters. And then the noise of their shouting and conversation broke out again.

Louis leaned forward and spoke above the background din. "Think I could get away for a couple days, head up to St. Joe with my cousin here?"

"How do I know you'd come back? We got unfinished business, don't forget it."

"I'll come back. You know I got to get back to Santa Fe. I promised that girl Lila I'd be there, and besides I've got to protect her from you."

"Oh, right partner. Our deal is share and share alike, remember."

"Only the wagon, the oxen, the costs and the profit. You remember."

"Yeah, I remember, just trying to see if you did." He seemed to be thinking for a long moment, and then said to Louis, "Tell you what. I'll take care of things here if you come back in a week . . . and bring me a St. Joe bride."

Abe met Louis at the stage stop near the edge of town. It was early and his cousin looked worse for wear from the night spent celebrating. Louis went to sleep for the first few hours of the ride to St, Joe, although Abe couldn't see how that was possible with the rocking and jouncing of the stage. Louis woke up when they stopped for a mid-day meal break and said he was finally hungry again after all that big meal the day before. They ate, and as they were waiting for the stage to roll again, they sat beneath one of the chestnut trees in front of the road-stop house. Louis pulled out a tobacco plug and offered it to Abe.

"No thanks," he said, "might have to kiss somebody when we get to St. Joe."

Louis laughed at that, and said, "Yeah, I'd be jealous of you, Cuz, but I got my own little something to look forward to."

They'd not had a chance to talk about this or much of anything else since their conversations of the day before were interrupted by the fight. "Tell me about this girl."

"Not much to say, except she's young and more pretty than the pure-blue sky and softer than the quilt on Mom's old feather bed."

"How'd you leave it with her?"

"Said I'd be meeting her in Santa Fe at the end of my next trip. Asked her to wait for me. Said she would. We'll see. Her folks didn't much seem to like me, but that just made her sweeter to me. And she can sing, sing like a lark, I'd say."

"Sound like you've got it bad."

"Hey, who's talking? Sarah Beth's boy?" He pushed on Abe's shoulder, and then used it to help himself to stand up. "My girl doesn't know about this," he pointed to his leg as he took the crutch from where it was leaning against the tree. "I imagine she'd be here now if she knew I was hurt like this." He hopped around the tree, spit and took a good leak. "When's your wedding, Cuz?

"Don't rightly know," Abe replied. "She was talking about it when I left. Why, you sure you want to be my best man?"

"Nah," Louis said when he reappeared from behind the tree, "I want to be the one gives you away." He laughed and started toward the ringing bell that was calling them back to the coach.

When they arrived at the home in St. Joe, there was a warm welcome and accompanying concern for Louis and his injury. Sarah Beth immediately wanted to know everything that had happened to him. Her father was more reserved, but certainly curious. Mattie fixed a delightful supper and when Louis didn't have his mouth full he was telling stories of his trek across the country and back. There were skirmishes with Indians, broken wagons to repair, dangerous river crossings and many other incidents to report. Abe noticed that there was nothing in his cousin's recap about the tragedy with the small wagon train and the girl he'd met, so he didn't bring it up.

Suddenly, Louis turned to Sarah Beth and bluntly asked, "So, when's the wedding? I've only got a week."

Sarah Beth gasped and covered her mouth with a napkin while Abe looked down at his hands in his lap. They'd had no time to discuss any of this since his return and neither knew what to say. Doctor Randall cleared his throat as if he were about to speak, but nothing came out.

After a few awkward moments, Mattie offered to dish out some more food to Louis's plate and asked, "Is it certain you must be leaving us again so soon?"

"Thank you," he said as he poured some gravy on the yams she'd served him. "Absolutely must return to business with my partner." He laughed, "Abe's seen him, not the sort of fellow you want to go up against, right, Cuz?"

"That's for sure," Abe mumbled.

"Well," Mattie said calmly, "then I think we should let these two young people have some time to discuss the matter. Doctor Randall, is there any time in the coming week when you will not be available for the ceremony?"

"No, only Sunday. I've never seen a wedding done as part of the Sabbath services." He smiled at the discomfort and silence of his daughter and Abe, "So I think you're absolutely right. We should let these two be alone while they have a talk together. Louis, would you care to accompany me and a bit of brandy to the outside porch? I don't believe it's cooled off too much for a few minutes spent with the oncoming twilight."

"Why sure." The young man stood and slapped his cousin on the back as he walked behind him. "No sense putting anything off if it's gonna happen, Cuz." And then he followed the Reverend.

Mattie bustled about clearing the used dinnerware and disappeared behind the kitchen door. After a few long moments of silence, Abe stood and walked around the table. He stopped behind Sarah Beth and gently eased her up from her chair to face him. As they looked into one another's eyes, they both smiled and brought their mouths together in a kiss.

"Ohhh," was Sarah Beth's first word. "I've missed you so much. Do you know that?" She reached up and traced the side of his face with her fingertips.

"It's been the same for me," he paused, and then went on, "there were nights when I couldn't sleep for thinking of you . . ." He could feel her pressing against him and perhaps for the first time he realized how shapely she'd become in the few years he'd known her. Then like lightning, he wondered if it was all right to think like that or should he feel a bit guilty? But then, for the first time, there came a new kind of feeling, that of a man thinking of a woman as his very own.

"Yes, yes, me too." She took his hand and led him out of the dining room and into the parlor where they sat together on a simple couch. "Oh, Abe, I've been so afraid."

"Why, nothing was going to happen to me."

"Do you still want me for your wife?" She was looking straight into his eyes.

"Yes, Sarah Beth, could I have changed so much?"

"Oh, I've been terrified that when you met up with Louis you'd become so fascinated with his adventures and not even come back to tell me it was over with us. Oh, Abe." She wiped a couple of tears away.

He placed his arm around her shoulders and drew her close, "No dearest, it's not like that at all. As a matter of fact, I've told Louis that if he returns to Santa Fe, and he assures me he will, then I won't be going with him because I'm now convinced that our direction is more northerly."

She nestled against him. "Oh, thank the Lord you're not running off."

They sat down quietly together, their intertwined hands gently twisting and touching, softly reacquainting.

"So, how does a place called Jordan Valley sound to you?" he asked softly.

"Jordan Valley? I don't know, sounds Biblical, like it's somewhere in the Promised Land . . . Where is it?"

"In Oregon, in the dry country, but where there are rivers, like one they call the Snake."

"Whatever you say, as long as we're together. Is it far?"

"Very far, but not so far as the other side of Oregon."

"Abe, I don't mean to change the subject, but we're supposed to be talking about . . . about a wedding."

"I know. When do you want it?"

"Right now."

He squeezed her tighter with his arm. "Shall I call your father?"

She giggled and said, "You know what I mean, as soon as possible."

"Well, Louis is leaving in a week and he wants to be best man. Can we do that?"

"Yes, yes. I'll tell father. Ohhh, Abe." She kissed him fully, and they kept at it for what seemed like a long time.

"Dearest, I have to tell you—I'm starting to believe all this is true," he said.

She laughed and threw her legs over his, pulling herself up into his lap. "It is. It just has to be. Now, when people ask what we want for gifts, what do we say?"

"What people?"

"Why the congregation here. They're all so excited and happy for us."

"You've told them?"

"Father announced our engagement during the service last Sunday while you were away." She kissed him again and then quickly pulled back. "Of course he asked my permission first. I knew you'd approve. So, what shall we ask for? Mattie said she'll take care of letting people know."

"It must be nice for her to be accepted here."

"Of course it is. But back to work, Mr. Saunders. The gifts?"

"All right, nothing breakable because everything has to ride in a wagon. And nothing that won't be useful either along the trail or once we settle out there."

"You're so reasonable," she said, leaning back to place her head on the arm of the couch. "And what would you expect me to wear at this wedding?"

"Pants," he said as he tickled her ribs. "Pants and boots, and carry a rifle so it looks like I had no choice in the matter."

"Oh Abe, you're so funny right now. For so long I worried that you were unhappy and you almost never made jokes, and . . ."

He tickled her some more and said, "Well, that's over now. I refuse to be serious about anything from now on. Except this." He pulled her to him and held her as close as he could, saying, "I love you." And kissing again.

"Me too," she mumbled through their lips.

Then she twisted out of his arms and jumped up, pulling at him. "Let's go tell them what we've decided."

The wedding was the next Saturday, and the streets near the church filled with buggies and horses. Close to eighty people showed up, by Louis's count. As Abe and his cousin stood at the front of the sanctuary with Doctor Randall, the congregation quieted and waited for the beginning of the ceremony. The small pump organ and its organist launched into the traditional bridal march and everyone stood and turned to watch Sarah Beth, followed by two of her new friends from the hospital, come walking slowly down the aisle.

As they neared the low platform at the front, Abe knew he had never seen such a woman in his whole life, and even though he was seeing her through the half-veil that gave a misty quality to the upper half of her face, he could see that her eyes were smiling at him and he couldn't help grinning back. He reached out, took her hand, and helped her up the two steps to stand beside him just in front of her father.

The organ went quiet and a low buzzing of whispers spread through the church from the back to the front. Abe looked and was not nearly as surprised as everyone else to see Lefty and his young wife Patsy standing to the side of the main door. He'd gone down to the camp two days before and made sure that they knew of his wedding, and that he wanted them to be there. Now as he watched the turning heads of the congregation, he realized that probably no one had ever seen Indians in this church, certainly not one in a dark black suit and the other in a buckskin dress. He nearly laughed out loud when Louis jabbed him in the ribs and nodded in the direction of the couple. Sarah Beth seemed oblivious to the commotion, which hushed as Doctor Randall raised both his hand and his voice in the opening prayer.

The ceremony was brief, as the bride's father had promised the newlyweds. The only unusual thing was before the final blessing, when Doctor Randall announced that he was especially proud that the young couple would soon be striking out for the West in answer to the urging of the small quiet Voice that God uses when he wants us to listen especially carefully to what He has to say. The doctor went on to say that making the journey, and their pledge to settle in a new land was nothing less than a reenactment following in the footsteps of the original Abraham and Sarah, as well as being similar in purpose to the God-guided sojourn of forty years in the wilderness experienced by the Israelites on their way to the Promised Land. He then asked a blessing on the two young people, asking for fruitfulness in the family way, and for safety and protection as they fulfilled God's promise to take care of those who follow in his pathways.

He then said, "I now pronounce you Man and Wife, in the eyes of God and all of us . . . You may now kiss the bride."

And they kissed with all the shyness that the situation brought out in them, combined with all of the thrill of their first kiss as one being. Then the organ burst to life and they nearly danced down the aisle, swinging their held hands and smiling to everyone on every side. They stopped briefly at the doorway, where Abe accepted Lefty's handshake as Sarah Beth received a shy embrace from Patsy. Then they were out the door and into the sunshine of a new life.

From the moment they saw Louis off on the stage back to Independence, their lives were filled with the flurries of preparation and activity. Making their decision and having Abe's cousin support it seemed to be all they needed to embark on this choice. Louis even suggested that he might be able to meet them north of Denver and continue on with them, if things worked out on the trail and when he reached his destination. This was a relief to both of them. To Abe it felt good because it meant that he wasn't being held responsible for breaking a deal with his cousin, and for Sarah Beth because it meant that she no longer needed to worry that her new husband would change his mind and leave for a separate journey out west and back with the freighters.

Over the next few days, one of the members of the congregation donated a wagon to them as a gift because, as he said, it had outlived its usefulness to his business. Although it was not of the Conestoga model and style, it would be easy to adapt it for a full canvas covering and its axles and undercarriage seemed to be in excellent condition. Another congregant who was a carpenter and wagon-smith offered to help them fix up and reinforce the wagon to withstand the rigors and distances of the trail. He said he wanted Abe to join him in much of the work and learn the wagon's parts and workings, an invaluable store of knowledge for such a trip.

Sarah Beth was sorting and packing their wedding gifts in categories of those useful along on the journey and those that wouldn't be needed until they reached their destination. She also consulted with other emigrants from the caravan they were joining. They'd met as they were all making preparations for the needs they were trying to anticipate. As far as these new acquaintances, and even their welcome acceptance into the next departing train, Lefty was even more invaluable. He provided advice and recommended sources of needed supplies. His connection with the wagon-master of this upcoming train was a good one, and the two of them had made the journey together once before. The plan was to leave St. Joe as a small party and then meet up with a group of Mormons coming out from Iowa. They would join up at Fort Kearney and head west to the Salt Lake country as a single large group. Lefty assured Abe that there would be no real problems getting from that destination in Utah to the southeast parts of Oregon, depending only on how much time was left before the first snows set in.

Although two oxen could have pulled the wagon, even with its heavy initial load, it was decided that a team of four was preferable, both for the ease of the animals and as insurance against the variety of problems that could occur along the way. Lefty suggested a livestock seller he trusted in St. Joe, and also provided the name of a rancher located near the trail in southern Wyoming who was known for having decent livestock that he sold to emigrants. Lefty suggested that if Abe was to need a replacement animal or two, he should ride on ahead of the rest of the train to make arrangements before the man sold out when the rest of the train arrived.

Abe found a decent four-ox team that had been well cared for over the winter, since its arrival from New Mexico the previous fall. As they didn't come with their own names, Sarah Beth was given the job of naming them. She simply called them Matthew, Mark, Luke and John, as she considered that to be a fine quartet of good examples.

As the time of their departure came closer, there was a quiet change in the mood among the members of their household. Sarah Beth's excitement and anticipation was tempered by the realization that she might not see either her father or Mattie for a long time, or even ever again, which she didn't want to think about. Mattie kept herself busy sewing things for whatever home the young couple would end up in, gathering kitchenware and blankets, and generally fussing over every detail of the packing. Doctor Randall was quite obviously trying to maintain an expansive sort of demeanor based on a combination of enthusiasm for their great future and an unspoken regret that he was no longer physically capable of such a journey. Abe continued to be as methodical as he could be, given that this was certainly the most important event of his life thus far. He continued to keep his emotions in check beneath the necessities of care for their two horses and the oxen, along with everything else that required his attention. Final steps included the addition of storage compartments to the wagon, and compiling a list of contacts, gathered from the files of the newspaper, for use along the way. He'd turned down the offer from the Independence paper out of loyalty to his own journal in St. Joe, and also because they'd promised that when his submissions were published they would be credited to him in his own name. He'd sent a letter to his cousin Flora, but no answer had been forthcoming.

Their honeymoon was delayed a week by the need for preparations and by Doctor Randall's sudden illness, which came on few days after the wedding. He was stricken with a respiratory ailment, and at first doctors were unable to diagnose its nature or its cure. They finally ascribed it to an allergy of undefined origin and kept him in a sealed-up room at the local hospital. The symptoms disappeared almost as fast as they'd come on and he was released to his home within a few days, but advised to stay indoors for awhile as whatever was currently blooming or pollinating passed on. The incident shook Sarah Beth deeply and almost curtailed their plans and arrangements for departure, but her father would have none of that and quickly regained his energy and positive attitude about the future and their opportunity to be a part of it. Mattie seemed to take all of this without a great deal of concern, although she confided to Sarah Beth that she'd long been concerned about the man's difficulty sleeping and the complaints he'd shared with her about his need to sleep nearly sitting up during many nights.

As the episode seemed to be resolved, Abe and Sarah Beth finally decided that the best way to celebrate their marriage was to take an overnight horseback trip away from the family home, and leave behind the preparations for the rigors of the upcoming overland journey. They packed a bedroll on the back of her saddle and a duffle of foodstuffs and cooking gear on the back of his, and set off in the direction of the trail they would be following in just a very short time. They made camp by a small stream in a grove of trees and hanging mosses, prepared a supper of dried meat boiled with potatoes and other vegetables, ate heartily, and laid out their bedding. It was a perfectly clear and moonless night and the stars were easily bright enough to shine through the light cast above them by their small campfire.

As they lay back staring upward, neither of them seemed to have any words to say. After a long silence, Sarah Beth began quietly humming and then singing a song about young lovers whose dreams were intertwined with each other's and whose love seemed impossible to attain. As the song went on, its difficulties gave way to a simple yet beautiful resolution and ended with the words,

"They never ever looked back to the past, they never ever parted or lost their way again."

The sound of the moving water rippling over its stones and a slight breeze in the treetops above seemed to provide a chorus of whispering echoes to her words and voice, and Abe softly asked where she'd learned the song.

"I made it up myself," she said, "once I was sure of us."

They'd been lying close, holding hands and now their hands tightened and Abe turned his face toward hers. The flickering light of the fire outlined her face and he knew that he'd never known anyone so beautiful. "Thank you, dear Sarah Beth," he said quietly. "Thank you so much for having me."

She turned toward him, pressing the length of her body to his and they kissed and moved in a gentle rocking against one another. It was almost as if they'd never been separate, never been alone. They felt the stirring of new needs, unknown feelings, and even impatience accompanied by the shared yet unconscious awareness that they were now on their own frontier with no experience to guide them, with only the mysterious rumors of youth to help them through this night. Then, almost at a signal from somewhere, their hands began exploring one another's bodies, slipping inside the loose-fitting garments they wore, encountering bare flesh. Almost without knowing what was next or how it was occurring, they joined together in a quickening rhythm that tangled the blanket as they tried to keep it wrapped around them. All of this led them to the touches of remarkable discoveries and the new experience and knowledge of the essential differences between man and woman. All of this joined in the ecstasy of finding the nearly unbelievable way this puzzle's pieces fit together, for now, for always . . .

As their motions and emotions peaked and then subsided and the sounds of the world around them returned to their consciousness, they found in the taste of one another's mouths what might have become a permanent connection had not one of the horses neighed sharply and sent shivers of apprehension up their spines. This reaction wasn't fear so much as the thought of being discovered in this position and the disarray that caused them to hastily pull themselves apart and gather their bedding together.

"Should I try to see what it is?" Abe whispered hoarsely.

"No, no, stay with me. It's probably nothing," said Sarah Beth in his ear. "Never leave me again." There was no other sound from the surrounding woods and once again they wrapped themselves in one another's arms and drifted in and out of a drowsiness of a kind that neither of them had ever felt before.

"Did I hurt you?" he said.

"Oh no, only for a moment. It was perfect."

Daylight found them shyly avoiding one another's glances while they made a quick meal and repacked their things. As they stood together, ready to return to their lives in town, they suddenly embraced and held on to one another for a long time. Again it was one of the horses that interrupted them, stamping its foot, impatient to be moving. They laughed and said "I love you" at the exact same moment.

They had a quiet and happy ride home. Later, Sarah Beth got out her diary and wrote only this:

My Dear Book,

I never imagined I would ever feel anything so good and so grand.

Then she closed the book and held it close to her heart, clasped in the hands that had just so recently been able to explore nearly everything about this beautiful man and make him truly her husband.

Part III

The Trail

May 1868-November 1868

CHAPTER NINE

Westward

When a wagon train left St. Joe for the West it was tradition to hold a celebration at the edge of town where last minute preparations accompanied all the chaos of the animals and their owners trying to follow the shouted orders of the wagon master and his assistants. With the clamor of livestock and the clatter of wagons and equipment it was nearly impossible to hear one another, but Abe and Sarah Beth were doing their best to follow the shouted commands and fall into some semblance of a line-up with the others. Most of the animals, as well as the people, were strangers to one another, so this attempt at order required much more than good intentions. The frequent tangles and unintended interference that occurred was constantly being sorted out, and the attempt to get all the wagons into a line was repeated over and over again.

Sarah Beth's father and Mattie stood as close as they could to their young adventurers, and there were tears aplenty. Abe had covered these events before on assignment from the newspaper, but Sarah Beth had yet to witness such a melee and neither of them had ever been actually involved in such a thing before. In some ways it reminded Abe of the few battles he'd been in. The difference was no guns were fired and everyone was supposedly on the same side of things and trying to work together. It was late morning by the time the wagon master, a big man by the name of John McFarland, was satisfied that they'd actually be able to move with some appearance of a wagon train. He gave a signal to the bandmaster of a small group of musicians whose brass instruments cast gleaming reflections of the sun into the trees behind them. The band struck up a rousing march, further disturbing the draft animals and adding one more element to the boisterous din of the send-off.

Sarah Beth had been perched on the seat of their wagon, but suddenly she leaped down and ran for one more hug with her father and Mattie. Now she was crying hard and Abe nearly had to drag her away from them and back to the wagon. He boosted her up onto the short bench, kissed her quickly, and then took his place at the head of the team of oxen. Their two horses were tethered to the back of the wagon and followed amicably in spite of the strangeness and noise of the whole scene.

The small train had at least twenty-five wagons, and rumors said they would link up with seventy more at the Fort Kearney rendezvous. Forward motion was a relief after the morning-long milling and confusion. The deeply cut ruts of the dirt road sent up clouds of dust as the wagons and their people settled into the motion and form of progress that would be their primary type of movement for the next few months.

A horseman reined to a stop beside Abe and jumped down. It was Lefty, and his eyes were shining brightly among the copper tones of his face. He smiled broadly and slapped Abe on the back with enough force to nearly knock him over.

"You done it," he said. "Damn if you ain't done it."

"Yeah," was all Abe could muster as a reply. "Yeah."

"Well, I'm pleased with you, and with Miss Sarah Beth too." He turned and gave a wave to the young woman on the wagon seat. "My woman sent this for her. Mind if I give it to her?" He unrolled and held up a simple buckskin dress with a circle of elk's teeth tightly spaced across the neckline.

"Of course, you can," Abe said, turning to watch as Lefty dropped back and handed the dress up to Sarah Beth, yelling something as he did.

He rejoined Abe and reached up into the saddle bag on his horse, pulling a small bundle wrapped in soft hide. As they walked along, he unwrapped it, revealing a bone hatchet with two large bird claws and some teeth hanging from around the neck where the wooden handle joined the sharpened bone of its blade.

"It ain't real," Lefty said, "so don't try chopping wood with it. But it's a good thing to have with you if you run into any hostiles, like some of my relatives," he laughed. "Take it out of its wrapping like this," he held it straight out in front and then touched it to the ground.

"Then tell them you are a friend of Left Hand Crow and that you are Big Bear Man. These bear teeth with speak for you and then they will listen to what you have to say." He looked into Abe's questioning eyes. "So, here take it, my young friend. I hope you do not need it for that purpose, but as the white man says, just-in-case." He wrapped the implement back inside its covering and handed it to Abe.

Abe took it, taking care with it as they kept walking beside the oxen. The chances of something unexpected were very much on his mind. "Thank you so very much, many thanks. I am sorry I have nothing to give you in return."

Lefty reached out and placed a hand on Abe's shoulder. "There will be time for that later. I also came to tell you that I will be going to Texas and then working to drive some cattle to Colorado, near Denver. When that job is done, we'll see. In any case, I'll find you and we will be together again." With that, he grasped Abe's forearm in a tight grip and said a few words in his Indian tongue. Then he mounted up and was gone.

Sarah Beth called to Abe and when he looked back to her, she was standing up in the wagon, and holding the dress up to herself. He couldn't quite hear what she was saying, but could tell that it was probably something to do with how perfectly it fit as she held it against herself. He raised his good hand and used it to trace a curving shape in the air. He laughed as she quickly took the dress away from her body. Just then, the oxen needed his attention as one of them had gotten a foot high enough to tangle in the rigging. He freed the foot and raised the strap higher so it wouldn't happen again. All part of the beginning, he thought.

It took the wagon train over a week to get to Nebraska, and then another week travelling along the north banks of the Platte River to reach the fort. The fort had been moved in 1850 to its present location at Grand Island. In the years since, a small and thriving town had grown up based on the supply needs of both the army and the emigrants. For most of the travelers, the trip from either St. Joe or Iowa was a test of their preparations and a chance to find out what they'd forgotten or hadn't known they'd need. The town at Fort Kearney was the last outpost for correcting this situation before the long and empty miles that lay ahead of them on the way to the next settlement, Fort Laramie.

The wagon train they were supposed to join up with had not yet arrived, so the wagon master took his party upriver a short ways to a long open plain beside the river. Here the livestock could graze and be contained by the younger men who were assigned to ride herd on the feeding animals whenever they made camp. Abe had volunteered for this duty, but McFarland asked him to instead work as the wagon master's informal assistant. There'd been a bit of an awkward moment when McFarland asked Abe what he'd done during the War. Abe tried to read into the man's question anything he could that would tell him how much and what he should say in response. Finally, after a long pause, he quietly began to tell enough of the truth to satisfy the man's curiosity.

McFarland's response was, "Tell you what, young fella. You and your wife have a bit of southern style of talking, but no more so than many others from the border states, or even Washington city itself. But I would advise the two of you to work together in private, listening to each other and speaking in practice for when and if it might be necessary to pass yourselves off as Yankees or at least sympathizers. Not saying it's going to happen, and far as I know it's not going to happen with this bunch or with the Mormons that's going to join up with us. But you never know. Just a word to the wise, so to speak. Now, all of that aside, Lefty spoke highly of you and your experience, and while I don't expect much trouble from the Indians on this trip, you never can tell. Once we clear the river valley and get organized and moving with that new bunch, and we're working together best we can, we'll make camp for a couple of days of rest before striking out to Laramie. That'd be the chance for a little training for these men. I'll let you know, and I'd appreciate your help. So, go on now, but I'll be talking to you soon."

The man stood up and dismissed Abe with a wave of the hand. He was over six-and-a half-feet tall, an imposing and powerful figure, but so far, except for trying to make himself heard above the noise of the wagons and stock, Abe hadn't heard the Captain raise his voice at anyone. When he returned to their wagon and settled into the supper Sarah Beth had prepared, he told her some of what had transpired between himself and the Captain, and he told her how impressed he was with their leader. Now, he said, he was the one wondering about another man's part in the War. Sarah Beth nodded as he told her this, and her only comment was that she hoped he wasn't going to talk to Abe about anything involving danger.

As they waited for the new party to arrive, they heard stories of this large group of Mormons, some said numbering five hundred, which had arrived by rail over the course of a week a few years back. They were trying to move onto the trail to Salt Lake, but there were nowhere near enough supplies, wagons, or livestock along the entire length of the trail in Nebraska to outfit them all, and many of them had to give up and turn back. Now there were rumors of another group, once again coming by rail. McFarland called a meeting of the train's leaders, but nearly every adult showed up for it.

"We have an agreement with the Mormons sponsoring the rest of our caravan that they are limited to seventy wagons and the families they carry. We will hold them to that limit. There's not enough feed for more than that number of livestock along our route this early in the year, and we can't organize or protect any more than what we've agreed to. I know! I've tried on a larger train when I was the number two on one of these in '66. Didn't work, so stand by me and don't make any promises or arrangements with anyone that don't come through me, not even if it's your own mother. 'Nuff said."

There was a hullabaloo of questions and shouts from the assembled group, but the wagon master just waved it all off and headed back to his own camp. For some time folks gathered in small groups and wondered back and forth at just what all this meant and what would happen to those additional people if they did show up.

Abe and Sarah Beth moved slowly back to their own camp and wagon, accompanied by another young couple they'd become acquainted with on the trail over the past two weeks. Guy and Norma Denton were from Maryland country, although Guy was the son of parents from England and still spoke with a recognizable English turn of phrase and a foreign sounding pronunciation. Norma and Sarah Beth were quickly and easily learning to share both cookware and their duties, and were very glad to have one another along. Guy and Abe had already hunted together along the way with no luck, but with time to get to know one another a bit.

"So what do you think of all that?" Guy asked as they reached the privacy of their own small area.

Abe explained his role as a reporter for the St. Joe newspaper and how he'd been privileged to gain a good store of knowledge from army dispatches and other sources. "And what the Captain said is true, far as I've heard it. There were some pretty bad fights over it that time and there were a lot of folks plumb out of luck. They either returned home to Illinois or wherever, or backtracked down the way we just came, to St. Joe and even Independence, and waited for another chance. I just hope the rumor's wrong this time, and folks learned from the last time."

Guy took out a plug of chewing tobacco, offered it to Abe who refused, took a bite and chewed hard to get it started. Soon as he could talk, he said, "On another subject, I don't think we should leave our stuff unwatched from now on. Take turns looking out for each other. What do you say?"

"Seems like a practical idea." Abe thought for a moment. "Do you and Norma need to be away for any time, soon?"

"Well, not that I know of, but if we do I'll let you know."

"Sarah Beth and I talked about taking our horses for a good long ride to keep them happy and in some kind of shape for the trip while we're laid over here."

"Good idea, long as you don't wear them out racing across these plains."

Abe laughed, "You're right, have to be careful with Sarah Beth. She and her horse are both pretty competitive."

"I'll talk with Norma, but I think tomorrow would be fine unless something comes up. Sure wish we knew when we're gonna move on, though. As you Yanks say, I just want to make some tracks."

"Righto!" Abe said in his best imitation of an English accent as they separated to go to their own wagons.

The next morning dawned with an overcast sky above them and darker clouds to the west. Abe had second thoughts about riding away from the camp, but Sarah Beth was obviously looking forward to it and made assurances that they wouldn't have to go so far as to not be able to return if the weather or anything else turned against them. So they saddled up, packed a bit of food and water, bid good-day to the Dentons, and left camp while most other folks were still lighting up their campfires for morning coffee and a meal.

The horses were eager to run and welcomed the freedom of the open ground along the low bluffs skirting the broad, slow-moving river. Just as he'd predicted to Guy, Sarah Beth and her horse kept challenging Abe and Bird to get out and run.

Abe shouted that it would be better to save their speed for the ride back, when they knew the way and were aware of any hazards they might encounter. Sarah Beth gave an exaggerated pout in his direction, but slowed Morning to a gentle loping gait. The beauty of the new green grass waving in the wind was a wonderful sight, mesmerizing in its reach to the far horizon. McFarland had informed Abe that this grassy bounty would only last until they reached the Sand Hills and then they would begin working their way through some dry, nearly desert-like conditions that would be their lot until nearly halfway through the Wyoming country. But for this day, it was beautiful in the somber gray tones of the sky and the waving motion of the green, green grass rolling and rising at the urging of the endless wind.

After about an hour of riding the bluff, they came to a small stream that cut down to the riverbank below. The footing was a little difficult, but they dismounted and had no trouble leading the horses down. There was a small grove of trees where the stream met the river and some large boulders that most likely rolled down out of the little canyon over the centuries. Abe tied the hobbles of the horses to each other with a length of rope and dropped their saddles to the ground while Sarah Beth laid out a small meal on one of the saddle blankets. She served Abe bread and cheese and a cup of fresh water she'd brought from camp. She ate something herself and very soon they were leaning back against one of the boulders together, staring up through the rustling leaves at the sky above. Dark clouds were chasing one another across the sky.

Sarah Beth took Abe's hands in hers and began humming one of her songs. Then she stopped and said, "You know, we're not going to have much privacy on this trip."

"I know, I've thought about that myself."

"So . . ."

He put his arms around her and leaned sideways to ease her down on the grass beside himself. "So?"

Instantly they were kissing. His hand fumbled with the buttons of her man-type shirt, reaching inside for the softness and warmth of her breasts. She arched her head back away from his lips and pushed his face where his hands had been. Her own hands fumbled for his belt, and within moments they were disrobed enough to press flesh against flesh, and to roll into a position of coupling and passion. They were young and very new at this, their frantic motions and urgency bespoke an impatience that neither had ever felt before about anything. Within the first few minutes of this they were lying back, spent for the moment and breathing deeply for the air they'd forgotten to breathe while locked in one another's embrace. Sarah Beth's gentle fingertips combed through Abe's lengthening hair and his lips brushed her neck between her ear and the collar of the open shirt. He pushed himself up on his good elbow to see that the horses were still nearby and calm.

Just then they heard shouts from the river and hurried to put their clothes in order. Men were poling a large raft downriver. Although the deck was piled high with bundles, the raft looked to be riding easily in the wide, shallow Platte. Now one of the men burst into a strident tune of praise to the river and its men. Another man spied the two now-clothed lovers on the bank and saluted Abe and Sarah Beth, raising his pole above his head.

The deep, rolling sound of thunder came from upriver. Sarah Beth quickly began packing up their few things while Abe saddled the horses. It still gave him a good feeling to be able to do this by himself after those years of disability. Just as they were ready to mount up, they heard the first raindrops striking the leaves overhead. They climbed on and turned the horses up the little canyon. It was safe enough to ride up it, even as it had been too risky to come down on horseback.

They reached the top of the bluff and felt the hard-falling warm rain slashing across the open land, driven by a furious wind. The horses were suddenly rearing and prancing about as the lightning flashed to the ground out across the plains, followed by nearly immediate claps of booming thunder. Abe shouted to Sarah Beth to give her horse its head and they added the thunder of their horses' hooves to the sounds of the crashing skies above. Abe led the way, hoping he would remember any hazard they'd encountered coming. But the horses ran with abandon and he probably wouldn't have been able to slow them even if he'd tried.

They reached the camp thoroughly drenched and nearly fell off their horses in exhaustion. The horses were blowing hard and the frothy sweat around their chests and necks was marked by the running rivulets of the rain. The wind was blasting against the canvas cover of the back half of their wagon, and Abe had to make a quick decision whether to pull it off or just lay it down on the cargo. He pulled it down as well as he could, but was having trouble lashing it in place when Guy showed up to help him fight against the wind. Sarah Beth was placing camp gear and other items under the wagon, although everything was already so wet that it wouldn't make that much difference.

When they got the cover lashed down, Guy yelled something and jogged back to his own wagon. Norma could be seen peeking out through the front opening of their cover. She waved to Sarah Beth and beckoned for her to join them in the relative dryness of their wagon. Both of the wagons had wooden built-over front sections and canvas over the rear parts. It was an improvement over the original Conestogas, but still nothing could do much to protect against the fury of this sort of storm. Sarah Beth waved back, but elected to stay in her own semi-shelter.

Then within a few minutes of their arrival back at the camp the rain passed over and the hot sun hit the plains around them, sending steam into the air like clouds of fog. The two women clambered down out of the wagons and got to work pulling things out and hanging wet things on rope lines the men strung between the wagons.

Next chance they had to talk, McFarland told Abe that storms like the one they'd just seen were fairly common. They could be seeing quite a few on their journey, but they usually didn't cause any real damage to the caravans. There were others he called "flashers": storms that hit high up and far away in the mountains and filled smaller creeks to bank-full currents on a perfectly clear day. The rush of water would tumble down slopes and turn to a raging wall of dark brown swirling waves that scoured the streambeds and pushed any debris ahead and out onto the floodplains. Then, he went on, there was also some danger from twisters or tornadoes. They were the worst thing that the weather could do out on these plains, but they were so rare and so contained in their fury that he'd only heard of one wagon train ever getting brushed by one of them.

Two days after the storm, a rider came galloping into camp, his horse spewing dust and him hollering, "We're here! We're here."

Folks gathered around as he dismounted and announced that he'd been sent ahead from the rest of his compatriots' train coming from Iowa and beyond. Someone handed him a jug of water and he gulped it down thirstily, then sloshed the remaining contents over his head.

His horse licked at the water running down his back, so he handed the reins to a youngster and asked him to take his horse to water, "if you please."

Someone produced an empty nail keg for the fellow to sit on and McFarland, his brawny arms across his chest, began asking questions. How far? How soon? How many? Any trouble gettin' here? Need some men to ride out and help them make it in? The stranger answered carefully and in detail and people began to wander off when it became clear that nothing out of the ordinary had happened along the other party's way. The real news was that when that whole group joined up, the camp would more than triple in size, and it could be as soon as by noon the next day.

And triple it did. There was no way for those who'd arrived first to judge how many new wagons were joining up with them. The chaos was reminiscent, but far noisier, than their departure from St. Joe. And this new group brought with them a sizeable herd of horses and cows that seemed surplus to the work of hauling the wagons. McFarland sent several of his hand-picked riders to begin driving this loose herd toward the west and the flatlands near the river. Meanwhile Abe, Guy and a couple of other men had been given the job of directing traffic as the newcomers jostled and struggled to find a place to park with some semblance of maintaining the order that had existed before they arrived. Children ran here and there among the wagons and the deafening din of roaring oxen and whinnying horses was nearly overwhelming. Norma and Sarah Beth stood up in the driving box of Sarah Beth and Abe's wagon, laughing and pointing at the sources of the confusion and the growing crowd of people on foot who were wandering through the original camp, looking a bit lost and nervous.

By nightfall all of the wagons were parked in a loosely arranged series of lines stretching in both directions along the river banks. Yoked and hobbled animals wandered outside the wagon area searching for mouthfuls of grass that hadn't yet been consumed by the first batch of animals to use the land during the past week. As the sun neared the horizon, the smoke of cook-fires joined the now settling dust to turn the sky a kind of soft orange and dirt-colored haze. Someone was playing on a fiddle, and somewhere else a man seemed to be hollering his loudest, probably trying to track down his kids. A few troopers from the fort rode into camp and found their way to McFarland. It was their task to see what kind of numbers had just descended on the small town and its fort, and to set out some regulatory framework for where and when the new citizens could wander about, and where they would feed their animals.

McFarland introduced Abe and several other men to the soldiers, giving Abe a sideways wink as he did. Abe acknowledged the introductions in a fair semblance of a Yankee accent and then kept his mouth shut for the rest of the discussion. The lieutenant in charge of the small group of "bluecoats" gave a short report gathered from dispatches arriving from Laramie and beyond. The weather was already quite dry this early in the season, and the Indians weren't causing much trouble as long as no one tried to keep them from stealing a few horses along the way. There had been unverified reports of gangs of white renegades operating out north of Denver, but they weren't a threat to a large party like this one. McFarland asked how many troops would be sent along with him as escorts for the train. When the lieutenant started making excuses about a shortage of manpower and other limitations, McFarland quietly reminded him that this was arranged far ahead of time and he had a guarantee from the fort's commander that included a patrol of at least ten troopers to accompany the train as far as Fort Laramie.

"And what was the name of that commander, sir?" the soldier asked politely.

"Was a Major Roberts. Here, I'll get the letter."

"I don't think it will make much difference, sir. Major Roberts has returned to West Point and been replaced out here. Fine man, but he was probably too valuable for this posting."

"Well, that don't mean his orders don't stand, does it. I mean, it's the same army even if it's a different officer. Right?"

"I suppose that makes sense to you, sir, and you're welcome to take it up with Captain Chamberlain, who's in charge for the interim. He'll be returning to the fort within the week. These are his orders we're following now."

"Damn," McFarland exploded as he pulled himself up to his full height and looked around the circle of his own men. "It's enough to make a man secede from his own country when it won't protect him and his people. Damn!" He stomped around in a small circle, obviously trying to control his anger. The troopers were backing away toward their horses. "All right Lieutenant, here's the deal. We're pulling out at daybreak, day after tomorrow and if there ain't ten soldiers ready to ride with us, then we're our own law from here on out. You got that, young fella? If you can't help us for what we need, then I guess we don't need you for anything else. You tell that to this Captain Chamberlain. Tell'im it was McFarland said so. What say, men?"

He looked around the circle at his own bunch and they all nodded in agreement. The lieutenant and his men mounted up and as they were about to pull away, the officer looked down and said, "I'll see what I can do."

"Daybreak, day after tomorrow," McFarland repeated.

The soldiers rode off as the wagon train men stood up and commented to one another, agreeing with their leader. Abe heard one man say, "Those fellas ain't much good out here anyway. Never want to get them pretty uniforms dirty." There were chuckles as the group broke up and the men began wandering back to their own camps. Abe had recognized the slight southern speech drawl when this man made his comment and was amused at the way the War was still playing out.

"Abe, stick around a minute," the wagon master said.

"All right."

"Remember our little talk about security for the train? Well, I'd like you come up with some kind of plan for what we'll be needing, now that we're on our own. I'm almost certain they're not going to give us any support. And say hello to that pretty little wife of yours. She looks like she can handle a wagon while you're busy. Thanks, son." And then he turned away and walked off toward wagons of the new campers.

When Abe got back to their campsite, he was a bit surprised to see Sarah Beth leaning over the cook-fire wearing a long skirt and puffy-sleeved blouse. For most of the time on the trail from St. Joe, and here in camp, it'd been her pants and shirts that she wore daily. He didn't know whether to comment or not, but she sure looked nice there as she stirred the food in the pot hanging over the fire. She set down her long spoon and turned to him as he approached. They embraced, even as he glanced around shyly for onlookers. He still wasn't all that comfortable with the easy public intimacy he'd seen in many of the train's couples, and was a bit nervous to show affection at such close quarters. But Sarah Beth seemed to have no qualms and planted a long kiss on his mouth and then quickly turned back to the cooking.

"What's going on over at McFarland's?" she asked.

"Oh, not much yet, but maybe it'll turn into something. Army says they can't supply us with the escort he requested. He says they promised. They say they can't do it. They've changed commanders so he doesn't have much to stand on."

"What will we do? And will it make a difference?"

He didn't answer as he took a dipper of clean water from the bucket hanging under the seat of the wagon. He wiped his face and said, "I'd best look after the animals, make sure they're all tethered and not tangled."

"Mr. Saunders," she stood with one hand on her hips and the other shaking the spoon in his direction. "you did not answer my question."

"I know. I guess there really isn't an answer, and I want to wait and see what will be done about it."

"Like what?" She smiled now that he'd answered, and went back to stirring.

"Like we may have to be ready to take care of ourselves."

"And . . ."

"And somehow it came up, when he and I talked before this all happened, that I'd done a little training for a patrol back in Virginia."

"And now he wants you to do the same thing. Did you tell him your wife is not about to risk her brand-new husband being his bodyguard?"

"Sarah Beth, there's nothing been decided and it's not just for him. Even with a squad of soldiers, we'd still have to be prepared for danger on the trail. You know that."

"Of course I do. But why does it always have to be you?"

He came back to her and put his hands on her shoulders and looked down into the eyes that were still flashing at him. "Because it means I can be sure you're well taken care of," he said as he held her close. "It'll be all right, my dearest. Whether I'm a leader or a follower, it'll be the same risk, and this way I can make sure we're as well prepared as we can be. And that's how I can be taking care of you."

"Oh, Abe, you can't always let people take advantage of you."

"I'm not. I'm just doing my part. Now you better do your part and watch that stew." He gently pushed her away and walked off toward the large rope corral that held his group's animals. He turned back and said, "You sure look nice this evening."

He went on to where young men had been scything green grass along the river and spreading it among the animals so that they were now eating peacefully. He walked out among them, feeling comfortable and checking each of their animals in turn. Matthew, Mark, Luke, John, Morning and Bird all seemed content as they satisfied their hunger with fresh-cut grass. As he stroked Sarah Beth's horse, he thought about what had just been almost an argument. If it truly qualified for that definition, it was their first since they'd been married. He'd known what her reaction would be, same as that first time back in Virginia, but this time it was even more important and it would take both of them working together, not just him out patrolling and her sitting at home worrying. She would have to do her part and drive the team, and if they did run into danger or hostilities, that job could quickly become difficult. He looked toward where the sun still caused the sky to glow in colors out where it had set just a few minutes before. The days were getting longer and that was a good thing for travel. As he kept watching the beauty of the dying light, he found himself praying for safety, for him and Sarah Beth of course, but also for everyone in this now large caravan of brave individuals, families and helpers, all hopefully committed to working together for safe passage and good fellowship along the way. Understanding Sarah Beth's concerns did not get in the way of his feeling that once again he'd been chosen to take on responsibility above and beyond his experience and his years, so he prayed for help in that as well, for guidance, and for the Voice to continue speaking to him when he could hear it and needed its counsel.

Once he was back at the camp, in the twilight of that day, the two of them sat by their small fire and ate heartily of the stew she'd cobbled together from fresh meat and dried foodstuffs. He asked her about her afternoon and was surprised by her eagerness to talk about it.

"Abe, you won't believe it. I was going to tell you earlier, but you had to go. But Norma and I and someone you don't know yet, name of Gladys, well we made the acquaintance of some of the newcomers, the Mormon women. It was so amazing. They're the ones you'll see now, the ones in long black dresses. We were almost scared to go near their camps, but Norma said it was our duty to welcome them. Of course when we got close enough to speak, one of them pointed at me and said, 'Young fellow, can you give us a helping hand with this barrel of water?' Well, I didn't know whether or not to say I'm a woman so I just let it by and helped them. Then I stood by while Norma and Gladys introduced us all. Gladys said my name was Sam.

We had such a laugh on our way back here about them thinking I was a young man. Anyway, they were very nice, and so polite. I think it's going to be just fine between the two groups. The girls and I are so relieved, because they are quite intimidating in those dark dresses and all their stern looks. Did you meet any of their men?" She ladled out another helping into the bowl on his knees.

"Not yet," he said, "but do you think they were laughing about the three of you after you left them?"

"Why?"

"Because it isn't hard to see that you're woman up close, even if you are in disguise." He reached over and tickled her ribs just below her breasts to make his point.

"Abe Saunders, you have such a mind."

"And you ma'am, have such a body."

Suddenly they were both quiet. This outburst of intimacy was a bit of shock to both of them, and since nothing quite like this had happened before, they weren't quite sure if it was allowed, or right or wrong, or whatever. Suddenly Sarah Beth burst out laughing.

"Yes I do," she said, "and you're not so bad looking yourself."

Just then, as if on a cue, they heard the far off yipping and howling of a pack of coyotes far out across the plain.

"I think they're laughing at us," he said as he poured some wash water into the empty stew pot. "Time to clean up and get some sleep."

After a few days on the Trail, the great size of the train became apparent one morning when they pulled up a hill and could look all the way back down the long line. The Captain had positioned Abe and Sarah Beth up near the front where he and his men rode with their own wagons, equipment and non-perishable supplies. The leadership of the two camps had met a few times, with the Captain attempting to iron out agreement over shared responsibilities and the division of labor regarding discipline, as well as the enforcement of certain rules of the road and customs that the Captain required anyone in his caravans to observe. The leader of the newcomers was a bishop named Bradley, and he seemed to run a pretty tight ship, with discipline well-developed and understood. He and McFarland agreed that the merger was coming along fairly well.

One evening as Sarah Beth and Abe were straightening up their camp for an early night's sleep, they got to talking about the newcomers and their strange ways. "Well, they certainly look different and seem to want to keep to themselves," Sarah Beth commented as she took their blankets off the rope where they'd been airing during the day. "It's almost as if those dresses of theirs are uniforms."

"You might say they are. Might be they're even required to dress that way," Abe replied. "And same for the men. Always look like they're ready to go to church at a moment's notice."

"I still think they're very nice. They have good manners, they keep their camps clean, and they're quiet enough, as a rule."

"Do you know anything about their religion?"

"Not much. Father told me they had a prophet who discovered a new gospel. Just dug it up one day and started preaching a new religion based on that Book."

"A new gospel, you say?" He snuck up behind her and wrapped his arms around hers from behind. "Guess we might have to get ourselves another ox, if there's five gospels."

She spun away from him and thrust the blanket into his arms. "Go put this on your bed, sir. The maid has more work to do."

Just then they heard shots from the other end of camp. Abe grabbed his rifle and waved a kiss at Sarah Beth as he ran off, joining a few other men hurrying toward the sound of the shots. She started to run after him, but stopped, realizing he wouldn't approve. Other women from the lead wagons appeared in the passageway made by the two circles of wagons in the front camp. Following the three or four shots there was now an eerie silence hanging over the shallow valley where they were camped for the night. Sarah Beth joined a small group of women, including Norma, who were talking quietly, wondering if there was any danger and if they shouldn't be doing something.

Sarah Beth commented softly, "There isn't much to do until we know what it's about." The others agreed and seemed to gather a little more tightly into their small group. The sun had been down for awhile, with dusk appearing to rise out of the hills that surrounded them.

When Abe and the men with him arrived at the intersection where the two camps were joined, they immediately saw two lines of men facing one another, guns drawn. The Bishop was calling loudly for Captain McFarland, as the face-off of men on each side kept staring across an open space at one another. Abe looked around. Seeing no one with any more authority than himself, he answered the man in the black frock coat.

"He should be here any time. I believe he was sleeping. Was up scouting ahead all night and most of today. What's the problem here?"

"Who we talking to? Seen you around, but we haven't met," one of the men hollered.

Abe looked around the area and saw more men in the deepening shadows. In his best Yankee accent he replied, "I am Abe Saunders, sir. Presently the drill sergeant of the Captain's security force. I've talked with some of these men already," he gestured at the line of formally dressed Mormon men. "We need help from everyone in maintaining order here," Abe went on. "So I'd appreciate it if you would tell me what's going on so we can work things out and all return to our own campsites."

Just then the Captain came riding up bareback. He jumped down and strode right in between the two lines of the stand-off.

"What the hell, 'scuse me Bishop, but what the hell is going on here?"

"Glad to see you McFarland. Remember hell is not a place to be taken lightly. But as to your question, one of your youngsters addressed one of our young women in a flirtatious manner. Turns out she's the wife of one of our true Disciples and he didn't take kindly to it."

"All right then," McFarland boomed out in his loud voice. "I hereby order your Disciple to execute the guilty man right here, right now. We'll have none of that kind of rudeness on this trip. Which one was he?"

"Well now, Captain. Don't rightly know, sir. She was carrying water past a group of these sinners and someone said something that made her run to her husband with tears in her eyes. Terrible thing for a poor child like herself."

"Child, you say? Thought you said she's married."

"Well, she is, but to me all of our young people are my children."

"All right you men, all of you, back to your camps. If this is just children getting in a little trouble we'll have an end to it. But the next time any of you pull a gun on any other person in this wagon train, you'll answer to me and this." He pulled a large pistol out from his waistband. "Now get some sleep. I want us moving before light. We've got one hell . . . I mean hoot of a long day ahead of us before we see water again. Go, now. Go. Abe, you and the Bishop stay here for a minute."

He led the two of them a ways away from the nearest wagon and camp and the three men stood together in the tall, thick grass. It was half grown by this time of year, half the height it would become when a man could get lost in it if he wasn't careful.

"Now gentlemen, we can't afford to let anything like this ever happen again. Bishop, and you, Abe, I'm making you two responsible to me for the law and order of this outfit. I'm Captain and my word goes, but I got a lot more on my mind and goin' on in my days than keeping track of who insults who and who lifts their skirt at who else. Abe here is from now on my sergeant-at-arms. He's in charge of the discipline and training of the two squads of men we're going to organize for our protection. And Bishop, don't be fooled by his baby face, he's done this kind of thing before and comes highly recommended. We're lucky to have him along."

Abe lowered his eyes and head and mumbled something that neither of the others could hear. The Bishop reached across and offered a handshake.

"Well son. I'm pleased to have you along as well. You handled that situation pretty well over there before this mountain of a man came into it and scared everyone." He smiled and shook hands with the Captain as well. "I'll do whatever you ask along these lines. My people want no trouble no less than yours. I'll appoint a man to work equally with Abe here and we'll make sure this wagon train gets where it's going," he smiled, "come hoot or high water."

"Good, sir. Now as far as training the men, I want them mixed up. Don't want to put together two bunches that would just as soon fight each other as Indians or renegades. There will be some patrolling of the camp, just kind of a precaution, and the men will do that two by two, one from each of the camps. Bishop, if I may, I'll want to know your beliefs about how we keep all these folks in line when things get hard. We'll follow common law about such as thievery and murder, but it's the other things like this one tonight that's gonna be the test for our methods."

"Captain, we have our ways and our holy laws. We take care of our own and that means in sickness and in health as well as in sin and troublemaking. Things will go a lot better if we're able to maintain our own rules and follow our own ways, and, we need to have the role of administering punishment and all that entails. As far as the Common Law, as you call it, when a conflict occurs between individuals of both

groups, I believe it will be best that you and I act in the office of a
two-judge court for decisions that require such a format."

"Sounds good to me. I'll have Abe here draw up an agreement.
You and me sign it, and we'll let folks know this here caravan is its
own nation with its own laws. Far as the Army of the USA goes, they'll
have to ask for our help rather than the other way round. Now I've
got a nap to catch up on 'fore I got to set out the route for morning.
Goodnight, gentlemen."

He was gone. The Bishop stared carefully at Abe, as if sizing
him up. "You know, young man, that we have our own ways and that
marriage is one of them. It's one of the reasons we're headed for the
Utah country where we can live in freedom to practice our own ways.
Now, I've already heard some grumbling about our men having more
than one woman. I want you to know that we will allow no intolerance
whatsoever when it come to the private affairs of ourselves and our
Church. Am I clear?"

"Yes, sir. I believe you have your rights and they will be protected
as long as I'm charged with looking out for the people of this caravan."
Abe paused and, thinking of how some clergymen are celibate, he
pushed his nerve to ask the man, "Are you married sir, or is that not a
part of your role as bishop?"

The man threw back his head and laughed, "Oh my son, oh my.
We are as far as you can get from the apostates of the Papacy on that
issue. As a bishop, I am responsible to set an example. As it is, I have
seven wives and, I'm pleased to say, not really looking for any more
at present. I am fortunate that the three eldest are sisters and have the
experience and shared responsibility to run my household. Answer
your question?"

"Yes sir."

"Then I'll excuse myself. I understand this night won't be long
for sleeping."

They both stood up, the older man slowly, and Abe awkwardly,
trying to push himself up with only his good arm.

The Bishop stood still for a moment and then asked. "War wound?"

"Yes sir."

As the man walked away, Abe watched him go, feeling a mixture
of respect and curiosity about this man and his ways. He dressed and
looked extremely formal, and his words were carefully chosen, but
there was a bit of twinkle to his eye and a slight familiarity of tone in

his voice that revealed something a bit less strict in his person than in his image. This will be interesting, he thought to himself as he turned and walked back toward his own wagon and his only wife.

As the days on the trail passed, the hard work and slow travel settled into the caravan's people with a kind of tedious rhythm that was offset by gratefulness that they hadn't encountered severe difficulties or attacks. Those at the rear of the line of wagons became accustomed to the dust, and the herd of non-draft animals learned to stick together for grazing and resting. A few thunderstorms were seen in the distance, passing them by, headed east. The routine of waking early and driving forward until the next spot to find sufficient water and forage for stopping became a hard kind of schedule for the emigrants, and they learned to rest whenever possible.

Abe was busy setting up the patrols he'd been charged with and was grateful for the able assistance of a somewhat older man named Benjamin Overstreet. The Mormon had once served as a supplies administrator for the Union Army, and was excellent at organization and administration, skills definitely needed for this new and rather unusual wagon train police force. It didn't take much working together and conversation for Overstreet to surmise that Abe was from the southern side of the recent conflict. But he was tolerant and confidentially explained that while most of the men on the trail with the train had served the Union side, it was his conjecture that it was more out of a sense of necessity rather than belief or loyalty to one side or the other. As a matter of fact, the reason most of these Mormon families were on the trail to Utah was because they felt betrayed by the Yankee side when their isolation and oppression continued with the same intensity after the end of the War in which many of them had fought.

Together they devised some rosters and rotations for the men. Two days previously, the train had stopped in the early afternoon for an overnight where there was plenty of access to sandy beaches along the river where the women could do laundry. There was also good graze for the animals and they could rest up for the next few hard days of mainly inclined roadways. Abe and Ben, as the man said he should be called since Abe was using the short version of his own name, took their small troop of twenty men out to where they could test and get used to weapons provided by the train to supplement their own arms.

Ammunition was carefully dispensed and accounted for, and some shooting practice was allowed. All in all, the session went well and the two leaders were pleased to find they had some good marksmen among the cadre.

Meanwhile, Norma had informed Sarah Beth that she thought she was with child. Though it was early on, she was apprehensive of how that would affect her ability to travel and keep up with the work expected of the women. Sarah Beth reassured her that most women were able to maintain their normal activities for at least the first seven months, and that Norma was a plenty strong enough woman to carry a child and keep up with the work. Sarah Beth promised to look out for her and help in any way she could. By the time the baby arrived, they would be settled in for the winter, wherever that was going to be.

That night was hot, and as she and Abe lay together beneath the wagon they didn't need coverings. They'd hung the blankets around them for privacy. Sarah Beth took Abe's weaker hand in hers and gently worked the elbow joint back and forth since she knew he was probably neglecting to keep doing that on a regular basis.

"Norma says she's going to have a baby at the end of the trail somewhere."

"That so? Hope the journey isn't too hard for her."

"It shouldn't be, if all goes well . . ." she paused for a spell, and then continued, "Abe, do you want me to have a child?"

"Of course I do. I mean, when the time is right, certainly. It would be better if we were settled first, but then that's probably not our decision, is it?" He laughed softly and reached over and tickled her ribs with his strong hand.

She giggled and pushed his hand away. "Maybe it depends on how busy you are with all these other things. And how much privacy we get along the way."

He leaned over and turned her face toward his, imagining how she looked in the light and tracing her features with his fingertips. "Maybe it depends on how much we love each other."

"Oh Abe, if that's true we'll probably have twins."

CHAPTER TEN

Desolation

The route they were taking was called the Mormon Trail and kept to the north side of the Platte River. They were often within sight of a railroad line, which was part of the new transcontinental route under construction. Once every couple of days, and sometimes more often, they could see the approaching cloud of smoke from the engines pulling loads of supplies west for the great project and for the towns along the way. The rumbling sound of the huge train could be heard at a distance and even felt as a low throbbing from the ground.

Most of the members of McFarland's section of the wagon train were counting on the Homestead Act to provide them with land and a new opportunity, unlike many of the Mormons who had some areas in Utah reserved for them in advance. The short history of the westward expansion was one that told of the need to dig in and develop farmland, but by 1870 that strategy required the willingness to settle in remote areas that had not already been claimed. The more isolated one was willing to make their claim, the better its quality would be, given what remained after these first few years of mobilization following the end of the War. The one thing held in common by this great exodus of refugees and citizens was that they were all, by and large, convinced that this would be the answer to the loss and devastation they were leaving behind, where battlefields lay scattered across the landscape and manifold hardships were the common order of the day. The dream was that settling the west wouldn't be as hard as staying in the east.

Abe and Sarah Beth often talked about their chances of finding the place of their own dreams, sometimes when they were alone together and sometimes with other companions on the trail. She was already drawing pictures of the house they would build and the great shade trees they knew they would plant and grow for their own comfort and sense of familiarity. Abe was more concerned about what kind of soil they would find. He had never actually farmed on his own before and he pondered what he would grow to help his new family to prosper.

One day when the trail passed close to the railroad tracks for several miles, a train heading east pulled to a long slow stop parallel to the wagon train. The locomotive and a passenger car were festooned with banners celebrating the building of the Transcontinental Railroad. There was one other car carrying passengers picked up at the line's end, as far west as it had reached, and several empty freight cars that had been used to carry construction supplies. As this was the first time a railroad train had stopped near them, McFarland summoned Abe and several assistants to ride with him to see what it was all about. Several men in dress suits climbed down out of a long black car and stood waiting to meet McFarland.

McFarland dismounted and approached the group cautiously. For all he knew, one or more among them could be law enforcement officers of the federal government. Perhaps sent to serve papers on him and some of the others for the manner in which they'd announced their independence from the authorities or for acting without any sort of permission or escort. He'd confided as much to Abe on their short ride to meet the visitors.

As they approached he let out with a "Hello" in his usual booming voice. "Can we help you out, or did you just come to wish us well and bring news from where you've been?"

A tall gentleman with an ornate walking stick stepped forward, removed his hat and bowed slightly, saying, "A little of both, my friend. First of all, let me introduce ourselves. We are board members of the Union Pacific. We've been out west of here to observe and inspect progress on the construction of the nation's first transcontinental railroad. Within a few short years we hope to be able to replace your more tiresome and arduous manner of travel with trains hauling both people and everything they need to the great frontier country beyond." He gestured toward the open plains to the west. "Sir, I'm certain that you yourself will look forward to that day and I invite you to consider seeking employment with our company, sooner rather than later. You seem to be a leader here and we can use that kind of man, isn't that right, gentlemen?" He looked around at his companions and they all gave hearty assent to his words.

McFarland looked around at his men, who were still mounted and said, "Hear that boys? We're gonna be replaced and I'll have to get me a shiny suit and hat just like these fellas here." He laughed and continued, "Can you give us any news about what's up ahead for a ways? That'd be more useful than that job right now."

"Well, yes sir. That is one reason we've stopped. West of here near where the North Platte separates from this river here, there's been quite a fire, many miles of it. Fortunately it was moving so fast it jumped over our tracks and very little damage was done, and of course the river stopped it from going any further. But you may want to cross over to the south side at some point because there won't be much for your animals to eat in those burned off areas. Just thought we'd warn you, as your good neighbors, so to speak."

"Thanks, Boss. Any sign of Indian trouble out that way?"

"None we could see, and none we've heard of. They are, however, a truly unpredictable breed and subject to hysterical outbursts such as we've encountered many times during our construction days. So remain alert my friend, and best wishes for your journey. Remember, 'the Union Pacific will always be just ahead of you, and always right on time.'"

As the men turned to board their train car, McFarland still had one more thing to say. "Wait a minute, *gentlemen*, we'd like to offer you a meal in our camps. Why, we've got plenty of the best dog head stew and buffalo testicle soup you ever tasted. Ain't that right, boys?"

"Yes sir! You bet!" there was a chorus of shouts from the wagon men.

The delegation from the train quickly climbed back into their car without another word.

McFarland mounted his horse and waited. As the train slowly heaved into motion, he and his men began to ride alongside, waving their hats and firing their pistols into the air.

After a few rounds, McFarland shouted, "That's enough shooting boys. Might need that ammunition along the way." Then he kicked his horse into a gallop and led his men around the front of the slow-moving train and back along its other side. Once they'd circled the train, they rode back to their wagons, laughing and hollering all the way.

Later that evening, Abe was sitting at McFarland's fire with several other men who'd been at the train. McFarland kept them focused on the business at hand, planning the route and stops for the next few days until they finished with it. Then he threw back his head in a great roar of laughter, shaking his long hair back and forth, and he said, "Bet them bastards are still talking 'bout us. What do you think, Abe?"

"Guess you're right. They've probably never seen such an ugly bunch up close."

The men laughed and made a few comments of their own.

"Sonsabitches, we should've taken them hostage."

"Traded them to the Indians for safe passage."

"Trying to offer Captain McFarland a job kissing their asses and shining their bald heads."

"All right, men, that's enough for tonight. Come daylight, I want you, Bill and Chester, to ride along the river and find the best place to cross. We may wait until we get close to it, but if there's a good place with decent feed on the other side, might as well use it sooner than later."

The men got up to leave. McFarland motioned for Abe to stay.

"There's an issue coming up you and me will have to deal with sooner or later. Might's well get ahead on it."

"What's that?" He said, almost adding "sir" out of habit.

"This camp's already divided into Mormons and us Gentiles, as they call us. But that's good long as we keep everyone busy and happy." McFarland bit off some of his chew and gestured out ahead of them toward the west where the slight glow of the sunset still shone dimly along the horizon. "But we're gonna start running out on the supplies they've all brought along, especially their dry meat. I've seen things get ugly when the food runs low, and the hardest most desolate part of the trip is comin' up once we get past Fort Laramie. From then on 'till we get down to the Green River country. Be lucky to spot an antelope or two. So, you're gonna have to start sending out hunting parties with your men. I don't want no free-for-all where everybody thinks they're the great hunter, or folks are just huntin' for theirselves. So we've got to control it by only us doing the huntin' and folks can do their own drying. Understand? You're gonna be a buffalo hunter, son, Chief Buffalo Hunter." He stood up and slapped Abe lightly on the back. "And it may come to us having to butcher some of our own stock. I've seen it. G'night, son."

Over a week went by before they crossed the Platte. The ford area was wide and mostly shallow, with buffalo chips on either side indicating a major crossing for wild animals. Children and women hastened to gather the dried chips for fuel while the men secured their wagons and shifted their loads. Before the train was ready to move, Abe sent some men across to see if they could find buffalo on the other side before the wagons ran them off. If they got any, they could kill, camp, and get the meat ready for drying while waiting for the train to catch up.

Within an hour of the men leaving, he was rewarded by the sound of distant gunfire. He wanted to join them, wished he'd been one of the hunters, but McFarland said he was needed to keep order on the crossing. He told Abe he hadn't seen anything yet compared to the chaos they could expect when the people started to panic and rush to get to the other side before anybody else. At the Captain's order and with him leading the way on his big red horse, the first of the wagons trundled into the river. Abe was to stay on the near bank and keep people from crowding their wagons into one another. At the rate it took the first dozen or so wagons to drop down the bank into the water, he figured he might be stuck at that post until after dark.

He heard his name called out in the sweet voice he was coming to know so well and quickly edged his horse over next to Sarah Beth and their wagon.

"How you doing?" he asked.

"Fine. Need a ride, stranger?"

"Naw," he said, "think I'll just swim."

She reached down and gave him her hand which he kissed and then held onto, pretending to try to pull her off the wagon seat. She laughed and cracked the whip to urge her team into the water to be drenched among the maelstrom of splashing, bellowing animals and shouting drivers. Abe watched her go until he felt confident that she would be fine on her own. He looked downriver at two wagons trying to push around all the traffic at the main ford where he was stationed. He kicked his horse into a run and pulled up beside them. He didn't know the folks in the first wagon but in the second wagon he saw their new friends Guy and Norma.

"Stop!" he yelled. "No good here, back in line."

Guy pulled up on his reins just as the front wheels entered the water. The wagon in front of him now pulled ahead, its team churning through the deepening water. Suddenly that wagon lurched and leaned over, almost capsizing. A child tumbled into the water. As the driver fought his team to keep turned upriver against the current, a woman leaned out the back of the wagon, screaming and waving her arms toward the child who was being swept away.

Abe yelled at Guy. "Keep your team out of the water and unhook them. See if you can lash onto that wagon and help pull it back out up here." And then he was gone, galloping down the riverbank and yanking on the reins to force Bird into the water at a spot he hoped was below the child, where the water was moving fast. His horse turned to face upriver and Abe stood high in his stirrups, desperately searching the water. Suddenly he saw a flash of fabric almost upon him and he reached to that side of his horse with his bad arm. It was his only chance. His fingers clutched at child's clothing, gripping as tight as he could. He pulled harder with his stiff arm and forced himself to bend it no matter what it took, pulling the passive bundle closer and lifting the child's head out of the water. It was a girl and she was gasping for air, sputtering and trying to breathe, now hitting him in the face with one of her arms. He held her across the saddle with his good arm and urged Bird back to the bank, then up and out of the water.

The girl was still gasping when he pulled up next to Norma, who was standing on the grass behind and above their wagon. He handed the little girl down to her, saying, "She needs to breathe. Help her if you can." Then he jumped off his horse and led it forward to where Guy had rigged ropes tied to his own team, and was just about ready to jump into the water to try to attach it to the floundering wagon. Abe grabbed it from him.

"You stay here. Got to use your team to pull that mess out of here. Unhitch them the rest of the way and turn them around. Hold on to this," he said as he handed Guy one of the thick ropes and grabbed the other, pulling it to himself.

Then he jumped into water that came up to his chest. Fortunately it wasn't moving fast at this spot. He fought his way toward the tipped wagon, yelling at the man, "Cut your team loose. Cut their harness, now!" Then he ducked under the water and tried to fasten the rope to the rear axle of the wagon. He had to come up for air before he got a knot made, but when he went back under he was able to get enough of a wrap to secure the rope with a fat knot, and to pull the extra into another loop around the chain holding up the tailgate of the wagon.

By then the driver had cut his oxen free and was frantically trying to herd them toward the bank. The woman appeared at the back of the wagon above Abe, hysterically hitting his head with her hands, screaming, "Is she alive? Alive?"

Abe backed away and shouted at the man to let the animals go, and to straighten out the tongue of the wagon and keep it that way. He'd just realized that there was no hope of pulling it back and out if its front wheels were turned against the direction of the pull. Then he stumbled through the water to the bank. By this time several other horsemen had gathered beside Guy and they were tying ropes from their saddles to his main rope. Now if only the rope held without itself breaking, or what it was lashed to.

They were able to inspire a tremendous effort from the animals. The men leaped into the water to help keep the trapped wagon from capsizing, and finally the back wheels slowly rolled up to the shallow water at the river's edge. Everyone paused and Guy brought his oxen back down to the wagon, re-hooked, and pulled the wagon up onto the bank. The woman leaped down over the tailgate and ran to where Norma was comforting the weeping girl. Norma got a blanket out of her wagon and wrapped both of them in it. Abe could hear men yelling from the point of crossing upriver. He pulled himself back onto Bird and hurried back, afraid he might be needed at his main job.

By the end of the day, as darkness was falling, all of the wagons were safely across, although many of them had broken parts, even wheel-spokes, but fortunately no broken wheels. McFarland spread word that there would be a day off for repairs and rest. He later told Abe that these crossings weren't all that unusual, but this one was more chaotic than most because of the accident and it being the first time for the two groups to really have to cooperate.

"But you did a damn good job, son. Don't know as I'd have tried to save the stupid sonovabitch, Mormon wasn't he?"

"The wagon in the river was, the second one was ours."

"Well, tell that Bishop next time you see him, keep a tighter rein on his folks, and you take care of that one of ours. Give'm what for. We can't afford any more of that goin' on."

When they reached the burned-over area, the scouts found it went on for miles and miles on the other side of the river, the side they'd crossed over from. The most appalling sight was the hundreds of vultures circling and settling on the small mounds the corpses of dead animals made across the landscape. Occasionally a breeze would come their way across the river and bring with it the scent of death and rot. Everyone was motivated to move along as fast as they could to get past it all, but even so it seemed the burn and the stench would never end.

The man and woman who'd almost lost their daughter and wagon appeared one evening at Abe and Sarah Beth's camp. They were dressed in the formal-looking Mormon apparel and carried a large bundle between them. Their daughter was hiding behind them as they came closer. They set the bundle down and the man said, "We don't have any way to thank you, sir. You saved our lives and all our possessions, well, the ones that didn't wash away. So we brought this for you."

His wife bent down and unwrapped the canvas away from the large shape and stood back to let them see it. It was a thick bed covering with a quilting stitch design crisscrossing its outer fabric. "It's for your bed," she said.

Her husband said, "Esther here made it herself. Its hair we brushed from a fine team of horses back in Illinois. We had to leave them behind and this is what we have left of them. It'll go good on your bed when you get to your new home. Esther says that design will help you make babies, didn't you say that?"

He turned to his now embarrassed wife and put his arm around her. "We were going to use it ourselves for another one, but right now we're so happy with our little Rebecca who you saved; oh thank God, sir, thank God for you and the strength of your arm. You saved her from the rushing flood and we'll never forget it. The Bishop says you'll always be welcome among us for that."

"Why thank you, my wife and I truly appreciate your gift and the sentiment it shows."

Sarah Beth broke in, "Are you sure you can spare it? We don't want to take anything so special from you."

The man nodded, and then said, "That river tried to take what's most special to us." He pulled the little girl around to face them. "And your man made a selfless and successful attempt to save her for us."

Abe looked a little embarrassed, but then he said, "I want you to know something that happened to me out there, something I got out of this. That was my weak arm I had to use. Elbow was smashed by a rifle ball at the end of that War and I hadn't been able to bend it ever since. Isn't that right, Sarah Beth?" She nodded and grasped his arm in her hands as he continued. "But when I grabbed for your girl there,

I couldn't raise her out of the water with my arm crippled straight stiff and locked like it was. Suddenly, with the effort I was giving it, the arm snapped at the joint and bent for the first time in all these years and I could haul her up onto my horse with that one arm. It was a miracle for me. So I thank God for helping to save you and your daughter, but I'm also giving great thanks for what He did for me."

"Praise the Lord," the woman said softly, speaking for the first time. "He loves you, even though you're a Gentile, He loves you and so do we." Then she turned and took her daughter's hand, walking quickly away. The little girl turned and waved back at Abe and Sarah Beth, and then the man held out his hand.

Abe shook it with his good hand and then added his other hand to the clasping, flexing his elbow as he did. "Bless you. But from now on I'd ask you to follow orders from those whose authority it is to give them."

The man nodded as tears began to fall down his cheeks and he turned away after his woman and the child.

Abe bent down to the mattress-quilt and rolled its tangled shape out on the ground. "Here, help me," he said. "Let's lay down on it right now."

"Abe," she said, moving to help, "what's got into you? You're so happy these days. Now you help me roll it up. It's beautifully made and so practical."

"So are you, my sweet, so beautiful and, unfortunately, much too practical at a moment like this. But I'm happy because nowadays I can hold you good with both arms for the first time. You won't ever get away from me now."

"Abe, shhh. People can hear you."

They reached Fort Laramie on the hottest day of their journey. The river had narrowed significantly and was getting lower all the time. They easily crossed over to the side where the small but booming town was located. When the railroad construction had passed through, Laramie was mostly a city of tents, including the Big Tent, a structure they bragged was the size of a city block in St. Louis. Now the signs and sounds of building were all about, and nowhere more so than in the stockyards, where workers were hastily building corrals for cattle by the hundred, preparing for the livestock trains that were part of the new traffic headed east.

McFarland ordered the wagons to set up in two huge double circles a ways from the settlement, with the draft animals to be left tethered to one another and allowed to move about the infields of the circles, while the rest of the animals, including riding horses, were to be picketed on the outside of the rings of wagons. He'd been here before and had been forced to move camp when the authorities determined that they'd pulled in too close to town—that the noise and insects brought by the train were a disruption—so to avoid any problems, he was setting up far enough away.

Once they'd settled into their formations and provided for the basic necessities of water, toilets and fire-pits, many of the emigrants were eager to head into town. Abe told Sarah Beth that he needed to deliver the articles he'd written along the way to the local telegraph office for transmission back to St. Joseph. He was pleased with some of his writing and with the subjects he'd chosen from the journey's seemingly endless trek. Sarah Beth said she would stay with the camp until he returned, but only if he didn't take his sweet time about it. He laughed and said that if she wasn't going to be there when he returned then what was there to come back to?

When he got to the telegraph office he was disappointed that they had no method for sending such large messages since it was all being done by hand and code and they weren't allowed to have the lines tied up for that long; with the wagon train just arriving, there were so many travelers waiting for the telegraph office to send their messages back home. Abe asked if and where there was a local newspaper office. He was pointed in the direction of the main street crossing and told to follow the boardwalk until he reached the office of the Laramie Sentinel; perhaps they could help him with their own connection to the telegraph line.

The Sentinel still had its "Grand Opening" banner stretched across the front window of a small shack with a canvas roof. Inside the open door were two men, one covered with ink stains and the other perched high on a stool at a writing desk. Abe entered, and then introduced himself in answer to the ink-man's question. He stated his business as briefly as he could.

"Ah-ha," said the man on the stool. "A fellow scribe, and as the playwright said, 'Hail fellow, well-met!' Come in, have a seat on that barrel and tell us what you've been through to get here. Did you have to escape that fire? Any Indian attacks? Go hungry? Fights among the travelers? Anybody die of disease or gunshot? I mean, give us the news, man." He sat with a notebook on his lap and a pencil poised above it.

"Well, sorry to disappoint you," Abe said, having to shout above the sound of the ancient printing press, which the ink-man had been starting as Abe walked up. "Not much out of the ordinary, but some good stories about the kind of people making the trip and why they're joining the New Crusade to conquer the West."

"Ahh, the New Crusade. Those your words, young man? Not bad. Make it the title of a series. Shut that damn thing off," he yelled at the younger man who was presumably his assistant. "We haven't even set the damn type yet, idiot."

The press clanked to a halt and the ink-man looked up and over the top of his spectacles. "Only way to see if it's clean enough to print off of later." He went back to cleaning and polishing the rollers.

"Well," the man addressed Abe, "we'll print what you've got if it's something unique and possibly unsettling, maybe some conflict, fear-inspiring, you know, the normal news crap."

"Yes sir, I'll see what I can do for you."

"Wait, what'd you say your name is?"

"Abe, Abraham Saunders."

"Wouldn't be related to a Lester Saunders, would you?"

Abe hesitated, surprised at the combined name, and then realized that he needed to know just a bit more before admitting that those were both his names. "Well, I am Saunders and I've a relative named Lester, so it might be me, might be a mistake, or," he went on, "could just be a coincidence."

"Well, I've got a letter come here addressed to Lester Saunders in care of this here newspaper, and it says it's from St. Louis, no other address."

"Oh, that explains it." Abe thought quickly. "My cousin's name is Louis, and his father was named Lester. He's either playing games, like he always does, or he's trying to make me guess who it's from. That's the way he is."

"All right, young fella, I don't want it around here anyway. If it's not for you, you find whoever it's intended for." He reached out and handed the envelope across the small room to Abe. "And come back when you've got something we can print." He turned and went back to his work at the desk. The ink-man saluted Abe, and bent back over his own work. Abe walked out wondering what the salute meant, but was more concerned about what Louis had to say.

Since this was his first letter since becoming a married man, he was wondered if he was bound to share it with Sarah Beth. He decided to read it first, before returning to camp, and let its contents make that decision for him. After all, who knew what Louis might have to say about anything. He found a place along the road back to camp where he could sit under a cottonwood and have a little bit of peace between all the bustling busyness of the fort, town, and their own camp.

Cuz,

I wrote this letter to you in both of your names half of each because how could I know what name you're using now? Buff said we made the best time he's ever had with a caravan. He also said when I told him what train you was on that he knows McFarland and that he's one of the best wagon bosses. I imagine you've got to know him by now. Me and my partner who you met, Mad Mountain Jace, him and me have bought some cattle, just a small bunch that we're pushing up to Laramie. I'm writing you from Denver and a fella's going to carry it up to the newspaper office up there. Hope you get it. Anyway, if you're there we'll meet. If you're not there, I'll wait. If you left, we'll sell the cows to be shipped out on the new train hauling set-up they got now. But if you're there when we get there, I'm thinking we can push these cows along with the wagon train and sell 'em to the emigrants when you all start running out of fresh food in the desimated parts you got to go through. Follow my thinking? Otherwise, we just push them west with us and we'll have a start once we get out there. Hope this finds you and Sarah Beth well and doing well. I know it's hard, but it's worth it.

Louis

Abe glanced up from the letter in his hands and tried to remember when he'd last seen Louis, in Independence. Always scheming something, this cousin of his. And this didn't seem like a bad plan at all if he made it in time. It could take some of the pressure off of Abe and the hunters, depending on how many head Louis was talking about, and how many made it here to the fort. Of course what mattered was if he could get here in the next couple days. In any case, it sounded like they would be seeing him sometime soon. And now that he'd read the letter, he was glad he felt comfortable to share it with Sarah Beth.

When he returned to the camp, Sarah Beth was already gone for the town. The little girl he'd saved from the river was sitting near their fire pit.

"Well hello, Rebecca, isn't it? What're you doing here, little miss?"

"My mom brought me by to visit your wife, and then she was leaving, but no one would be here, so my mother said that I would stay to watch things until you returned."

"Well, thank you for doing that. It's nice to see you again, you look all better now."

"Yes. I had the chills for quite some time after you saved me from the river, but I'm just fine now."

"How old are you?" Abe sat down on a nail keg he'd been using for a stool since he found it along the trail one day.

"I'm nine years old, but small for my age."

"And are you called Rebecca, or Becky, or anything other?"

"Everyone calls me Rebecca, but once I read a book with a girl named Becky in it. I wish that was my name. But they won't let me change it"

"Well, just between you and me, I'll call you Becky when no one else is around."

"Thank you. I need to be going now. And thank you for saving me."

"I'm glad I could do that. I must tell you I was really afraid I wouldn't have the strength or the position to pull you out of the water"

"But God helped you and you did it. Good day now." She tossed her braids and ran off toward the other camp.

Abe watched her go and thought about how wonderful it was going to be when he and Sarah Beth had children. One like this Becky would do very nicely.

They stayed in the same camp for three days while they made repairs on the wagons, almost every one of which needed something.

Horses were re-shod and the oxen allowed to graze down along the river where they found a good growth of the year's early grasses. Abe checked his animals for soundness and was pleased with the way they'd managed to come through the past several weeks of hard work and travel.

On the first of those days, McFarland told Abe that he was restless to get going before the early summer heat brought snow melt down to fill the rivers they would be crossing, but people seemed to be needing the rest and since the next couple of weeks would be the most difficult of the journey, he was willing to stay on for another two days. Abe told him about Louis and his cattle, but there'd still been no sign of him. McFarland allowed that it would be good to have some beef on the hoof moving along with the train, but said it wasn't worth waiting extra time for, since there was no telling when Louis would actually appear.

Sarah Beth was pleased with the news from Louis, although she did mention that if he came along with them it would be one more limitation on their privacy, but then she added, "There's not all that much privacy to lose when you're in a fish bowl." Abe never heard that saying before and asked her what it meant. She asked him if he'd ever seen fish swimming in a bowl in a store or in someone's house and he said he hadn't. She promised him that once they built their own house she'd get one for him if he promised not to go after the pet fish with a hook and line. He promised and then invited her on a horse ride the following day since their wagon and oxen were ready to go for the next stage of the trip. She smiled and mumbled something about fish jumping out of the fishbowl, then gave him a kiss and said she'd be happy to ride with the man she called her husband.

That next morning broke clear with a slight chill left over from some time earlier in the year. One of the men who'd been on the trail before said it meant a scorcher coming later in the day. Abe and Sarah Beth saddled up. After stopping by their neighbor's wagon to ask them to look after camp, Abe and Sarah Beth trotted out through the livestock area and headed to where rolling hills began rising out of the plain. Before the sun was hardly above the horizon they found themselves galloping down the other side of a long, long hillside until they finally pulled up near a small creek, which wound through willow patches and other brushy vegetation. Near the creek they found a clear space where beaver had used the willows to build a small dam.

The water was backed up a ways, and the horses eased forward to wet their noses and take some water.

Sarah Beth climbed down from her horse and pulled off the bridle so he could graze. Then she pulled off her boots and stockings, sticking one foot into the water and leaning over to check her reflection. "It's not very cold," she said, "and it's so long since I've bathed." She sat at the water's edge and began removing her oversize shirt. When it lay on the ground beside her, she stretched her arms over her head and then loosened her bound-up hair, shaking it down over her shoulders.

Abe was still mounted and from habit he scanned as much of the countryside as he could, thinking that even if you feel safe, it doesn't mean you are. He'd checked everything he could see from the top of the long hill, but as he dismounted he was still looking, now for hoof or boot prints in the soft ground at the water's edge. Then he looked up and saw Sarah Beth as she stood and finished disrobing, and he instantly thought how he was the only man who'd ever seen the full beauty of this woman, at least since she'd become a woman. Him and God, he thought with a smile. Then he, too, set his horse loose and kicked off his boots, sat and removed stockings that were worn to the point of holes appearing at the toes.

Sarah Beth splashed her way out to where the water was a couple of feet deep and lowered herself slowly into the water, face first. She kept her head under as long as she could, knowing Abe was watching her, and that maybe this was the first time he'd seen her completely naked in the daylight. It gave her a sense of pride that she could be under the water and yet still visible to this man she loved. Then she pushed herself up, turning over as she did and sitting up with her breasts being floated by the rippling water. She kept her eyes lowered, but could still see his face by looking out under her lids.

"Come on in," she said sending a splash his way with her hand. "It's actually quite wonderful."

"So are you," he said, pulling his over-shirt above his head.

Then quickly he was standing over her with his hands on the top of her head. She couldn't help thinking that this was like him giving her a blessing, almost a baptism, and she hoped it would bring them all that they both wanted. She reached her hands up to his waist and then drew them slowly down his legs, urging him to his knees with her eyes and touch. As he knelt and leaned against her knees, she reached up and pulled his head down into her kiss. Then, with no more delay, they were laughing and wrestling in the water, rolling over and over, kicking one another and splashing until they had to stop to catch their breath. Abe disentangled himself and began crawling toward the bank, but she was on him in a moment, riding astride his back. He bucked once or twice, then relaxed as she lay down on his back and reached under him to gently rub the muscles of his chest. He slowly rolled over beneath her and with her kneeling on top of him he was able to enter and feel the mystery of this moment in all its fullness and release.

Sarah Beth thrust onto him from above, making small sounds deep in her throat. They were soon spent, collapsing into the water and then slowly crawling out onto the bank. By now the sun, part-way up the sky, was beginning to send its own heat into the earth. They lay there calmly for awhile, breathing deeply and stroking one another with their fingertips.

Abe pushed up on both of his elbows, and said, "First time we've done that since I could use both arms . . . I wonder what the beaver thought?"

Sarah Beth sat up and looked down into his eyes. "Probably wishing they had long legs so they can do like we do."

When they returned to camp there was a message for Abe to report to McFarland's wagon. Abe was hungry, but thought he'd better go right away. When he got there, he saw a stranger seated next to McFarland, and several of the other men listening intently to the man's words.

"Sit, Saunders. This here's Wes Stevens, just rode up from Fort Collins south of here. Says there was a shoot-up between some cavalry and a small band of Indians. They took a couple of soldiers prisoner and sent a message they'd give 'em back for some beef cows and being left alone to return to their camp in the mountains. Now, go on, Mr. Stevens."

"Did you say his name's Saunders? Wouldn't have a cousin named Louis would you?"

"Yes sir, I do."

"Well, you don't know it yet, but you're right in the middle of this. I'm bringing you a message from your cousin. It's his cattle the Injuns want. He and a partner was driving them this way and they got blocked by the war party. The fort commander sent me to get help from Fort Laramie, but your cousin sent word to have you come down and get your share of the cattle before the Injuns take them away from him . . . And I sure could use some water."

One of the men jumped up and brought a small bucket with a dipper.

"How far is it to where he is?" Abe asked.

"He said to tell you, he's sorry he's late to meet up with you, but he's been delayed." The man laughed and took another drink of the water. "I'd say it's not more than thirty miles. Halfway back to where I come here from."

"Well, Abe, what do you want to do?" McFarland asked. "I was about to have us move out tomorrow. We're rested and ready."

"Like I told you, he wrote me he was trying to bring the cattle along to join up with us for when we need fresh meat, up ahead where there might be no buffalo."

"So that makes this the business of our train here. Mr. Stevens is waiting on the colonel over at the fort to see if he can get a troop to ride back with him. Maybe we should send you and some of your patrol. We can wait one more day. If you're not back, we'll start off and you catch up. Sound all right?"

Early the next morning a troop of ten cavalry waited at the edge of camp while Abe and his men saddled up and collected provisions and goodbyes. As Abe hugged Sarah Beth, she began to cry softly and he held her face in his hands and held her slightly away.

"It's my duty and God's will. He will protect me."

"I know," she said, "but protect you how? Here take this," she held out a small medallion, a floral design stamped into a golden circle. "It was my mother's. She'll be watching out for you too, in case God gets too busy." And then she smiled brightly, wiping away the few tears that had escaped the corners of her deep and loving eyes.

"Thank you, dearest. And I'll take good care of it." He kissed her once and turned to mount his horse, calling out as he did, "Mount up! Can't keep the army waiting."

As the men moved out, the women gave a cheer and began returning to their camps. Sarah Beth fell in with Norma and they held each other's hands as they walked briskly back to their camps and their chores. Norma was beginning to show some growth around the middle and Sarah Beth patted the rounded belly.

"Coming along," Sarah Beth said.

"Yes, when Abe came by last night to talk with Guy, he also noticed and said it was a blessing for the whole caravan to be escorting a new life to the frontier. He's so poetic, don't you think?"

"Yes, sometimes, and other times he's all down to business . . . Well, here we are, I have more to do to be ready to move out. We unpacked and repacked almost everything"

"I know what you mean."

It was actually about forty miles of hard riding to the site of the stand-off. They made camp at dusk, when they were most of the way there. They were up and on their way again before dawn. The soldiers kept to themselves, and so did the wagon train men. Abe and the lieutenant in charge held a brief meeting to coordinate their different signals and to discuss command roles and strategy. It seemed the cattle were bunched in a small canyon along with Louis and his partners, and that the Indians held positions above them and across the mouth of the enclosure. It was a simple natural trap, according to the reports from the army scouts, but there was still no good estimate of the number of Indians.

It was early afternoon when the lieutenant pulled up his horse at the top of a rise and raised his arm in a signal to halt. Abe walked Bird up beside him and looked down at the open ground below. A small creek wound through the land, brush and cottonwoods growing along its path. The lieutenant took out his field glasses and scanned the area. Suddenly his arm shot out as he pointed to movement down near an outcropping of rock. A figure was moving several horses back into the sheltered area by the creek.

"They're down there somewhere. Probably their spare mounts," he said to Abe. Just then they heard a strange warbling whoop from another bit of high ground across from them and they watched as a lone rider charged down the slope on his horse.

"They'll come out and face us now," the lieutenant said. He turned and called for the flag carrier who immediately rode up beside him. "Put the white one on, below our flag," he said, as he handed the glasses to Abe. "I think we'd best try and talk with them first.'

Abe watched closely in the area where the rider disappeared. He also swept the glasses over the entrance to the canyon, looking for any sign of cattle or his cousin.

The lieutenant took the flag staff and turned to Abe, "Coming with me?" Then he called for another soldier to come along. "Man knows signs," he said, and the three of them kicked their horses into motion. About a dozen Indians appeared at the edge of the wooded area and rode slowly in a circle. The lieutenant stopped about a hundred yards away from them and held up his arm that wasn't holding the flagstaff. "Show them your hands aren't holding guns," he said. Then he moved his horse slowly forward. "Be ready to run, they've already captured those men and might try for us."

One of the Indians separated from the rest of the bunch and came slowly toward them. He stopped halfway and raised his hand in greeting. He made signs which the soldier translated. "Says they have us outnumbered. More men and more guns than we have. Wants to know what we want."

"Tell him we want our men returned. Now."

More signs back and forth. "Says he let them go already, on foot."

"Tell him I don't believe him. Ask him what he wants."

"Says he only wants half of the cattle to feed his women and children, Then everybody go back where they came from, back where they belong. He says he loves the white man, but his families are hungry. White man scared away all the buffalo with their guns."

"Tell him those cattle are for our families, not for his."

More signs.

The Indian burst out laughing. More signs. "He says he lied about the soldiers, and they will have to eat them if they don't get any cattle."

Abe leaned over and spoke softly to the lieutenant. "I don't think my cousin will go along for half. Offer him a fourth of the herd and I think I can get Louis to agree."

"Go ahead," the lieutenant said. "Offer one-fourth." The soldier held up one finger of one hand and three on the other.

"He says then they only eat one soldier." The Indian laughed again. Suddenly he slapped his horse and came closer.

"Watch him," the lieutenant said.

Now the Indian pointed at Abe and at his horse. Then he touched one of his own horse's ears. Then he pointed back at Abe's horse and made a motion as if using a knife and then touched his horse's ear again.

More signs. "He says he knows this horse, the one you're on."

Now the Indian grabbed his left hand and shook it with his right. He shouted something and kept shaking the hand and then pointing at Abe's horse.

"Something about his hand and the horse. I don't get it."

Abe reached forward and touched Bird's ear where there was a notch cut from it. As Lefty had told him, it was an Indian way of branding horses,. He turned to the lieutenant and said, "I got this horse from an Indian who is called Lefty."

The lieutenant turned to the sign-maker soldier, "Ask him if he's talking about an Indian named Lefty?"

The Indian nodded his head vigorously and made quick signs.

"He says that was once his brother's horse. It was sold to another Indian, a left-handed Indian."

"This is very strange," Abe said. "I got the horse back in St. Joe. There was an Indian camp outside town. Man gave me the horse. He's been a guide for some of the trains on the trail." He turned to the soldier. "Ask him the horse's name."

The Indian made a series of quick gestures with his hand.

"He makes the sign for a small bird," the soldier said. "Don't know what kind."

Abe smiled and said to the lieutenant, "He said he'd help me out by giving me this horse named Hummingbird. It's almost too uncanny to believe." Then he reached down into his saddlebag and pulled out the hide-wrapped hatchet Lefty had given him. He slowly unwrapped it and held it up by the head so as not to be threatening with it. "Soldier, tell the Indian this is a good horse, tell him that we trust him because of the man who gave me the horse. And that he also gave this to me," he said as he held it out toward the Indian. "If that's all right with you, sir," he said to the officer.

"All right, go ahead, soldier."

The Indian wouldn't take the hatchet from Abe, but he signed back with both hands held palms up toward Abe, shaking his head, yes, and then more signs. The soldier interpreted, "He trusts any man that receives a horse from the left-handed one." Then he held up one finger on one hand and two on the other. "He'll trade our men for one-third of the cattle," the soldier said.

"Well," said the lieutenant, "this is almost too good to pass up, Saunders. See if he'll let you ride into the canyon with two of our men and talk to your cousin. The army will compensate him for the cattle he's giving up when we get back to the fort."

It was agreed to give Abe and the two men safe passage into the canyon. When they rode in, they immediately saw the cattle bunched up against one of the rock walls that surrounded the small enclosure. Two mounted men were keeping them there.

"Louis," Abe called out, as he waved his hat in the air. "Louis, it's me, Abe."

One of the men rode toward him, handgun drawn. "Is it really you?" he shouted as he came near.

"Yes it's really me," Abe hollered back. The two of them jumped down off their horses and ran toward each other.

"Damn, I'm glad to see you." They embraced briefly. "Indians still out there?"

"They are. But they'll let you go for a third of the cattle."

"What? That's impossible! Them cattle is all I've got to my name. Worked hard for them. Gonna sell 'em to your wagon train folks."

"Can't help it," Abe said. "You're in a bad situation and that's the best we could do. They started out asking for half."

"My partner isn't gonna like it at all. You remember him, Mad Mountain. He'll just get mad, and . . ."

"It's OK, the army will pay for the cattle."

Right then the mouth of the canyon was filled with Indians and cavalry, as well as Abe's men. They were still in separate groups, but they were all riding abreast with guns held at ready.

"Guess you're right, doesn't look like we've got much choice," Louis said. They mounted and with the other rider they moved to cut out twenty of the animals and push them toward the group of riders. The Indians circled the cattle, and with much whooping and shouting they drove them out and away from the canyon. The captive soldiers emerged from rocks in the canyon wall and scrambled down.

By afternoon, the soldiers and the wagon train men had the remaining cattle on the move back toward the caravan. They sent a messenger to McFarland, and then camped that night with several riders taking turns watching over the animals while the rest slept. By dawn they were on their way and by next nightfall the soldiers turned off ahead of the rest, going back to their fort. The lieutenant promised to send a courier after the wagon train with the money for the ransomed cows. Abe and his men kept a lookout for trouble as they moved along after the train, but they encountered none. Abe told Louis about the Indian and his horse and what a strange coincidence it had been. When Louis asked him more about it, he just said it was a case of God and his Indian friend working together to protect them.

"When we get a chance, we must give thanks," Abe said.

CHAPTER ELEVEN

The Big Empty

It had been two weeks since they left Fort Laramie, and the countryside was more empty and barren than any other along the journey since leaving St. Joseph. Sarah Beth and Norma were down washing clothes beside a small creek that was barely flowing toward the river. Apparently there'd been some problems with one of the wagon master's supply wagons and it was necessary to stop while it was repaired. A cookout for the whole train, using three of Louis's animals, was planned for the evening.

Norma held up a dress and then pushed it down into the water. "That was one of my favorites. Wore it all the time. Guess I'll just pack it away now," she laughed as she struggled to bend toward the water from her kneeling position on the grassy bank.

"Abe said this is probably the last almost clean free flowing water we'll see until we get to the Green River country. The main river's going to be mostly mud. "

"And how far is that?"

"I don't know, but far enough that the men are all filling water barrels upstream from here and lashing them to the wagons." Sarah Beth gathered her long loose hair and knotted it out of the way behind her head.

Other women were scattered along the creek, all busily scrubbing clothing on the small boulders that lined the channel. It was easy to distinguish the Mormon women by their heavy dark dresses.

"I don't think I could put up with those dresses all the time," Sarah Beth said in a low voice. "I'd probably get so hot inside one, I'd just shuck it off, no matter who was looking."

"Oh my," Norma said, covering her mouth. "You are a shocker, aren't you?"

"Not really, I just think shocking things sometimes. I'd certainly never do anything like that, because I don't want to embarrass Abe. He's so level-headed."

"Guy gets angry once in awhile. Oh, I don't mean to where he hurts anyone like some of these brawlers we have along with us, but it's more that he gets sullen and fuming. I don't think I've ever seen Abe upset, even when he was rescuing our wagon."

"He holds it in mostly, I think. He did tell me he was a little impatient with some of the folks on the train who keep trying to do things their own way."

"That would be Guy, wouldn't it?"

"No, he likes Guy, and he thinks he learned his lesson . . . How does Guy like the idea that there's a baby's coming?"

"He's all right with it, at least he says he is, but sometimes I think he worries about the added difficulty. Coming at this time."

They gathered the clothing that was bundled up around them. As they prepared to start back to their wagons, Sarah Beth said, "Sometimes I get the feeling that Abe is a little envious. I know he really wants children, but he says it's not the time for it, that it's better to wait unless God makes it happen sooner." She fit the last of the wet laundry into her basket.

"Well, I don't think ours was up to God." Again Norma covered her mouth with her hand, stifling a sudden laugh.

"What do you mean?"

"Oh nothing, just that Guy was all over me before we joined the train. Kept saying we wouldn't have any opportunity once we were all crowded together, what with the Mormons too."

"Well," Sarah Beth said in a hushed voice, "they certainly seem to have plenty of children, even when it's only one man for several wives." They exchanged smiles.

Norma finished packing her basket of laundry and leaned over to whisper, "Imagine if it was the other way around, one woman to several men," she again tried not to laugh, "I think I'd become one of them, if that was the case." And now she couldn't hold it back and giggled quite loudly, loud enough that some of the other women looked their way.

"Shhh, they're looking at us," Sarah Beth said, also trying to hold back her laughter. "I can't believe you said that. And you thought I was a shocker."

"Well, I didn't mean anything by it, just a wild thought."

They picked up their baskets and headed back toward the wagons. Suddenly Sarah Beth was quiet and serious, and said, "I think part of it is the privacy thing, we're both very shy. But I know he's thinking about it, just from the way he looks at me, and from the way he's always so happy to see you."

"Well, ask him. Ask him what he's thinking."

"I couldn't do that." She shifted her basket and turned to walk back toward the camp. "After all," she smiled broadly, "we hardly know each other."

A few days later, they reached the South Fork of the Platte River by evening. McFarland sent out word that they would hold over the next day for a rest where they could feed the animals along a small dry riverbed, where grass grew amid the willow patches. Abe helped Louis and his partner push the shrinking cattle herd some ways ahead so they could feed without using up what was needed for the draft animals of the caravan. It was dark when he returned and Sarah Beth had already turned their oxen out with the rest of the animals and staked Morning alongside the wagon. She was cooking a fine-smelling stew made from the neck bones of one of the cattle they'd feasted on. They'd been cooking a little of the leftovers every day.

"How's everything?" Abe asked as he lowered himself to sit near the small fire.

"Good enough, I suppose," his wife replied quietly. "Did you put Bird near my horse?"

"Pretty close."

"There are two women getting near-term to deliver their babies, and I'm not sure if McFarland will stop the wagons for them to be born."

"Any idea when?" Abe was struggling to pull off his boots and she bent over to help. Then she seemed to cheer up and pushed him over onto his back. He grabbed her and pulled her down on top of him and they wrestled on the ground for a few moments. From the nearby camps came some shouts and cheers, and the two of them immediately separated while still lying on the ground.

"No privacy around here," Abe said loudly.

One of his neighbors hollered back, "Go ahead, we promise not to watch." And then there was laughter from the camps nearest them.

Just then the stew began to bubble over and Sarah Beth jumped up to tend it, brushing herself off as best she could. She was wearing a cotton skirt she'd sewed up the middle to make pant legs for herself. She called it a compromise. The first time she'd worn the old work pants she liked there had been some mixed comments from other ladies as to how it wasn't proper, and Norma had informed her that some of them were quite upset. Sarah Beth's answer had been that those women ought to put on some pants sometime and see how comfortable and practical they were out here on the trail. Still, she hadn't worn men's clothing again except when she would ride off with Abe, and now around the camp she was settling for this kind of outfit she made for herself out of her most durable skirts. After all, she thought as she rescued the stew, what would have happened if she'd been in a skirt a few minutes ago, rolling around on the ground with Abe? She smiled as she thought of the shock it would cause if her dress flew up over her head while that was going on. And of course the whole incident just brought home how little privacy they had, for anything.

The next morning George, a young man responsible for watching the draft animals, rode into their camp. He jumped down and removed his hat as Abe stood up to greet him.

"Bad news, Mr. Saunders. Looks like one of your animals got snake bit, went down and we don't think he's gonna make it. Breathing real hard and all."

"I'll be right with you. How far away?"

"Well, some of 'em went off on their own during the night, so it's a ways."

"I'll get my horse."

Sarah Beth was standing near her fire holding out a cup of coffee to him. He waved it away and grabbed his saddle and bridle and hurried to catch and rig his horse.

When he and the young man got to where the animal was laid out, two other men were there. One from his patrol and the other a stranger to Abe, one of the Mormons. The stranger held out his hand and introduced himself a Dr. Ferguson, animal doctor from Illinois.

"See over there by those rocks," he said. "The men saw five or six snakes heading into those holes this morning. An ox this size can usually take one or even two bites and recover, but from the look of that swelling on both front legs, I'd say he stepped into the batch of them and was bit several times. I'm sorry."

Abe knelt down beside the animal and looked into its eyes. It was the one called Luke and he'd been a favorite of both Abe and Sarah Beth. "How soon can we know for sure there's no chance?" he said.

"I'd say there's none, but I've not worked out this far west before, so I couldn't be sure."

Just then the animal heaved itself into what was almost a sitting position, struggling to get up, and then collapsed back with a long, loud gasping that got more and more irregular. "Might be your answer right there," the Doctor said.

"Yeah," Abe said, and then asked George for the use of his sidearm. He mumbled a brief prayer, then placed the gun to the ox's head and fired the shot. The animal struggled some more and slowly subsided into a quivering carcass. "Any idea about the meat? Can it be eaten, or is it poisoned?"

"I really don't know. Maybe some of the veterans of the trail would know, having had more experience with this kind of thing."

"Right, I'll ride back and ask McFarland. Meantime, George, if you could keep an eye on it 'till I get back, just to keep any wolves away."

"Yes sir."

When he approached the wagon master and told him what had happened, he was assured that if the meat was cooked good, no one ever got sick from the venom in the carcass.

"But you'll run sideways with only three in the harness," McFarland commented.

"Yeah, but I think we're too heavy for just two to pull."

"Well damn, aren't you the lucky man with your bad luck. Just up ahead, not more than forty miles, there's a livestock man. Sells to folks on the trail just like you. Been doing it for more than twenty-five years I know of. Name's Bradford. Him and his son got some pens and corrals up ahead, off the trail a couple miles, and if I know them, they'll be waiting for us. You're not the only one on this train needs a new animal or two."

"Reckon I'll just re-fit the harness and put the single ox in the lead until we get there, then. You're right about that being good fortune, but I'd like to think God had a bit to do with letting me get this far with no trouble at all."

"You and the Mormons. Hell, I can just relax and be my old sinner self and we'll get by just fine with all you kinda folks along."

Abe smiled, "I'll take a couple men and we should be back with the meat in a few hours."

"Don't let the wolves know about it. Or Indians neither," McFarland waved him away.

Abe went back to his own camp to share the news with Sarah Beth. He knew she'd be upset, and he was right, but as soon as he mentioned that they'd been fortunate enough to have this happen in a place where there'd be a replacement animal, she brightened up.

"Good," she said, "I guess we'll have to call him Peter so he'll fit in with the other disciples."

Abe gave her a good long kiss, and then set about gathering some knives and a jug of water for the job. "Be back soon," he said as he mounted Bird and turned away, calling for Guy to come with him if he could get away.

The Bradford stockyards were set back against a bluff that rose sharply out of the sagebrush plain. A spring flowed out of the side of the hill and the sound of animals lowing and bawling met Abe's ears when he and several other men approached, driving a batch of the weakest animals from the train. They'd been told that this Carlton Bradford had built up quite a business trading his healthy stock for the weak and worn out animals from the people on the trail, and from the looks of the stock in the pens, he was doing quite well when it came to recovering the health of the castoffs he took in.

As they drew close to the first pen, a young man rode quickly up beside Abe and the other man in the lead. "I'm Brace Bradford, You fellas must be from the Trail."

"Yes, we're from the Trail, for sure," Abe said, smiling.

"My Dad's not here right now, but I'll work with you."

"Well, thanks. Sure glad you're here. Don't know what we would've done."

"Yeah, gets worse from here on. You'll need your animals to be in as good a shape as you can. Who's your wagon master? McFarland, isn't it?"

"It is," Abe said. "He spoke highly of your father."

"We've done him some favors over the years. Probably why he keeps sending folks to us. That and because there's no one else out here . . ." He laughed and pointed to an empty pen, "Let's put yours in there and see what you've got and what you need."

Within a couple of hours, the men who'd come with Abe, representing both themselves and others, were satisfied with the deals they'd made and were preparing to drive their purchases back to rejoin the train. Abe had selected a large reddish steer, partly on young Bradford's recommendation and partly from his own instinct. Even though he was thinking it would stand out among the other three in their team, them all being black and white.

When they'd sorted the animals and arrived at deals, they paid, and were getting ready to release the newly purchased animals from the pens to drive them back to the wagon train. A somewhat older man rode up, and tipped his hat. "I'm Carlton Bradford. Glad to serve you fellas. Hope you'll be satisfied."

"Yes sir, pleased to meet you, sir," Abe said. "We tried your competition, but you seem to have the best livestock around these parts."

Bradford smiled and said, "Guess you're right. Only competition I got is the army and they buy more from me than the trains do. Well, hey, you got any time to visit, or you headed right back?"

"I think we'd best be going. What's the best way back to the trail, seeing as how they've been on the move since we left them?"

"Suppose you'd want to go around the ridgeline over that way. Brace," he said to his son,

"why don't you ride with them a ways in the right direction." He drew his horse up close to Abe and reached out to shake hands. "Don't get many visitors out this way."

"Where's your ranch?" Abe asked.

"Bout twenty miles up that way, laid in under those hills with the forest on'em. Just didn't see how I could live without some trees to look at."

"I understand." Abe said. "Pretty barren out here."

"Go on Brace, get'em going. And take this man's animal with the rest. He can catch up . . . that is," he turned to Abe, "if you don't mind keepin' company with me for a bit."

"That'd be fine." Abe's curiosity and what he'd learned about accepting opportunities urged his mind to take up the invitation, especially since Bird seemed anxious to run all the way back to the wagons.

"Come, let's sit in that shade." He pointed to the one lonely tree in the whole area. "Picked this spot because of that tree."

They led their horses over to the small patch of shade beside the tree and Bradford offered his guest a seat on a boulder where he could lean back against the trunk. He himself rolled a small log into the shaded area.

"Thanks for stayin' around," the older man said when they'd settled. "Like I said, don't get much company out here, and when we do they're almost always in a hurry."

Abe stayed quiet, nodding his agreement. Bradford had a keen set of eyes looking him over and he tried not to shift under the man's gaze.

"I see something in you, son. That's why I asked you to stay. Mind if I ask your name? I'm Carlton Bradford if you didn't know by now."

"Abe, that is, Abraham Saunders."

"You're carrying a big name. I'm a Bible man myself and that name means a lot to me. I'd say you're from a little ways south of north, from your speech."

"Yessir. Can't help that, I guess.'

"Don't worry about it. Wife and I are from Missouri ourselves. Missed the War, though, being out here and all."

"Yes sir."

"Mind my questions? I mean, I'll be glad to answer yours if you have'em."

"No, I don't mind. How long you been out here?"

"Dropped off the Old Trail in '49. Oxen wore out and there wasn't no Bradford stockyard in those days," he smiled. "My wife had it in her mind to stop here if she couldn't take all her stuff with her and we knew she had to let the heavy things go or quit. Cast iron stove woulda had to go, but here we're still using it. You married?"

"Yes sir."

"Name wouldn't be Sarah, would it?"

"Yes, how'd you know?"

"Told you I'm a Bible man, always looking for the similarities between then and now. You'd be surprised how many there are. Once something happens for the first time, it's bound to happen again, probably many times, even though it don't always look the same. That's what makes the Bible so useful, to me at least. Besides, I told you I see something in you. Your wife, I imagine she's young and pretty."

"So they say. And I've always thought so." He paused as a hawk screeched above, circling and diving near the corrals. "But I'm inclined to favor her anyway."

"Well, she should be, because that's one of the things I see. I'm not trying to intrude on you here, and I ain't no prophet, but I've been known to see things coming."

"Yes sir, it kind of shows in your eyes."

"Maybe so. Now, about you. I can see from the way you are with your men. You been an in-charge man before, even at your age. Comes natural to some men. Be careful, it brings jealousy every bit as much as respect. They come together at a man. So, where you headed?"

"Like to think we could settle in a place called Jordan Valley, Oregon territory."

"I like the sound of that. Bible sounding. I heard about it. Kind of rough out there, once gold was found. There's never enough of it, and the fightin' starts. But it might be good country for a young man to settle. Heard it's got good grass. Bible says 'He built towers in the desert, and digged many wells: for he had much cattle, both in the low country, and in the plains.' We can claim that promise, young man, it's what I'm doing here, 'and He provided Hezekiah flocks and herds in abundance.' It's happening, slow but surely."

"Well, I surely hope so. I've heard there's not much good land left further west, over the mountains. Mostly taken since the Homestead Act."

"Ahhh, Mr. Lincoln's gift to the veterans of his war. Well, I'd say you shouldn't try and make it there this year. Be too hard to start from nothing and be ready for that kind of winter. Best to find a place to hold over in Utah, except for the Mormons."

"The Mormons?"

"Well, you're travelling with them, aren't you? They're not the kind to provide a helping hand to their non-Mormon neighbors. And they're always after new wives, especially pretty ones. Not to mention you being a Southerner. You did fight some didn't you? Got a military look to you and probably got the wounded elbow that way."

"Yes sir." Abe was feeling more and more comfortable with the friendliness of the other man, in spite of his somewhat prying questions. At the same, it made him a little anxious to have so much known about himself without him even having to tell it.

"Well, be advised, those guys'll try to take your wife before they'll take your horse. Same time, if they like you they'll allow you to be around in case they need something from you. I only bring it up because your namesake had to give up his wife to Abimelech, the king of a strange country he was passing through. He said she was his sister. Course it worked out all right when God scared the king and told him to 'restore the man his wife, for he is a prophet, and he shall pray for thee and thou shalt live.' So the king gave her back along with sheep and oxen and servants. And then he let them stay in his land wherever they chose to. If you don't believe me, look it up, Genesis, Chapter Twenty. Now, I'm not saying that's what's going to happen to you, just 'cause you dropped by and bought a red steer from me and I can see what a fine young man you are, and I can see you for what you are. But I'm warning you that the Bible don't just happen once and be all done with it. Happens over and over again, different but the same. Now enough of that. 'Less you have something else to say about it."

"Well, not sure what to say, but I guess I'm grateful for your words. And I appreciate the chance to meet a real Bible man clear out here. Haven't had much time to talk about faith and such on the trail."

"Like you say, 'faith and such.' That's what I see in you, son. I see the kind of faith of a Jacob who became Israel, the faith of the founding fathers which is a questioning faith, and a working it out faith, and if I'm wrong about you, you'll find out before I do, but the last thing I'll say is that I knew you were comin' and I just had to wait for you. Now here you are." He stood up a little stiffly. "Better get you on your way before I make you lose your fellas and your animal. You'll be able to see my son's dust cloud coming back at you as you go, he don't ever ride slow if he doesn't have to. He'll point you the way to catch up to your men and the Trail."

Abe stood up and tried to find some words of thanks, but Bradford cut him off and held out a hand to shake. "Give my best to Sarah," he said as they shook. He mounted his horse, stopped a few paces away and raised his hand in blessing, then rode off without looking back.

Abe took one last look around the stockyard, admiring the efficiency of the bent-wood fencing and obvious care given the animals within. Beyond the corrals was a large area where other animals grazed. Like the man said, "herds in abundance." Abe mounted, tapped Bird on the neck and gave her loose reins; she broke into a smooth canter. He doubted that the others would be very far ahead of him. They'd have to move slowly with the new stock. He kept his eyes out for the dust cloud that would be the man's son coming his way, and he settled himself into the ride, trying to sort through the conversation he'd just had with Mr. Bradford.

As he rode through the sagebrush, he kept turning things over in his mind, like the part about Sarah Beth being at some kind of risk, and him as well. So far he'd seen nothing resembling that kind of threat on the trail with the Mormons, but he was acutely aware of the numbers of women clustered around every one of those men's camps. It made him wonder where all the other men were, as there didn't seem to be a lot of bachelors along on the caravan. Maybe they were all out west already. As for him and Sarah Beth, it was already somewhat risky being in this company as Southerners, and while he'd worked on his speech patterns in order to sound neutral if not northern, his wife still sounded very much like the Virginian she'd grown up as. He knew there'd been Mormon battle groups fighting for the Union, men from as far away as Utah even, but he didn't recall any on the Confederate side, although there were rumors of a few small contingents.

It wasn't long before he saw the son's dust up ahead, and within a few minutes, the man became visible to his eyes. He pulled up and waited. When the young man came alongside him, it was with a holler and a smile, "Whoop-whoop . . . hey, how is it out here all alone? That's the way I like it best myself."

"It's good. My horse appreciates the chance to open up and move along."

"Yep, most horses would prefer either runnin' or walkin' and nothin' in between. So my Dad talked to you, did he have anything good to say?"

"Yes, he did."

"Bet he went Bible on you. He's kind of bent that way, to a fault, I'd say. Did he make any sense?"

"Some. He's done a lot out here, and he gives God a great deal of the credit."

"That's fine, but without me and a couple others working all the time, year round, God hadn't done much with this land before we got here. Some call it the Big Empty. I just call it Happy Hell."

"That bad?"

"No, that good. Our whole lives are hell in my mind, so having it as good as we do, makes it a happy one. I'm Brace, by the way. Didn't get your name."

"Abe, Abraham."

"He must've liked that. Did he ask if you're married?"

"Yes. And I am."

"My mother makes him ask every young man he meets that. See, we got two girls at home, both younger than me, and she's worried for them, having no young men out here."

"Laramie's not so far back."

"She don't want them to leave our place, needs their help. Wants them to find young men to bring into home to help out. I doubt we'll see it. No more likely than I find a girl out hiding in this sagebrush. Anyway, good talking to you. Come back anytime." Then he whooped again, jabbed his heels into his horse's sides, and was off toward the distant ridgeline to the north.

Once again Abe was left with many new thoughts rolling through his mind. He urged Bird back into a loping run and tried not to think about much at all. There would be time enough for that later, out along the emptiness of the trail's meandering route.

Within a few days, the new red ox had worked into their team quite well, although the harness needed enlarging for him. He was exceptionally docile for an animal who'd been described to Abe as mostly wild but very strong. As the train moved along, the desert and its winds became more and more of a challenge. They headed into rolling craggy hills with an extremely rocky road surface. For the first time, Sarah Beth became conscious of children crying during the long hot days. Many were forced to leave the wagons and move on foot, as every pound of weight seemed to affect the draft animals. The water they were packing with them also added to the weight of each wagon and when some of the animals began stopping in their traces rather than continue, McFarland gave the order to reduce the loads in each wagon enough to have only half of each team pulling at a time. Many resisted this order, but when they tried to move ahead with the rest of the train, they could not and had to recognize the necessity. Even so, the half-teams made progress much slower and the constant dust that filled the air seemed like the curse of a mean-spirited deity, at least according to some of the emigrants.

Sarah Beth and Abe walked alongside their wagon like the rest of the folks, but with the strength of the new steer and the relative health of their other three animals, they hadn't needed to begin discarding stoves or anvils or other weighty objects, as so many of their companions did. While these things would help make life tolerable and would be of use at their destinations, there was no sense holding onto many of these possessions if they prevented the animals from being able to pull the wagon up the long, heat-parched hills. The days passed slowly, with the dreadful heat and dust combining to create a general sense of futility and despair among the members of the wagon train.

The Mormons held prayer meetings and singing times as dark fell on their exhausted folks, but, by and large, the only real hope was provided by the wagon master McFarland, who would daily ride up and down the train on his great horse, yelling encouragement and reminding everyone that this was no worse than it had been for everyone on every train he'd ever commanded. Privately, he admitted to a few of his men and to Abe, that this trip was a pretty bad one, one of the worst he'd seen, but he held out the promise that Rock Springs would signal the end of the Big Empty and the beginning of the last stage of the trail into Utah, closing in on the destination of so many of the folks.

A kind of madness sets into the brain when the wind never stops and the dust fills your eyes and every other opening. Some of the people on the train went silent, some talked only to themselves, while others yelled or sang to keep their spirits up. After a week that seemed like a year, they were told they were nearing Rock Springs and there had been a recent rain in the area.

Sarah Beth was becoming more and more concerned for the women coming due. She'd been able to talk with a Mormon midwife who assured her the Mormons would be taking care of their own. This left Sarah Beth responsible only for Norma and Gloria, the two expectant mothers in their part of the train. If all went well, the train would reach somewhere in Utah with civilized medical care by the time they were ready to deliver. Gloria was a very small woman, originally from Tennessee country, but she already had two children of her own, and could have this one at any time.

"How are you feeling?" Abe asked his wife on the evening before they were supposed to make it to a camping spot near the outpost of Rock Springs.

"I've never been so tired in my life," she said softly. "Sometimes during the past week, I just wanted to give up. Abe, am I weak? I want to be strong, but I feel so helpless these days."

Abe sat down beside her and gently rested her head in his lap. He traced the shape of her face and tucked some stray hairs behind her ears. "You're the strongest woman I know. Think how you've been helping the others, carrying their water for them, taking care of their children so they could rest in the evenings, all on top of taking care of me and helping with our animals. No wonder you're tired. You never seem to stop."

"But I feel like nothing makes a difference out here. The wind and the dust, even the stars at night seem to be laughing at us. And I can't help worrying about my father. We haven't been able to hear anything."

"The time is coming when we shall rest, and not much longer now, when we shall rest. And then we'll have to decide whether to push on for the Oregon land or spend the winter in Utah. That man I told you about, Bradford, he advised against arriving somewhere too late to get settled for the winter. He said we'd be better off if we could find a place to stay over and make a temporary home. And I've been thinking about that a lot."

"Oh yes, please, let's stop somewhere, even if we have to live in our wagon. I just want to stop hearing the screeching sound of the wheels and the hard, hoarse breathing of the team. They're so willing, but they've got to be even more tired than I am."

"We'll have to see. We need to do some asking around about good places to stay over, and good people as well. I'm a bit concerned about us being in all-Mormon country once we get out of this terrible desert."

"I think my father would say something about the forty years in the wilderness, and how we've hardly had to put up with forty days."

"More like 100 days," Abe said, lightly touching her lips with his finger. "Now, I have a surprise for you."

She sat up and looked at him, "You don't need to try to make me happy, Abe. I'm so happy with you—you're why I can do all this."

"Well, it's not really from me. Lefty's youngest wife gave it to me to give to you when the time came we were nearing her country. It's a bit early, and I was going to wait until we got closer, but I think you need something to lift your spirits." He reached into one of his shirt pockets and pulled out a small piece of folded leather and handed it to her. "She said it would help protect you when you reached their country and passed among her people. I haven't seen what it is yet. Go ahead."

She held the small packet between both her hands. "Is it dangerous there," she asked. "I mean, I hate to worry, but if she thinks I need protection . . ."

"Open it."

She carefully unfolded the leather wrapping and stared silently at the object in her hand. It was a necklace with a delicate braided thong. A pendant of shell and stone hung from it. She held it up and the setting sun caught the stone with its light and there was a quick bright flash of orange from the reflection.

"She said it's for a Dreamer. Dreamers are greatly honored among her people and when I told her about you, she somehow knew to ask about your dreams. I didn't tell her any of them, but I did say that you often have dreams of people coming to you with questions, and of those who are seeking help. I did tell her that you feel sorry you cannot help them in your dreams. She said this will help you to help others, not in your sleep but in your waking life. She said she thought you must be a Dreamer and that someday you will be able to dream help for others when they ask you for it. Then Lefty told me all of that is true, but that you will always have to help yourself because no one who is not a Dreamer knows how to help a Dreamer. Then he laughed and said 'not even her husband,' but his woman said that wasn't true because the Dreamer and their mate are like one person, and they help one another without even realizing it."

"Abe, I believe it's true, and some time I will tell you how you have helped me without even knowing it."

"Well, enough of this, what's cooking in that pot?"

"Wait, should I wear it or put it away?"

"I think the safest place for it is around your neck. This whole time I've been afraid I would lose it, but I didn't, thank God. So yes— wear it from now on."

Rock Springs was little more than a village of shanties, mostly canvas shelters and a few wooden buildings in different stages of partial completion. The sudden influx of money and folks brought on by the recent construction of the railroad passing nearby was only just beginning to have an impact on the town. Coal was the biggest business in the area now, as the railroad would need it all along the line, and Rock Springs had one of the better sources. Once the coal was mined, it could be transported to any section of line where it was needed, back to Fort Laramie and even further west, down into Utah territory.

The wagon train made camp to the north of town. There wasn't a lot of forage for the animals, but the open space would allow for some dispersal without the herders losing track of any stock. Rock Spring's closest thing to a mercantile was a large tent-like structure opened for business by an enterprising pair of brothers known as the Frazier twins. It was here that the wagon folks crowded to push and shove for turns to make purchases on their first day after arrival.

Sarah Beth and Abe stood in a small group with some of their friends while they waited their turn. There was little worry about a scarcity of goods, because word had it that the twins kept fully restocked with weekly cargoes coming in for the rail line work. Whereas, as McFarland informed them, before the building of the railroad there had been little chance of any new supplies until the train had reached the Salt Lake basin.

"Where's Louis?" Sarah Beth asked as they stood waiting in the line.

"Don't know, haven't seen him since we got here. Could be out with his cattle, or I heard there's a makeshift saloon here. I hope he can stay out of trouble."

"Me too. I thought we'd see more of him."

"He's been mostly staying out with the cattle. Says he doesn't much like crowds unless they're in a town."

Sarah Beth touched Abe's arm and then said, "I was thinking that we won't have it so hard for the rest of the trip and it might be nice to get some additional fabric I could sew on while I'm riding on the wagon."

"And what would you sew?" he asked.

"Oh, you know, just things we need. And I could patch the things that are wearing out and can't be replaced."

"Well, that would be good." He smiled. "Maybe you could make yourself a new pair of pants. I don't have any more to give to you, mine are all wore out."

Sarah Beth put her hand on his shoulder and spun him around to face her. "Are you making fun of me, Mr. Saunders? Because, if you are, I'm not liable to make anything at all for you, just pretty dresses and curtains for me."

"Shh! There's people can hear you," he whispered. "Besides, you know I think you're the best looking woman that ever pulled on a pair of pants."

Just then they heard the sound of a shot from the central part of the small town, then several more. Abe pulled away from Sarah Beth, looked around and called out the names of two of his men standing nearby. Over his shoulder he said to her, "Get whatever you need. Have to make sure none of our folks are in trouble."

When he reached the center of the built-up area, he saw a small crowd gathered in the street. Louis was one of them and he held his gun pointed down at a man on the ground. His partner Mad Mountain held his gun pointed at the crowd. There were also two strange looking persons cowering near the entrance to a storefront. It took Abe a few seconds to realize that he was looking at the first two Chinamen he'd ever seen in his life.

"What's going on here, Louis?"

"Kinda hard to explain, Cuz. This here ruffian was inside when me and Mad Mountain stopped by for a breakfast drink. Lo, and behold, these two Chinee come into the place and started sweeping the dirt floor. This one hollered at'em and threatened to run them out. They backed out the door and next thing I knew him and his partner were shooting at these fellas' feet and hollerin' at them to do a Chinee dance."

The man on the ground struggled to get up and Louis kicked him back down. The man was mumbling something about how he wasn't about to sit in a place that had that slit-eye kind coming in and he had a right to his privacy when he was drinking and paying for it, or something like that.

Abe looked more closely at him and recognized him as one of the more troublesome men from the train, always complaining about something or other. "Best let him up," he said to Louis. "We'll let McFarland deal with him, and I doubt it will be pretty. Get up fella and get back to your camp. Don't want to see you in here again. You'll be lucky to be allowed to stay with the train." Then, as an afterthought, he said, "Better think of your family, Mister. They might not be happy to have to go on alone without you. Now get." He turned to Louis and said, "Where's the other one?"

"Run off, I guess." Louis seemed reluctant to let the one man shuffle away, but he holstered his gun and offered to buy Abe a drink. Abe said no thanks and walked over to where the two Chinamen were huddled past the entrance to the shaky building. He held out his hand, but they both turned and ran off down the street.

"All right folks, get back to your own business," he said loudly. And then to Louis, "Any idea how they got here? It's a long ways from China."

"Heard tell they brought a pack of 'em in for the coal mining. The saloon keeper told me they're good workers, work hard for dirt cheap."

"Maybe they're some of the ones I heard worked on bringing the railroad out to Utah from California. Anyway, I think it's good what you did, standing up for them like that."

"Didn't have nothin' to do with them. I just very much dislike the bastard that was causing the trouble. Had a run-in with him once before, never told you about it."

"Want to tell me now?"

"No, I just feel sorry for his wife. She's a pretty little one, but looks scared all the time. He was pushin' her around and I knowed I shouldn't have stood up for her, but I did. The sonofabitch said he'd kill me if I did it again. Guess he'll probably try this time."

"Watch yourself then, and let me know if he does try anything," Abe said. "We do have some regulations on this here trip."

When he got back to the big tent store, Sarah Beth was nowhere to be seen so he supposed she'd made it inside. He talked his way up the line and told those he knew that he had to help his wife who was inside. Folks were courteous and most of them recognized him as someone with authority on the wagon train.

He found her between some counters with her arms full of goods and cloth. She immediately handed it all to him and told him to wait right there. While he stood there he remembered that the small patrol force he was responsible for was low on several kinds of ammunition. He figured he'd have to get some cash from McFarland and come back later, but for now he should ask to see if they had what was needed. As he edged his way through the crowded aisles, he caught a glimpse of someone familiar, someone from his army days. He turned away out of reflex and then set himself where he could see the person more fully. If it wasn't one of the corporals who'd served with him at President Davis's headquarters, it was his twin. He wanted to reunite with the young man, find out what he was doing here, but his cautious old habits warned him against it.

Sarah Beth came up to him just at that moment with more things in her arms. "I think this better be enough for now," she said. "Otherwise we'll need a wagon to take it back to camp."

They paid for their goods and started back to their wagon. He was still curious about the young man and had remembered his name, Struthers. Then he saw him in the street with a young woman beside him as they put their supplies into a one-horse cart. He asked Sarah Beth to wait for a moment, and walked over to the man.

"I think I recognize you, Phillip Struthers," he said.

"Yeah, that's me." He looked up. "Lieutenant Saunders. What are you doing here?"

"I'm making my way across the country, looking to settle a bit further west. Yourself?"

"Oh, I've got a job with a coal company from Virginia. They opened up mine out here and sent me to help run the thing." He nodded to the woman who had finished putting her parcels in the back of the cart. "My wife Eleanor. Honey, this is Lieutenant Saunders. I knew him when we were both with the President."

"Pleased to meet you," the woman said in clearly southern speech.

"Likewise." Abe turned and beckoned for Sarah Beth to join them.

They ended up together heading back to the wagon train camp with the Struthers cart carrying all the supplies as a favor to Abe and Sarah Beth. The two women fell easily into comparing family histories from their roots in Virginia, and the two men talked about the way it was for Confederates in the western country.

"It's been mostly all right for me," Struthers said. "A little prejudice here and there, and some gloating on the part of a Yankee or two, but overall, nothing real bad. I hear it's a little tougher down in Mormon country. Most of them, the ones that fought, were on the Union side. From what I hear, they're still fighting us Southerners."

"Interesting, because I'm travelling with a wagon train that's over half Mormon, and, far as I know, we haven't been bothered or singled out. Certainly some of them must know about me and Sarah Beth by now. But we are headed for Utah, and I was advised that it might be better to lay over there rather than push on and find a place in Oregon before winter."

"Good advice, but be careful where you settle for the winter. It's hard country and you'll need some friendly neighbors."

"Thanks for the warning."

They unloaded the goods at their camp, served supper to the young couple, visited some more, and then said goodnight.

It turned into a totally clear night. The light from a nearly full moon filled the sky with a soft, shimmering glow. As they were preparing for sleep, a boy ran into their camp calling, "Miss Sarah Beth."

It was Gloria's oldest son and he said his mother needed her, quick.

Several hours later, as she was cleaning herself and the mess that was the necessary accompaniment of the process, she again experienced the wave of relief that came to her after a successful birth and being witness to the miracle that it could even happen at all. And once again she was nearly overwhelmed with the power of the feeling that had its source deep in her own center where the empty womb cried out for a purpose and seemed to be calling out in deep loneliness for its function and its right. When someone like Gloria could be so brave in facing the challenges of another mouth to feed and a tiny body to hold, and as Norma got closer and closer, Sarah felt much more often the ache of failure in her own self. Because even though Abe sometimes expressed his apprehension at the timing of such a thing and cautioned about the need to wait until they were more settled, and even though her own thoughts were fraught with fears both small and large, she had tried any and everything she knew, within the lack of privacy due to their travelling situation, to overcome whatever it was that was holding them back from God's own gift of conception.

As she walked around the edge of the camp, she kept thinking that Abe wasn't the problem. His unwillingness and fear of discovery by others was easily overcome by some simple and gentle stroking of his body, things she had learned from their intimacy together, and their ability to perform the act in silence and near motionlessness was almost a miracle in itself. No, it wasn't for lack of trying, and it wasn't for her lack of prayer. Sometimes she felt selfish when she realized she'd finished her prayers without any mention of almost anything or anyone else. 'Dear God,' her heart cried out. 'You need our child, I am willing to give you the best of my life, to give anything and everything you ask in return, please, please . . . ' And often she was astonished with herself and this overwhelming intensity of need and desire. 'Dear God, if only, if only . . . '

When she reached their camp, she was surprised to find Louis there with Abe, sitting by a small fire. She answered their questions quickly even as she felt the heavy exhaustion of her past few hours and her need for sleep. There was some stew for her to eat, and her curiosity about Louis's business with her husband kept her attention.

"That's good. I'm glad she and the baby are all right," Abe said. "Louis here has been talking with me about what happens when we come to the end of this part of the journey and the Mormons separate off. And should we try to keep going this year, or wait somewhere?"

Louis interrupted, "We've got the start on a good herd of animals, but I don't think they should move much farther if they're going to make it through the unknowns of winter. They've got to get settled in time to put on some weight and recover from this trip so far. And I've got to head back to New Mexico, got a job drivin' freight back to St. Louis in a pretty big hurry, and then back out in the spring." He paused and turned to Abe. "So what say?"

Abe continued, now looking at Sarah Beth, "I say, if we could find a place with some of these folks to winter over, take care of the animals, then we could all move along together to Oregon when Louis gets back in the springtime. Depending on how it goes, I might even be able to make a quick trip to explore this Jordan Valley and we'd have some idea if that's truly where we're headed or not. We want to know what you think, Sarah? And you don't have to say anything tonight, dearest, I can see how exhausted you are."

"I'm thinking about it," she said, as she moved toward their bed under the wagon, but not really thinking as she crawled under the covers.

CHAPTER TWELVE

First Stop

The wagon train pulled its way up a long incline out of the Green River plain and crested the line of hills that separated Wyoming from Utah. When those in the first Mormon wagons glimpsed the land of their promise, there were loud shouts and cheers and even a few gunshots, all rising into the crisp air that spoke of the autumn time coming.

Later, in the evening, Sarah Beth received a summons from the Bishop regarding a birthing situation. It wasn't urgent, the messenger said, but even so, could she please come?

As she gathered up her things and kissed Abe goodbye, he said, "You're lucky. I've always wondered what their camp life is like. But hurry back, I'll be missing you."

He was drowsing by the fire when she returned. "Boy or girl?" he asked.

"Neither," she said, placing her kit of supplies and the bundle of clean rags under the seat of the wagon. "The baby isn't due for another two months or so, but the woman's young and been having some bleeding. They're worried. I am too. The only thing that can help will be getting her to where she's able to lie still and rest, after they get where they're going."

"Who's her husband?"

"The Bishop himself. That's why this is so important to them over there. And I'm a little concerned that if I don't do things right, and have some luck, I might get the blame." She knelt down beside him and took his hands in hers. "Oh Abe, I'm so tired of this traveling. Can we stop soon, can we just stop and stay somewhere . . . anywhere?"

"Of course." He eased her down beside him and took her in his strongest arm, gently pulling her over into his lap. "I know how tired you are, how tired everyone is. But we'll make it. We're getting close and maybe the Bishop or someone will let us stay the winter in some kind of structure or shelter. We'll be all right, Sarah Beth, you're the strongest woman on the train."

"You're just saying that. You should see some of those Mormon women work. Besides, it's going to take more than either one of us to make whatever happens for the two of us."

"I'll make up the bed," he said, "and let's go to sleep. Tomorrow morning will be a grand new day . . . I love you, Sarah Beth." He lifted her off his lap and stood up, moving to unroll their bed and make it as comfortable as possible. The half-moon was dropping toward the far horizon. In the distance some wolves were howling

He helped her under the covers and crawled in, wrapping her in his arms and nuzzling her hair with his chin. After a few minutes he said, "Well, even if you don't think you're the strongest, you can't deny you're the most beautiful." But she was already mostly asleep and probably didn't hear him.

The next day they crossed the Green River and climbed a small range of mountains. That evening, McFarland sent word through camp that they would be holding up for two days when they emerged onto the flats below. He wanted to reorganize the train into the groups that would be heading off in different directions. Most of the Mormons would take off toward the Salt Lake, where they would probably spend the winter before heading out to their allotted lands. Of the remainder, one group was headed for California, and the rest to Oregon. They were all mostly folks who had land or family waiting. These would be small caravans, but the Indians and roads ahead were supposedly tame enough to be negotiated without much danger.

The next two days were spent in the repair and maintenance of wagons and in resting the stock on the wide grasslands that had appeared on the down slope side of the crossing into Utah Territory. During the afternoon of the second day, the Captain and the Bishop both held meetings with the men of their respective groups. Most of that time was spent giving out instructions for organizing the new alignments of the procession, and assuring everyone that, in the time remaining with the whole group together, they would continue to follow the rules and processes that had gotten them this far.

This included hunting parties and the security patrol under Abe's leadership. A rising level of excitement was felt throughout the entire train. Even the children seemed to grasp that something was going on; their whooping and racing about increased in both noise and intensity. The cooler weather was also a blessing and a relief.

When most of the men's questions had been answered in the non-Mormon group, the meeting was adjourned with a shared round of handshaking and backslapping, interrupted briefly by McFarland's shouted warning that it wasn't over with yet. Then he said, "But it's close enough. So have a great evening and be ready to pull out early."

As the group was breaking up, he called Abe aside and asked him to wait around for a few more minutes while he took care of some other business. He was back soon enough, and the two of them sat against a large boulder. McFarland rolled a cigarette, lit it, and then asked, "Have you got your plans worked out yet?" They had discussed the various possibilities once before, but they hadn't made any decisions. "Because I'm taking the bunch south to California and I still could use your help."

Abe was quiet for a few moments, and then said, "Pretty sure we're headed for the Oregon area, part they call the Jordan Valley. But I'm thinking it would be better to hold over if we can find a way. Get a good early start in the spring so's we'd have time to settle in and get ourselves something built for the next winter."

"And your cousin? Heard he's headed back New Mexico way."

"Says he's obligated to a freight train trying to make it back to St. Louis by fall."

"Leave you with that bunch of cows?"

"Yes sir."

"Seems to me you're looking for some help finding somewhere to hold over. I mean, you can't just settle into these Mormons' territory and expect to be left alone, or, even more important, get the help you might need."

"Funny you should mention that, but the Bishop himself has showed a bit of concern that Sarah Beth be close enough to help that youngest wife of his with her baby coming. Seems the young woman's been having a bit of a rough go, and my wife's been seeing her nearly every day, trying to keep her rested and fed the right things. He's even offered some space on his place out there by what's known as the Logan Canyon country."

"Not sure as I'd want to tie my wagon to that bunch. They'll help you when they can, but you'll be on your own soon as hard times come. They take care of their own first and always."

"Yes sir, well we haven't decided, but I was going to go see the man this evening and find out just what he's got in mind. So far it's just been the women talking about it, I mean telling Sarah Beth about the Bishop's idea."

"Well, if your heart's set on Oregon, and you've got those plans, don't guess I can offer anything that would change your mind. You've been a damn good hand and I hate to lose you, but that's the way of these things. Every train I've ever run ends up all scattered out across the land, no matter how close we get coming through it all to get here. So, thanks, son, and be sure to come see me before you split off." He stood up and strode off toward his own wagon without looking back.

Abe suddenly realized just how much he'd come to rely on the man's judgment and felt a bit of chill at the realization that they'd be going off on their own, but as the man said, it was the way of this land and its people. He pushed himself up off the ground and walked slowly toward his own campsite.

By evening Abe had finished the job of greasing the wagon wheel hubs, a laborious process that required propping them up and removing them one at a time. He cleaned his hands and arms as well as he could from the dark, sticky compound he'd been using, and he was ready to eat when Sarah Beth returned to say they'd been invited for a meal at the Bishop's camp. This was to be in preparation for the talk between them that had already been arranged.

When they arrived at the camp, the Bishop and a couple of his men were sitting near one of the wagons and three women were cooking over two fires. The women greeted Sarah Beth, who immediately went to one of the wagons and climbed inside. Abe stood still, not sure what to do next, and then the Bishop called out his name and beckoned to him.

"Welcome, to our humble camp, young man."

"Thank you."

"Boys, this is Abe. You'd know him as the security man for the Captain; I'm sure you've seen him around. This is my brother, and one of my sons."

"Yes, sir."

"Pull up rock and have a seat."

Abe adjusted a flat rock and settled on it as best he could.

"Been wanting to let you know how much I appreciate young Sarah Beth's attentions to my woman. We've been worried, but she helps out and makes it seem not so bad."

Abe nodded, but didn't have an answer ready.

"Wondering where you're headed next? Which train you'll be hooking onto?"

"Well, sir, that's not an easy question to answer. I plan on looking into that part of Oregon they call the Jordan Valley. But it's already a bit late in the year for settling in."

"Yes it is, unless you've got a lot of help. One thing about us— we've always got folks to help each other out. That's our way."

"Yes sir."

A woman approached and quietly said the food was ready.

"Well then, we best eat it," the Bishop said. "We'll talk more after we've fed the animal appetite part of ourselves."

The men got up and moved over near the cook fire, where they were handed plates of steaming meat stew and corncakes.

The Bishop held his plate out in front of him and said, "Lord almighty, bless this sustenance to our bodies and aid us in performing your work here in this savage land. We rejoice in our fellowship with our family and our neighbors, even as we ask your Holy Spirit to touch the souls of the unbelievers. Amen."

The men sat on logs around the fire. Abe took a seat as well, thinking that he'd just been prayed for as an unbeliever and that it was a strange way to welcome a guest. Probably it was a part of their customs whether he was there or not.

Sarah Beth came out of the wagon and went to eat with the women who were standing a short ways away. No one spoke while waiting for the food to cool and then eating. Abe noticed that the women seemed quite friendly to Sarah Beth and he couldn't help wondering if they, too, considered her an unbeliever. Most likely.

The stew was good, flavored with the small turnip-like bulbs people gathered along the way. Abe enjoyed watching Sarah Beth among the women, thinking that she was always able to fit in anywhere, with anyone. As the group finished eating, she moved to collect some of the plates, but was gently pushed aside as the youngest of the Mormon women took on the task. That girl gave Abe a kind smile as she took his plate and quickly turned away.

The Bishop cleared his throat, and spoke, "Seems to me, young man, you must need somewhere to settle for this coming winter before you think about what comes after that."

"Well, yes sir, I've had that on my mind. I would also like to take a short time to ride up to that Jordan Valley sometime this fall, just to see if that's what we want, and what, if anything, is still open for homesteading."

"Sounds like part of a plan. Now as to the other part . . . where will you stay? I need the young woman to stay nearby to mine. I fear for this young wife, this child she's trying to have might be difficult for her. Your young woman has been a great help and I'd like to have her close by. So I'm thinking we could provide for your temporary needs where we're going in the Logan Valley area. Think about it. We'll talk details in the next couple of days." He stood up and started to walk away. "It's a bit of an unusual situation, young man. We don't often take in the Gentiles, but in this case I might be able to make it work. G'night."

And that was it. The man and his companions walked off toward another part of their camp. The women were still cleaning up and putting things in order for the night, and Abe and Sarah Beth were left alone to themselves. They gave each other a look that said, "Let's go," and they walked back to their camp together.

Once they were back at the wagon, they both started talking at once.

Abe let Sarah Beth go first, and she asked, "What did he say to you?"

"He said he wants you nearby for the birth and that, even though we're 'unbelievers,' he'll consider helping us set up a temporary place to stay this winter. We didn't go into details."

"Unbelievers? He said that?"

"Earlier when he said a prayer while you were still in the wagon, and then just now he mentioned the Gentiles. How's the woman?"

"Her name is Grace, and she's the sweetest thing. I know she's having pain, but she won't let it show through her smile and her calm. I worry, though. It's too early for some of what's going on with her."

"Are you able to help?"

"Doing everything I can, but I'm not a doctor and maybe I don't know enough. It worries me that something bad might happen . . ."

Abe moved to her side and placed his arm around her. "It'll be all right, and no one can blame you, anyway. You're doing everything you can."

When Abe told Louis about the new plan, his cousin said it suited him fine, because he really did need to leave for New Mexico right away. Mad Mountain had already lit out, and their caravan headed from Taos to the east would be leaving any time now.

"As it is, I'll have to ride like hell."

"You know the way?"

"Yeah, it's pretty well marked. Only hard part is those mountains where you got to cross over. Besides, there'll be other travelers. I'll find someone to partner with."

"What will you do then?"

"Probably hole up near St. Louis over the winter until the first caravan lights out for New Mexico again. Then do pretty much the same thing. Hustle up a small herd and drive it this way. You'll be ready for me by summer, right Cuz?"

"I can only hope so."

"Unless that Bishop decides you ain't righteous enough for his folks and gives you the boot." He laughed and said he wasn't really serious.

The next day they rode away from the wagon train together and checked out the cattle. There were only twenty-one of them left now, one a bull, and most of the rest due to calve in the spring.

"Well, Cuz, take care of them, they're my babies, y'know."

"I will, but I won't be surprised if there'll be some call on all that walking meat. What do you want me to do about that?"

"Sell what you have to if it helps you stay friendly with these folks, but only the young ones. Keep the rest of them mommas 'cause they've proved themselves to pretty hardy, and that's what we want to start out with once we get our own place. They're worth more as mamas than as meat."

They were quiet for awhile, watching their cows moving among the rest of the train's herd. They looked to be in pretty fair shape given what they'd been through to get this far.

"I best move out," Louis said with a grunt to his horse. The two men leaned out from their saddles and had a quick embrace. Then Louis was galloping across the wide open grassland, scattering cattle and horses as he went, whooping and hollering all the way to the far ridgeline where he disappeared from sight. And that's that, Abe thought.

The next few days proved to be easy enough with fairly level ground and a well-travelled trail. They were now on what was the main route to the Salt Lake from the north, and began coming across other wagons and travelers, although no other large caravans.

The Bishop had clarified his offer by suggesting he would put them in an unfinished cabin his men would help with and which could then become something he'd need in the future, once they were gone. They could work on it as much as they wanted to, make it more suitable. Abe was fine with that, although he wasn't sure how bad the winter could get or what exactly unfinished meant. The other issue was land and feed for the herd, but that didn't seem to be a problem once they'd agreed on a certain number of animals in trade. He reminded the Bishop that he still wanted to take a short time away to check into the Jordan Valley country if that could be a likely possibility.

The Bishop agreed, but said it would be best to get the shell of the cabin ready for Sarah Beth, and plenty of firewood stacked up before he left. Once those things were taken care of, and if the weather hadn't turned too harsh, he said he'd even send one of his sons along for Abe's company and protection, since it wasn't good for a man to be alone out there. There was just too much could go wrong.

Sarah Beth was happy with most parts of the arrangement, but wanted to know how long he thought he'd be gone. She didn't like the idea of being alone, even with the rest of the Bishop's folks nearby. He promised to find out how long a quick trip would take, and also promised not to even go at all if it would take more than two weeks.

That night they set up the big camp early to take advantage of some springs, and the two of them rode off as soon as they'd done some laundry and refilled their water barrels. They rode out to low hills that were covered in patchy forest with white-barked aspen and strong-smelling pines. They found a nice hollow where the horses could graze and, within the matter of a minute or two, they were rolling on the ground in each other's arms. They made love with an urgency that spoke of how long it had been, and then when they'd spent that pent up energy, they lay back and watched the dusk deepening the color of the sky. Sarah Beth sang softly, a song from her childhood in Virginia. When she finished, or at least paused, Abe asked her if she missed the old home and its way of life.

"I miss it because I don't yet have anything to take its place, but I know that's coming, so I just make up pictures in my mind of our new land and our kids running around, and . . ." She stopped and leaned over to give Abe a kiss. "Besides, you're out here, so I'd be really lonely without you if I was back there."

He pulled her over on top of himself and ran his hands through her hair. "I love you Sarah Beth, and I wouldn't be here if you weren't here with me."

"Where would you be?"

"Probably riding like crazy trying to keep up with my cousin, getting in and out of scrapes and scraps, who know?"

"Well, I'm glad to know I'm the reason you behave yourself."

They sat up and unwrapped the bread and meat they'd brought along for a cold supper. Colors filled the sky overhead and the evening's bird songs built up and then faded away.

The next week went by quickly, even though the train was moving more slowly now as it came closer to the goal for many of the emigrants. No one wanted to break down at this point. Spirits were lifting with each day of progress, and even the unspoken tension between the two distinct groups seem to have somewhat evaporated in the pleasant days of what felt like an early fall.

The Bishop had placed his own people, his family and immediate congregation, together as a kind of unit and invited Abe to join up as soon as he was ready. McFarland was aware of this, but continued to maintain that until the actual separation of the groups, Abe was still his "officer" and needed to be in the front formation with the Captain and his other assistants. When Abe explained this to the Bishop, he gave reluctant approval, but only on the condition that Sarah Beth be readily available for any needed assistance to the pregnant young woman. They'd brought their two horses in from the general herd and had them moving with the wagon on short ties, to be staked out at night. Due to the curving nature of the trail, the train stretched almost a mile; Sarah Beth would need her horse if and when she was called, and for the daily calls she made on Grace. That possibility meant that Abe needed to stay close to their wagon as well.

Finally the day came when they reached the fork where one trail led to the Salt Lake and the other cut off to the Logan Valley. It was to the latter that the Bishop had been assigned by the Church's higher-ups for the purpose of strengthening a new congregation and initiating the building of a local sanctuary.

The parting was rather perfunctory for most of the two groups of travelers, since they had very little to do with one another over the course of the journey. However, there was some emotion involved in the separation of the Mormons who were turning off and those that were continuing on. Sarah Beth and Abe had one last supper with Guy and Norma, and Gloria and her husband and newborn, and they all pledged to find a way to visit sometime in the future if there were any way to make it happen.

The next morning, Sarah Beth drove the wagon to its new place in the Logan Valley line. Abe rode out to round up their cattle and get them moving in the right direction, separated from the rest of the herd going south or west. One of the Bishop's men also owned a small bunch that would be combined with his and moved out along with their much smaller caravan.

Sarah Beth was relieved when someone told her they had fewer than two days of moderate travel before they would stop, at last. Grace seemed to be in good spirits and capable of remaining in stable condition for at least that long. Once they arrived at their destination, Sarah Beth's first order of business would be to seek help in creating some kind of sanitary accommodation that would serve in any of the several possibilities which might occur. If it came down to a difficult birth, either early or even on time, she would be on her own. The only doctor on the entire train had gone on with the California-bound contingent. It did make Sarah Beth feel better to know that most of the Mormon women had been through childbirth, either their own or helping someone close to them.

Abe returned at mid-day, saying that the other man was able to keep the cattle moving with little trouble and he wasn't really needed for that work. He tied Bird behind the wagon and climbed up next to Sarah Beth and asked her to sing some kind of "Here We Are in the Big Country" song. She said she certainly didn't know one and if he wanted something like that, he'd have to make it up himself. She was quite surprised when he started singing those words and adding some other nonsense about "from the mountains to the valleys there was no prettier woman than the one that sat beside him on the old wagon seat." She shushed him and playfully covered his mouth so he had to mumble through her hand to keep on singing. She hadn't seen him so light-hearted throughout the entire trip and it instantly spread to her, as they both giggled and laughed for several minutes. Just as their gaiety was subsiding, a rider from the Bishop appeared by Abe's side of the seat.

"Bishop'd like to see you, sir." And then he was gone again.

Abe said quietly to Sarah Beth, "I guess we're about to find out if I'm working for him or if we're some kind of partners. I have a feeling he's only used to having people working with him as subordinates. Kind of like the army." He leaned over and kissed her and then climbed down and saddled his horse. "Now, you keep working on that song for me, while I'm gone," he called out, then off he rode off along the line.

When Abe reached the Bishop's wagon, it was time for the mid-day stop. A small stream flowed across the road to where they would be going, and folks were carrying water to their draft stock so as not to have to unharness. The order had been given not to unhook anything, as it was to be only a brief break, only enough time for a short meal.

The Bishop and Abe both climbed down off their mounts at the same time and found a place to sit on some boulders.

"First thing we're going to need is building lumber. I have an arrangement with some fellas have a small sawmill twenty some miles from where we're locating. Need you to drive one of the wagons after some of that material so as we can get started building places as soon as possible. We'll make some simple frame structures for this winter. They'll turn into outbuildings when we get to setting up log cabins in the spring, but by then I guess you'll be gone on. Agreed?"

"Yes, sir."

"All right then, better get yourself back for something to eat. It'll be nearly dark before we can stop again."

As Abe rode the short distance back to his own wagon, he thought about how easily he'd slipped back into the "Yes, sir" habit, and how he felt actually rather relieved not to have to make decisions at this point in the trip. He also realized just how much McFarland had relied on him for not just consultation, but the actual taking on of responsibilities. But all that was behind him now. What came next was just a question of getting along and doing what he was asked to. No problems there, he hoped.

When they arrived at their destination, Abe didn't quite understand the arrangements regarding the land. It seemed that the Church acquired or claimed it somehow and then allocated to its members. If "outsiders" attempted to follow homestead laws and take some land for themselves, it wasn't clear how it would be settled, either in the legally constituted courts, which were far away, or by frontier justice. Most likely the latter. So he was pleased when one of the Bishop's sons took him for a short ride away from the big family's headquarters that had been selected on the first day. He was offered a couple of different spots where he could settle temporarily, and chose the one closest to what appeared to be a spring that looked like a steady source of fresh water. The best location for a structure was on a flat that had exposure to both the east and the west with a small rise to its south. Although the grass was sparse in among the brushier plants, it still retained a green hue at this time late in the summer. He thought that was a good sign. As for the "unfinished structure" they'd been promised, there was no sign of it.

It wasn't until the next day that he was able to take Sarah Beth and the cattle out to that spot, but she instantly loved it and immediately started planning just where she would place the wagon so they could stay in it, and where the structure would be. Abe asked her to please leave some room for a covered space for the horses, wagon and equipment. That was the kind of outbuilding that the Bishop was most interested in seeing constructed, because it was the one he'd said they would go on to complete for a permanent part of their ranching operation after Sarah Beth and Abe moved on. From the look on his wife's face, however, he began to wonder how difficult it would be to convince her to pull stakes in the spring, especially once they'd settled in.

The days spun by in a full round of hauling lumber, gathering firewood, and building structures that seemed more like wooden camps than anything else. The cattle wandered toward higher ground where the grass was less dried out, but there was enough that they didn't go farther than a half-day's ride. The two small herds had been combined so that one man could round them up if necessary; the dog the family acquired from one of the new neighbors helped out a lot.

The days were growing shorter, so the harder everyone worked the more work there seemed to be. Nights were cool and even a bit frosty, and the signs of what was coming became clearer to them all. Abe and Sarah Beth actually built on and around the bed of their wagon, after removing its cover. This gave them a kind of sleeping loft with storage beneath. The walls and roof rafters were the first thing completed, and, although they had nothing to make it really waterproof, the roof was pitched at a steep enough angle to assure that most of the rain or melting snow would run off once it was covered with whatever they could find. Then one day, the Bishop's freight wagon showed up in their yard and unloaded a large roll of oiled canvas. It took only a day, with help, to get it unrolled and fastened down over the whole roof of the small half-built structure. They even got to see how well it would work when, the next day, a crashing thundershower visited the valley.

Every day required a trip by Sarah Beth to visit her charge, the young Grace, who seemed to be somewhat improved now that she wasn't subject to the jarring motion of riding in a wagon all day, every day. Her one room was the first part of the bishop's complex to have been constructed and now, with the cold nights, it was the first to be heated by a tiny kitchen stove that also served to warm food for her, and to boil water for the teas that Sarah Beth prescribed.

One day, as she was changing the bedding and the girl was standing near the open door, Sarah Beth was taken completely off guard when Grace turned to her and asked, "Do you think I'll die?"

Sarah Beth kept her attention on the pillows she was fluffing up and placing at the head of the bed, trying to think of a response. "Well, I suppose we all die sometime," she said softly.

"No, I mean now, from this," the girl rubbed her belly, "from this baby?"

"Well, we're certainly doing everything we can to make sure nothing goes wrong. And now that we've stopped traveling, you seem to be doing much better."

"Well, one of the wives said I would probably die from this."

"Why, and what business did she have saying that?"

Grace didn't say anything

"Who was it?" Sarah Beth asked.

"Oh, I can't say, but she said it would be God's will if I died and the baby lived."

"Well, I think that's a horrible thing to say. And don't you believe it." She went over and took the girl's hand and led her to the side of the freshly made up bed. They both sat together. "Grace, I know we don't have the same ways, or even the same Church, but I think it's the same God we worship, and I know that my God, who is also your God, just isn't like that. Besides, I also know that many of these folks are praying hard for you and this baby, and I know that I'm going to do everything I can to see that you and the baby here are going to be just fine. Now why don't you just lay down here and take yourself a nap and stop thinking about what cruel, jealous old ladies are saying. I'll even sing to you for a few minutes. You like that, don't you?"

"Yes ma'am." She lay back and Sarah Beth covered her with a blanket and softly sang one of the old hymns from her choir days. The girl was quickly asleep, and Sarah Beth left to return to Abe and their own hurried preparations for the coming winter weather. As she and the horse trotted back to the new home, she realized just how angry she was at anyone who would torment a young girl like that. Then she realized that although in her own mind she always referred to Grace as a girl, Grace wasn't really more than a year or two younger than Sarah Beth herself. She tried to chase all of that out of her mind and get back to concentrating on the ever-growing mental list of things she needed to take care of before Abe left, and before winter came with all of its unknown hardship.

Abe was again off on one of the lumber runs when she returned to their camp, to what she was calling a house-camp. She busied herself rolling bits of fabric to seal the cracks between boards in the new wall sections. They would have enough blankets to cover the two walls with the most open exposure, but they still had to worry about the whole area behind and under the wagon. While she was working she couldn't help letting her mind return to the afternoon's revelation from Grace. It wasn't unusual for women to be mean to or about other women, but the Mormons had cast themselves as so much above that kind of thing that she was still a bit surprised by what she'd heard. But then, as her father had always said, "human nature is just that, humans and nature." Suddenly she felt a wave of longing for him. It had been so long now since they'd left all that behind with no way to find out what was going one, with him, with his health, with Mattie. She promised herself that she'd find a way to mail and receive letters as soon as they could get connected to the nearest town with postal service.

The other thing that came into her mind without her bidding was the short conversation she'd had with Grace soon after they met. The girl had been delirious from the pain and fear caused by her bleeding, and was mumbling over and over again, lightly slapping her belly, "I didn't want you, I didn't want to do it, I didn't want you." She soon calmed down and become more at ease from the combination of caring assurances and soothing tea Sarah Beth provided her. When

Sarah Beth gently asked what she meant by those things she'd said, she wouldn't answer. Sarah Beth urged her to accept that a baby was God's gift to a mother. As she spoke it wasn't hard for her to translate her own deep longing for a child into a kind of disbelief that this girl or any other could feel that she didn't want such a gift from God. The girl wouldn't explain it, except to say "He made me do it." And then she was quiet, and hadn't mentioned it again.

Abe was eager to leave on his way to check out the Jordan Valley country before the winter set in and made it impossible. He'd found a companion for the ride when he was shopping for hardware in the closest town. The young man, whose relatives were actually settled near the Jordan Valley, was not a Mormon but was working for one of their ranchers as a blacksmith and was about to head back to his home country. They'd been introduced by a storekeeper who knew that the Bishop was doing a lot of building and would need quite a bit of metalwork. Abe arranged for the young man, Blair Grimes by name, to meet the Bishop. It went well enough that Blair committed to returning in the spring for the work that would be needed then. He quickly set to work on some immediate needs for stovepipe and hinges, but thought he would be ready to head out when Abe was.

The way this had all fit together was one more confirmation of his father-in-law's formula for matching needs to opportunities. The only concern that lurked in the shadows of this arrangement was the possibility that Grace might come to term while he was gone, putting extra burdens on Sarah Beth, but the Bishop promised that one of his sons would look after the cattle, and they'd make sure that Sarah Beth was provided for and taken care of over the next couple of weeks. The son was an earnest young man around sixteen years of age, named Paul, and it seemed he liked the opportunity to be around some of the "others."

As Abe prepared for his departure, he and Sarah Beth made use of the nighttime hours. They now shared a commitment to seriously try for a child; they planned on returning to the trail in early summer, and it would be easier on Sarah Beth to travel with a baby than to travel pregnant. They had seen quite a few women with nursing infants on the journey from Nebraska to Utah, and it seemed to be a satisfactory situation. Of course Abe pretended he wasn't really into this arrangement and would prefer to have them wait for a couple of years. Sarah Beth obviously didn't believe him and jested back at him: "Fine, if that's the way you want to be, I'll just sleep alone. It'll help me get used you being gone, anyway." And that was the signal for them to climb up into the wagon bed and proceed to wrestle about until their pleasure and purpose became serious lovemaking, followed by the ensuing deep sleep.

The few days remaining until Abe's departure passed quickly, even as Sarah Beth found herself spending more time with Grace. Grace hadn't bled since they'd stopped travelling, but she was still weak and Sarah Beth wondered if the girl would be strong enough to put up with the stress and pain of labor. Sarah Beth tried to reassure herself by reflecting that millions of women had babies under all sorts of conditions, and that God created women for this. She should just she should just have more faith. The problem was that no one else seemed inclined to share her responsibility for both Grace and the baby. The other women in the household had all successfully borne children, but they acted like it was nothing they'd ever been a part of except as the delivering mother. None of them seemed to want to spend any time with Grace.

The dawn of the day when Abe was to leave came with the first frost of the season, and a clear blue sky. He woke in the dark, started a fire in the small cook-stove that doubled as their heater, and then quietly packed his saddlebags, his guns and ammunition. Sarah Beth watched him from her reclining position in the bed. She was already missing him, but vowed to herself to be a good wife and help him on his way with no undue sadness or second thoughts about the worthiness of what he was doing for them both.

His plan was to meet young Blair where the wagon-road diverged from the trail west to the small town. He was quickly as ready as he would ever be, went out, caught Bird, saddled up, and returned to the small shelter. With no words between them, they held each other closely for a long, long moment, then kissed deeply . . . and suddenly he was gone. She threw a blanket around her shoulders and went outside into the coming light to watch him until he vanished.

"Oh God, please be with him and bring him back to me, just as soon as you can." Sarah Beth was surprised to realize that she'd spoken the words aloud, which was not her usual custom for prayer. Guess I just wanted Him to be sure and hear me, she thought.

It wasn't yet the middle of that day when young Paul rode up and jumped off his horse. Sarah was washing the last of her own laundry and getting ready to hang it on the taut line that stretched between their structure and the one tree in what passed for their yard. The boy took a moment to catch his breath and then said, "Miss Sarah Beth, you'd best come along now. Gracie's calling for you."

"Well, is she all right, has anything changed?"

"I wouldn't know, ma'am. They don't let the menfolk and boys in there right now."

"All right, can you saddle my horse while I get some things together?"

"Yes'm."

She quickly wrung out the remaining clothes as best she could, and hurried to gather up what she thought she'd need if, worst case, she wouldn't be able to return home that night. When Paul brought the horse around, she was ready to go and the two of them galloped off as if they were racing.

When they arrived at the Bishop's growing complex, Paul took Morning and led him away as women urged Sarah Beth inside and led her to Grace's space. It wasn't exactly a room yet, with two walls made up only of fabric where final walls would someday be.

Grace was looking feverish and rolling her head from side to side. Sarah Beth took her hand and tried to calm her with soothing sounds and soft questions. It was clear that something had changed and that the discomfort was coming in the kind of waves that point to early contractions. There was no doubt that the baby was trying to be born, Sarah Beth was quite sure of that. She let go of Grace's hands and busied herself preparing the small space for what was coming. She called for the linens she'd had the women tear into strips, and let them know that warm, but not boiling water, should be ready from then on.

She went back to Grace's side and pulled the only available chair next to the bed. It was likely to be a long wait until things really started to happen, so she thought she might as well make herself as comfortable as possible. It amazed her that it wasn't but a few hours after Abe left and now this was happening. Well, it wouldn't have mattered much if he was still around. There wasn't anything for him to do in this situation, and although the girl looked feverish, she wasn't at all warm, maybe even a little cool to the touch. Sarah Beth could hear muted voices of the other women out in the rest of the building, but they weren't speaking loudly enough for her to distinguish any of their words. Suddenly, Grace reached out for her head and pulled it close to hers.

She whispered hoarsely, "I'm going to die, I know it, but you should know why." She shushed Sarah Beth when she tried to object. "Yes, I'm going to die because of what he made me do . . . Thank you for being with me, I can trust only you . . . Thank you for helping me die . . . Please help me . . . He can't make a baby any more . . . so he had someone . . . it's not his and he made me sin even when I was his wife . . . that's why I'm going to die, but I had no choice . . . he forced . . ." Suddenly she sat up straight as a real contraction seized her body and seemed to lift her almost out of the bed. Sarah Beth held on as the shaking spasm passed and the girl fell back against the pillows.

The next hour passed with only a few more contractions, but each time Grace twisted and fought against Sarah Beth, who was trying to restrain her. Sarah Beth wondered how the weak young girl could possibly have the energy to withstand hours more of this effort, especially as the violent contortions and contractions would only increase in strength and frequency. One of the women came into the small space and beckoned for Sarah Beth to follow her out through the hanging blankets. The woman leaned close and whispered, "Our Bishop wants to have a word with you, outside. I'll stay with the girl."

Sarah Beth crossed through the roughed in spaces of a future house and went out through what would become the entryway. The Bishop was standing near the well that had just been put in. She walked over to him and waited for him to speak.

"How is she?" he asked softly.

"It's started. But she's so weak . . ."

"It will be too much for her perhaps?"

"Perhaps. Oftentimes women have more strength than it seems they do." Sarah Beth continued looking down as she spoke.

They were both quiet. Somewhere nearby two men were yelling back and forth to one another, but their words were lost in the distance.

The Bishop placed his hand on Sarah Beth's shoulder and said, "If you have to make a choice, save the child." And then he turned and walked away.

Sarah Beth's thoughts fought back against what she'd just heard. Did this Bishop really have the power over life and death for his people? How could she decide? Whatever was going to happen would happen. It wasn't her choice. Why did he put it on her? And what would he be able to do to her if it went the other way?

She walked slowly back to the unfinished building, thinking that the only thing she could do was what she was supposed to do, try to save them both, the mother and the child. She looked upward and said in her softest tones. "Please, help me now, help me. I can't do this alone . . ."

Grace was just falling back from another contraction. Two women were with her, one on either side of the bed. Sarah Beth stood at the parted blanket curtain, realizing that the frail young woman on the bed might not even have milk for the child. Who would nurse, whether the mother lived or died? It was horrible to have to think like this, to try to be practical when lives were at stake. The two women backed away from the bed and stepped around Sarah Beth to leave the space. Suddenly she was remembering something Abe had said to her about being in the army. He'd said he never wanted to be in command of any troops because then it would be up to him to decide who lived and who died. And now here she was, almost being asked to face the same kind of decision.

She uncovered the woman's legs and looked between them. She saw mucous discharge, but no blood, a good sign, a very good sign. Just then Grace kicked out with one leg, nearly catching Sarah Beth in the face. Another shuddering contraction passed through both of them as they clung together, the one trying to thrash about, the other trying to hold her down.

Hours of increasingly difficult contractions went by, time seeming to go slower and slower and the labor pains increasing in frequency with each episode. Grace seemed to be unconscious for all intents and purposes. This was probably for the best. Her screams could be heard outside, but it seemed to Sarah Beth that those shrieking sounds were almost separate from the woman whose glazed eyes still looked peaceful. Someone brought Sarah Beth a plate of food and she realized that lanterns were being lit as darkness fell. She ate a bit of the food. It tasted good, but she had no appetite for more. Suddenly Grace opened her eyes wide and covered her mouth with her hands, as if she were gagging.

"What is it, what is it?" Sarah Beth leaned over to place her ear close to the young woman's mouth.

Hoarse and exhausted, the young woman's voice spit, "I have to do this . . . this is Jesus's baby. He told me so." She coughed and fell back, twisting her head and pulling at her hair as her body went almost completely rigid and then settled into a shaking and shivering that seemed to threaten the whole bed.

Sarah Beth thought her words were an improvement; at least she wasn't talking about dying. Oh, how she wished for Martha to be here by her side. Martha had been the nurse and midwife at the fort, who took Sarah Beth on, first as an apprentice and then as an assistant. Oh please Miss Martha, she thought, please tell me something more I could be doing. There has to be something. But there was only silence and the sound of Grace's heavy breathing. Then Sarah Beth remembered something, something she'd seen Miss Martha try. It would mean tying a sash tightly around the woman's belly and then working it slowly, slowly down her body, possibly forcing the baby to move down into the birthing canal. It was something she'd seen used only twice, and both times it was when the women seemed too exhausted to deliver their babies.

Sarah Beth looked around the small space for something that would serve that function, but there wasn't anything. She called out of the little space, asking for a shawl or something like one. She was remembering now that it was risky because if the binding was too tight it could cut off the flow of blood to the woman's lower limbs and even to the baby, but if it wasn't tight enough it wouldn't do any good. In this case, with Grace's strength failing at every contraction, and them coming more and more often, each one with less of her strength and greater pain, it was worth a try. Nothing else Sarah Beth knew could help. And the worst thing that could happen would be to lose both of them, which God forbid, she was beginning to think might happen anyway.

She knew she would need help to be able to perform this kind of a maneuver and still be able to restrain Grace during her contractions. She pushed the blanket aside and looked out into the other room. She caught a glimpse of a girl she'd noticed several times but never been introduced to. She was strong-looking and appeared to be trying to stay close to what was going on, without getting close enough to be sent away. The girl stared at her, holding out a shawl.

Sarah Beth beckoned to her, calling out, "You come here, I need your help." The girl looked around and behind herself, but there was no one else nearby. She pointed at herself in a questioning way.

"Yes. Hurry in here."

When Sarah Beth and the girl were alone inside the small space, they were just in time for another jolting and thrashing episode with Grace. The girl looked on but did not seem afraid. Sarah Beth held Grace down on the bed and prevented her from throwing herself off onto the floor. This was becoming more and more exhausting for both of them.

"What's your name?"

"Helga."

"I'm Sarah Beth. Have you ever been at a birth before?"

There was a pause before the girl answered, and Sarah Beth looked over to see a smile flit across the girl's face. "Only my own," she said softly.

"That's funny. I didn't expect you to say that . . . All right then, I need your help. Can I ask how old you are?"

"They tell me I'm almost seventeen and I should act more grown up," she whispered, "but I don't know when my birthday is."

"That's all right. I need help with this. Will you?"

"Yes. But I don't know what to do."

"I'll tell you. First of all, you know Grace, don't you?"

"Yes." She moved closer to the bed so Grace could see her and then the young woman took the girl's hand in her own.

"All right," Sarah Beth said. "Grace is having some trouble pushing the baby out. And she's getting weaker. It's very hard work, so we have to help her do this. I'm going to wrap this shawl around her and tie it just above the baby. You're going to hold Grace's legs down so she doesn't kick. Think you can do that?"

"Yes ma'am." The girl moved to the foot of the bed and gently touched Grace's ankles.

"You'll know when it happens. We call them contractions. When we have to help her, I'll be pushing the shawl down each time, trying to help move the baby down and not let it go back up. Understand?"

The girl nodded her head and then tied her long hair back into a knot behind her head. Sarah Beth got her first good look at the girl and was surprised at how delicately beautiful her features were, given how strong her body looked.

A contraction began suddenly and the girl leaned down onto Grace's ankles. Sarah Beth cinched up on the shawl. As the contraction shuddered its way through the young woman's body, she eased the shawl down as far as she could. When the contraction had passed, she quickly loosened the knot just a bit. There was really no way to know if it was going to do any good. If it were, there would only be a small gain each time.

"That's good," she said to the girl. "That's exactly what you need to do. Also, in between contractions, I want you to dampen that cloth, come around and wipe her face with it. It's gotten hot in here and she doesn't need sweat running down into her eyes."

Each time the young woman's body tensed and began to shake, the two of them reacted and held on, Helga to the legs, and Sarah Beth to the shawl. As the time went by, Grace went from screaming to moaning, weaker with every contraction. But now it seemed like the bulge of her belly was moving a little downward, a bit at a time. The blanket at the little room's entrance was pulled back and two of the other women looked in, and then backed away, letting the blanket fall closed. It was strange that they didn't offer to help, Sarah Beth thought to herself, but then this whole situation was strange. Especially the things Grace had told about herself and this baby. Whatever that was about still wasn't clear.

Sarah Beth rinsed her hands in the hot water that someone had just left. It was now time to see if she could feel the baby, to see if it was headfirst or not. There was almost no hope for either one of them if it was breech. She eased Helga out of the way and leaned in from the foot of the bed. She carefully inserted her fingers and gently pushed them inside until she felt an obstruction. The head! Thank you, God. Another contraction was on its way. Now she stayed at the foot of the bed and leaned forward to pull on the tied shawl with both hands, one on either side of Grace's belly. Helga instinctively moved to hold Grace's shoulders down and that seemed to help.

"You can push. Push!" Sarah Beth said. "Now." And as Grace pushed, she pulled on the shawl and tightened it. There was movement now, another contraction, and she could see for the first time a tiny patch of the baby's scalp. The head was close now. She eased her fingers around it, softly giving just the slightest help to the already tightly stretched opening . . . Another contraction, another pushing and pulling . . . and another. Then a long pause.

"It's all right Grace, we're almost done," she said, "now see if you can really push this time." Sarah Beth pulled on the shawl with one hand while the other hand was helping to stretch back the opening for the head. "Helga, push down, push toward me on her belly."

Grace screamed louder than she had at any time so far, and longer, longer, and then it suddenly stopped and there was no sound in the space besides her whimpering, sobbing moans. Sarah Beth now held the tiny head in her hands. She cleaned some mucous off the face with her thumb.

"Now, again, Grace," and there came another push and pulling. Sarah Beth got a hold under the baby's arms and pulled it out into her own waiting arms. She brought the head up close to her face and sucked on the baby's nose and mouth, spitting out what she'd gotten in her mouth. The baby opened its own mouth, struggling to breathe. Sarah Beth held it upside down and tapped on its back. There was a tiny whoosh of air with the first breath, and then more gasping little breaths. Then a cry. Sarah Beth quickly handed the baby to Helga, checked for the color of the bleeding between Grace's legs and saw no bright red blood, just the normal mess. Then she moved to lean over Grace's face and felt the woman's breath on her cheek.

"It's done," she said. "You have a girl."

The baby was crying, making healthy first sounds and Sarah Beth took her from Helga and laid her gently on her mother's chest. The door blanket opened again, and now there were three women staring into the space.

"You can tell the Bishop they're both alive." Sarah Beth said. "And get me more water, but not too hot."

Part IV

Journey's End

November 1868-April 1869

CHAPTER THIRTEEN

Trapped

The Bishop's wives began helping with the cleanup, swarming around Grace and the infant, now that the birth was accomplished. It seemed to Sarah Beth that they'd only waited to be sure it wasn't going to end badly. She had the impolite and sarcastic thought that they'd stayed out of it just to make sure they wouldn't be blamed if anything went wrong. She pushed that thought away as unkind, and actually welcomed their help as they gently changed the soiled bedding beneath Grace and took turns holding the baby. Sarah Beth stepped back from most of this activity, only adding a comment or a direction when it was needed. She did check the tied-off cord again, and was pleased that it clotted well. She was so tired now that nothing mattered except getting this done, and getting herself to a place where she could sleep. It had been so long since she'd said goodbye to Abe.

One of the Bishop's wives, Ella, even told her in a sweet voice that she was no longer needed, and if she wanted they would get one of the boys to ride with her over to her place. She was immediately torn by the call of responsibility to stay until she was sure things were truly going as well as could be expected, and the desire to be in her own space. She felt she needed to see that the baby was nursing and Grace's discharges had stopped, but as she watched the three women working to restore order in the small space and saw how exhausted Grace was, she realized that there really might not be anything for her to do for some time. If she might be needed again, she'd better get some rest.

She held on for another hour or so and then got her things together, whispered good-night to the sleeping new mother, and went out into the chilly night with one of the Bishop's sons. Her horse was already saddled and waiting. Another young man, standing nearby, carried a lit lantern. He handed it up to her companion rider. They rode slowly across the area between the compound and her place. The young man helped her inside, lit a fire in the stove, brought in more wood, and then offered to stay if she needed anything else.

"No, that's fine. Thank you so much. Can you let my horse free? And tell your mother and the others, I'll be back in the morning sometime, unless they need me before then."

She knew she couldn't fall asleep without washing herself, so she drew a bucket of water from the barrel and set it on the heater to warm. She stripped off the clothes she'd been wearing for what seemed like forever and pulled a blanket tightly around herself. It wouldn't be much of a bath, but it would have to do. For the first time in hours, she had time to think of Abe and wonder how far along the way he was and if he was all right. Please God.

By the next day, some color had returned to Grace's face, she had a little milk coming in, and the baby, though perhaps abnormally quiet, seemed to be moving all her limbs in a normal fashion. She was even beginning to look around and turn her head to sounds and voices. All to the good, Sarah Beth thought. Thank you God and all of you angels whose energy it took to bring this about. She stayed until evening, was fed a warm meal that she could hardly stop eating as her hunger insisted on its due, and then she once again returned to her own place. They had named the child Rachel.

Sarah Beth spent the next days catching up on home chores and doing what she could to make their little shelter warmer and tighter. Two evenings later, one of the young sons summoned her to the Bishop's area of the group camp. At first she was afraid something had gone wrong, but when she got there, she was reassured that all was well. The boy pointed her to a large army-style tent pitched near the construction site.

She made a scratching sound on the canvas of the structure and was called inside. Immediately two men stood up and left. The Bishop motioned for her to sit in one of the chairs they'd vacated. He didn't say anything as he turned down the lantern so it cast only a dim light into the corners of the tent. He sat down in his own chair and the light was behind him so he was only a silhouette to Sarah Beth.

Finally he spoke, "I've been watching you," he said. "You're a good woman. Did you know I've been watching you?"

"No, not really."

"I think the man you call husband has noticed. I was surprised he would leave you here behind, alone. Are you all right? Is there anything you need?"

"I'm all right," she said, growing more curious.

"Good. Because I want you to be all right, even better than all right." He paused for a long time and then continued, "I want the best for you, so I want you to be my wife."

His words made no impression on her until she had time to understand them, then her hands flew to her mouth and a small cry escaped her throat as she cast her eyes around the enclosed space. It was just the two of them, and now she realized he sat between her and the tent flap doorway.

"I am quite aware you had no way of knowing about this, so it will take you a little time to become accustomed to the idea, I am sure."

She started to stand up, but there was no strength in her legs and she sank back down into the chair. "But I'm married," she said. "You know that."

"You thought you were married," he said, calmly. "As you may or may not know, our Church has an entire research administration, experts in tracing families, those both missing and found. Since early on in our journey, I've had a search conducted about you and your husband. It seemed the right thing to do when I first realized how important you might become to me and my work here in this New Land. And just as I suspected, you Southerners are a lot more closely related than any of you ever know. The man you call your husband is a relative of yours, too close for marriage by our laws, and those are the laws we now live under out here."

"That's false," she said, "false and impossible. We don't even come from the same state. Abe's from the Carolinas and I'm a Virginian. Our families never even met, never, never."

"What you've never known is that your mother's grandparents were cousins to Abraham's great-grandparents. When they died they gave away his grandfather for adoption. It was never talked about again until our researchers found the evidence."

She found the strength to stand up, and said, "I don't believe you. And now, if you'll excuse me, I want to return to my home place."

"You have no place of your own. Might I remind you that you are here at my behest, and from this time forward we are betrothed?

There will be a formal marriage ceremony in three days. You may choose to remain in what you call 'your place,' but don't become too attached to it. As far as the young man, I'm sure he will understand the impropriety of being married to someone who is almost a sister to himself. If not, and if he isn't willing to leave this place and leave you behind, things will not go well for him, I can assure you. You may go now—you have much to think about. I am sure you will grow to respect me, even if you don't think you like me at this moment. We'll see. You may go now." He stood and stepped out of the way to the door.

It was dark outside, but there was a quarter moon near the western horizon. She got to her horse and rode off into the night. She rode fast, reckless. She didn't want to be around anyone right now. She pushed Morning right on past her place, the place the Bishop now had claimed and taken from her. She rode down into the valley, now screaming, "God, God," remembering and using the words of His Son, "Why have you forsaken me?"

She finally pulled her horse to a stop and leaned forward over his neck while he blew great breaths out through his nostrils, his sides heaving with the exertion of the ride. Her mind was in turmoil, a churning storm of thoughts and wishes and desperate plans. She would ride after Abe. Maybe she could catch him, somewhere, somewhere along his way. But he would be making fast time and be far ahead of her. She should go somewhere else and just hide and wait, taking food to last her until he came back, until she could reunite with him, tell him of this terrible thing.

The horse caught his breath and stretched down to nibble at patches of grass. The moon was dipping closer to the far away ridges. If the Bishop meant what he said, there was still time before his plan was carried out, before it was over for her, for her life, for Abe. She pulled Morning's head up and around and urged him slowly back toward their place, the place that had been taken away from her tonight, just like everything else. There was the rifle. Abe never left her without one. She could shoot something, someone, the Bishop or herself . . . No, this horrible insult required more than simple revenge. Alone as she was, she knew it would take all of her skill and wits to escape this situation, and now, for the first time, she realized the threat in the Bishop's words about Abe, a threat to kill him if he didn't go along with all of this. Morning raised up his head and his ears shot forward. She caught a glimpse of a small lantern on the rise beyond their little camp. They would be watching her, of course they would be. No way she could escape now. It would take something else, something she alone could do to save Abe and free herself. But what?

Somehow she slept, and in the morning, with a fresh mind, she was able to think more clearly. And she suddenly remembered the conversation, or at least the words Grace whispered in her ear. The Bishop hadn't made her baby . . . Whatever did that mean? She was relieved there were still some coffee beans to pound and grind. Although she hardly ever drank it, and it was mostly Abe's treat, she wanted something to help make her sharper than she'd ever been, alert and thinking hard.

What had Grace meant? What was she trying to say to her? And why? She thought about asking her to repeat what she'd said, to explain it, but she was afraid that now the girl would be frightened and stay silent about the subject. But now Sarah Beth had to know. How?

The trip was going well for Abe and Blair. The weather was mostly good enough. There'd been a couple of showers, but nothing heavy, and the creeks and rivers they needed to ford were all still low and passable. They passed a few merchant's wagons along the way, most of them headed back to Utah from delivering goods to the Idaho and Oregon border areas. The Oregon Trail was now used more for trade than migration.

They made good time and within a couple days they were camped outside the small settlement of Boise. At the stables in town they learned that they had another couple days of hard riding ahead of them to reach the Jordan Valley area, but there shouldn't be any problems along the way. The Indians were headed toward their winter camps to the north in Palouse country or south into Nevada, and when Abe asked about the possibility of marauders or veterans of the War preying on riders, the proprietor told him he'd never heard of such, at least not in these parts.

He and Blair were getting acquainted and finding that their desire for their own land and a chance to try out the cattle business gave them a lot in common. They got into enjoyable arguments over which breed was best and whether Texas cattle were any advantage over those from Kansas and Nebraska, but since neither one of them knew much about it, the arguments were usually short-lived and more for fun than for competition.

Two days later, they crested a steep hill and a new panorama spread out before them. They saw an island of mostly green land with several strips of shrubby brush running through it. There were mountains to the west; a couple still had snow from the past winter.

"I think this is it," Abe said softly. "Jordan Valley, the Land of Promise."

"Yeah it is. Gonna be dark pretty soon."

So they gave their horses their heads and let them find their own way down the rocky semblance of a trail that led into the valley below. As the darkness crept into the lowland, the sun was still lighting up high plumes of smoke from the cook-fires of homesteads in the area.

"Best we camp this evening, then see where we are and where we go from here."

"Be all right with me," Blair said. "Long as somebody don't mind us."

"Well, we'll stay here at the edge. Should be allowed."

"Your call," Blair said, and they rode down a short ways until they found a small flat near a puddled seep coming from the rocks. "This'll do, you think?"

The next morning they rode into the very small town perched on a bluff above the creek that meandered through rocky desert. Along the stream banks, willows struggled to grow and songbirds made their homes. Abe and Blair had directions from a rancher near where they spent the night. He told them to make for the newer of two small towns because there was more going on there than in the older village a few miles away. The new town was booming as a result of the gold mining, even though it was called Silver City.

They tied their horses in front of a general store and decided to walk around for a few minutes. It didn't take long to go up one side of the single street and back down the other, and by the time they'd made that circuit, it seemed like everyone in town knew they were there. They could see the fingers pointing at them and hear the buzz of small conversations that followed them along as they walked.

"Must not be many strangers come here," Abe said.

"Either that, or the ones that do are all miners."

"Well, let's see what we can find out."

They entered a small eating establishment that was a part of the town's two story hotel.

A tired-looking woman came over to the table they chose and said, "Got no breakfast, it's gone, but you can have dinner, which is lamb stew and fresh bread."

"Sounds good," Abe said, and she was off to get the food.

It was the first real meal that wasn't trail food since they'd left. When they'd finished it off, Abe called the woman over and asked, "Who do I see about ranch land around here?"

She looked down at him and said quietly, "Depends if you want to fight the Indians for it, or pay too much money for what's for sale. All the good homesteads are already gone. That'll be two dollars please." As she turned away, she said over her shoulder, "You might talk to Mike Skinner. He's about five miles out along the river."

"Is that the river down there?" Abe asked.

"No that's just the creek. Follow the river to the first side-creek and then head upstream."

"Thanks."

"Don't say I told you," she said and then vanished through a swinging door into the kitchen.

"All right, I won't," he said. Then, to Blair, "Want to try it?"

"I'm just along for the ride, except I've got to peel off to see my folks. Maybe you ought to head out alone. That way I can get my business done and won't hold you up. I know you're in a hurry to get back."

"Where will I find you?"

Blair explained how to get to his family's place. Abe had the thought that it was strange no one in the town seemed to recognize or speak to Blair, and asked about it.

"I never really lived here. Grew up in Wyoming and I helped them move here, but then I took off on my own." He mounted up and waved, "So, seeya soon." He rode off.

The river was low, but Abe could see high water marks from the spring thaw and the small log jams that were now high and dry on the banks. The nearest mountains had no snow at this time of the year, but they looked like the kind he'd heard could carry quite a load of it during the winter. The wagon road followed the river and Abe thought it must get treacherous during high water, if it stayed passable at all. The road forked when it came to a fairly large creek and he turned up that fork. He rode for several miles and then came around a bluff that jutted toward the creek. There was a ranch, a few low-slung buildings, corrals, and some high stacks of hay. It looked livable, but it didn't look like easy living. He wondered what Sarah Beth would have to say about this country. As he sat looking down the slope from the road toward the ranch, he wondered how she was and whether Grace had her baby yet. Well, no way to know. Sooner he got back the better.

He pulled up in front of what was obviously the main building, but no one appeared and he sat there on his horse for awhile, not sure about what to do next. Then he heard the ringing of metal on metal coming from one of the barn structures. Someone in a smithy, perhaps. He tied Bird to a railing and walked toward the sounds coming from the barn. A large man was swinging a hammer at a piece of rod iron. When he stopped pounding long enough to thrust the rod back into the forge, Abe cleared his throat and spoke up.

The man turned slowly around and looked him over. "You lost or found?" he said.

Abe smiled and said, "Remains to be seen, I guess. Looking for Mister Mike Skinner."

"Well, he might be here if he knows what you want. Excuse me." He pulled the red-hot iron rod from the forge fire and began banging on it again. He was working to flatten it. When it cooled again, he stuck it back in the heat and said,

"You got business with him, or just curiosity?"

"Trying to find a place for me and my wife to settle. Someone said to ask you."

"Don't know why me. What do you want it for? Cattle, sheep, fruit trees? There's some land around here yet, but it's no good without a lot of hard work." He used his tongs to grab the hot metal again, flattened it some more and then dropped it in a water barrel. Steam blasted and the man whipped off his leather apron and waved it at the hot air. "You can get scalded that way, know that?" he said. "C'mon with me."

A few minutes later they were sitting on a bench under a small tree, passing a jug of cold water back and forth.

They were silent for awhile and then Abe decided to answer the man's question. "Got a small bunch of cattle back down in Utah."

"Well, hate to discourage you, but there's nowhere to sell cattle around here except the mines, and they mostly buy from me and a couple of other guys. You come through Boise area?"

"Stayed south of the big river."

"That place is growing and might be a lot better for you than here. Besides, this ain't no place to raise a family. My wife run off second year we were here. Said it was too lonely, said it wasn't human to live way out here. I kind of like it myself, but I could see her point. Women like company, and if they can't get it, they'll run off and find it."

"I was thinking about just that while riding out here," Abe said, "but I'm thinking you don't know until you try."

"Have it your own way," the man said as he stood up. "Head on out that way, follow that creek. It's small now, but it runs all year. You'll come to a series of beaver dams. Most of the beaver been trapped out, but their dams are still there. Indians too, they camp there sometimes, but they might make you a deal," he laughed. "Otherwise, not much else."

"Well, thank you sir. I appreciate it."

"Don't thank me for nothing. Leastways not until you find out if I've helped or not. Most likely not." He walked back toward the barn, not even turning to see if Abe was leaving.

Abe followed the man's directions and easily found the series of beaver dams. He kept working his way along the creek, sometimes having to climb up and away in order to get around thickets of brush. Then, at a certain point he noticed a thin column of smoke up ahead. Somebody, but who? Mr. Skinner only mentioned Indians, so it was either them or some other stranger that Skinner didn't talk about. Abe debated whether or not to go on and find out. He reasoned he didn't come this far not to know what was going on hereabouts.

He came to a large open meadow of some size that stretched on both sides of the creek to meet the steep hillsides that closed in the little valley on the north and the south. Across the creek were two tipi lodges, one of which was the source of the smoke. Some children came running out, but when they saw him they disappeared into bushes on that side of the creek.

He hollered, "Hello, hello there." And got no answer.

He climbed down out of the saddle and stood by the edge of the clear bubbling water. Someone else must be over there; the children wouldn't be left alone. Still, no one appeared. Just then Bird jerked her head and nearly pulled the reins out of his loose grip. He turned around to see a man standing only a few feet away from him, an Indian dressed in a combination of buckskin and flannel.

"Ho!" the man said.

Abe replied, "Ho." and stuck out his hand. The man folded his arms across his chest and stepped sideways so that he too was standing next to the water.

"Lost? Want something? Nothing for you."

"Ah, you speak English. Good. No, I'm not lost. Looking for a place to live someday. Mr. Skinner pointed me this way. Told me you Indians might be here. I come in friendship."

"Don't have many English." His hands fluttered and made a motion of flying away. "But know horse like this." Then his hands fluttered again. "Bird."

"That's right. This horse belonged to an Indian. He gave it to me."

"Horse like this." The Indian pointed to the one of Bird's legs that was almost all white.

The dark hide over her rear half also had several white spots, which to Abe had always been the horse's significant markings, but since he'd been west he knew there were many Indian horses with similar spotted coats, but he'd seen none with a white leg like this. "Good horse," the man said. Now he walked around the horse and then back again. Then he vigorously pointed to his left hand with his right.

"Yes, Left Hand," Abe said, although this was too much of a coincidence that another Indian, just like the ones in Colorado, would recognize Lefty's horse and know Lefty.

The Indian kept shaking his left hand and pointing to it.

Abe finally said, "Lefty? You know Lefty?"

"Yes, yes. All know. Name is," he pointed to his left hand again and gave the cry of a crow. A perfect imitation, Abe thought.

"That's right, Left Hand Crow. I can't believe you know him. I mean," Abe pointed at the man and then at his own left hand, "you, him, you know him?"

"I say, all know, Indians, whites, all. Great man. Good horse. Why you have horse?" He stepped back a couple of paces and placed his hand on the knife at his waist. "You kill Lefty? You steal horse?"

"No, no, he gave her to me. He said she would take care of me and he was right, why, back in Colorado . . ." He stopped talking suddenly, realizing the man had no idea what he was saying. He reached back into one of his saddlebags and took out a wrapped plug of tobacco. He never used it himself, but found it useful as a gift to most men he ran into out here. He offered it to the Indian, who took it and bit off a piece, chewing vigorously, then spitting.

"HaHo." The man offered the plug back to Abe.

"No," he refused to take it, "for you."

"Yes?"

"Yes."

"Come, eat." The man stepped into the creek and quickly walked across it. Abe mounted and followed on Bird, thinking, he had the horse everybody knew, and Lefty was the man everyone knew. He wondered how Dr. Randall would interpret these fortuitous connections and their happenstances. And yet, he thought, although the west was a huge place, there weren't all that many people, so maybe it wasn't that unusual. Suddenly, he couldn't wait to see Lefty again.

The lodge was smoky inside, but the air was clear down low where the two men sat. Sleeping platforms at the rear were covered with what looked like elk hides. The two women inside the lodge appeared to be nearly the same age, and looked like sisters.

"I, Hawk Man," the man touched his large curved nose and laughed. "I Hawk Man. My wifes," he said. Then he looked at Abe curiously, "You wives?"

"I left her with friends so I could look for a home for us."

Hawk Man waved his hand in a gesture of dismissal as if he didn't understand, and didn't need to. One of the women handed Abe a wooden bowl of steaming meat. He thanked her and was treated to a flashing smile.

The women sat off to one side, apparently waiting for the men to eat first. Abe and Hawk Man blew on their bowlfuls to try to cool them, snatching morsels from the broth with their fingers. Neither spoke. Finally the food was cooled enough to swallow, and it disappeared quickly. Hawk Man turned down another bowl, but tried to get Abe to accept more. Abe turned his bowl upside down to sign that he'd had enough. The woman who served him came and took their bowls and filled them for herself and the other woman. Again, she gave Abe a bright smile.

Hawk Man gestured toward that woman as she sat down to eat in the back. "She have English. Name Mary Wolf Woman. She talk you." He gestured to the woman and said a few words in their own language.

"He say tell you I am Mary Wolf Woman, name Mary by mission people at school, name Wolf Woman by father who sees wolf near camp night I am born. He says tell you I was taken to mission school for this many years." She raised one hand, fingers extended to sign the number five. "Then come back to my people." She stopped and looked back over at Hawk Man, who spoke some more to her.

"He say where your wives? How you have Left Hand Crow horse?"

"I'm pleased that you can speak my language so well. Tell him my wife is waiting for me in Utah country. Lefty gave me the horse when we became friends back in Missouri, before I came west. He said . . ."

The woman cut him off, laughing, "Too much, speak too much." Then she repeated what he'd said to her husband. Hawk Man spoke for awhile, nodding all the time. The woman covered her face with her hands, and shook her head, no. Hawk Man urged her to speak to Abe, and she said, "He says you are friend of Lefty, you stay here with us. He say," and she paused while the man urged her on. "He say you have no woman, you will have me because nights are cold." She kept her eyes on her hands while she said this.

Abe didn't have any idea what to say, and stumbled a bit before replying, "That's all right. Tell him thank you, but I will be warm enough and my wife would not like that." She translated and the man laughed and said something, then laughed some more, waving at the woman to continue.

She kept looking down while she said, "He says your woman will not know, because he will not tell her."

"Tell him I thank him and I think you are lovely, but the ways of my people are different. We only have one wife and she is our only woman for sleeping with."

She again translated. Hawk Man waved his hand as if to brush away a fly or some other nuisance, and then he spoke softly. The woman translated his words as "How unfortunate for your women. Only one woman take all care of one man."

There was silence in the lodge for a few minutes while the women ate their food and Hawk Man prepared his pipe for smoking. Abe was beginning to wonder how, if at all, he could bring up the subject of land and its availability. He was incredibly glad that this man knew Lefty and was an admirer, but how did that fit in with God's will for his and Sarah Beth's lives? Obviously these coincidences kept revealing to him something of a Divine design, but what was it exactly and would he ever know it? Once again, he found himself missing the wisdom of Dr. Randall.

Mary Wolf Woman took the other woman's bowl and her own and bowed out of the lodge. The other woman followed her out, also bowing.

Hawk Man pointed at Abe with his chin and held the pipe out. Abe wasn't sure whether to take it, but when he reached for it, Hawk Man pulled it back and began lighting it from embers in the small fire in front of him. He smoked, and then held the pipe above his head, then passed it to Abe, who carefully took a small puff, and then also held it up and handed it back. The Indian smoked again and turned the pipe around, pointing in several directions around the lodge. Then he spoke some words and smoked some more. He offered the pipe once more to Abe, who smiled, took it, turned it around, and then handed it back without smoking. Hawk Man grunted, but seemed pleased. He continued smoking until the coals in the stone pipe were gone, then he used a small sharp stick or bone to empty the ashes out beside the fire.

He put the pipe away in its bag and placed it behind him. Then he said, "Horses," and got up to leave the lodge. Abe followed him and watched as Hawk Man tied his five horses to willows. Abe hobbled Bird, hoping she would still be able to eat some during the night without getting into any trouble. He realized he hadn't decided to stay the night, it just happened that way. Well, hopefully morning would bring an opportunity to talk about the business he was here for. In the meantime, there would have to be some arrangement for sleeping that didn't include him lying next to the woman, for both of their sakes.

Two days later, Sarah Beth was informed by messenger that the wedding would be held next day. She'd spent the past two days by herself, alternately crying and fuming over her situation. She'd taken Morning on a short ride to see if she would be followed, but hadn't been able to tell. She had no doubt that this man meant it when he said Abe would be in danger if she went against his demands. It was very apparent he really was the only law in this place. At the same time she was fearful of what could happen when Abe returned and found out. Would he go crazy with anger and get both of them killed? Or would he just take it on with some sense of pain, and hope that it all would somehow get better? She couldn't be sure in this instance how he would react, but she knew that whatever he did would be based on trying to save them both. Her best feeling came from the idea that he would find some way of escape.

Finally, she decided that the only thing she could really do about it for now was whatever it took to find out from Grace just what had happened, and what her words meant. So early in the afternoon she saddled Bird and rode over to the Bishop's compound. She knew she would not be welcomed by the other women, but she planned to say it was necessary for her to check on Grace. In truth, something could still go wrong and Sarah Beth actually wanted to make sure that the young woman was all right, and under adequate care.

She tied Morning to one of the few small trees, and went straight into the structure without speaking with anyone. Once she got near the tiny alcove where the birth took place, she was surprised to see the curtains and bed removed. She spun around, looking everywhere in the half-finished house, but she found no sign of the young woman or anyone else. Sarah Beth hurried back out, but again saw no one. Then she caught a glimpse of the girl, Helga, who seemed to be hiding around the corner of the building, but hiding as if she wanted to be seen.

Sarah Beth walked toward her, but the girl gestured with a negative sign and pointed up toward the hill behind the buildings. It wasn't far away and Sarah Beth saw a trail leading upward. She caught the reins of her horse, mounted, and trotted Morning in that direction. When she was out of sight of the structures in the clearing, she stopped and waited, hoping this was what the girl meant her to do.

A short time later, Helga appeared, running up the trail and out of breath.

"Miss Sarah Beth," she gasped out as she tried to catch her wind. "So glad you came. Grace is gone."

Sarah Beth slid down from the saddle. "What do you mean, gone?"

The girl was breathing easier now. "They sent her away to another family. When she heard about your wedding to the Bishop she got angry and started screaming all kinds of things. So the women tied her up and they took her and the baby away."

"What kind of things was she saying?"

"About the Bishop being evil. And about they better not hurt you. And how she never wanted the baby, but now no one could take it away from her. She said she would die to keep her baby . . . Then,

I can't believe it, but she said the Bishop wasn't the baby's father, and that's when the women tied a scarf around her head and in her mouth. Then she seemed to faint and they took her and the baby out to a wagon and one of the men drove it away, with another man riding alongside, holding the baby."

"Poor girl, poor sweet girl."

"I have to go. They'll beat me if they know I'm with you. The women say the Bishop is making a mistake, that you will cause him trouble. I have to go." She turned and ran down the hillside, not taking the trail, but plunging through the shrubs that grew among the rocks.

One part of Sarah Beth didn't want to know that this was true. She knew she was in real danger, and Grace as well. She looked around for a trail across the top of the hill so she could work her way back to their place without having to cross through the growing settlement below.

She thought as she rode, letting Morning pick his way through the rocks and brush of an animal trail. If the Bishop wasn't the father of Grace's child, then who was? Or did it matter? What mattered was that the Bishop must have forced her into something because either he wasn't able to give her a child, or because the other man was more powerful than the Bishop in some way or other. He was getting on in years and a man loses his abilities, or so she'd heard. But forcing a young wife to make a child with someone else didn't make any sense to her. Suddenly she realized it didn't need to make sense; these people had their own strange ways. But she'd better be aware. It might be what he had in mind for her. Oh my God, she thought, praying, what can I do to protect Abe, to protect us? She breathed deeply and tried to think calmly. First things first, she knew she had to get through this false wedding and then face the Bishop in his own quarters, for whatever that might mean when it happened.

She wore pants on the day of the wedding, trying to look as unattractive as possible. One of the Bishop's sons came to get her in a buggy. She still couldn't keep the young men sorted out by name, and she didn't even know how many sons there were. The two of them rode in silence back to the compound. When they arrived, one of the wives escorted Sarah Beth to a spot near the Bishop's tent. He and three other men stood there, all dressed in their formal black suits, waiting for her. The woman stepped back a ways at the bishop's gesture, and then he motioned for Sarah Beth to come stand next to him.

One of the men stepped in front of them and read some words from a text. It went on for awhile; when he stopped reading, she realized she hadn't heard a word of it. Then the Bishop took her hand tightly, and placed a ring on her finger. She was glad she'd taken off the one Abe gave her at their wedding, fearing that it might be taken away from her.

The Bishop said softly, "Now you are my wife. Go with her," he nodded toward the other woman. "Eat, and come back to this tent and wait for me here. Go now."

She turned away slowly and walked toward the half-built kitchen area of the new house. One of the other wives pointed to where she was to sit at a table where some food was set out. They left her to eat alone. Now the reality of it all began to come over her, the insane reality of it. She gagged on a mouthful of some kind of dumplings, and realized she was sick inside, and shivering on the outside. She fought back tears and looked up toward heaven, hoping against hope that something would change. Then she suddenly realized that any time now Abe would be on his way back, coming closer, perhaps even watched and followed. She wanted to scream, but at the same time she didn't want to show any weakness in front of these women. Although she knew it had nothing to do with any of them, she could feel they resented her for the very last thing in the world she would ever want to happen to her. She fought off the trembling and shortness of breath, and tried to compose herself. She knew at least one of them was watching her, had been ordered to keep an eye on her, so she pretended to be eating, and eventually was able to swallow and even feel some hunger. She'd hardly eaten for days and it was actually kind of a relief to feel food going down her throat.

She ate as much as she could, trying hard not to think about Abe. It would only make what was coming worse. How could she save him? Was there any other way than submission to this horrible man? What, if any, chance did she have now that she was a hostage, and now that Abe was threatened?

She got slowly to her feet. Like a condemned person walking to the gallows, she hesitated at every step that took her out into the yard and then toward the Bishop's tent. She realized she had just been married to a man and didn't even know his name. If only all this wasn't so horrible, that would be some kind of a joke, or at least something to make light of. But it was all real now, all too real, and she felt herself frozen inside the moment of entering his tent, not knowing if he were there or not, desiring only to flee, to escape, but knowing that path risked both her life and Abe's. There was only one thing she could do now to buy time and that was to submit, or at least appear to, even as she knew she would never ever willingly give anything to this man, this awful man so deranged with his own power.

She pushed aside the flap on the tent. She saw no one inside, only a chair, a tiny box, and the bed. The stark emptiness made her think of a jail cell and she could almost feel the irons around her arms and legs. "Dear God," she whispered, "please, please protect me, your child; protect me, I pray in Jesus's name." And then she had the thought: what if this was all God's will? But how could that be possible? If this was allowed to happen to her for no reason that she could understand, she knew that it would be hard for her, if not impossible, to ever again believe in a God of justice.

She sat down quietly on the chair, staring at the horror of the man's bed and struggling as hard as she could to somehow to ignore all of this, and think only of the day that she and Abe could be rejoined, when the terror of this awful nightmare ended.

Perhaps an hour went by as the tent darkened with the fading light of the evening. Then she heard his voice outside, telling someone to leave him alone now. The flap opened and he was inside. He took two steps toward her. Before she could move, he gripped her by the shoulder with one strong hand and pulled her out of the chair. He was carrying a lit candle that he used to light the other two. He let go of her and he sat on the chair.

"Are you afraid?" he asked.

She didn't want to answer, but she shook her head, "No."

"Good, you have nothing to fear . . . as long as you are obedient."

She found herself huddling against the tent wall farthest from him.

"Come here, into the light."

She slowly did as she was told.

"Come closer . . . Now turn away from me, bend over . . . . Bend over and touch the ground."

Again she did as she was told, having no idea what this was about. He pulled the chair closer to her, now sitting very close behind her. If she twisted her head slightly she could see him between her legs, see up to his knees, up to where his hands were now reaching inside his pants at his crotch. She shifted her weight from one leg to the other.

She felt his nose touch her and his face press against her buttocks. She was almost pushed over forward and reached out one hand to steady herself against the foot of the bed.

He made a low moaning sound, and then said, "Since I first saw you . . . this is what I wanted. This . . ."

Her legs were beginning to ache and even tremble from the strain of holding this awkward position . . . she realized that perhaps he was telling the truth, that this was all he could do to her, that Grace was right, and he couldn't do any more than this. Suddenly he pushed her forward onto the bed, and sharply commanded, "Turn over."

She rolled over with her feet still on the ground and her back arched over the end of the high bed. She held her head up with her arms and hands, watching him now, fearing that he would lunge forward onto her, knowing she would fight him.

But he stayed where he was, seated in the chair with his hands down the front of his pants. And he said quietly, "There's nothing harmful I can do to you now, but you must never speak of that, to anyone. You are my wife, and that is enough. I will have whatever I want from you. Now slowly unbutton your shirt, your man's shirt."

Sarah Beth sat up slowly, facing him. She forced herself to speak, "I know what you did to Grace, and now I know why."

"Don't speak of her," he said in a near-shout. There was a long pause, and when he spoke again it was softly. "She is a harlot."

"And you made her that way." Sarah Beth felt some of her strength returning.

"I did not. She is a sinful, lustful wench who has no right to everything I have done for her. I rescued her when she had nothing."

"But you made her do it." Sarah Beth felt the thoughts race through her mind as if they were gusts of wind, each one blowing harder and harder on this sudden revelation.

The man was nearly collapsing in the chair now, as if the air had gone out of him, but his hands inside his pants were still moving. "She is nothing but an ungrateful sinner, an adulteress, and a harlot."

"But you made her go with another man because you were ashamed of what you have become." She stood up now, looking down at him. "And what you have become is an old, old man, a helpless old man. You don't want anyone to know, but now I know."

"She took pleasure in it. I was watching them, she had what she wanted, and she took pleasure in her sinning. A harlot, I say." Now he stood up and they were face to face.

"You will let me go, and you will not harm my husband, or I will tell the world that you are nothing more than an evil old whoremaster."

He stepped back and looked closely into her face and eyes, perhaps for the first time, and said, "And if I get rid of you and your husband, who will know?"

Her mind raced to deal with this, and she slowly said, "I have left a letter to be opened if I disappear or am killed." She tried to think fast enough to complete the lie, and then went on, "It will be given to the Church authorities in Salt Lake and a copy to the court and," she paused and added, "there is someone who hates you enough to make sure it is delivered."

He took another step back and said, "And what if there are no witnesses, no harlot, no unbelievers like you and that young man, what if you no longer exist? What if there is no one to say any of this happened?"

"Take your chances, old man," she said as she pushed past him and left the tent, now running for her horse.

On the way back, Abe and Blair rode into some snow showers as they passed through the higher ground. They made their way slowly, and Abe found himself thinking about the unusual and surprising turn of events that occurred with Hawk Man that second morning as Abe prepared to leave the camp. The Indian man had taken him and Mary Wolf Woman to a place slightly above the small valley so that he could show his new acquaintance the land that he still held in some kind of trust for his tribe.

"He says to tell you all this, from those trees at the top on one side and those rocks on top other side is his people's place, for longer than the old ones can remember. His people came here to camp every year, but not so much anymore." Hawk Man was talking and his woman was also talking and translating at the same time. "He stays here when the grass is green and the snows are far away."

Abe nodded and the other man reached out and took his shoulder in one hand and turned him around. Mary Wolf continued translating. "One day the white man will try to take this place for himself. But we cannot let that be. It is our people who must have this place. You are the left hand man's friend so you will help us, because he is one of us. His great-grandmother was also my great-grandmother." Hawk Man sat down on the ground and motioned for Abe to do the same. The woman remained standing. "He says he will make you one with this land to live here with your woman so no other white man will take it," she said.

Hawk Man pulled a knife out of his belt and scraped away the grass and pebbles from a spot on the ground between them. He handed the knife to Abe and made a gesture of cutting his own third finger. The woman said softly, "He say he wants you to give your blood to this place so you will live here."

Abe felt the sharpness of the blade, a store-bought knife of good quality. The edge was like a razor. He turned it over and over in his hands. He understood what was expected of him and he knew that Hawk Man was waiting. He pulled the knife blade slowly above the middle joint of his finger. Blood dripped onto the ground. With lightning speed, Hawk Man grabbed his wrist and squeezed the finger to make it bleed even more, still dripping into the ground. Then he pinched dirt between his forefinger and thumb and pressed it into the wound, held it there with his thumb. He said some words in his own language, and then said in English, "You welcome here now."

After a few minutes of silence, the three of them walked back to the camp. Hawk Man explained through Mary Wolf Woman that other white men might be angry with Abe, but the Indian people would say he was working for them. He could build a house for his wife and have cattle. Only he must allow the Indians to have their camps and visits with Hawk Man and his family. Then he said this was all because he prayed for a way to keep the land before the white men took it away or there was a big fight. He said that if his new friend must sign paper to belong in this place, paper with white judges, that was all right, as long as he remembered whose land it really was.

Abe still couldn't understand how all of this could be coming about simply because of his own curiosity tracing back to an Indian camp in Missouri, and Lefty's friendship, and the horse. But rather than question it too much, he knew he should simply be grateful, give thanks. He couldn't wait to share the news with Sarah Beth.

After that, the days of the ride back home were uneventful until they got within twenty miles of the Logan Valley. Just as they turned away from the road to Salt Lake and were feeling good about being almost home, they were accosted by two of the Bishop's sons and another man. Abe had been experiencing a growing excitement ever since they'd started out before daylight that morning. Now, suddenly he was confused. What was this about?

"I know you," he said. "What's going on?"

The two younger men stared at him, and sat still on their horses, their hands near the pistols they each wore. The other man, a stranger to Abe, spoke first, "You're young Saunders."

He didn't say anything else so Abe answered what might have been a question, "Yes, that's me."

"We're to escort you to that woman you came with, and then we're to make sure you both leave these parts as fast as you can. Bishop's orders."

'What?" Abe felt a tremor go through Bird as if she too felt the threat in the man's voice. "Please explain."

"The Bishop wants you gone, gone for good. You'll find out why when you reach your camp and that woman you call a wife."

Then they ordered Blair to get on his way and stay away from the Bishop's compound.

CHAPTER FOURTEEN

Moving Again

Their reunion and the first moments of Abe's homecoming had been so sweet and such a relief for Sarah Beth that she didn't want to tell him anything. He'd nearly flown off his horse, sweeping her into his arms. But then, as soon as they'd had a long, long kiss, he suddenly held her away from him, and said he needed to know what was going on, what had happened. Then he gestured at the three men who were still mounted and watching some distance away.

"They escorted me here. Said we had to leave as soon as possible. Tell me."

She was starting to cry, not knowing if it was caused by Abe's safe return, or from the built-up despair she'd been living with for the past few days. She took his hand and led him into their little camp room, out of sight of the watchers, and sat him down in front of her. He reached out, wiping the tears from her face as she knelt in front of him.

"You won't believe it, I don't know where to start . . . I can't."

"It's all right, Sarah Beth. I already know we have to leave here, those men told me, but they wouldn't say why."

She started by trying to tell him everything, from the threats to the marriage, and then the terrifying night she'd been alone with the Bishop in his tent. She tried to tell him everything she could, but it was hard since her sobbing was shaking her so hard, and she was getting it all mixed together. Finally, he just pulled her to him and told her to stop trying to talk, it would be all right, he could wait, all he cared about that she was safe and they were back together again. Besides, he had good news, news that the Bishop couldn't spoil, couldn't do anything about.

"Oh, Abe, it was all just so awful!" She pulled him out of his chair so that they were both kneeling together face-to-face, and she said, "I never want you to leave again."

He stood and pulled her up, then kissed her, and again."Sounds like we've got some packing up and moving to do." And then he gave her a look she'd never seen before. "Dear Sarah Beth," he said, "you've got to help me. I have to get out of here before I kill that man for whatever he's done."

"Oh Abe, no, he isn't worth it. He's old and mean and I just want to leave here."

"We will. Let me put Bird away. Wait until you hear how she's helped us now. It'll cheer you up, I promise." He turned and went outside, stopping to turn back and say, "I'll be right back so don't go anywhere." And then he was out the canvas flap-door.

Later that night, Abe told Sarah Beth the story of Hawk Man and his plan, leaving out the part about him offering his wife for the night. She was amazed.

"Abe, I don't know how you do it. You must be the most blessed man alive, or at least the luckiest. You found us a home. Thank you, thank you."

"Thank Lefty and Bird, that's who's doing all this for us."

"And God."

"Of course, God works in mysterious ways, they say, and one of those ways is a spotted horse with one white leg."

Abe went out and took one more look around to make sure there weren't any watchers close-by, and then he went back in to find Sarah Beth already in their bed with the quilt pulled up under her chin. He quickly undressed and pushed his way in with her. They made love fast, and then slow, and then they fell asleep, once again at home in one another's arms.

The next morning, Abe strapped on his handgun and saddled up their two horses.

"Come with me," he said to Sarah Beth. "I need to find Blair to see if he knows about a place we passed back a ways. It had been started as someone's home, but it looks abandoned."

So they rode off at a gallop. They looked back every once in awhile, but seeing no one following, they slowed the horses and settled into their ride. Sarah Beth asked Abe again to describe what this new place was like, "in every detail," she said.

He did his best to paint a picture in words for her, but ended by saying, "You'll just have to see it to believe it."

They asked around in the small town where Abe had said goodbye to his travelling companion and were told that Blair was working on a place a short distance west of the town. They followed the directions and soon found a small group of men branding calves. Blair was among them.

He looked up when they appeared, saw them, but had to keep on working. They waited until he was able to take breather and found a place to sit in some shade. Even though it was well into the fall, the sun still had heat to give on this summery day. Abe quickly skipped through the story of what happened while they'd been away, saying only that the Bishop demanded that they leave his settlement for certain unspecified reasons. Sarah Beth kept her eyes on the ground in front of herself, worried that he might say something about what came down between herself and the Bishop, but he squeezed her hand reassuringly and didn't mention anything about it.

"So, I'm asking what you know about that abandoned place we passed, or how to find out something . . ."

"You'll need to talk to the judge in the next town, Judge Harcourt, I think it is. Funny name for a judge, huh? He keeps all the land records for the government, and for the Church. Pretty much the same thing here, huh?"

"What's he like?"

"They say he's a fair man, what some of us 'unbelievers' call a Good Mormon."

"Thanks, Blair. Well, we better keep moving so we can get back and protect our things. I don't trust that Bishop or any of his folks either. Thanks for your help. If we get settled nearby, you'll have to come see us . . . Oh, and don't let that Bishop take advantage of you."

"Right. I'll come see you if I can. Good luck. Ma'am, it was good travelling with your husband. He kept me cheerful."

Abe and Sarah Beth mounted and rode off toward the next small settlement.

The Judge was easy to find. The first person they asked pointed down the town's one bumpy street and said, "He always has court outdoors unless it's raining, or snowing."

They found the court in session under a large tree. The Judge was a big man with a broad smile on his face as he listened to what appeared to be the question of debt between two agitated men. They were both raising their voices and their fists at one another when the Judge finally had enough and banged an old cow's bone on the small table in front of him and called for order in the court.

"You're both wrong, boys, and you're both a little bit in the right, so following my predecessor Solomon's example, I hereby order you Mr. Thompson to pay back one-half of what Mr. Bisbee says you owe him, and Mr. Bisbee, I don't want to hear another word about this matter from you or anyone else. Case closed." He hit the table again. "Court is now in recess until I start it up again which most likely won't be until tomorrow."

Abe took Sarah Beth's arm and the two of them moved up to stand near the Judge. The man looked like he was almost asleep, then he shook himself and looked straight at Abe.

"You're that young couple had some misfortune over there at the Bishop's place.

Sorry to hear about it, but there's nothing I can do for you. The man may be difficult, some say impossible, and he don't know our ways out here yet, but he's got the law on his side, even if he violates the spirit of our Church. Now is there anything else I can do for you? Because if not, it is time for my nap."

Abe and Sarah Beth looked at one another, surprised that he already knew about them; neither was sure how to proceed.

"Sir, we didn't come here for legal help," Abe started saying, but the Judge interrupted.

"Might be the only kind I got to give." Then he laughed and put his feet up on the small table, nearing toppling it over."Well, speak up."

"Sir, I recently rode by a place not far west of here that looked as though it was off to a pretty good start. Now it looks abandoned."

"Well, you're right on both counts. Good start, now abandoned, and you'd like to know if it's available and somebody told you I'm the man to see. Well, I might be, then again I might not be. Those poor folks left the country in a hurry when a Texas Marshall showed up looking for a murderer or some such thing. They weren't believers among us, but the fella had been given the right to try his hand at the place because he was, or said he was, an animal doctor, and we surely do need one around here. So, I guess I need to ask what good are you to a community of us Latter Day Saints?"

"Well sir, first of all it'd only be temporary. We've got a place waiting over in Oregon, but it's too late to get there now, especially with the cows we've got to move."

"I see. Anything else to put up, besides offering to leave as soon as you can?"

"Well, my wife here helps bring babies into this world."

"So, I've heard. Saved that poor girl over at the Bishop's place. You know, he sent that girl packing too. Up to me to also find her a place, which I did. You know, that man is causing me more trouble every time I look around. Tell you what I'll do, let you stay out there if you can make it without help, and if you give two beef animals to the local folks at what we call our temple. And if this woman is on call for birthing business."

"Thank you sir, I don't think we have much choice. Your terms are certainly generous enough, and we are in kind of a hurry."

"So I've heard. Well, get moving. I'm late for my nap."

"What if someone doesn't like us being there?"

"You leave that part up to me. I don't think you'll have any problems with that."

Riding back, Sarah Beth pulled up alongside Abe and leaned over to say, "Abe Saunders, I don't know how you do it, but you must be the most fortunate man alive."

He reached out for her hand and said, "You mean because I have you?" Then he leaned to try and kiss her and she pulled away, laughing and almost yanking him out of the saddle.

They packed up and dismantled what had been the beginnings of their more permanent camp. They were ready to move out by the third morning after their return from meeting with the Judge. Once again, they were on a trail with everything they owned in the wagon, pulled by the oxen and driven by Sarah Beth. Abe had been able to recruit Blair to help with driving the small herd of cattle, but as they moved out they heard a sudden commotion at the top of a rise toward the Bishop's settlement.

Abe signaled Sarah Beth to hold back the wagon while he investigated. As he got closer he could see that it was two young men driving a small bunch, maybe half a dozen or more, of cattle. He pulled up, waiting for them to turn aside toward the meadows. Instead, they circled up the cattle and one man held them there while the other came up to Abe. It was one of the bishop's sons, the one Abe knew as Phillip. He raised his hand in greeting to Abe and held up his horse a little ways away.

"My father says he wants you to take these cattle with you. Says he doesn't want anyone thinking he treated you poorly. And he said he hoped you wouldn't say anything except things didn't work out and you moving on was for the best. That's what he said to say. And he said you'd know what he meant." Then the young man spun around and rode off, joined by the other rider. Abe turned and waved back to Blair to join him. There wasn't time to think this over if he was going to gather these cows and combine them with his own. After a bit of hard riding, the job was done and Blair took over moving the whole bunch along by himself. Abe rode back to Sarah Beth to explain what had happened.

"Bribery," she said, almost spitting out the word.

"Yeah," Abe said, walking his horse alongside her, "but a good bribe."

'Well, good for you, and I guess for me. What he doesn't know is that what happened is so shameful that I wouldn't talk about it to anyone besides you anyway."

"Well, I promise not to say anything either, but we'd better have the same story about why this happened. Let's just say he owed us for work we'd already done for him."

"All right." She flicked her whip over the backs of the oxen and shouted to him, "Let's get going, daylight's a wasting."

Abe waited for a look from her before he rode off, and she did finally give him one, with a kind of secretive smile, then she was back to her driving. He rode off to rejoin Blair and the herd, which was now a third larger.

Blair yelled out to him, "What happened?"

"Bishop owed us for some back work, guess he decided to pay up. Have to admit, I didn't think he would, but he wants things square between us." Then he urged Bird into the job of pushing the three or four cows who wanted to turn back where they'd come from. All he had to do now was find enough forage to take this many animals through winter, and pray for it to be a mild one.

That night they made camp near a small lake and made sure the cows were going to stay together before they took a break for supper. Sarah Beth was cooking over a fire when the two young men returned to camp.

"Guess I haven't forgotten how to do this," she said.

"Hope not," Abe said, "and I hope you remember I like my biscuits a bit soft."

"Who says you're getting biscuits?" she said as she used a glove to grab the Dutch oven and remove its lid to check on the biscuits.

The three of them ate quietly, and then Blair left to take first watch on the cattle. The night was cooling fast. Abe dragged in more wood for the fire while Sarah Beth finished cleaning up. Blair was out watching over the cattle. Suddenly they both heard a horse coming closer and closer, moving at a gallop. Abe grabbed the lantern from where it was hanging on the wagon, and held it up to see what or who was coming.

The horse stopped just outside the ring of lantern light and someone yelled at it to go back where it came from. Then a girl walked into the dim light of the lantern and the fire. It was Helga. Sarah Beth rushed forward to meet her and the girl fell into her arms.

"What are you doing here?" Sarah Beth asked.

The girl was out of breath from her ride, but managed to say, "I was so afraid I wouldn't find you."

Sarah Beth helped her closer to the fire and sat her down, and then unwrapped some of the biscuits and meat left over from their supper. "Here, you must be hungry."

Now the girl was crying and trying to eat at the same time. Sarah Beth sat down beside her and put an arm around her shoulders. Abe built up the fire, not really sure who this person was, though he could see that Sarah Beth certainly knew her. Finally the girl seemed to catch her breath and push away the food long enough to say something clearly.

"I ran away. Please don't send me back. I took a horse, but just now I sent it back. Oh, I hope they don't come after me, but Miss Sarah Beth, please don't let them take me back. I'll do anything for you."

"There, Helga, that's enough now. You'll stay with us," she glanced at Abe and shook her head yes as if asking him to agree with her.

"Of course," he said.

"Now you just settle down and eat something. I doubt if you brought any food with you."

The girl began eating, slowly at first and then her hunger came alive, and Sarah Beth had to find more food for her. When Helga seemed to have had enough, Sarah Beth asked her what had happened.

"Right after you left, one of his sons caught me in the shed they made for their things, you know the one," she said, still fighting back tears. "I was sent to find some bedding for a new bed they made. It was that one named Thomas, do you know him?"

"Not really, I never could tell them all apart," Sarah Beth said.

"Well, he pushed me into a corner and said now that you were gone there was no one to take up for me. I don't know how he knew you were good to me when Grace was having her baby. Those wives must have been talking. And I never got to thank you for that either. So thank you, Miss Sarah Beth. That's why I came to you. I knew they would make my life like the Devil's own Hell on earth. They hated my mother."

"How did you end up with them? I guess I thought you were their relative."

"I am. My mother was the Bishop's niece, but she ran away when she was young and had me. When they found her they threw her out of the family, but took me away from her. When I was growing up they told me never to turn out like my mother who left the Church and had a baby without a husband . . . That baby was me. So they took me away from her and made me do their work for them, as much as I could do. I didn't mind the work but they were mean too, and I used to dream of running away. I never had a chance until now . . . Please, please don't send me back. I'll just stay a little while and go on my own if you don't want me around, but please."

"Well, it's all going to be all right. And this is Abe, my husband. I don't think you ever met him before. So can you tell me what happened with that Thomas?"

"I hate him so much. He was pulling at my clothes and I was pushing him away. He's not so strong as me, but I was against that wall. Then I felt something dig into my back and reached behind me and it was some kind of tool. I never saw what it was. I grabbed it and hit him on his neck and he yelled out and fell down. I hit him hard."

"And were you able to get away?"

"Yes, but when I was leaving the shed he said if I ever said anything he'd beat me so bad . . . Then this morning I did get beat. See?" She leaned close to the fire where Sarah Beth could now see a swollen bruise on the girl's cheek.

"I'll get you something for that, but tell us how it happened?"

"This morning, the Bishop called for me to come to his tent. I was so scared that Thomas had told him some lies or something, but when

I went in he started yelling at me about a letter. About a letter from you and I better give it to him. I told him I didn't have any letter and didn't know anything about it. That's when he hit me with his fist, hit me so hard I fell down. But I was screaming that I didn't have any letter. Then he kicked me and told me to get out and stay out of his sight or he'd beat me some more. And I'd better come up with that letter."

"Oh, Helga, I'm so sorry. I told him I was leaving a letter with someone about what he'd done to us. I made that up so he wouldn't harm us, and I never said who I gave it to. I'm so sorry." She put her arm around the girl's shoulders and held her close. "You must be so tired. I'll make you a place to sleep. We'll get going early, so we all need to get some sleep now." She went to the wagon and pulled out some bedding and made a place near the fire. "You'll sleep here. Abe will have to take a turn watching the cattle in the night, so if he wakes you up, don't worry about anything, just go back to sleep. We'll see what we can do to help you in the morning. And here, hold this cold rag on your face."

Sarah Beth and Abe walked a ways away from the fire and had a whispered conversation about this latest turn of events. Abe's concern was that this might be enough to rouse the Bishop and his people to pursue them and take the girl back by force if necessary. Sarah Beth told him how poorly the girl was being treated and how she didn't think anyone really wanted her there, in spite of all the work she did.

"Well, we'll see. That horse may find its way back and they might think she fell off somewhere, who knows."

"Abe, from what I know about her and the help she gave me, she's a good girl, and I just couldn't send her back to them."

"OK, my dear, we'll see what we can do in the morning."

By the time their small party reached the abandoned place that was to become their home for the winter, both Blair and Helga had become useful and even essential to the challenges of moving the cattle and maintaining everything on the trail. The country around the new place was nearly all flat and stretched away for a few miles in every direction. They could see thin plumes of smoke some distance away, probably from other people's homes. Abe decided to call the place Moab after the Plains of Moab, where the Israelites stopped before they entered into the Promised Land.

"That way," he said, "if someone asks us where we live, we can tell them we call it Moab and they may think we're Mormons as well."

They pushed the cattle along to where the grass was still somewhat green near a small creek, and then they all set about cleaning and fixing up the small half-finished cabin that was the only real sign of the previous inhabitants. Later on, Blair left to return to his job on the ranch nearby. He said he'd be back soon for a visit. Sarah Beth made him promise to make it for Thanksgiving, a holiday she was determined not to miss, both as a reminder of home and a sign of occupying a new home in this land.

"I'll try," the young man said, "but I don't even know when that is."

"Do they have a calendar at that ranch of yours?" she asked.

"I think so."

"Well you just be here on the last Wednesday of November and we'll celebrate the next day, just like everybody back in Virginia."

"Yes ma'am, I'll do my best."

As he rode away, Sarah Beth saw Helga give a wave and him return it. Well, she thought, why would it be otherwise? They were the only two young people in sight.

Abe was able to find a sawmill nearby and borrow a flat wagon and horse to haul some boards of random sizes back to their place. They put up a small roofed shed with no walls for their horses and then added a couple of rooms off two sides of the existing cabin.

About then, Abe said he was going to have to take a break from that work and start finding some wood for their fires or they'd go hungry while they were freezing to death.

He was surprised when Helga asked if he would let her help.

"Actually," he said, "if Sarah Beth can spare you here, you might be able to help. I bought another horse and have to go pick her up tomorrow, then we'll see how she suits you. I know you can ride from the way you showed up at our camp that first night."

"Yes," she said, "I can ride."

The next day Abe rode off after the horse he'd bought, an older mare named Ginger, and was back before mid-day. Helga and Ginger seemed to get along from the start, and Abe decided there was still daytime enough to do some scouting for the wood he was after. Although he didn't need any help for this part, he allowed Helga to come along so she and the new horse could get used to each other.

He'd bought the mare mostly for pulling things like a hauling sled and their wagon once they could move out of it, but when he saw how well Helga could ride, he realized that the two newcomers had a lot in common and should be paired up for the time being.

They rode down along a larger stream that wasn't far away, and he was pleased that it didn't look like anyone else had been there for awhile. There was quite a lot of dead wood piled up along the banks from flooding of the recent past. Abe got down off Bird and motioned for Helga to dismount as well. He wrapped a rope around the saddle horn on the new horse, tied the other end to a log that was somewhat balanced on the bank of the stream, and then told Helga to lead the horse forward while he made sure the log didn't hang up on anything. Before long they had quite a bit of wood stacked and ready to be either hauled or cut up. Helga pulled off her knapsack and took some wrapped food from it.

"Miss Sarah Beth sent this for us. She said you haven't eaten all day, and neither have I."

They sat down on one of the logs they'd pulled and ate in silence. When they were finishing up the bread and meat, Abe asked the girl how long she'd been living with the Bishop and his family.

She snapped out, "Too long." And then she apologized and said, "I shouldn't talk like that, it's just that I've never had anyone who was even a little bit nice to me. That's why I was so happy when Miss Sarah Beth came along. She let me help her and even said thank you. In all those years, I had never heard those words . . . Oh, and to answer your question, they found me and my Mom when I was four years old and came after me, so I hardly remember her."

"Well, I'm glad Sarah Beth had a chance to be nice to you. From what she's told me, she really needed your help, because those women wouldn't do anything for her."

"That's because the Bishop told them not to help in any way. He wanted Grace to die, I know he did."

"That's a pretty strong accusation, don't you think?"

"Not for what he's done. But I'm going to forget him from now on, him and all of them, and if you'll let me, I'll do anything I can to help you and Miss Sarah Beth. You'll see I can be a good helper, and I'm strong too."

"I've noticed, and I'm sure we can use the help. It's going to be a hard winter for us since we've had no time to get ready, and it's almost here."

"How are we going to get this wood back to the place?" she asked.

"Well, I was going to build some kind of a sled to load up with the wood. As long as it stays dry and doesn't snow, it should slide pretty good on this grass and the dirt's still hard."

"Do you have some extra rope in your saddle?"

"Yes why?"

"I have an idea. There's no sense wasting a trip back there without some wood. When you said sled, I remembered something I saw when we were in Illinois. Where's your rope and a good knife?"

He got the rope from the saddle-bag and handed it to her with a knife. She asked him if she could cut a couple of short pieces and he said yes. Then she got him to help her line up two rather thin logs a few feet apart. She laid some shorter pieces crosswise and lashed it all together.

"Kind of a sled," she said, "at least it'll work like one," and she began piling limbs and branches on her handiwork. Abe pitched in and soon they had quite a load. Helga used the rest of the rope to tie the load on, and went off to catch Ginger, who was grazing a short distance away. She brought the horse back and looped another rope around the horse's neck in such a way that it would neither tighten up nor tangle in the saddle rigging. She urged the horse into motion and after two tries the load was sliding forward. Abe watched all of this in admiration and realized right then that this was no ordinary girl. Then he asked her if she thought it would help to have Bird tied onto the load as well.

"I don't think we need to, but you could lead Ginger from your horse and that way I can just run along."

"All right." He took the lead rope and pulled ahead on Ginger and they all started heading for home. Abe watched Helga running along, even jumping and skipping, and he knew that she was happier than she'd been in a long time, as well as turning out to be useful. The only drawback he could see in the situation was the lack of privacy for him and Sarah Beth. There was no way to build an extra cabin or shed for the girl, and he knew that he and his dear wife would be very shy about making any attempts to have their physical unions.

The next day Abe went ahead and built a more durable sled out of scrap lumber, since Helga's invention was temporary and nearly falling apart by the time they got it back the their place. It had made it though, so she was right about not wasting a trip back without a load. When they did get the rest of the wood back, the three of them chopped and sawed it into stove-lengths for the winter supply. Helga was quite good with an ax, and Sarah Beth and Abe took turns using the saw and piling the cut pieces. Although each of them had asked other people what kind of winter they could expect, there'd never been a clear answer. It seemed that the winters varied almost as much as the landscape stayed the same, brown and green all year long.

The sun was warming them all that afternoon, even though the nights were becoming very chilly. They stopped for a break and Sarah Beth went after some minted water she'd put out in the sun the day before and then left in the relative coolness of the little stream since the night before. It was great refreshment, and they had to resist gulping all of it straight down. Sarah Beth said they could have as much as they wanted as long as they picked some more of the mint, which was either wild or had been planted out by their predecessors.

Helga suddenly spoke up, "What will you do with your freight wagon when the cabin is finished?"

Abe looked over at her and said, "Probably need it once in awhile for a supply trip, but with only one horse to pull it and the oxen being too slow, maybe I should try and find an old buggy to borrow or buy. Once we've got most things we'll need, I don't think we should count on the weather allowing us to haul much with it. Why?"

"Well," the girl said slowly. "One time I was in town over here and I saw a tiny little heater-stove in the mercantile that would be just right if I could use some left over boards and some canvas to make a little shelter using the wagon. Just a thought."

Sarah Beth looked at her, and said, "Probably a good idea, but how do we know if you'd be warm enough?"

"Miss Sarah Beth, you have no idea how cold I've spent some nights. Those people never let me in a house at night, always the barn, or if there wasn't a barn, I'd be under a haystack. A tiny amount of heat would do me just fine. Besides, I want to be away from the two of you. You need to be together without me right there in your way. Back when I was little they did bring me into their rooms, but that didn't stop them from doing what they do at night. I'd just as soon not have to be in the way for you, if you don't mind."

Abe and Sarah Beth exchanged looks and then Abe said, "Well, that's kind of you, but I don't know how comfortable we can make you in that wagon."

"I'll be fine, besides, maybe I can get a dog to stay with me. Don't you think we'll need to have one?"

With that she got up and went back to her ax. Sarah Beth was looking a little embarrassed and Abe didn't know what to say. He was almost thinking the girl could read his mind since this was exactly what he'd been thinking about on the ride home pulling the sled the day before.

"Well, she's thoughtful, I'd say."

Sarah Beth looked at him and then smiled. "Unless you put her up to this."

"I surely did not, but I'm kind of glad she thought of it . . . And the dog idea is a good one. We need to find one that can help me keep track of those cows before they start scattering."

"Whatever you say, Mr. Saunders. I think I better start fixing some supper. I have an idea there's a couple of hungry hard-working people around here somewhere."

By the coming of the first real storm, what they would have called a blizzard back home in Virginia, they were fairly well closed in and spending more and more of the dark hours inside their shelters or even covered up in the beds they'd made. Helga continued to behave in the most respectful way and to keep to herself when she wasn't needed to help out in some way. She and Sarah Beth always seemed to be able to find something to talk about when they were together and the few years that separated them were no more than what was usual for many sisters. Abe worried a lot about the cattle and spent many of his days out moving them to higher ground where the wind would sweep aside the frequent dry snowfalls. Then the cattle would move back down into whatever passed for hollows out in the mostly flat landscape, trying to get out of the cold wind as they huddled together for the night.

Abe had also been over to visit Blair on the ranch where he was working. Sarah Beth made sure that he reminded the young man about their Thanksgiving, which was little more than a week away. When Abe returned he had a smile on his face that made both of the young women curious, but he wouldn't say a word about what could have caused him to smile like that.

"You'll see," was all he would say.

When Blair arrived for Thanksgiving, they did see. As he climbed down from his horse and undid the bundle strapped across his saddlebags, it turned out to be a small dog or puppy who was whimpering in surprise or unhappiness at being in such strange circumstances. When Helga saw the little animal in Blair's arms she ran from the cabin door and snatched it from him.

"Oh, Mr. Abe, It's so beautiful," she said as she inspected it, "and it's a little boy puppy. Oh thank you, thank you." Then she saw that Blair was still standing where he'd been when she grabbed the puppy from him. "Oh, Blair, thank you for bringing him."

Sarah Beth was watching all of this from the doorway with a big smile on her face. She loved how Abe had been able to keep the secret, knowing how pleased he must have been with himself. Now she walked slowly toward Helga, enjoying the happiness that was all over the young woman's face. When she got closer she held out her arms for the puppy. Helga reluctantly handed him to her.

"Just for a second," Sarah Beth said, "I'll give him right back . . . Ohhh, you make us so happy, and it's all right puppy, puppy. Look we're all smiling. This puppy is a good sign for us, a Thanksgiving gift of happiness."

"Then I'll call him Happy," Helga said, as Sarah Beth handed him back to her. "It's a good name for you, isn't it, Happy, Happy." And just then the little fellow started wiggling all over and even looked like he was smiling too. Then he peed on Helga's arms. "Oh you little mischief, here." She set him down on the ground and shook off her arms. The puppy ran around in little circles.

"Well, I have to get back inside," Sarah Beth said. "That turkey Abe shot isn't going to cook itself. And of course, if anyone else is available I could use a little help with the rest of the meal, Helga."

"I know, I know. Can I bring him in, can I?"

"As long as you clean up after him," Sarah Beth said as she turned and went back inside.

The meal was good and substantial. Sarah Beth had been able to gather some surplus vegetables and other things from folks the Judge had introduced them to. It was amazing how nice everyone was to them. It seemed that they wanted to make sure she and Abe knew that the Mormons who lived around there weren't at all like the Bishop and his group. The Judge had even told Abe that it wouldn't take long to straighten the kinks out of the man's bitter ways. A good hard winter would show him how much he needed his neighbors, Believers or not.

Blair admitted that he'd never been to a Thanksgiving dinner before, and Helga commented that she'd never been at one where everyone seemed to like each other. As soon as the girl cleared the table, Sarah Beth uncovered the pumpkin pie she'd made. The pumpkin had been a gift from a lady who'd seen Sarah Beth admiring the garden growing alongside the road, on the way back from town.

"Why, Sarah Beth, I believe you are a miracle worker," Abe said. "I haven't even thought about a pumpkin pie since we left Virginia, and I certainly had no idea there was one anywhere this far west." He looked over at Helga and Blair, "Have either of you two ever had pumpkin pie before?"

Blair mumbled something that sounded like "never" and Helga shook her head yes, but said she didn't remember when, it was so long ago.

"Well, you are in for a treat. Looks like there's enough for two pieces for each of us, and four for me."

Just then the sound of shots broke in on them, loud and coming closer. Abe leaped to his feet, grabbed the rifle by the door and was outside in a matter of moments. He was quickly followed by Blair. Helga grabbed the puppy hiding under the table, and Sarah Beth went to the door and pushed aside the heavy curtain.

Two riders galloped toward the shed and pulled up in a cloud of dry snow and dust. One dismounted.

"It's me, Cuz, me Louis!" He half hopped toward Abe, grabbing him by the shoulders in a long and strong hug. "I found you, I found you . . ."

"Louis, what a surprise," Abe turned to look back at Sarah Beth who'd come outside followed by Helga and the puppy.

"Well, I guess there goes your extra pie," she said as she stepped up to Louis and gave him a big hug. "Welcome, and Happy Thanksgiving Day."

"Really." And then almost as if he'd forgotten his companion, he limped back to help a woman down off of her horse. "This is Maria Angelina, we got married in Santa Fe." He led her toward the little group, "She's the sweetest gal I ever met," he paused, "except maybe you, of course, Sarah Beth."

The woman was dark-skinned and rather small with a long a black braid hanging down over her chest. She was wrapped in a blanket and wearing pants underneath it. She smiled shyly, holding on to Louis's arm.

Louis took a long look around, and said, "She doesn't have hardly any English, but she's learning . . . Nice land here, but not much for a house and buildings. You were easy to find once we got close enough. Everybody seemed to know about the soldier and his woman. So, I see you didn't make it to Oregon yet."

Abe started to answer, but Sarah Beth interrupted, "Well, I don't know if there's enough room inside, but why don't we try and get out of this cold?" Sarah Beth said, turning to go back inside. "Helga, can you help me get these two some of the food we were eating?"

"Yes, ma'am." She handed the puppy to Blair and followed Sarah Beth inside. Abe led the two tired horses over to the shed and began unsaddling them. Just then a pack animal showed up on its own and came over to join the rest of the horses. It was a mule and Abe yelled over to Louis, "This one yours, too?"

"Yeah, come with the roan. They can't be separated."

"Makes it easy to lead him then."

"It's good unless you don't want him to go where you're going."

Louis walked over and started to undo some of the packing ropes.

Abe gave him a slight shove on the shoulder, saying, "Kinda like you. Always showing up where I am."

Louis shoved him back. "Somebody's got to look after you." Maria stood nearby.

Abe was pouring some grain-feed into buckets for his three and putting three piles on the ground for Louis's as well. "Don't usually treat'em this good less they're working hard or it's real cold, but I guess they might as well have Thanksgiving too. So, what happened to your leg?"

"Gunshot. Seen a guy pushing Maria around down in Santa Fe. She worked in a kind of a hotel down there and the guy must have thought she was in a different line of work. Wanted more than housekeeping and she was standing her ground and screaming at him. He hit her and the fight was on. Kinda like those Chinese guys all over again . . . Except this time, I got shot in the leg and had to kill the bastard."

"Whoa. Any charges from the law?"

"No, hotel clerk said it was self-defense, and Maria claimed I saved her life."

"Is that how you met her?"

"Not really, I was staying in that hotel place myself. She cleaned my room, and I guess you could say we took a bit of a liking to one another."

"Before or after the other guy?"

"Before."

"What ever happened to that other girl, the one you went back for?"

"Never showed up. Couldn't wait around forever."

Just then Helga came out with the puppy in her arms and called them to come in and eat, reminding Abe about his pumpkin pie.

They turned all the horses out together and watched them awhile, but there didn't seem to be any trouble among them, and they headed for the small building.

"Who's the girl?" Louis asked.

"That's Helga. There's a story to it. Tell you later. She ran away from some Mormons and came to stay with us."

"And the guy?"

"Helps me out some. Works on a big place out that way," he gestured.

Helga moved herself and a few things back into the house-shelter with Abe and Sarah Beth, so Louis and Maria could use her place in the wagon. The wind blew hard all night, but it wasn't a real cold wind, just the sound of winter on its way. Blair took advantage of the nearly full moon to ride on back to the ranch.

The next day, Louis and Abe spent some time catching up on where they'd been and what they'd done since Colorado, and the women folk gathered some kind of berries and mashed them out in layers to dry above the heater. Abe told Louis about the opportunity out in the Jordan Valley area, the deal with the Indians, and Louis commented on the number of cattle he'd seen riding in, as having grown considerably.

"Well," Abe said, not wanting to go into all of the facts around Sarah Beth and the Bishop, "It was kind of a separation settlement from this Mormon Bishop that took us on while we were still on the trail. Sarah Beth delivered a baby and saved a woman's life doing it, and I helped them out quite a bit when they were getting settled . . . but it wasn't really comfortable for any of us. We're a little different than them."

"Guess so," Louis said. "They're the most standoffish and rude people I've met yet. Just as soon live with Mexicans than Mormons."

"Well, we've met some good ones. Matter of fact, most of them out this way are pretty nice folk. Like to keep to themselves, but they've been more helpful than I expected."

Louis and Maria stayed for a couple of days and then they headed north toward Montana where there was work for both of them for the winter.

"Gonna be cold up there, Cuz," Abe said.

"Yeah, but we'll be all right. I'll try to get back down here before you head west, maybe I can help you make the move. And if you're gone already, I'll find you." He smiled and said, "I always do." They shook hands and said good-bye.

Sarah Beth and Helga had become friends with Maria, even though they shared very few words in common. They all hugged, helped the woman to her horse, and gave her some gifts she could put in her saddle bag. Then Maria and Louis were gone, the mule following right along behind.

As the dry cold of winter settled in around them, Sarah Beth set about making the inside of the little building they called a house as comfortable as possible. She'd been given some old blankets in town and was ripping them into pieces to stuff into cracks in the walls and around the two windows. Abe had filled in the roof and was spending his days moving the cattle farther and farther away for forage, and then going out and bringing them back at night. He was also still bringing in some firewood, knowing now that that it was going to take a lot.

One night Sarah Beth again brought up the subject of their having children, for although they'd had privacy since Louis left, and Helga seemed to be doing fine in her own space, they hadn't had any success.

"I just have to wonder if there isn't something wrong with me," she said as they were getting ready for bed. "I've even made sure we were following the times of my month like I read in a book back at the hospital in Virginia."

"Maybe it's not often enough," Abe said as he threw his arms around her and tumbled her into bed beside him. "Or maybe something's wrong with me."

"I don't think so, but you could find out if you really wanted to."

"How's that?

"You could leave me, and try someone else." She was fighting back the tears that these words brought to her eyes.

"Never," he said. "It's not that important to me, not enough to lose you."

"Abe, I know it's important to you. Ever since we started being together it's been on your mind." Now she was crying. "I can tell whenever I go off to help someone else have a baby. I can tell, because as soon as I'm home again, you try so hard with me . . . And I'm the same way, every time I've helped a baby be born, I almost get angry at God, oh forgive me, but it's true. I help everybody else and can't have it for myself . . . and for you."

"Sweet Sarah Beth, please don't cry for this. It's going to be all right. Maybe we should have you see a doctor, or me too. Maybe they could tell us something."

"Not around here," she snapped. "They all talk to each other and I don't want everyone to know about this."

"All right, all right. Take it easy. I love you. You, and I always will. Now let's just lie here together in each other's arms and try to get some sleep. It's late and the wind is howling like we still have a lot of work to get done still. I love you so much!"

They kissed and he gently licked the tears from her face. Soon she was asleep and he kept holding her, waiting for his own sleep. It was strange, he thought, looking back at all the women who she'd helped with their babies. It was almost everyone they knew who was her age, and she did seem healthy enough. They would just have to keep trying, and at least that wasn't a chore, it was very much his favorite thing.

Snow came down for two days, but the wind kept blowing it around so much that there were open spots between the drifts. Abe had Helga help him move the cows to the highest places, where the wind was strongest and the bare ground still held some remnants of vegetation.

When the road came clear, Sarah Beth made a ride to town for supplies. She was able to make the whole trip in the short daylight hours, but it wore her out and she was resting when Abe came in from his day. She lay in their bed and Abe saw she clasped a paper to her chest. Once again he saw tears glistening on the side of her face in the light from the lantern that sat on the table.

"What is it?" he said as he pulled off his boots and wet coat.

"A letter. It was waiting for me at the store. But you should eat first."

"I can wait. Who's it from? Who knows you're here?"

"It's from Mattie. She says Father's ill. I wrote to them when we first moved here. I was missing them so much after that business with the Bishop. Here, you can read it."

Dearest Sarah Beth,

It was wonderful to receive your letter and to hear that you and Abe made it to a place to stay for the winter.

It has not been easy for us here. But, Praise the Lord, there have been none of the problems with the congregation such as those we faced back home.

However, I am sad that I must tell you that your Father is ailing. He is getting weaker all the time, and although he has his good days, he also has days when he is worse. The doctors don't seem to agree or even know what this condition is caused by.

He asked me not to notify you because he doesn't want you to be concerned, but I just felt you would want to know. We are praying for his recovery, and wisdom for the doctors.

Please give our greetings and best wishes to Abe.

Wish we could see you, but understand that is impossible.

Love, Mattie

Abe sat down on the edge of the bed beside her, and placed one hand over hers. "I think maybe you should go."

"But how? Like Mattie says it's impossible."

"The new railroad. A stage goes from Ogden to the end of its line coming west, and Ogden's not that far from here."

Sarah Beth gently lifted his hand away and sat up, swinging her legs to sit beside him. "I doubt it runs in the winter. Besides we have no money for that."

"I'd wager that if we sent a telegram to Mattie, and asked for some help, she'd find a way in a minute." Sarah Beth was quiet, holding her face in her hands. "What?" he said. "What is it?"

"I said I never wanted to be parted from you again."

"But this is different. This is for you and your father. It may be . . ." He stopped.

"My last chance." She finished it for him. "I know, but it's too hard."

He placed his arm around her and said, "Let's not decide anything now, not until we find out if it's even possible. Now, why don't you stoke up the fire and I'll put the horses away. I was wondering why Morning was still saddled, now I know why."

"Oh Abe, I wasn't thinking. Only about the letter."

"You had more important things. And let's not tell Helga until we know more. Don't know how she'll take it if you go away."

"Well, if I have to go I wish you'd come along. Maybe Blair . . ."

"Just don't think about it now, not until we find out. I'll ride to town and send a telegram as soon as I can, and I'll check on the train . . . And, Sarah Beth," he turned back from the door, one boot on and pulling on the other, "I'm very sorry to hear about your father. He means a lot to me as well." Then he went out, and she went over to tend the fire, wiping her face on her sweater sleeve.

Within a week, Abe made the roundtrip trip to Ogden in two days and a night, in spite of the dry cold that made it extremely uncomfortable for both horse and man. While there, he was able to send a telegram to Mattie and Doctor Randall, and miraculously he received an answer the next morning. It said they were overjoyed at the prospect of seeing Sarah Beth again, and were only disappointed that Abe couldn't come with her. They arranged to send money for the ticket to a local bank. The train was only running once a week in the winter, weather permitting, but if he could get Sarah Beth back to Ogden within the next week, it would work out. He hurried to the train station and made arrangements, reserving a ticket without paying for it.

As things seemed to be falling into place he realized that he was disappointed to be unable to return to the East for a short time. Although he never had any second thoughts about emigrating, and was satisfied with their progress this far, it would be nice to see the old places and experience firsthand some of the striking differences between the two regions and peoples. As he was thinking about the trip and what Sarah Beth would need, he realized that they didn't have a way to carry the things she would want to take along to the train. After all, even a portmanteau or small trunk couldn't be easily trussed up on horseback. Besides, gentle as she was, he had no idea how Ginger would react to any load other than Helga or another rider.

Then, almost as if the moment had been designed, he found himself standing in front of the town's livery stable and staring at a small one horse buggy that looked like it hadn't been used for awhile. It struck him that it would be an ideal addition to their assets. He was glad, due to the friendliness of the clerk, that he didn't have to pay any money on the ticket, but he was quite sure he wouldn't have enough to buy this buggy. Of course it would be useful . . . First for this trip, but also for supply trips to town. A buggy would cut down on the number of trips and allow them to stock up for times when the weather might prevent any travel at all. Well, he thought, it couldn't hurt to ask.

He went into the stable and asked to speak with the owner. The young man working on some harnesses said he wasn't in, but since it was his father, he might be able to help out. So Abe asked if the buggy might be for sale.

"No sir. Belongs to the Mayor's wife. Doesn't use it much, but she's right proud of it."

"Anything else like it around?"

"Matter of fact, there is. Just the other day Father said he'd like to get rid of the old buggy out back; it's just in the way, he said."

"Can you show it to me?"

"Guess I might. This way."

The buggy had a torn canopy and ripped cushions on the seat, but the wheels were sound, and the hardware looked to be all there. "What about a harness?" Abe asked.

"Well that one I'm working on is gonna be for sale. You take it off my hands now and you'll get a good deal. I'm sick of working on it."

"Is it all there? Can it be used the way it is. Then I guess I could finish the work?"

"I believe so. Ain't nothing a little wire and rope can't fix."

Abe went back to where he was staying, a small rooming house on a back street. He collected Bird, who was hobbled in an open field across the road. By the time he returned to the stable the owner had returned, and within a few minutes Abe was the partial owner of a buggy and harness. Now all he had to do was pay off the rest of it when he returned next week and figure out how to hook Bird up to the thing to pull it home. The money would have to come out of their savings, but it would be an investment in something that would help them on their way when the time came to move again. Besides, he thought, if Sarah Beth did get with child, it would be a better ride for her than either horseback or their wagon.

CHAPTER FIFTEEN

Winter's End

The blizzard began late at night soon after Abe and Helga came back from putting Sarah Beth on the stage. Within three days Abe was unable to even find the cattle, much less move them to a place where there was any food. He hardly saw Helga at all, except when she came over from her place to fix their supper. She had begged to go along when he took Sarah Beth to the stage for the train, and since there was room in the buggy for her if he rode Bird, they had decided it would be a nice thing for her since she hadn't been anywhere since joining up with them. While Abe and Sarah Beth were saying goodbye at the stage depot, Helga was left at the local mercantile, and began choosing individual lengths of fabric for a project she had in mind.

As soon the stage left, Abe came looking for Helga at the store and found her with an armful of different colors of cloth. "And what's this about?" he asked.

"Oh, I just want so badly to make a quilt, Mr. Abe. One of the wives taught me about it, but only so I could help on her project. I don't have any money, or any way to get some, but if you would buy this for me, and some thread, I could do extra work for you, like mending your clothes or making something for Miss Sarah Beth; or if I make quilts good enough to sell, I can pay you back. Please, Mr. Abe, I'll make it up to you."

He looked at her for a long moment, making her impatient, but she was polite enough to hold her silence. Finally, he said, "Seems like a good proposition to me, but do you need that many kinds of fabric just for one quilt?"

"Oh yes, you see, I want to start by making a Joseph's quilt. It's a pattern kind of like a crazy quilt, but more orderly. It's named after

Joseph's coat of many colors, in the Bible, in your Bible, not just the Mormon's book. I promise you, Mr. Abe . . . And I know what I'm doing, I won't waste a single bit."

"All right, you've convinced me. Now let's get the rest of the things we need and head for home. It's still early enough we should be able to make it by dark, and I don't like the look of the weather out of the west."

On the way back home, Helga drove Ginger, pulling the buggy. Abe rode alongside. Every once in awhile he could hear the girl singing, and he was glad that she was finding some happiness. From what he could tell there hadn't been much in her life. Then he thought back on the recent moments at the stage depot, Sarah Beth crying as he helped her up the steps into the stage. When he asked her why she was crying, even though he thought he knew, she surprised him by saying "I'm afraid."

"Afraid of what?"

"Afraid of what I'll find when I get there. Oh Abe, I'm just not strong enough if I have to face the worst alone."

"Yes, you are, dear. You're the strongest woman I've ever known, and your love for your father, and his for you is even stronger. God will help you through anything. Please try to remember that."

They kissed until the driver called down from his seat and told Abe he'd have to get back or get run over. Now, as he rode toward home beside the buggy, he wondered how long she'd be gone. Sometimes when he wanted to put things in God's hands it seemed to him that God was so busy that it took a little longer that way. But in this case, there was nothing else he could do.

The snow stayed on the ground for four days, then the sky broke open into a brilliant blue and the air froze to the point of being painful to breathe. One day of that and suddenly there was a warm wind blowing hard from the southeast, blowing the still-frozen snow crystals into swirling piles and drifts. Then hard rain melted the snow and ran across the ground in rivulets, and the stream beds filled with muddy water.

As soon as he could, Abe was off on Bird looking for the cattle. It took most of the day, but he had to admire the herd for finding a narrow shallow ravine that he hadn't known existed. It had given some shelter from the storm and all but two moved quickly ahead of him when he circled the herd and began pushing them back toward home.

One yearling didn't get up. He could see she was too weak; there was an old one already dead. He got off the horse and tried to stand the yearling up, but she couldn't make it. He shot her out of mercy. He figured if it froze up again, he could drag her back for soup bones and some for Happy. The old one was mostly just skin and bones.

As he neared the home place, he heard a sound almost like the howling of the wind, but the air was still as could be. He urged Bird forward at a run and was surprised to see two horses and their riders standing on either side of Helga. As he got closer he could see she was swinging her arms at the two and now he could clearly hear her screams. They saw him, and one man grabbed again for the girl while the other aimed a rifle at Abe, who swung over, hanging on the side of the horse away from them, Indian style. He charged straight at them, thinking only that he was risking Bird's life, but thinking nothing of his own

He yanked the horse to a stop and swung down so he was flat on the ground with his pistol pointed straight at the man with the rifle. Helga kept up her struggling and screaming, and Abe yelled at the man to drop his rifle. The man went down to one knee and took aim. Just as he fired, Abe rolled over and came up firing a single shot. The shooter crumpled as the other man wrestled Helga into position as a shield. Apparently he was not armed with a gun, but Abe realized that he might have a knife. Just then Helga bit the man's hand with all the strength of her jaws, and the man screamed and loosened his grip. She turned and gave him a knee in the crotch. He went down. Abe moved toward Helga, handed her his gun, and said, "Cover him," as he went to see what had happened to the other man.

The man was bleeding from just below his shoulder and a rasping sound came from his throat. Abe couldn't help thinking that it sounded just like the yearling before he'd put down an hour earlier. Two in one day, he thought. He picked up the man's rifle and pushed at him with his foot, but there was no recognition in the man's eyes of much of anything. Abe recognized him as one of the Bishop's men or sons, one who'd followed him home that day when he returned from Oregon.

He went over to Helga and took the gun from her hand. She threw herself against him and began choking and sobbing out phrases that he couldn't understand. "If you hadn't . . . it's the one, he's . . . the one . . . kidnapping, he said you kidnapped me . . ."

"Whoa, settle down. You're going to be all right. I recognize the other one, not sure about this one."

"He's the son, Thomas, the one who tried . . . to hurt me. Why I ran away."

Abe looked down at the man she'd hurt, who was finally able to stop his writhing and push himself up to his knees. "Well, it looks like you gave him what he deserved. Listen mister, you've about two minutes to load your partner on his horse and get the two of you out of here and gone. And if I ever see you again, you won't live to tell anybody it was me that done it. Now get up, and move out."

He placed his arm around the girl and backed her away toward the little house, keeping his pistol aimed at the man who was now limping slowly to catch up their two horses. "Here," he said to the girl, "you go inside and wait. I'll be right in."

"Oh, Mr. Abe, I am so glad you got here. They said they were taking me back."

"Go in now, and heat some water. We'll have a cup of something and then make some supper, once I get this mess cleaned out of here."

He watched as the young man struggled to push his partner up and over the saddle. Then he tied the wounded man on so his legs hung down on one side of the horse, his head on the other. Abe watched with some detachment and no desire to help. He was beginning to feel the anger he hadn't had time to feel during the confrontation. The crazy nerve of these guys to come in here like that. He wondered what they'd planned to do if he'd been here. Just kill him and take the girl?

Finally the man climbed on his own horse and began leading the other away. It was difficult at first because the horse was shying and trying to see what was behind him, what was hanging off the saddle. He probably smelled blood as well, since it was still dripping on the ground as they trotted away.

Abe watched until they were just small images nearing the line of low hills that defined where the little creek was. Then suddenly he began to shake all over. He tried to steady himself by holding his hands together and then moving toward the little half-made barn. He knew he needed to cover the puddle of blood, but the ground was still too frozen to dig into. Instead he gathered up horse manure in a feed sack. It was still frozen as well, but he was able to separate the chunks and gather enough to do the job. He didn't want Happy getting into that blood.

The puddle was already stiff and he realized he was still shaking. Was it from the act of shooting a man, or the aftershock of fear?

Or was it both? He wiped the crumbs of manure off his hands and then raised both arms high over his head, thanking God for one more miracle in his life and the lives of those he loved. As he lowered his arms he realized that the shaking was going away and he was mostly just chilled now as the evening dropped into dusk and the darkness in the east began coming their way. It could just as easily get cold again as warm up some more. He turned back toward the house and was pleased to see smoke coming from the stovepipe. The warmth would feel good, and as soon as he'd unsaddled and put Bird away, he could rest from what had been a terrible hard day.

There was no way to know when Sarah Beth would return without going into town and checking for a message. He deliberated on the risk of leaving Helga behind, and decided it was better to leave the place unattended than to leave her alone again. At first light he harnessed Ginger to the buggy, on which he had done quite a bit of repair work, and they set off for town. Hopefully, they would be able to meet the stage, or find a message telling them what to do.

It was not quite mid-day when they arrived in the small town where they'd met the Judge. Helga waited with the animals and buggy while Abe checked in with the telegraph office.

"The stage will be late to Ogden," he said when he returned to her. "How about I treat you to a breakfast at that little food place at the hotel? We didn't really eat much this morning."

"Oh," she said, "that would be so wonderful, Mr. Abe. I've never had a meal fixed by strangers."

He laughed at that and said, "You mean in a place where they serve food to customers?"

"Yes, that's what I mean."

They tied up the horses, walked the short distance to a hotel restaurant and found a table. It wasn't quite time for the mid-day meal, so they had the place nearly to themselves. They were ordering the "Late Breakfast Special" when the Judge walked in with a small group of men. He noticed Abe and waved, said a few words to his companions, and came over to their table, sitting down opposite Abe.

"Mr. Saunders, how are you and how are things going for you out there?" He shook Abe's extended hand.

"First, Judge, this is Helga. She lives with us out there as well."

"I know all about Helga. Pleased to meet you, Miss. Listen, Saunders, we have something to discuss. Is it all right to speak frankly in front of the girl here, or should you and I move ourselves to another table?"

Abe glanced at Helga, and said, "I believe she's pretty near growed up, so speak what's on your mind. She's a member of our family now."

"Well, that's what I want to talk to you about, and I'm glad I didn't have to come all the way out there to do it." The serving-girl brought a plate of biscuits and they each took one.

"Like I said, sir, speak what's on your mind, sir."

"You can stop calling me sir if I can call you Abe. Just call me Judge Harold. Now, it seems that I've had a charge of kidnapping filed with my court not very long ago, just the other day, in fact. Know anything about it?"

"I'm not sure."

"Well, it was filed by one of your Bishop's boys regarding the girl here, and then he added the charge of attempted murder of his brother. You may be glad to know the young man didn't die, at least not yet. What would you have to say in response?" He took another biscuit, leaving only one.

Abe held the basket out to Helga and said, "Well, sir, I guess I'd have to ask you if it's kidnapping when a minor runs away from being assaulted by her so-called family members and seeks refuge with someone she trusts."

The Judge started to speak, but Abe continued, "And then I'd have to ask if when the perpetrators of the assault on the young girl come after her to do her more harm and one of them pulls a rifle on me when I'm trying to help her, and I fire back at him after he fires the first shot, if that isn't defined as self-defense in your court, Judge Harold, your Honor." He motioned to the serving girl with the empty basket, seeking a refill.

"I believe your legal arguments have a bit of truth to them, but are there any witnesses to any of this, other than yourself and the girl here, and of course the other two parties? That may have a bearing."

"Not unless you count some horses and a dog, Judge."

"Well, the facts of the case seem to be that this girl had taken up residence with you and your wife, not necessarily legally, may I say, but out of some kind of fear for her person. That much can be allowed. However, before we go any further I would like to ask you to sign this affidavit." He turned over the one-page menu of the place to its blank side and scribbled something on it with a pencil. "This here says you and your wife are the girl's legal guardians. Don't worry about the date unless you know when she first showed up to be with you. That should take care of the kidnapping charge." He pushed the stiff paper across the table and handed Abe the pencil.

Abe signed his name, "There."

"Good, I'll file it in my office when I return. And, since the other fellow isn't dead, we don't have an attempted murder charge. Given that I know a bit about your military background, I'd rule that if you wanted to kill the man, you would have succeeded, so it was just a little gunfight and not 'attempted' anything. Happens fairly often around here, actually. Now, I don't think this will make the Bishop happy, or maybe he doesn't care. We don't know. But," and he placed a hand on Helga's wrist, "if I was you, Abe, I'd make sure this young woman and your wife both carry a piece of protection with them out there, and that they know how to use it. Just a word to the wise. I will also give a word to the wise to that bunch that they are violating this court's legal restraining order if they go anywhere near your place, and I will inform them that you have the right to run them off if need be. This is about the best I can do in the circumstances, Abe, and don't bother to say thank you, it's my duty. Besides, we don't know how this will all play out. By the way, where's your beautiful wife?"

"Coming back home on the train. She went to visit her ailing father. She's taking the stage into Ogden. We're on our way to pick her up. "

"Well best wishes, Abe, and try not to cause me any more trouble, if you can help it."

"Yes, sir, your Honor."

The Judge stood up, placed a kiss with his fingers on Helga's arm, and bent to speak softly to both of them, saying, "Remember, all us Mormons ain't as bad as that bunch. And a man like that so-called Bishop can be a bad one, no matter what his religion." Then he went to join his party at the other table just as several more folks came into the place.

"Well, Helga, that man has helped us out twice now."

"He seems nice." Their food had arrived and she was digging in with the hunger of a still growing girl. Abe joined her with the hunger of a man who hadn't eaten yet that day.

They made the rest of the trip to Ogden in good time, although it was late in the evening. They went to the same place Abe had stayed before and were up early in the morning to wait for the stage to arrive. After breakfast they went to wait at the stage stop, where a small crowd of people waited.

When the stage arrived and unloaded its passengers, Sarah Beth immediately saw Abe and pushed through the crowd, throwing herself into his arms.

"Abe, oh Abe . . ."

She began weeping immediately. It was as if she'd been holding back a flood of tears. Helga also put her arms around the shaking woman who was now her best friend. The three of them stood there wrapped around each other until, after a minute or two, Sarah Beth shook herself free from them, saying, "My bags, must get my bags." She pointed Abe in the right direction and he was quick to retrieve them.

"What have you got in here," he asked, "cannon balls?"

"I'm sorry dear, and there's more coming to Silver City on a freight wagon. I don't know how we'll even get all this home. It's not too late to try to get back, is it? I want so badly to be home."

"There should be a pretty big moon tonight and the weather looks like it's holding. We can try. We've got the buggy now and Helga here is quite good at driving it. If you're not too tired. I suppose it's been a hard trip."

"Abe, it's been the hardest thing I've ever done, but we'll talk about it later. I don't want to waste any daylight right now."

Each of them picked up luggage, but they couldn't get it all, so Helga stayed behind to watch over what was left.

As they reached the buggy, Sarah Beth said, "Abe, Father passed away three days after I got there. It was good to see him. Oh Abe, if I hadn't gone, I don't know what I'd have done. But I don't want to cry now. That's all we need to say until we're home. Now, you should go back for the rest and I'll watch all this. You and Helga can manage?" She pushed him away and turned to look the other way, hiding another wave of tears as she wiped her face and blew her nose in an already soaked handkerchief.

They arrived home a few hours after the darkness had settled in. The horses were put away and fed. Fires were started in both the house and in Helga's shelter, and some soup made from the bones of the yearling was being heated up. Helga politely offered to leave the two of them alone, but Sarah Beth would have none of it.

"You stay right here and have supper with us. I missed you too, you know."

"Thank you, Miss Sarah Beth. I missed you as well."

When the meal was finished, Helga began cleaning up, but Sarah Beth stopped her, saying, "Mattie wouldn't let me lift a finger while I was there, so let me do this. It is my kitchen, you know."

"All right, I guess. I'll just go now. I have things to do and Happy is waiting for me. We've been gone since before daylight."

As soon as she was gone, Abe stepped up behind his wife, who was leaning over the basin of dirty dishes. "Let that be, I want you to tell me what you can, whatever you want to."

She turned and looked up into his eyes, "Abe, I missed you so much; like I said, it was the hardest thing I've ever done." Then she remembered the Bishop and said, "Well, almost the hardest."

"Come," he said. He led her over to the bed and gently sat her down. He wrapped a blanket around her shoulders and then set their one chair opposite her, so he could look at her. He took her hands in his own. They were silent for a very long moment, and then he said, "Whatever you want to tell me."

"He asked about you. He wanted to know if God was leading us on this way and if we could hear His Voice in the opportunities and in the wind. I thought it might be delirium, but he was so clear about everything right up until the end. Oh, Abe, I didn't know what he was talking about some of the time, and sometimes I couldn't hear him, but his eyes were alive and he was struggling to whisper . . ."

"That what he said, it's something he taught me. It's about God's Voice. I'll explain it to you sometime, but it shows me that he was still very much alive when you saw him. Go on, if you can, if you want to."

"Well, Mattie was an angel through it all. It must have been so difficult taking care of him before I got there. She said he'd been failing for quite some time. And then when . . . when he was gone, she finally just fell apart. I'm so glad I was there for her. She was just so hurt, so hurt. And, and . . . I love her so much for loving him all those years. She told me that ever since my mother began treating him badly about the War, she'd been trying to keep from loving him, but she couldn't help it, and now here she was alone again. But she's coming here sometime. Maybe not right away, there're things to settle, but she's coming, maybe after we get moved to our new place. I want her with me, I want us to be with her. Besides you, and Helga, she's the only family I have now. Oh, Abe, it was all so horrible, and so beautiful at the same time. I have to say that he died with a smile on his face and holding mine and Mattie's hands in his. Then there was just a kind of a shudder went through him and he was gone."

"I'm so glad that you were there, dear. I'm sure it meant everything to both of them. And was there a service for him?"

"Oh yes, but I'm so tired. Can we talk about that tomorrow? It was nice. So many good people from the church and from the town. Oh! And I saw your friend Lefty. He sent his best wishes and said we'd see him next summer, but there's more to tell tomorrow, not right now. Right now, I just want to lie in bed and have you hold me the way that you do. Ahhh, so good to be here, home." She stretched and then stood to undress.

He also got up and went to stoke the fire and shut off the lamps, leaving only a candle burning next to the bed. Then they were truly together again, their bodies curled into one another, and he felt her slipping into sleep in a matter of moments. It was good to have her back, he was thinking as he blew out the candle, and that was his last thought of the night.

The next morning they awoke together, and Sarah Beth asked if Helga would be coming in for breakfast. Abe told her about the quilt project, and how that seemed to keep the girl busy whenever he didn't need her for some work.

"So we can be alone for a few more minutes," she said.

"I think so. I'll have to ride out after the cows. Haven't seen them since day before yesterday, but they can wait."

"They'll have to wait," she said as she rolled over on top of him, looking down into his eyes and pushing his shoulders down with her outstretched arms. "I have something else in mind." And they melted into one another with the anxiousness of too long a separation and the happiness of a well-deserved reunion.

Sarah Beth was the first one to climb out of bed and when she went to revive the fire, he said he'd do it, and so she started making coffee and biscuits. "It was the day after the services they had for father when I saw Lefty and his young wife. She is so beautiful. They were in town and he was getting paid some money and buying something for his horses when I went into the bank. I had to do some of the complicated and unfinished banking Father left behind. Lefty didn't seem to know who I was at first, but I was almost certain it was him. Then I saw him sign a paper with his left hand and I knew it was your friend. He was dressed like anyone else, but his dark skin and the feather in his hat set him apart. He was happy to see me and to find out how far we'd made it. There, now they just have to bake for a few minutes," she said as she closed the oven door and sat down on a small barrel to have coffee with him.

"You said he's coming this way?"

"Yes, I told him about where we would be going and how Bird had helped us more than once along the way. He said we were being helped because you are a spirit man, and that's why he gave you the horse, so his people would recognize you."

"Just like he said you're a Dreamer."

"Oh no Abe, Abe, I had such a horrible dream while I was gone. I almost forgot it until you said 'Dreamer.' It was terrifying. Two men, and I didn't know them, these two men had you and Helga and they were tying her up and one of them said she was lucky they weren't going to burn her at the stake. The other one hit you with the rifle he was carrying and you fell down and he was kicking you. In the dream I didn't know where this was, but I heard myself screaming, and then I woke up and it was me really screaming. Mattie was at the doorway, asking if I was all right. I told her it was just a dream, but Abe, it was more than that. It was almost too real. I was so afraid for you, for days it kept coming back to my mind, and I was so afraid because I was helpless and couldn't do anything, in the dream or in real life."

"Dear Sarah Beth, that's truly amazing. Because there was something like that happened to us. It goes to prove you're Dreamer, like Lefty said. I was going to tell you later, but . . ." And he went ahead and gave her a brief outline of what happened to him and Helga and how the Judge was trying to resolve it. He added that all three of them should be wearing guns from now on and he'd bought out one for her, a small one with a holster.

"But, I'm pretty sure it's over, and the Judge said he'd warned those boys that if he found out they were ever around here again, they'd be taken to Laramie and put in the soldier jail. So that should keep them away from us."

"Oh Abe, I must have known somehow. Even with everything that was going on back there, with Father and all the people who came by to speak of their sympathy, and they brought us more food than we could ever eat, but I kept worrying so much if you were all right. Oh, I'm so glad to find out you're safe, you and Helga."

"Well here," he reached out to the dresser they'd brought all the way from Virginia and opened a drawer, pulling out a small pistol and holster, "might as well start now. I have to ride out and push those cows somewhere they can get a day's worth of feeding in before dark. Half the day's gone already."

"But you are glad I'm back aren't you?"

He jumped up from his chair and grabbed her, lifting her up and spinning around in the tiny space.

"Abe, careful, you'll break something."

He set her down, kissed her deeply and then grabbed his own gun, hat and coat and headed out into the mid-day cold. He called back over his shoulder, "If you need help unpacking or something, call Helga."

Later that day, Sarah Beth did need some help and went to Helga's small space, built from their wagon and some additional lumber and canvas. It was more complete than when Sarah Beth had left. She knocked on the canvas and Helga instantly stuck her head out, looking surprised.

"Uh, Miss Sarah Beth, um, do you want to come in? It's not great, but it's good enough for me." She held aside the heavy canvas door and beckoned.

Sarah Beth smiled and stepped inside. There were things stored underneath the wagon and it reminded her of all the nights on the trail she and Abe slept underneath it. A little ladder climbed into the wagon bed, and in the rest of the space was a small homemade table and two tree stump chairs. The small stove was in a corner and seemed to be quite enough to keep the space warm.

"Sit down. Would you like some tea or something? I can heat water."

"No, Helga, I came to ask your help putting away a few of the things that I brought back. Some of them might go nicely in here, make it a little more comfortable for you. So tell me about your project. All Abe said was that you had him buy some material for making a quilt."

"Oh yes, he was so good to do it. I'd helped the wives on their quilting projects. I've worked on every part of it, but I never was allowed to make my own, and I wanted to so badly. Now look, I'm doing it. Look." She held up a bundle of squares, all the same size, but of various colors, each one made of nine smaller squares. "It's a Jacob's quilt named for his many-colored coat. I wanted my first one to have a pattern with as many colors as possible, but not just one of those with no order that they call a crazy quilt."

"I've never done anything like that myself," Sarah Beth said, taking the bundle that was being held out to her. "Such perfect stitching. Maybe I can help you sometime and learn something about it."

"Yes, you can help me do the final quilting stitch that holds it all together, the front side to the back side. But we should go now so I can help you."

"Helga, wait, Abe told me about what happened with those two men from the Bishop's group. It must have been so terrible for you. I almost feel like I should have been here to help protect you. Although I don't know what I could have done . . . I wouldn't have had this then." She pointed at the guns they were both wearing, hanging from their waists. "But now look at us."

"No, Miss Sarah Beth, they might have hurt both of us if you were here. I was just so lucky that Mr. Abe showed up when he did, or I don't know what would have happened to me. He was so strong and just took care of those two. They are awful. When I was younger they always tormented me and threatened me that if I told anyone, they'd beat me and leave me for the wild animals to eat. I was so scared of them, but this time I was just angry."

"Well, it sounds like you got a little bit of revenge for all that. Come on, let's go get started. And we can have tea while we're working." As they walked across the space between the two dwellings, Sarah Beth put her arm around the younger woman's shoulders and they walked together to the other house.

They spent the rest of the afternoon unpacking her luggage and one whole trunk of things she'd brought from their home in Missouri, including individually wrapped dishes, curtains and bedclothes, and even a couple of cookbooks. Helga was thrilled to see the fine housewares, and they both enjoyed trying to find places in the small space for it all.

"There's much more arriving on the freight wagon from where the train had to stop. We might as well unpack it all when it gets here," Sarah Beth said, "because it will have to all be repacked anyway, for the wagon ride when we move on in the spring. And here, you should take any of these things you want for your little room. A blanket, a mirror, a pitcher for water, a lamp, whatever you'd like."

"Oh I don't need anything. I wouldn't know where to start, but I do love this blanket, it feels so warm and the wind does blow into my little place."

"Take it, and here take a couple of place settings, in case you ever have company to serve supper to, or just to have."

"Oh, I won't ever have any company."

"What about Blair? He seems to have taken notice of you."

"No, he's just a lonely young ranch hand. He's probably got himself a girl in town anyway. But I will take the two plates to put on my wall. They're so pretty."

After what seemed like months, there finally came a warm day with almost no wind. The sky was filled with fluffy white clouds racing across its big blue dome, hurrying east. Abe had lost two more of the weaker cows, one to a miscarriage, and one whose carcass was surrounded by the tracks of wolves, but he was pleased that it had been no worse, and most of the female cows looked pregnant and were nearing their term.

Sarah Beth was still showing no signs of conception, although the cold winter had been an incentive for them to spend plenty of time in bed together. Neither spoke of it, both waiting for something to change. In the meantime, it was time to start thinking about the move they would be making. Abe said he wanted to wait for at least a month after the calves were born, to be sure they could stand the long distance, and so there would be plenty of fresh grass along the way. Helga was nearly finished with her quilt, and Sarah Beth was enjoying helping her with the finishing touches. It gave them time together to begin planning what they would need to do for the move west. Abe wanted to build crates for the more fragile things and the two women were sewing some canvas bags for the clothing, bedding and other cloth goods to be stored in. There had been no sign of any trouble from the Bishop's people, for which they were all truly relieved.

On one particularly warm day, when the little creek was overflowing from snow melting somewhere in the faraway mountains, Abe saw a single rider coming closer and closer. He'd been checking a newly born calf to see how strong it was, since he hadn't seen it nurse from its mother. It seemed to have its leg-strength and followed the mother cow when he let it go and rolled up his rope. He mounted up and rode toward the rider, alert to any strange move the man might make.

When they were close enough he yelled across the space between them, "Who is it? Can I help you out?"

"Would you be Abe Saunders?" the man hollered as the distance between them shortened and they could see each other's faces.

"Might be," Abe said as he pulled Bird to a stop and kept one hand on his sidearm.

"Well, that's who I'm looking for. Got a message from a fellow named Louis."

"All right. You know Louis?"

"Spent the winter with him, up Montana way."

"Was he alone?"

"No, had him a pretty little Mexican woman, said she's his wife."

"Yeah, that's him all right. Come along, we'll ride over to our place and I'll hear all about him."

They broke into a comfortable loping run and pulled up near the corral where the other two horses were waiting, suspicious of the newcomer. The men loosened and pulled off their saddles, hung them over the railing, and then shook hands.

"Name's Rogers, Spin Rogers. Came out from back Indiana way."

"Well, I am, as you know, Abe Saunders, and this here," he pointed over at Sarah Beth standing in their doorway, "is my wife, Sarah Beth. Dear, he says he's brought word from Louis, can we feed him something? If you're hungry, that is."

"Oh, I wouldn't want to intrude, trying to make the next town by dark."

"Well, I'm sure we've got a slice of fresh bread and dried meat for you, haven't we?"

"Of course," she said and disappeared inside.

Abe pointed to a couple of rounds of firewood set up for stools, just outside the doorway, "So what's he up to now?"

"Well, we been fightin' blizzards and wolves all winter, but now it's time to move the herd up to where there's fresh grass is comin' in the foothills. The owner's got his own boys and didn't need us anymore. So I headed out and Louis said he'll be along in a week or two. That's about all he said, except that he sure hoped you were all right and made it through the winter best as could be expected."

"Oh, yes. We're fine. And I'm glad you showed up, because we didn't know when to expect him, whether to wait or just head off without him. He isn't one of your most predictable type of fellows."

"Well, you might be surprised. That little woman seems to have settled him down some. I'd heard about him from his days on the trail with the caravans, and he don't hardly seem the same person now, although he does have some roarin' good stories."

Sarah Beth appeared with some thick slices of bread and dried meat, gave them to the men, and then stood behind Abe.

"Any children?" Rogers asked.

"No sir, not yet."

"Well, Louis said you might or might not, but don't worry. I say, once you get settled, they'll come along. I've seen it happen more than once."

"Well, yes sir, that'll be fine. When we're ready."

"That is one fine piece of bread, a whole meal in itself, ma'am. Haven't had anything like that all winter, just those flatbread things Louis's woman made for every meal. I find I always appreciate a good piece of bread, believe you me. But now I best be going on if I'm going to find a bed for the night. Haven't slept in a bed since last summer. Looking forward to it, so thank you much." He stood up and stuck the dry meat in his jacket pocket. "Think I'll have that along the trail somewhere since you gave it to me . . . Well, pleased to meet you, tell that scoundrel cousin of yours I done what he asked, and tell him to remember that his woman promised me her sister," he laughed loudly, and walked off to saddle his horse. And then he was gone.

"Well," Abe said, "that's good news. I was wondering how we'd make it to Oregon, just the three of us, with the cows and all our things."

Sarah Beth put her arms around his neck and pulled him into a kiss. "I was just counting on you to figure all that out. My job is to get things for us, your job is to figure out what to do with them all." She laughed and turned back to the little house. "I think I'd like to go for a ride with you, Mr. Saunders, if and when you're available." And then she was gone back inside. "I'll be back in an hour," he called. "Be ready." And then he saddled up and took off, hurrying after the cattle, which needed to be moved to the other side of the creek before it got any higher from the snow-melt.

A few days later, Blair came by, wanting to know if they were going to need him to make their journey west. Abe had asked him to find out if he'd be available, since it would take an extra hand to move the number of cows and the anticipated calves. That was before he'd heard from Louis.

"Well, you're welcome to come with us, but I just found out that my cousin will be coming back here from Montana in a couple of weeks. Some of the cows are his, so I expect he'll be helping me out."

"Well, that's fine, Mr. Abe. I could get away, but only if you really needed me. I also got an offer to work for a surveying crew that's headed south from here, down to where Utah and New Mexico meet up."

"Are you interested in that sort of thing?"

"I was good at the arithmetic part of school, but that's about all. And a fellow needs to have some kind of skill, other than riding and roping."

Just then Abe caught sight of Helga leaning out from behind her little building. She knew he saw her and motioned him to "Shhh." Abe smiled, and then went back to his conversation with Blair.

"I agree with you. This frontier is changing fast and if you don't own the land and the cattle, you might be out of luck before long. That's why I'm so set on getting this move on, but I admire you for your ambition and wish you the best. Will you be staying for supper?"

"Probably not. I said I'd be back to the ranch tonight if possible. So, could you tell Helga I'm sorry not to be travelling in her company, but this is a better way to go for me right now."

Abe smiled and said, "Well, why don't you tell her yourself. She's right over there by her shed, and I think she's been listening to us."

Helga stepped into sight and looked quite flustered. Abe knew he'd hear about it later, but he couldn't just let the two of them not have a chance to say their goodbyes, although from the way it looked they were both so shy maybe neither one would say much of anything. He turned and left, going back out to the barn to finish repairing some harness he was working on.

The wind was blowing dust for the first time that spring when Louis and Maria showed up, followed by their mule and another horse, both carrying packs and tied together. "Hiyeee there, Cuz . . . We are back, returned from the North Pole, survivors of the Arctic winter." He slid down off of his horse and ran, limping, over to Abe, nearly knocking him down with the vigor of his handshake.

"Well, you do look like a survivor of something or other."

"Here, Maria, let me help you." As he helped her down off of her horse, it became clear she was a carrying a baby. Louis put his arm around her with a proud look and announced, "We're going to have us another member of our family, Cuz." Maria kept looking at the ground.

Sarah Beth and Helga came outside and hurried over to greet the returnees. "Well," Sarah Beth, "you did say you'd be back, didn't you?"

"Just like birds in the springtime," Louis said. "How are you?"

"Well, I'm doing just fine." She looked at Maria and said, "Let me take her inside, she must be exhausted. Helga, heat some water for us to have coffee or tea. This is cause for celebration."

The two men took the animals over to the corral and began unloading the pack animals and unsaddling the two riding horses. Just then it began to rain.

"Might settle this dust," Abe said. "Been dry ever since it stopped snowing."

"Well, we've got ourselves a good army tent, so let it rain, let it pour. Where should I set it up? I can unload these packs after."

"Well, you'll want flat ground, I imagine, and the flattest place around here is right over there next to that clump of sage."

"Looks good to me," Louis said as he led the pack horse that way, and then dropped the rest of the animal's load on the ground. The horse shook himself all over and then immediately started trying to graze on the bare ground. "He's always hungry."

"We can take them over by that little creek and hobble yours if they need it. Mine don't go far."

"I imagine they'll all stick together. So how's it been here? You-all all right, Cuz? When I left you'd had yourself a bit of a run-in with the Mormons, but now you seem all right to me."

"A couple of them came around and I actually had to shoot one of 'em, but far as I know, he didn't die."

"You have trouble with the law over it?"

"Turned out the law took up for me. The Judge that let us stay on this land is a right nice fellow. Wants us to always remember most Mormons are good folk, but he says that bunch we tied up to is going to have to change if they're trying to stick it out around here."

"Well, good for you. You always did have a way with folks, making friends and all. Me, I'd a probably been run out of the country by now."

"So how soon you expecting a little one?"

"Oh, could be any day. No, seriously? It'll be a couple months yet. Hopefully time enough for us to get where we're going."

"Should be. Come on, let's have some coffee and you can tell me what you been up to. I'm curious about this Montana country."

After a few days, the rain and the wind passed on over them, and the weather seemed made for their next move. Having Louis and Maria around made it both easier to get things ready, and more necessary, as it was now a bit crowded. Abe and Louis worked hard on the harness and wagon and buggy, while the women wrapped and organized their belongings. They accumulated an extra pile of clothing and cookware that would not fit in their limited space. Sarah Beth and Helga loaded it in the buggy and took it into the nearest church.

The day finally came when they were packed and loaded, the cattle rounded up, and the place they'd called home for the winter was locked up as tight as they could get it. Abe made one last quick trip into town to talk with the Judge, thank him, and get his instructions for how to leave the place.

"Mighty thankful for what you've done for us, sir."

"That's all right. Kind of hate to see you go, but I understand how you could want to move on, given what some of our renegades have put you through. Just remember what I said, most of us aren't so bad."

"Yes, sir, you've taught me that, and more."

"All right son, have a good trip to Oregon. If anyone asks, I'll tell them you headed out for Arizona or somewhere south of here."

"Thanks, for that and for everything. Maybe we'll meet again."

"Doubt it, but I won't forget you."

Then Abe had come back out to the ranch they'd taken care of and that had taken care of them, and the little group got ready to depart. Maria was getting bigger all the time, but Sarah Beth said that she was a very strong, if quite small, woman and should have no trouble with the birth. Helga wanted to drive the buggy, but Abe decided she should take the wagon and the oxen so Maria and Sarah Beth could have the gentler ride behind Ginger in the buggy.

Louis seemed to be everywhere at once, lashing this, loading that, and circling up the cattle every time they started to spread out. When it was finally time to put the party into motion, Abe sat on Bird and took a long, long look at the land and the little shed they'd called home, and gave silent thanks to God for His protection and constant care. Then he added a request for more of the same if that wasn't asking too much.

While he was in town, he'd overheard a conversation in the mercantile about some Indians out west a ways causing trouble, but when he recalled it later, he just dismissed it and placed his trust in Lefty and the white-legged "spirit horse." Sarah Beth actually felt relief at being on the move again at last. She was counting on the stranger's words, that she would be much more likely to become pregnant once they'd settled somewhere. Helga had one more visit from the young man, Blair, and although he said he came just to say goodbye to the whole family, it was obvious he mostly had eyes for the younger woman. When Sarah Beth asked her about it, she claimed she hadn't noticed anything, and that they'd exchanged no particular plans about the future.

Once they were on the move, the rain seemed to threaten them from the south down toward the big Salt Lake, but it blew on past and they were greeted with beautiful warm sunny weather as they moved west, finding the trail they needed. They camped only very temporarily at night until they'd put a good distance between themselves and the place they left behind. After nearly three weeks of that, at what Abe figured was a little over halfway, they were close enough to a town called Twin Falls to take a rest for themselves and the animals. They found a good campsite and settled in for a few days.

It was there that they were joined by a travelling fiddler named Gentry and his four daughters, who sang when he played in towns they travelled through. The girls were extremely shy, and would barely speak with Helga or Sarah Beth, but when they started singing, they seemed to have no fear of anyone or anything. Helga confided in Sarah Beth that she'd always wished she could sing that kind of popular music, but that "those people" considered such singing to be the same as Devil worship, and she'd never been allowed to sing anything but what she called "dried-up old church hymns."

When the girls and their father held their practice sessions in their own camp, she sat, transfixed by their presence and talent, and could even be heard singing softly along with the melody, although she didn't know any words of the songs. The next afternoon, Gentry and his daughters got ready to go into town and perform at the local music hall. The man had arranged it the day before. One of the girls, the oldest one, quietly approached Helga and asked if she would care to come along and help the girls with their clothing and hairstyles. Helga could hardly believe it at first, but asked Abe and Sarah Beth if she could please go. Sarah Beth though that it would be better if one of them went along, but said she didn't much want to as she was busy trying to get started on a quilt of her own. Abe said he had a few other errands that he could do in the town. Then they wouldn't all have to make a stop on their way past, day after tomorrow, when they started up again. So he saddled up and rode alongside the wagon with the words "Gentry Girls" painted on the side. He could tell that Louis wanted to come along, but felt that he should stay with Maria in case anything changed in her condition.

Backstage at the music hall, Helga was nearly beside herself with excitement, fluffing out dresses, brushing hair and humming the melodies of the songs the girls would be singing a little later. When the show finally started and the crowd gave a big cheer at the entrance of the girls, she had the strange feeling that this was something she'd always dreamed of doing, but never knew about. And far from wanting to be on stage herself, she was completely happy just to be in the background and know that she had helped the show in many small ways.

The next day when Gentry and the girls were about to load up and make their way south, the man asked Abe if he wanted to spare that girl and let her come along with him on his "minstrel travels" as he called them. Abe turned him down, but not without first asking Helga what she thought about it.

"Oh, Mr. Abe, I would love to go, but I'd never leave you and Miss Sarah Beth, not now when you'll be needing so much help getting settled. Besides, we're family, and they're their own family, and there's just too big a difference."

And that was that. Abe thanked Gentry and then said he hoped they'd meet up again someday further on along their own trails.

CHAPTER SIXTEEN

Jordan Valley

The rest of their journey, from Twin Falls to the Jordan Valley, was mostly uneventful with the exception of a broken wagon wheel that happened on an extremely rocky stretch of the trail. They were going downhill toward what was called the Owyhee River when they all heard the cracking sound and the shrill screaming of the hub. Louis and Abe were able to prop the wagon up just enough by using leverage, as heavily-loaded as it was, and remove the wheel. Abe remembered a blacksmith in a very small community that he'd passed through on his first trip, back in the previous fall. They lashed the wheel, with its cracked metal hub, onto the back of the buggy. Sarah Beth decided she wanted to go along with Abe, and he and Louis both agreed that it was probably all right for the two of them to be gone at the same time, since there wouldn't be much of anything that could get done until they moved out again.

After a final check on Maria, who was still showing no signs of even the earliest stages of labor, Sarah Beth climbed into the buggy, Abe mounted Bird, and they were off. The day before all that happened, Louis shot a young buffalo that seemed to be lost or separated from its herd. He and Helga planned to dress it out and salt the meat. If they were lucky and there was enough heat in the sun, they might even be able to quick-dry some of it. Despite the setback with the wheel, Abe was in good spirits and welcomed some time alone with Sarah Beth. For her part, a letter from Mattie had come just before they started out, and the two of them really had no time to discuss it during the preparations and the hard work of travelling.

The two of them got an early start, and were ready to stop for a break at mid-day. Both horses needed to be watered and allowed to browse for awhile. Abe hobbled Bird so she wouldn't wander too far, and Ginger was not likely to leave her once they settled into some spring grass along the stream near the trail. While he was taking care of the animals and re-checking the wheel's lash-up to the buggy, Sarah Beth laid out their lunch in the shade of a cottonwood.

As soon as they'd eaten a bit of the food she brought along, she began talking about what was mostly occupying her mind, the concern she felt for Mattie. "I told you what she said in the letter." She paused to make sure that she had Abe's attention.

"Yes, she's afraid to come all this way alone, but doesn't really have anywhere else to go now that your father's gone."

"I just wish she'd written before now, so she could have gotten out here before we had to move on. I know you were set on leaving now, and I know the reasons why, but if we're all she's got in this world, we have to help her somehow."

"Is there anyone, or maybe a family from the church that she could stay with until we get somewhat settled in out here?"

"Probably, but she so much hates taking anything from anyone."

"Well, there's a post office out where we're going, in Silver City. The mail is slow, but I think we should write her and ask her to find somewhere to stay, and maybe she'll even find some work with a family. Then just as soon as we're ready, the new train might be running and you and myself, or you and Louis could make the short trip down to that place with the funny name, that Winnemucca. It's not really that far and it's the closest place the train will stop."

"I like that idea," she said. "I hope she's willing to do it. I was only thinking of getting her as far as Ogden where I travelled from and that will be too far away. I didn't know about Winnie-mucka." She smiled for the first time in the conversation.

"Does she have enough to pay her expenses?"

"Abe, that's the other part of the letter that I didn't read to you. It turns out that father's estate was more extensive than any of us knew. There's the property he had in Virginia, which the Union has returned to us. And after we moved out to Missouri, he became a silent partner with one of the church deacons in a construction firm. They were contracted to build a new bridge across the Platte River right there in St. Joseph. And when he knew his health was failing, he sold his share for quite a lot of money. The Will was finally opened and just became official last month. Mattie says he was very generous with her, and that you and I have a good amount in an account under my name at one of the banks back there."

Abe looked at her for a few moments, and then said, "Well, I wish you told me this before we started coming this way. I might have changed my mind and gone back to St. Joe, become a businessman, maybe even a banker . . ." Then he rolled over in her direction and grabbed her by the shoulders, pulling her down on top of him. She pushed herself up and was laughing now, pretending to slap his face with her hands and fingers. He reached up and got his hands on each side of her head and pulled her down to a long kiss. Just then they heard a rifle shot. There was no way to tell from what direction. Abe pushed her off, away, and quickly got to his knees. He crawled over to the buggy, pulled out his own rifle, and quickly checked its load.

There was a high ridge set somewhat back from the stream and silhouetted against the sky was a single rider. Abe beckoned Sarah Beth to join him and quickly pushed her behind the buggy. The rider on the ridge disappeared, and they waited for several minutes, not knowing what might happen next. Finally, Abe felt it was safe to gather up the horses, and he hooked Ginger to the buggy again, saddled Bird and mounted, this time with his gun ready.

"Let's cross the stream down there where the banks are easy and we'll move away from that ridge." He led the way, often glancing over his shoulder, but seeing nothing.

Sarah Beth spoke up, saying, "Why do we always seem to get interrupted? I mean when we're having a serious conversation."

Abe pulled Bird over close to her and said, "Because, it just makes us want each other more."

"Why, Mr. Saunders . . ." She brushed the buggy whip across Ginger's rear end and started her trotting ahead. Abe took one more look around, and then caught up with her.

"How much farther to that little town?" she asked.

"If I remember right, we're close."

Within an hour they arrived at a small collection of buildings situated on a low bluff above the confluence of two streams. Abe led the way along the single roadway to the smithy. The wheel was fixed by the end of the afternoon, and they were told of a place where they could spend the night, if they chose. It was a small cabin next to a church. The church was not in use, as the minister had moved on and his replacement never showed up. Abe thanked the smith and paid him, and they settled into the lodging for the night. They were both tired, but not so they couldn't take advantage of this small interlude of privacy.

By morning they were back near the place where the shot had been fired, and once again the silhouetted rider was visible against the morning sky. The day before, when Abe told the blacksmith what had happened to them he was informed that it was just a solitary Indian named "Christian Eagle." It seemed that he kept an eye out on travelers coming along that part of the trail. He wasn't known to be hostile, just keeping watch. No one seemed to know where he lived or who his people were.

This time when they saw the rider, Abe waved his hat and the figure held his rifle high in the air. The stranger then began riding down the side of the bluff toward them. Abe told Sarah Beth to get down behind the buggy and stay there while he tried to deal with the situation. As the rider came closer, he raised both arms above his head, showing that his rifle was not in his hands. He galloped his horse in a wide circle around the buggy and then stopped a ways away. Now he held his left hand above his head and pointed at it with his right. Then he gestured toward Abe's horse, and gave a hoarse yell.

Abe dismounted and laid his own gun on the ground, beckoning for the other man to join him on the ground. The Indian climbed down and warily approached within a few yards. He pointed in the direction of the buggy and made a sign that he knew there was someone else hiding there. Abe called to Sarah Beth and told her it was all right to show herself, but to stay where she was.

The Indian then pointed at Bird and ran his hand up and down his own leg, and pointed at the horse's white leg. Abe held up his own left hand and made a sign for receiving something with his arms. Then the other man startled him by speaking in English, saying, "Where is he, why you have horse?"

Abe slowly answered, "Lefty is far away, but he will come here soon." As he spoke, he tried to make what he thought would be explanatory signs with his hands.

"You see him, say you see Jesus Eagle man."

Abe said, "Christian Eagle?"

"Yes, yes." The man pounded his chest and pointed to heaven and then to his heart. "Jesus man, eagle man." Then he quickly stepped backwards to his horse, threw his leg over its back and galloped away.

On the run, he pulled his rifle from under the saddle blanket and fired one shot into the air.

Abe watched him go and then turned back and went to Sarah Beth. "Well, that was strange," he said as he put his arm around her.

"It certainly was . . . Do you think everyone in this country knows Lefty?"

"Seems so, doesn't it. We'll have to ask him about this strange Indian when we see him. I hope it's soon." He laughed, "I don't want to forget all the questions I have for him."

By the middle of the next morning they had the wheel back on the wagon and were underway. Maria seemed to Sarah Beth more sluggish than usual, moving slowly around the morning cook-fire and unable to help pack up as much as she usually did. Louis came and gave her a gentle hug before he rode off to get the cattle moving. Helga got back on the wagon seat as soon as the oxen were harnessed. She started them off down the trail. This route was nowhere near so heavily traveled as the Oregon Trail, and in some places it almost disappeared under fresh new grass that heralded the birth of the spring in this country.

With no one to talk to and all the wide open space to keep her eyes on, Helga had plenty of time to think or sing as she let the oxen move at their own pace. Some part of her felt a little regretful that she hadn't taken the opportunity to go along with that Gentry family, but she knew realistically, she would not have been much more than a servant to the girls, and she'd had enough of that role with the Bishop's family. Maybe if there had been a chance of her being included in the singing and the show, but that was highly unlikely. Besides, she thought, Abe and Sarah Beth were not only the most handsome couple she knew, they were the nicest people she ever lived around. There was something else new for her too, and that was that both of them always made sure she was included in the discussions concerning their daily work and their futures together. For the first time in her life she truly felt she had a family, and even though she was almost their ages, it was sometimes comfortable to just relax and pretend they were her parents and would just go on taking care of her.

Abe told her about the mighty Snake River last fall when he got back from his trip to Oregon, and again the day before. Now, as the sun came up behind them she thought about how that river was just over the next ridge to the north and how the valley they were travelling through would open up into another one before the end of the day. Abe said he was very glad they didn't have to cross the big river because it was bound to be flowing high and fast with the melting snows of the mountains beginning to fill its banks. They would be staying on this side, as it turned away to the north. There were times like this, when she sincerely wished she was able to attend a school so she could learn about things like maps and numbers. The Bishop's wives barely taught her to read, and it was a difficult time as they used a switch on her whenever she made a mistake reading from the Bible out loud. They always said it was a worse fault if she made a mistake reading God's Word than if she had been reading a newspaper or something, but they wouldn't let her read or practice on anything else.

The warmth of the sun made her feel like singing, so she did. It was one of the songs she'd learned from the Gentrys, one she really liked. She didn't realize how enthusiastically she was singing or that her voice was carrying until Abe rode up beside her and asked where she'd learned the song.

"From those girls, Mr. Abe. But I didn't realize you could hear me. I'll sing softer or not at all if it's a bother to you."

"No Helga, it's wonderful. You have a beautiful voice and your singing will help pass the time. Please go on, I want to hear more when I return," he said as he and Bird turned away. He waved as he rode off to check with Louis and the cattle.

Although Abe and Blair had taken a more direct route when they returned home from that first trip, this time it was clear that for this big a group they'd need to take the longer route, close to but not on the same side of the Snake as the towns of Boise and Nampa. While this route would eliminate much of the rough, rocky trails and climbing through mountains, it was longer and would take a few more days. Louis was beginning to get more and more impatient with the slow pace at which they were moving because of Maria's condition, but even he realized that there wasn't much they could do about it. He even suggested selling off some of the cattle, but Abe convinced him that unless they got rid of them all, it wouldn't make any real difference how fast they could move. Besides, he said, they would need the cattle for their income once they got to their destination.

Maria was learning more English, mostly from Helga, and now she could describe to Sarah Beth what was going on inside her belly.

In exchange, Helga was learning some basic Spanish vocabulary. She joked with Sarah Beth that it might come in useful for her in case she met and married a prince from Spain who would then become King of Spain and make her the Queen. Sarah Beth thought that was really funny and from then on kept asking when her prince was coming. Helga's usual answer was, "Any day now."

One evening when the others had gone off to their bedrolls early, Abe and Sarah Beth had a chance to talk about some of the circumstances they might find themselves in once they arrived at the land in Jordan. She was especially concerned about the legality of them just moving onto a piece of land when it wasn't theirs, nor was there any way to claim it. Abe admitted that it could become a problem, but more than likely it would work out and hopefully Hawk Man would show up before any problems did develop.

"But you did say other people wanted the land."

"Well, it's a pretty good place, and one of the few, I guess, that are still not taken."

"That's why I'm worried."

"We won't being doing anything that looks permanent until after Hawk Man and his family come back for their summer camp. In the meantime, we'll just say that we're stopping temporarily, to rest the cattle and wait for Maria's baby to be strong enough for traveling. Now, what else is on your mind?"

She got up and added a few pieces of brushwood to the fire. It snapped and crackled as the twigs caught the flames. She sat on the ground beside Abe and snuggled up next to him. After several long moments, she spoke, saying, "Abe, I'm getting impatient . . . for our child to come, I know you believe in it, and so do I. But nothing's changing for us, and whenever I'm around someone like Maria, I'm guilty of some sinful thoughts, jealousy and the like. I love her, she is so sweet and helpful, even in her condition, but I can't help it. God doesn't answer my prayers, yet others have no trouble . . . I can't stand myself sometimes, and what if I'm to be barren for my whole life, forever helping other women have their babies, but never any of my own . . ."

Abe held her tightly to himself and stroked her hair with his other hand. He could feel the soft tremor of her quiet sobbing and was at a loss as to know how to comfort her. He too, was beginning to wonder, and yes, to feel pangs of impatience even though he knew that this still wasn't a good time for them. They really needed to get settled into their new lives, at least in some ways, and be able to stop this nearly endless travelling.

"Dear, sweet Sarah Beth, we have each other, and I have my faith that this will all . . . be all right. This isn't the right time for us. We're not ready, we need to have more of a home for you to feel comfortable and safe. There's still too much that's unknown, and I'm sure those things have as much to do with it as anything else. You and I think too much, think about the future when we're not even settled in the present. I doubt that Louis and Maria ever considered the question of what would happen to them and a baby if they were still without a home . . . but we're different than that, and I think it might have something to do with this, this delay. So, we'll just keep on loving each other. Why don't we get some sleep. I'd like to put in a long day tomorrow, if we can. We'll be crossing a river, not the Snake, but it could be a little difficult."

He turned her face up so his lips could meet hers in a careful kiss, and then he softly licked a few of the tears from her cheeks. They kissed again and he got up, helped her to her feet so they could take care of the final duties of the night, and then they got into their bedroll for the sleep they both needed.

By next morning, it was raining, not hard, but enough it would make the cattle a little more difficult to get moving. Abe and Louis both went to take care of it, and left the women to load the camping gear into the wagon and get moving. While Sarah Beth and Helga were lifting the crate full of their cooking utensils and dishes up into the wagon, Maria gave out a muffled but high-pitched little scream. They shoved the crate into its space in the load, and rushed to Maria's side.

"Es nada," she said, pointing to a hole in some nearby rocks where the black and white tail of a skunk was sticking out.

Sarah Beth quickly led her away and they all hurried to get everything packed away and left as quickly as they could. "Well, that was fortunate," Sarah Beth yelled to Helga from the buggy once they were on the move. "We were there all night and it didn't get us. I am so relieved."

"Oh, I know," Helga said. "That was such a close call. And I really thought it was Maria's time when she cried out."

"Well, it will be, soon, but hopefully not when one of those creatures is around." Then they both pulled up on their reins to slow the pace at which they'd been driving the animals in their panic to get away from the threat of skunk. "Maria, are you all right now?" she asked. The woman nodded her head up and down vigorously and held her nose closed.

"Yes, I know."

Later in the day, they crossed a river with a small, crooked sign that said it was the Bruneau. It was wide and shallow at the place where they crossed and not moving very fast. The cattle balked at entering it, but Louis started firing his pistol right behind them and some of the older cows plunged in and found footing. Then it was just a matter of staying downstream from them and forcing them to take the shortest distance across. There was good spring grass on the other side, and both men were able to leave the cattle and ride back to help the women and the wagon and buggy across. Louis took the lead with the buggy, riding alongside Ginger and frequently brushing her rump with his coiled rope. Abe stayed back until the way was clear and then fastened a loop onto one of the oxen and led them and Helga into the water.

He turned back to see if she was all right and yelled, "Now's the time for a song."

She shook her whip and began singing something he couldn't make out over the splashing sounds of the water. At one place there was some kind of a hole at the bottom of the river. One of the oxen stepped into it and nearly went in over his head. Abe shouted for Helga to pull up and he was able to force the team sideways and back them up a little so they could be guided around the deep spot. From then on he stayed just ahead of them, counting on Bird to avoid any more of those holes.

That night they made a large fire and strung ropes around it to help dry out the clothes that all of them had gotten wet. Maria laid down right after supper and Sarah Beth spent some time with her, lightly massaging her belly and serving her some tea she'd made from a supply of herbs she brought all the way from Virginia, and had used many times before.

Louis was getting more and more nervous and kept leaving with a lantern to look after the cattle, even though they were bedded down already. Helga and Abe sat by the fire wrapped in spare blankets and he tried to get her to sing some more. She resisted by saying it wasn't the time for it, that she didn't feel like it, and besides, maybe Maria needed to get sleep.

"Then sing softly, like a lullaby," he said.

So she smiled and then stared into the fire and began humming a melody he'd never heard before, or at least didn't recognize. When she stopped after awhile, he asked what song that was.

She said, "It was something I learned from the women. Their songs were the nicest thing about them. I remember being sung to when I was very little. Maybe even by my mother."

"Well, go on then. You have a wonderful voice."

Sarah Beth came back to the fire and sat beside him. When Helga stopped her singing again, Sarah Beth said, "I think it could be any time, but since it's her first, it may take longer. Do you know any good places we can camp for a couple of days if we have to?"

"Well, like I said, Blair and I went a little south of here, through those mountains we saw today, but I'm sure we could find somewhere. There are settlers all along this side of the Snake."

"Any idea how much longer until we'll be close to where we're going?"

"Maybe a week, four days, if all goes well."

"Well, keep all your fingers crossed. I'm going to fix our bed."

"She seems a bit tired, I guess we all are," he said to Helga, and then noticed that her eyes were closed and her head was nodding. "Hey you, Helga, wake up. Time to get yourself in bed."

Several days later, they skirted the small town of Silver City and a smaller community, and found the poorly maintained road that led out to Mike Skinner's place and on past it to their goal. Abe kept looking for Sarah Beth whenever he could, to try and catch a glimpse of her expression, hoping to be able to read her reaction to the area. But she was mostly concentrating on Maria, often reaching over to feel the woman's belly and to hold the woman's hand in her own. At one point, several hours later, he saw Maria leaning back against the buggy seat, arching herself up from it. He rode over next to Sarah Beth's side of the buggy and asked in a low voice, "About two or three more hours, can she hold out?"

"I think so."

"Maybe I should have Louis stay here with the cattle and Helga, while we make our way as quickly as we can."

"I don't think he'll go for that, he's pretty worried. He told me so this morning. And I don't want him to come and to leave you behind."

"All right, we'll push as hard as we can. You just keep going on this trail here, and I'll ride back and forth between you and the cattle. Helga will be in between us. There's only one homestead between here and where we're going. I told the old boy to expect us arriving about now when I last saw him."

A short ways further on, Sarah Beth signaled to Abe to come back to them.

"She's having some contractions, but they're far apart and not at all regular. What can we do to make her more comfortable?"

"We'll see." He waved for Helga to pull up near the buggy and when she stopped the team, he began removing some of the items stacked behind the seat of the buggy and pushing them into the few open spaces left on the wagon. Then he told Helga to grab as many blankets from the wagon as she easily could, and hand them down to him. Within a few minutes, he and Sarah Beth had made a small bed for Maria and helped her up into it.

"Good thing she's small," he commented.

"Lengthwise," Sarah Beth said, "but awfully big around."

"Well, let's get going and see if this baby waits for us to get there."

He rode off to join Louis and give him an update on what was going on with his woman. Louis looked worried and wanted to know if he should go on ahead and catch up with her.

"Let's just push these cows as fast as we can. That's the best we can do now."

With a few whoops and hollers they got the herd moving again, and glancing ahead they could see the buggy and the wagon moving along.

The main part of what could hardly be called a road went close by the Skinner place, but Abe and Louis pushed the cattle on a wide curving path around the buildings. Sarah Beth and Helga kept on the more direct route. Then Abe came back to be with them in case anyone came out of the buildings. Although it looked as occupied as when Abe was there before, no one appeared and there was no smoke from either the house or the smithy in the shed.

"Must not be home," he said. "How's she doing?"

"Not too well. This road is so rough . . . and I remember one woman I helped back home at the Fort. The baby just wouldn't come after hours and hours, so her husband, he was some kind of an officer, took her and loaded her into the back of a supply wagon and drove out on the roughest road he could find. Pretty soon he was back with her and the baby came soon after."

"That's a good trick," he said, "but I think we've got the opposite problem. How to make the little one wait 'till we get there."

"I know. You're right. How much more?"

"Just past that low ridge up ahead, a couple of miles, but should be easier going along the creek now, more flat ground."

She reached back and felt the belly of the now moaning woman. "I'll just make it as fast as I can," she said. "How will I know where I can stop if we make it that far?"

"There's two really big, old cottonwoods down along the creek. It's near where Hawk Man says his family have always camped. Stop there if you make it that far."

She gently tapped Ginger on the rump with her buggy whip and set off, trying to steer the horse ahead onto the smoothest ground she could see. Helga pulled up beside Abe in the wagon and yelled, "What's going on with Maria?"

"She's all right yet. Just keep moving and we'll make it."

Then he rode over to the cattle, and to report the situation to the agitated Louis.

The next hour passed slowly for Sarah Beth as the moaning and occasional screams of the woman behind the seat kept getting stronger and louder. She often reached behind herself to feel the contractions and try to count the seconds they lasted and minutes between them. They were still irregular and randomly spaced, but she had enough experience to know that every delivery doesn't necessarily go by the rules. Whoever made up the rules anyway? Every birth was different as far as she'd seen. And that thought made her wonder about her own, how would it be for her, would she be strong enough, would she weep or laugh, scream, or be silent with teeth gritted against the recurrent spasms and pain. It scared her, but there was nothing in God's world that she wanted more . . .

They rounded a bend in the trail that was caused by the outcropping of a low hill. As they moved along the creek, she could see two huge trees with the bright green of new leaves filling their crowns. She drove until she was under them and pulled the horse to a stop, jumped down and grabbed a bucket and ran for water. Within minutes she had a fire going, was heating water and making a cushioned pile of bedding on the ground for Maria. By this time, the woman's eyes were rolling back in her head and her breathing was coming in sharp gasps. Sarah Beth softly whispered a short prayer of thanks for having been able to make it this far. Then, another prayer asking for safety and a strong baby. She poured some of the heated water from the bucket into a couple of pots taken from under the buggy seat and washed her hands and face. She was glad she had done some things in preparation for this, and started soaking some of the strips of cloth she'd already torn. When she'd done all she could to get ready, without realizing it, she just sort of collapsed to the ground next to Maria, took the woman's grasping hand in her own and then took as many of her own deep breaths as she could. She remembered one of the nurses back in Virginia telling her that you have to take care of yourself as much as you're taking care of the mother if you're going to be able to help her all the way through. Right then this made perfect sense, because she knew she was exhausted and was fighting to keep from dozing off.

She heard the sounds of the wagon pulling in, then Helga was beside her, asking what she could do to help. Sarah Beth showed her how to hold the woman's feet so they could brace against the girl.

"Remember, you did this with Grace."

"Do you think this one is going to be that hard?"

"I hope not, and I really don't think so the way it's been going."

The labor progressed in what Sarah Beth told Helga ways that were better than the norm, and after less than two hours of it, she whispered to Helga that it was already almost time for Maria to begin pushing. "So, why don't you refill the pots near the fire, stoke it up, and then bring us a full jug of fresh cold water. I think we'll all be thirsty when this is over."

Helga hurried off to do as she was asked and Sarah Beth took over holding the woman's ankles. Just as Helga was returning, they heard the sound of hoofbeats and within moments, Louis had joined them.

"Is she all right, has it happened?" he asked loudly, jumping down from his horse.

"Yes and no," Sarah Beth replied. "She's doing well, and you're in time, so catch your breath and kneel down there by her head. Here, wipe her face with this cloth if she wants it."

"Abe said I should come on ahead. He's still bringing up the cows, not far back."

He knelt beside Maria and leaned over to give her a kiss just as she screamed, arching her back up and away from the padding beneath her hips. Helga quickly took Sarah Beth's place at the feet as the kicking of the legs became almost too much to hang on to.

Sarah Beth pulled back everything that was covering the woman's mid-section, but Maria fought to push her loose dress back down. "You'll have to leave it up now Maria, it's the only way I can get in there to help you."

Maria whimpered and allowed her coverings to be pushed out of the way just as her body was wracked by another contraction.

"It's coming . . . now, Maria push hard . . . push . . ."

After a few more of the heavy, fairly violent thrashings, the top of the baby's head appeared, its dark hair wreathed by Maria's own darkness. Sarah Beth gently eased her fingers into position to help with the next burst of energy when, hopefully, the head would crown. Then in moments the head appeared, twisting back and forth as Sarah Beth wiped the mucous from its face. The baby was very dark. Sarah Beth felt the cord wrapped around its neck and she quickly loosened and pulled it over the head. The dark color of the baby was a bluish brown, and Sarah Beth reached around the head with both hands to be able to pull on the infant's shoulders, clutching with her fingers under its armpits. One arm came out, and then the other. She pulled some more until its body flopped out into her waiting hands and she rapidly untangled the rest of the cord, held the baby upside down, holding it by its feet and swinging it gently back and forth. There was a choking, gasping sound and Sarah Beth placed her mouth over the baby's and sucked at a plug of mucous that came out. She spit it to the side and eased her finger into the baby's mouth, causing it to choke some more. When she removed her finger, there was a hoarse squalling and coughing sound. Then there was a sound, a real baby cry. Sarah Beth turned it right side up and held it against her own bosom for a few moments, rocking back and forth, making sure the breathing hadn't stopped. Maria was reaching for her baby, but Louis was gently holding her down.

"You done it, girl," he was saying, "you done it good."

Sarah Beth was remembering a birth she'd been at where a white woman's baby came out an odd shade of blue, again from the cord being wrapped around it's throat and most likely cutting off some circulation to the head. That baby had stayed blue for a couple of hours while the blood cleared itself. That's what must be the source of the strange color of this one, but she was beginning to feel that it would be all right just like that other one. Then although she was reluctant to give it up, cherishing the moment of holding the most precious thing she could ever imagine, holding on carefully to a moments-old newborn, she eased forward and gently handed the little girl to her mother, placing the baby on the mother's breasts and covering both the mother and child with their softest cotton blanket.

Maria was crying, and saying over and over again, "Gracias, gracias," and "Madre de Dios, Madre, Madre, gracias . . ."

Even Louis was shedding a few tears and wiping them away as if there were flies on his face, "Is it gonna be all right?" he asked, lightly placing his big hands on the precious lump of baby lying on Maria's chest.

"The baby? Yes, she is. We'll just have to watch her carefully for a few hours, just to make sure she doesn't have any trouble breathing."

It was then that they finally noticed the sound of cattle in the distance, just as Abe rode up, looking down from his horse with a question on his face.

"All right, they're both all right," Sarah Beth said as she stood up and moved over to lean her face against his leg. He ran his hand over her hair and gently pushed her out of the way so he could climb down. He yanked the bridle from Bird's head and let the horse go. Then he took Sarah Beth in his arms and held her tightly.

"Good job," he said, "good job. A great way to start things off in our new home." Then he felt her sobbing against his chest and he knew she was exhausted. And he knew once again, this had to be the hardest thing in the world for her, this helping other women bring life into the world, and wanting nothing less for herself. "You're a miracle worker, my dear sweet one. You're so special."

"It's Maria and God did the hard work," she said, trying to catch her breath and stop her crying.

Abe looked over her head and saw Helga still sitting at Maria's feet, looking as if she was in a trance. "Helga," he said, "are you all right?"

"Oh . . . yes, Mr. Abe. I'm fine, just too happy to think. I'll get things going for our supper, I surely will."

"That's all right, it's early enough yet. I think we'll all just enjoy being in our new home together for a little while. There'll be a nearly full moon tonight and we can unpack things as we need them. The only thing is, we need to clean up all this and make a safe and snug spot for Maria and whatever the little one's name is."

For the first several weeks they were at the new home, it stayed dry with cold nights and warm days. Once again they made a makeshift camp, only this time it was Maria, the baby and Louis who had the use of the wagon as a 'bedroom' and shelter. Helga was happy to build her own lean-to using evergreen branches and pieces of old rope. It faced the rising sun so that, as she said, she'd be up early to enjoy the peace and quiet of the daybreak hours. For some reason, this reminded Abe of something Doctor Randall had said to him back in Virginia.

Abe went into the mining town, Silver City, right off and purchased a good-sized tent for himself and Sarah Beth. He was surprised, given how small the town was, that no one asked him where he was from or where he was living. He was able to surmise from the conversations he overheard that there was a great deal of turnover in the town, but as one older clerk at the dry goods store said when he asked about it, "folks hereabouts don't much care where someone comes from or where they're going, long as they pay their bills."

Abe and Sarah Beth spent a good amount of time the next few days exploring the place and its possibilities. He showed her where Hawk Man and the other families had their main camp on the other side of the creek. They found a nice place not too far the giant cottonwoods for their temporary camp, and then they began looking for a house site for themselves that wouldn't be too close to the Indians. On the other hand, it needed to be close enough to be on the same property, if there were such things as property lines that came with the place. They'd decided on three considerations; nearness to the stream and its water but upslope above any possibility of flooding, a view and exposure to both the east and west end of what was actually a kind of valley formed by the low-lying hills to both the north and the south, and they wanted enough flat land close to the house they built for their outbuildings and a barn where Abe wouldn't have to be too far away when he was working. He joked with Sarah Beth that a man might need to get away from the household and its women once in awhile.

She laughed and said, "That's exactly why I want to make it hard for you to get too far. You'll be gone enough as it is, and I'm getting tired of having to wear this gun all the time to take care of myself."

He grabbed her arm and spun her around, reaching behind and pulling the small revolver from its holster. He lifted her up and then laid her down on the ground, tossed both of their guns aside and knelt down straddled across her. "Now, Miss Sarah Beth, what are you going to do with me if I am around you all the time?"

"Well, not this. I'll just keep you working while I read a book or something."

"What's wrong with this?" he said as he leaned forward, pinned her arms back and kissed her gently at first, and then more and more.

She responded, not resisting, and then twisted her head aside so she could say, "Well, there's nothing especially wrong with this, but it won't get all my chores done for me. Yours either." Then she reached up and pulled the front of his shirt open. "Uh-oh," she said, "now who's going to have to sew that button back on."

Their bodies responded to the soft ground, the warm sun and the longing that was always just below the surface for both of them. As they made love Abe tried as hard as he could to keep his mind on making a child with her, for her, thinking, please God, please God . . . please . . .

After they'd rested, when he finally stood up and straightened out his clothes, minus the one button, he helped her up and took her into his arms and said, "Seems like a fine place for a bedroom to me."

She smiled up at him. They kissed again, then began walking back toward the camp. When they got there Maria was cutting deer meat into strips for drying and Helga was holding the little baby, who'd been given the name Conchita Margarita, after Louis's father Conrad, and Maria's mother, Margarita Sanchez.

When Abe was in town that first time, he'd asked after Mike Skinner, their closest neighbor, and found that the man was gone, north to the Columbia River country to pick up a woman who was his second cousin, and whom he planned to marry. Abe told Sarah Beth what the man said about women getting lonely in these parts, but she tossed her head and said she wasn't worried about that since there were probably plenty enough miners in Silver City that would like a young wife from Virginia. That was, if she couldn't keep her own husband home for companionship. Abe had looked closely at her to make sure she was joking and she assured him that the last thing this girl would ever want was a dirty old miner. So he promised not to ever be gone for very long, no more than a month or two.

"Fine," she said, "you might just come home and find me with an Indian husband."

"That's funny, I guess I never did tell you about the Indian who wanted to give me one of his wives. Turned him down, though, I said one wife was more than enough trouble for me."

They ended up laughing and kissing as they usually did, and went back to discussing their neighbor and whether or not the man would be back in time to make some of the hardware they'd need for their house and building, and whether he might teach Abe how to do it himself and let him use tools and the forge until they could get one of their own going.

The day after they'd chosen their new home-site, and blessed it with their loving, a small wagon pulled by two horses arrived near their camp. A man climbed down and by the time Abe recognized him, Mike Skinner was yelling a hello. Abe waved back, and called for Sarah Beth who was down at the creek behind their wagon washing clothes with Maria. Abe waited for her and then took her hand, leading her to meet the neighbor, Just then, a woman climbed down out of the back of the wagon and came walking to join the three of them. The men shook hands and then stumbled over their words as they both tried to introduce the women at once.

"Go ahead," Abe said,

"Well, this is Martha Skinner, my new wife, brought her down here from up Pendleton country."

"And this is Sarah Beth, my wife, all the way from Virginia."

The two women smiled at each other, and then they both gave polite small curtsies to the men they'd just met.

"How many more of you is there?" Mike asked.

"Well, there's my cousin Louis and his woman, Maria, and they've got a newborn, and then there's Helga, a girl, or I guess she's more a young woman, and she's been with us since we stopped down in Utah for the winter."

"Well, it's nice to have neighbors at last," Mike said.

Sarah Beth motioned to the other woman, saying, "Come along and we'll fix us all some coffee or tea, and I'm sure we've got something edible." She took Martha's arm and the two of them walked toward the covered kitchen space that was next to the big wagon.

Mike and Abe walked back to the Skinner's wagon and team and he asked if he could unhook them if they were going to be there awhile.

"Sure, let me help."

Mike hobbled one of the two and then went to the wagon and pulled a small bottle out of a bundle. "Need to welcome you proper," he said, handing the half-full bottle to Abe.

"Well, thanks . . . appreciate it, but I don't usually . . ."

"Don't usually don't matter. This is a special occasion, the answer to one of my prayers, or wishes, or whatever a non-church-going man uses for asking for things. Drink up, won't hurt you a bit."

Abe took a small swallow and passed the bottle back as the burning liquid flowed down his throat and warmed his belly. He said, "We've been wondering when you'd get back. Heard you'd gone north after a woman."

"Well, I'm back and what I'm talking about is how glad I am to see another woman or two here. Martha made me promise she could go back home if there wasn't anyone here for her besides me, so I sure was hoping you'd still be coming" He'd taken a large pull on the bottle and offered it back to Abe who waved it off.

"I'm just happy you remembered me, and maybe you can help me make sure folks know I'm not a squatter or anything."

"Well, Hawk Man tried to tell me about you and him making some kind of a deal, but I just figured to wait and see if you showed, and then try to figure it out. That Indian don't have the best English for talking about things. Said something about you came from the left hand of the Creator and it was meant to be."

"Oh, yes, but that's not quite how it is. We have a common Indian friend whose name in white man talk is Lefty. I met him back in Missouri and he gave me that white-legged horse. Seems every Indian I've met knows him and that horse, and some of the white folks as well."

"Now I get it," Mike said, taking another swig. "I've met the man myself when he come through couple summers back. Had a couple of wives and now that you mention it, I'm pretty sure he had that horse with him too."

"I'd imagine so."

Mike offered the bottle to him one more time and this time Abe took another small taste and handed it back. The man put what was left under the seat of his wagon, and they walked toward the cook-fire and the women. Sarah Beth had set out their only two chairs and she and Martha were talking away with each other. Helga was holding the baby and obviously fascinated by the tall woman stranger.

"Coffee or tea, gentlemen?" Sarah Beth asked.

They both asked for coffee, but refused when she urged them to take the chairs, and they hunkered down on some rocks. The four of them talked among themselves for quite awhile, long enough for second cups of coffee and tea. Abe explained to Mike that his cousin was out making sure their cows were moving up and away from the lush but low-nutrient grass along the stream. Maria had glanced out from behind the wagon, then quickly disappeared after calling to Helga to bring the baby to her. Helga came back and sat on the ground near the new woman, trying not to be impolite by staring at her with so much curiosity. Martha was saying what a happy surprise it was there was someone else out here in a place where she was fearful they'd always be alone except for the Indians.

Abe and Mike had a good talk about things they could help each other with, such as the use of the forge for Abe, and the idea of allowing Mike's small bunch of cattle to join theirs for easier management. The women soon had their own conversation going, finding out about each other's relatives and backgrounds and what they thought about being out here in God's own nowhere. Helga just kept smiling and weaving strands of grass together.

It was the middle of the afternoon when Mike stood up and said it was time for them to get on home, but they'd sure appreciate a visit soon when the new folks settled in a bit more.

"And Abe, I'll try to notice if I see anyone coming this way, maybe explain to them that one of your women just had a baby and you're just staying over for a bit. We'll let Mr. Hawk Man do the real explaining when he gets here . . . And thank you, Miss Sarah Beth, that sweet bread was delicious.

"Why thank you. Actually, Helga here made it."

He smiled and said, "We could use a small bakery around here."

Then they all walked the Skinners to their wagon, and when Mike had hooked up the team, they waved them goodbye, everyone promising to see each other again soon. As the neighbors were driving away, Abe commented to Sarah Beth that the man was much nicer than he'd been when he saw him on his first visit to the place.

Sarah Beth smiled up at him, and said, "Having a woman will do that to a man."

Part V

Settling In

May 1869-September 1869

CHAPTER SEVENTEEN

Building

As springtime turned the grass a bright green and the leaves on the cottonwoods burst their buds, the little family began planning for the future and the way of life that now, after all of the dreaming, waiting, and the travail of the trail, was finally becoming reality. Some of the cows had already calved, and Louis was happy with their success. However, it was becoming clear that he had little or no interest in building a house for himself, Maria and the baby, and it was time for Abe to confront his cousin about the issue. After talking it over with Sarah Beth, he went for a ride with Louis on the excuse that they needed to find another source of water above the place for the bone dry months of the coming summer.

They did find a place where a couple of springs came of out of a rocky hillside and merged into one channel that led down into their stream, the one flowing down through the spot where they were camping. There was also a kind of natural bowl of rock nearby, and they could see that with some hard work it could be made to suffice as a pond of sorts, if it would hold water. This would be something to investigate when it rained again. They would also need to see if they could make a change in the channels of the springs to feed an improved natural depression. Once again, it was clear from the difference between Abe's enthusiasm for the project and Louis's reticence that something else was going on besides them making plans for their future in this place together.

"So what's going on with you these days, cousin?" Abe asked when they were back on the valley bottom and they'd climbed off their horses to eat the small meal the women had packed for them.

"What're you talking about?"

"It's just been a little strange with you, you know. For example, when I went off to meet that man with the lumber mill. I invited you to come along so we could see what he has on hand that we might get for our houses."

"Yeah, well I didn't think it was a good time for both of us to be gone from the cows, them starting to calve and all, and I think I seen some wolf, so I want be checking them or know you're here to do it. There's time enough to build a house. Got all summer don't we?"

"Guess that depends on what it takes to get ready for next winter. I know I'm going to need your help, and you'll probably need mine."

They ate in silence for awhile. Then Louis cleared his throat and started to say something, stopped, and then said, "What'll you give me for my share of the cattle?"

"What?'

"You heard me. Just wondering what I'm worth these days."

"I have no idea, but we agreed we're not selling until we've built up the herd."

Louis rolled a cigarette and lit it. "Well, cousin, there's two things going on and you were right to ask," he said. "Maria's homesick as hell for Mexico, or at least Santa Fe if she's got to stay in America. And I miss the work on the caravans, miss the travel and the money. That's where I've got work waiting any time I want it. Besides," he stood up and began pacing back and forth, "just like today, we're looking for enough water for the herd and the houses. How we going to handle enough cattle here to make a living for both of us? No way in hell we can support our families, build houses and grow the herd at the same time. This country looks good right now, green and all, but it's going to dry out, I know it is. Then, cousin, it'll be hard times for the livestock, and that ain't my idea of happiness."

Now Abe stood up just as Louis sat back down, having put out his cigarette. "I can hardly believe this, but when I think about it, it does make some kind of sense. You never have been one to settle anyplace and I guess that's what we're talking about here, isn't it?"

"Maybe that, but also what's practical? Besides did you ever tell your Indian friend, the one who said you could stay here, about me, about having another family, more folks, being here with you?"

"No, but I don't think that should make any difference."

"Maybe not to you cousin, but I'm not about to settle on some Indian's land when he can just up and kick me off from one morning to the next."

"Best thing we've come across so far. Nothing's ever real secure in this life."

Louis got back up and started walking toward his horse which had wandered a short ways off. He stopped and turned back to face Abe. "Ain't about security, Cuz. It's about snow, if you really want to know. Me and Maria barely made it through last winter up in Montana and I had to promise we wouldn't do that again. Thought she might get over it, but now I'm feeling the same. Don't ever want to go through anything like that again. She don't hardly talk to me about much a else these days, and I guess I love her enough to listen."

He mounted and started riding back toward their headquarters. Abe went over to the prospective pond and stood there for some time. He couldn't help but think about how much harder it would be with only one man doing the work, but then, when he thought about it a little more, he could see some sense in what Louis was saying about room enough for two families. What with both of them trying to live off the same herd, off the same land. And then he realized that it wouldn't just be him working here alone, both Sarah Beth and Helga could work alongside him if that's what it took. On top of all that, Louis did have a point about Hawk Man. What if he didn't want another white man's family here, or even backed out on Abe?

Later that evening when he and Sarah Beth were alone and getting ready for bed, he brought it up, carefully at first, and then it all kind of spilled out of him. She was quiet until he finished, then she led him over to the bed, sat him down and pulled off his boots.

"When we get a real house with something besides a dirt floor, you're going to have to take your dirty boots off when you come inside."

"Thanks," he said as she set his boots outside the tent flap, "but what about what I been saying?"

She sat down on their low bed next to him. "I had a dream last week. There were way more cows than we have now, and some horses. There was a wolf circling them into a bunch, only one wolf, but he could get them all so they were facing him wherever he went, circling round and round. Then suddenly there was another wolf and then some more and the first one turned and just stood staring out at the others. His eyes were like fire and the rest of the wolves backed away, then turned and trotted off. That first one slowly turned into a bear and lay down. Soon the cows went back to eating." She paused and then asked, "Did he say how much he wants for his share of the herd?"

"No, just asked me what I thought they were worth."

"Did he ever get the money from the army for the ones the Indians took from him back in Colorado?"

"Yes, they sent it with a courier who met up with him out with the wagon train's herds."

"Maybe start by offering him the same amount, by the head." She was crawling under the covers.

"That's probably fair. But who do you think that wolf-bear in your dream was?"

"If you don't know, I won't tell you. Now get in this bed with me, if you don't mind." She spoke sternly, but was smiling as she said, "It's always cold without you."

Once the decision to separate had been made, it didn't take long for Maria and Louis to get ready for leaving. Abe and Sarah Beth promised to send them a share of money to pay for their cattle as soon as they received it from the bank in St. Joseph. There was no telegraph in Silver City, but mail came somewhat regularly and a bank draft was possible, if difficult. Then, as if it were more than some kind of coincidence, Mike Skinner showed up with a letter to Sarah Beth. It was from Mattie; the hotel manager in town, who was also the postal clerk, had given it to Mike for delivery. Mike said the clerk hadn't known the person it was addressed to, and it had been waiting there for over a month when he asked Skinner if he'd ever heard of the Saunders folks.

Sarah Beth quickly opened and read the letter while the two men visited and discussed the plans for the new house and what kind of iron-work would be needed.

> *My dearest Sarah Beth,*
>
> *I have sold everything that your father left for me to take care of. Your share is quite a significant amount, and I don't really want more than a little for myself for traveling on and to bring with me to help me pay my*

way however things turn out to be. The bank people here said I should have no trouble with their money draft once I get to a bank in Nevada.

I am trying so very hard not to presume on your kindness. You and your father have always done the right thing for me, and now I have no one else and am excited to think of being a pioneer lady. Even if I can't join with you, I know you can point me in the right direction to find a home and a job. Please. You don't know how lonely it has been for me since your father passed away.

I love you my special girl, Mattie

p.s. They told me the train just opened a line through a funny sounding place called Winnymucka, so I will travel to there and wait to hear from you. I hope they have a postal service office.

When Abe asked her what was in the letter, she passed it off as being just news from Missouri, and decided to wait until she could have him alone for that news. Her thoughts were whirling as she tried to adjust to the situation. With all that had happened since her father had died and she'd returned west, it was small wonder that she'd nearly forgotten about her promise to Mattie. Now she recalled the eagerness the woman had shown to join them as soon as they were able to settle. It was happening, and maybe there was a way to combine Cousin Louis's leaving plans with a way to bring Mattie here. Sarah Beth was excited to tell Abe about this development, but also cautious as she thought there was no way to know how he would take it. Especially since it meant another woman for him to have to take care of, unless they could find some other arrangement for Mattie. Deep inside though, she knew that Mattie was as close to a mother as she had now, and she herself needed the woman as much as she needed them, at least for the time being.

When they were alone together and could talk about things, Abe was quite honest about having forgotten Mattie's plan to join them at some point. As far as the money was concerned, he wondered whether they could get enough of it separated from the rest to pay Louis for the cattle, and then bring what was left to the bank in Silver City. That would be much more convenient for them than any other alternative. Then when he started to talk about how to arrange to meet and bring Mattie to their place, Sarah Beth interrupted.

"I do like the way you start right away thinking about all the details and arranging things in your mind, but I think there's a bigger issue here. Mattie has never lived away from towns and cities, never put up with this kind of living, and we don't even have a house for her."

"She was a slave, wasn't she?"

"Well yes, but what's that got to do with it?"

"I just mean that when she was younger she must have got used to living under some pretty harsh conditions."

"I really don't think she was a field worker. She never talked about it, but it would be a surprise to me if she wasn't either a housemaid or perhaps even lived in a town."

"Well, summer's coming and we want to have our house built by the fall. It's just going to take one more room."

"Oh Abe, you're so practical about all of this. I was afraid you wouldn't want her to come here."

"She's family, Sarah Beth, more family than any I have left, what with Louis now taking off. Don't worry, we'll make it work. Now, how do we go after her?"

"I wish there was a stage from this Winnemucca to here."

"But there isn't, and I can't let you go and come back alone."

"We can ask Louis to at least go that route, especially if he wants his money."

"That would work, but you and Mattie can't be travelling back here alone. I won't have that happen."

"Perhaps we could hire someone down there, someone who's trying to come this way."

"That's taking too big a chance . . . I know it sometimes seems like things often work out for us, like God's always on our side, but we can't just jump off a cliff and expect to be able to fly before we hit the ground."

"Oh Abe," she was laughing, "sometimes you say the funniest things."

"Well, right now I'm going to say I'm hungry, and that's not the least bit funny."

"Oh yes it is, because I was just going to ask you what you were cooking for supper."

He looked at her, and now it was his turn to laugh, "You better hope I'm not the cook. We'd probably all be sick for a week."

"Oh, all right, Mr. Hungry Man, we'll get something together." She turned and called for Helga who came to the doorway of her shelter carrying her quilting work.

"Yes?"

"I found this starving stranger wandering around the place and I think we better feed him before he collapses."

"All right, I'm coming." She went back into her space.

"Now give me a kiss, stranger, so I know it's you," she said.

Before he and Maria left, Louis made a couple of trips with Abe and a flat wagon they borrowed from Mike Skinner to get lumber from that small local mill about ten miles away. It was the one thing that Abe needed help with the most. While they were traveling back and forth, Louis finally asked Abe if he was angry at him, or disappointed.

"I don't usually get angry if I can help myself, and I learned in the army not to be disappointed by anything another man does or doesn't do."

"Doesn't answer my question, Cuz, but I want you to know, I am sorry it had to work out this way."

"No," Abe looked intently at his cousin, "you shouldn't feel sorry. I don't expect you to. Besides I've seen how cheerful Maria has been since this was all decided."

"She has been, hasn't she?"

"So it's good for you, and for the baby, as well as for her."

The next day, on the trip home with the second load, Abe was driving the team and Louis was riding alongside when he leaned down and asked, "Been on my mind for some time. Hope you don't mind me asking, but you two ever want to have some young'uns?"

Abe looked at him for a long time before answering, "Nothing we want more, but it doesn't seem to be happening yet."

"So what you doing about it?"

"We have our times alone together. And I pray about it."

"Yeah, takes more than prayer. But sometimes it doesn't take much. Me and Maria never even talked about having a kid. That baby just showed up."

He started to ride ahead again, but Abe spoke, "I know it comes easy for some people, maybe most people, but could be something's wrong with me."

"Or her."

"And there's no way to know."

They rode along for awhile in silence. Then Louis looked down at his cousin and said. "Not unless you both try it with other people." And then he gave his horse a little nudge and rode on ahead.

It wasn't as if that thought had never crossed Abe's mind before. But it always came back to the reality of his love for Sarah Beth and their love for each other, "Until death do us part . . ." He knew there was no way he could leave Sarah Beth for someone else, even if it was the only way to have a child. It just wouldn't be right. And maybe if nothing came along in the next year or two, they could take on another little child, like they'd taken on Helga. Although she was only a few years younger than the two of them, it seemed to be working out to have her with them, even though she wasn't a baby or a young child. He couldn't help it, but suddenly thought about the Bishop and how he'd gotten someone else for that young woman of his because he couldn't do it himself. Suddenly there was a gunshot, and Louis was dismounting up ahead and looking at the ground. He fired another shot straight down.

He yelled back to Abe who could barely hear him, "Rattler!" Then he got back on his horse and kept going.

Abe's thoughts took up where they'd left off. What if it was him that got with another woman, almost like a second wife? If Sarah Beth wanted a baby in their home, would it be all right? After all, most of the people in the Bible had more than one wife, and just because we've changed our customs in these modern times, he thought, it doesn't mean . . . He tried to shake off these thoughts and realized he too had better keep an eye out for rattlers. It was the time of year they came out of their dens and began sunning and foraging, and an open roadway made a good place for both.

By that evening, he hadn't been able to stop thinking about the matter of a child for him and his wife, especially Louis's comment that it takes more than prayer. He almost wanted to talk more about this with Sarah Beth, but there were more important things of immediate concern, besides, on second thought, it would probably hurt her to know he had these things on his mind.

It was soon time for Louis and Maria to move out and start their journey south. Abe's cousin was in a hurry because he was anxious about being able to get on one of the early caravans heading east, and Maria was quite obviously packed up and ready to go. It was also clear that Louis didn't want to be delayed by having to accompany a buggy and all the potential problems they could face on the rough trail going from Silver City to the middle of Nevada. The day before, while in conversation with the sawmill owner, Abe learned that the stagecoach route from Winnemucca to Boise actually was in full operation for the summertime. While there were still Indian and outlaw threats, located on the border between Nevada and Oregon, Fort McDermitt supplied patrols to accompany the coaches in both directions. Abe knew that this method of travel would be safer for Mattie and better than if either one of them went after her. Sarah Beth agreed and was just worried that even now Mattie might already be waiting by herself in Nevada.

"We could ask Louis to go that way and stay with her until she can get on the stage, and he can ask among the other passengers for someone willing to kind of look after her," she said.

"Well, I guess it's either that or one of us going and coming back and that might take at least three weeks. That's if nothing goes wrong. And I need to be getting our house started. Also, from now on I'll surely need your help with that and with the cattle."

"I'd be pleased to be your assistant, as long as you help me with the laundry."

"I thought Helga did that," he smiled. "Now, how about we go to bed? It is the right time of the month according to your moon, and me."

Final arrangements for the departure were made. Louis purchased another pack mule and could tie its lead line to the one they already had, leaving their other horse behind. Maria had sewed herself a leather sling arrangement for carrying the baby horseback. It was made so it worked either on her front or on her back. Sarah Beth gave them some cookware, and Helga had somehow found the time to sew a baby-sized quilt in a kind of circular rainbow pattern with bright colors. Abe waited until the little party was mounted up to give his gift, a new rifle with a hand-made leather sling. He handed it up to Louis.

When there was no more putting it off, and it really was time for them to leave, Maria reached down to take the baby from Helga, who obviously did not want to let go of the little one. The baby was playing with her hair and the young woman was clearly shaking from sobbing. Finally, as Maria was having some trouble holding her horse still and close, Helga kissed the little girl on both cheeks and slowly handed her up to her mother. Maria took her daughter and fixed her into position in the sling, and then when her hands were free she removed the cross necklace she wore and handed it down to Helga. Helga gripped Maria's hand for a long moment and then turned, running to her own shelter and disappearing behind the canvas door.

Louis gave a long loud rebel yell and the little group began moving off. Abe put his arms around Sarah Beth and they stood together watching until the party was very small on the horizon. Then Sarah Beth went over all the items they'd given Louis regarding Mattie.

"The letter about giving Louis money and bringing the rest with her in a document to the bank here in Silver City? The name of the hotel for when she arrives there? And the note I gave you for her? Did that all go with him?"

"Yes, everything. It'll be fine. In a month or so, we'll be able to go get her and bring her back here to the fine house I will have finished building by then, with your help, of course."

"Exactly. You know you are my dear hero of the fantastical imagination." They kissed, and then she said, "Poor Helga, did you see her?"

"Yes. I knew she was attached to the little one, but she really is taking it hard."

"Oh Abe, it was good for all of us to have a baby in the family, you know that." And then she made a little sniffling sound herself and turned away from him to go back inside their shelter.

Abe was left alone, staring out toward the south where the little family had by now disappeared. Then he addressed God in a low voice, "You gave us a little one for a very short time. You let us have that, and now You've seen fit to take even that away from us. Now I am left with two very sad women, and there's nothing I can do to help them through this, nothing. Only You can help them and only You can give us the little one we so desire with all our hearts and with all of our prayers. Please give my Cuz and his woman and child a safe trip. They are as your own Son was as a little one traveling with His mother Mary and His father Joseph. Please, if it is in your plans for us, hasten to help us and bring us our heart's desire. Please dear God, not for my sake, but for my wife and our young girl. Please. We are incomplete; we are not yet a family. If it so be Your will, Amen . . .'"

With that, he went and hitched Ginger to the wagon load of lumber that still had not been unloaded and drove her to the house site. He turned the horse loose on a long rope to graze and threw himself into the work of unloading and stacking. When he was done unloading, he dug his tools out from under the wagon seat and began notching one of the largest of the sawn timbers. He'd already placed and leveled the cornerstones, and was ready to lay-out the foundation perimeter.

By noon, the first srtrings of all four sides of the building plan were in place and secured both to the ground and each other. He'd never built much before, and was somewhat proud of the accuracy and the substantial appearance of what he'd already accomplished. Now, he thought, just put a house on it.

He heard the neigh of a horse and turned to see Sarah Beth riding toward him. When she climbed down from Morning's back, she handed Abe a basket.

"Knew you'd be hungry, so I thought it better you didn't waste any time coming back for your meal. Here." She removed the cloth the food was wrapped in. "Now tell me what I can do while you're eating."

"Well, first of all, thank you. I really am hungry."

"It's all right, but don't think I'm going to make it a habit every day. Now, what can I do to help?"

"Remember where we said we were going to put the fireplace? Over there, near the back wall. It needs to be dug out to be level there so we can place rocks for the hearth. We'll need good flat stones to build a kind of platform. Then the floor will surround it, when we get a floor."

"Remember, I really do want a floor, not just dirt."

"I haven't forgotten," he said with his mouth full. "It's just that getting the roof done is more important than the floor for right now."

"Of course," She grabbed a spade and went to where the work was needed.

"How's Helga?" he asked when he'd finished most of the food.

"I think she'll be all right. She made up your meal and seemed anxious to be doing something, anything. She asked a lot of questions about Mattie. Now don't bother me, I'm working," she said with a smile as she started digging.

"Yes ma'am." He packed up the basket and went after Ginger. When he'd caught and hitched her, he called out to Sarah Beth. "Long as you're here, why don't we both go after those stones? I've got a good idea where we can look, and it would be best to have both of us lifting them into the wagon." When she got closer to him, he added, "We can get bigger ones that way, with two of us lifting them. Besides, it's over near where I think the cattle are, and we'll be able to check on them at the same time."

"Should I bring Morning?"

"That would be good. Then you can go back on your own while I bring the wagon back and leave it over here with the stones. I'll ride Ginger back later."

Over the next few weeks the building project made good progress. Their neighbor Mike used his forge to fabricate the hardware they thought they'd need, starting with the fireplace bracing and its swinging pot-holding arms. Then there would be coat racks, hat racks and boot scrapers, hinges and handles. Abe tried to offer payment for the work, but Mike said he would only take money for the materials. Beyond that, an informal work trade between the two of them would be good enough. He also quietly mentioned that it was definitely in his interest that his new woman be happy in her friendship with Sarah Beth and Helga. That had turned into one of the best things he could have hoped for, and it seemed to be working out quite well, what with the women all getting friendlier all the time.

Then one bright spring day, filled with the sounds of returning birds, Martha came riding up to their place, and dismounted, looking for Sarah Beth. Abe happened to be standing in the yard tying a loop in the end of a rope he was planning to use for dragging stones. He nodded toward their shelter.

Martha hurried that way, saying over her shoulder, "Message from someone named Mattie. Mike saw her in Silver City."

The next morning Sarah Beth and Helga set off for town in the buggy, both excited and eager to make this trip. Abe tried to read off a list of things he needed them to pick up for him and for the building project, but Sarah Beth just grabbed it out of his hand and said, "I can read your writing by now, you know." Then she kissed him quickly and promised they'd be back by nightfall of the next day.

As they climbed into the buggy, Helga looked back at him and said, sounding serious, "You will be all right by yourself, won't you

Mr. Abe?" and then the two women broke out in laughter and drove away. Ginger also seemed excited to be leaving.

The next day, while he was placing stones in the shallow bed they'd dug for the hearth, Abe had the strange feeling that he wasn't alone. He looked all around the house site, which was on a slight rise, and then went back to his work. A few minutes later he heard the loud whistle of a hawk, the sound they make when diving for prey. He again looked around, this time into the sky, but again nothing could be seen other than the blue emptiness of the sunlit day. Then suddenly he heard the galloping of a horse and saw the shape of a shirtless man riding his way on a paint horse with its mane flying. The man was waving both his arms, apparently holding on to the horse's bare back with just his legs.

The horse slid to an abrupt stop right at the edge of the string markings for the new house. The man jumped off onto the ground, laughing loudly. "It's me, friend. Me, Hawk Man. You look like you see enemy."

Abe dropped his pry bar and rope and quickly stepped toward the man. They gripped each other's forearms in the Indian way of shaking hands. "I am happy to see you," Abe said, still trying to recover from his fright at the man's wild approach.

"Good. Me too, see you. You alone?"

"No, my wife and our . . ." he hesitated and then said, "our niece, have gone to Silver City to pick someone up, another woman who is coming."

Hawk Man looked at him carefully and then said, "Your other woman?"

Abe smiled and said, "No, my wife's stepmother. I told you, I only have one wife."

"I feel bad for her, no one to help take care of you," he laughed.

"That's what you said before, but she doesn't seem to mind it. And our, uh, niece works hard. What are you doing here, where's your family, your people?"

"I come now. Want to see you here, see you all right. I go back now to family. We come here in one moon. Help you make your camp." He gestured at the site. "Good place here. I like for you." He squatted down, still holding the single rein to his horse. "Any white man trouble for you?"

"No, none so far. That neighbor, Mike, is very good to us, helping us. Haven't seen anyone else around."

"Good, you have trouble. I tell Lefty. He comes."

"Have you seen him?"

"No, but his mother say he coming soon."

"That's great. I'll be glad to see him."

"I go now. Me, too many women. Hard keep all happy." He laughed and made a gesture of helplessness, went back to his horse and leaped on. "Take care yours. Only one you got." And then he was galloping away, once again with both arms held straight out, not holding on to anything.

As Abe went back to work he realized this was a very good sign, that he'd been more anxious about the arrangement than he would admit to Sarah Beth or even to himself. To take a stranger's word for some kind of vague agreement, then to move his family here and start settling in, and even start building on a house, involved a lot of risk. In some ways it still looked rather impossible to him, but once again, here was God's confirmation being delivered by his benefactor. That afternoon as he wrestled with the stones and their weight and their odd shapes, he was reminded of Jacob wrestling with the angel and having his faith tested. Tested and then passing that test and becoming the fulfillment of those promises made before him to the first Abraham and Sarah. At one point, Abe stopped work for a long moment and simply listened to the birdsongs, silently giving thanks for all the blessings they'd received since leaving Virginia.

Now, God, he thought, still in a prayerful manner, about this child of ours.

Later, he was just about to start cooking a stew of some kind when Sarah Beth and the others drove into their little compound. Helga was perched on top of a large trunk and other luggage; Mattie and Sarah Beth were on the seat. From the dust and the tired stance of Ginger, he could see that it had been a hard trip for them. He hurried over to help Mattie alight from the buggy and was surprised and pleased by the strong hug that she gave him.

"Welcome, welcome," he said.

"Yes, oh yes, and thank you so much for having me." She stepped back and surveyed the surrounding country. "Beautiful," she said, "beautiful, and very empty."

Sarah Beth came up behind him and covered his eyes with her hands, "Hello you, what's for supper?"

"Oh, it's you," he said spinning around and giving her a hug. "I was just getting started, but I was afraid, with three women coming home, nobody would eat anything I cooked, so I was putting it off. I did shoot a coyote, though."

She pushed him away. "Ugh. Then that's what you'll have for supper. We'll have the lamb roast that's in the buggy. I bought it from a wonderful family along the way home. They have plenty more; we just have to tell them ahead of time what we want."

"Good. Coyote and lamb stew. Good combination. That'll take awhile, so we should get Mattie settled in. I've been working on her place. After you left yesterday, I used the old army tent and then built a couple of temporary walls to protect from the wind. I hope she'll like it. And it is just for now."

By then Mattie and Helga were walking arm in arm toward the family's outhouse, laughing and picking up speed as they approached the little building. Abe and Sarah Beth could hear Mattie saying, "Haven't used one of these since I was a girl."

"What have you used since then?" Helga asked.

Mattie went on inside the little building and spoke loudly, saying, "I've always had what they call a chamber pot indoors and then we take it outside to empty it."

Helga looked back at Abe and Sarah Beth with a big smile on her face and gave a hugging sign that said she really liked their visitor. Sarah Beth turned and started unloading parcels from under the seat and giving instructions to Abe as to what else needed to be carried in to the kitchen area.

"Then you can have Ginger pull the buggy over and unload Mattie's things. I do hope she's going to be all right here. She told me she doesn't have anyone else in the world besides us. And she wants to work. She said that since Father passed away she hasn't had anything to do and she's so anxious to be busy again."

While Abe was unloading her trunk and luggage, Mattie came up beside him and looked into the small space he'd made for her, of canvas and boards. "Why I love this," she said. "It reminds me so much of when I was a happy little girl, on the plantation."

Abe tied back the flap that served as a door so they could get her things inside. "I wouldn't have thought those would be good memories," he said.

"Oh, but when they're the only memories one has from childhood, they have to be good, don't you think so?"

"Well, yes ma'am, I guess I do. I'll leave you now to settle in. Sarah Beth told me you brought your own bedclothes. I hope that makeshift bed is satisfactory until we can get you something better."

"It will do, young man, it will do just splendidly."

As he walked away, he could hear her softly singing about "Crossing over Jordan," and he smiled to think how good it was to have someone else who was happy to be with them.

The following day, Mattie began to take over some of Sarah Beth's work, freeing the younger woman up to spend more of her time helping Abe with the new house. Cooking, washing clothes and keeping Helga company seemed to be what Mattie most wanted to do, though she told Sarah Beth she was also looking forward to the opportunity to take long walks. And she wasn't the least bit put off when they told her she should carry a small pistol with her, mostly for snakes.

A couple of days later, when they were working on the main doorway that needed to go up before the walls could be attached to it, Sarah Beth pinched one of her fingers between two boards. She screamed, and then pretended it was nothing. Abe took her hand and held it as the bruise rapidly appeared between the two knuckles on one finger.

"I'm so sorry," he said. "Let me run down and get some cold water for you."

When he came quickly back, she dipped her whole hand into the cold stream water, freshly fed from still melting snow on the distant mountains. "Abe," she said, as he sat down beside her with his arm around her. "Mattie asked me if we were going to have a baby anytime soon, said she's anxious to be a Grandma. I had to tell her we've been trying, but so far . . ."

"Maybe now that she's here, she'll bring us good luck."

"Maybe. She went on to tell me about her life back then and how she had three babies that lived out of the five that she carried, how none of them had the same father because at the time she was forced to lie with whoever her owner wanted her to have a child from. Just like the horses, as she said."

"So she really was a plantation slave."

"Until she was almost thirty years old, then she was taken into the big house. A few years later, when it looked like the War was coming, her family moved to our town in western Virginia and she became, as she says, civilized."

"When did she come to work for your mother and father?"

"I remember it very clearly. It was right after the War started. Her people, her owners, had been members of Father's church and when the man died of pneumonia, his family moved away, and she was left with us."

"That's an amazing story. Now she's with us on the frontier, about to get all uncivilized again."

"Abe, we are not savages."

"No, but who knows what will happen to us? Speaking of savages, Hawk Man showed up while you were gone. He was making sure that we arrived here all right."

"Do you really think he's a savage?"

Abe waited before answering. He was thinking about the man's civilized behavior in most things except the matter about being willing to share his young wife with Abe. "Oh, I only meant that in jest. Wait until you meet them. They're quite civilized. Just different than us. How's your finger?"

"Hurts, but it will heal, nothing broken. I'll have to more careful working with you. But back to Mattie. When I told her how hard we'd been trying to have a baby . . ."

"You said you told her that."

"Well, yes, she's like my mother now, you know . . . Anyway, she said the strangest thing. That back on the plantation if a woman didn't conceive a child when the owner wanted her to, they tried both the man and that woman with other partners to find out who was barren or whatever. And whichever slave couldn't have a baby with someone else, then they were sold."

"So you're going to sell me?" he asked with a bit of a smile.

She made as if to punch him, and he took the bowl of water from her and refilled it with colder water from the bucket. Then she said quietly, "Maybe you need to sell me."

They were sitting on a stack of lumber and he quickly got up and went to one knee, looking up into her face, "Please don't be like that. You are the one I love and will always love. I shouldn't have joked about that just now."

"Well, something good's going to happen or we'll grow old, just two of us."

He kissed her hands, gently avoiding the hurt finger and then stood up, saying, "You just sit still and let that pain die down. I've got to get back to work."

Later that evening, when he rode out to check on the cattle, Abe couldn't help thinking about their conversation. Of course he wouldn't give up on Sarah Beth, child or no child. Besides, the only other women he even knew out here were Mattie and Helga, one too old and one too young. That didn't count Hawk Man's offer, but knew he would never do that.

He found the cattle, did a quick count, and then began moving the herd away from the small creek to a higher spot where grass grew amid the sage. He'd noticed the herd wouldn't leave the greener areas along the water unless forced to, but then when they found some better grass in another place they were content to graze there for awhile, at least until it was gone or they were thirsty again. He wondered how many other things he still had to learn about taking care of his livestock, and how many mistakes he was bound to make in the future before he'd gained enough experience to get it right. It was a bit like the situation with Sarah Beth. How long would it take until they became familiar enough with one another to have God bless them with a child of their own?

Two days later a storm blew in with hard sheets of rain and gusty winds. Abe was kept busy lashing and strengthening the little shelters for Helga and Mattie, as well as the larger one for Sarah Beth and himself. None of the structures leaked, but they all seemed to be just waiting to collapse if the wind came on any stronger. He was running out of rope when he remembered a long coil out at the house-site. He caught and mounted Bird and galloped bareback out to the site. When he got close, he suddenly pulled up at the sight of two horses near the partially constructed building. He urged Bird forward and slid off when he came close to the other horses. He dropped the reins to the ground.

Then he saw two men standing behind the one completed wall where he couldn't have seen them before. "Who's there?" he said loudly.

"Just some visitors," one of the men replied.

The frenzy of the storm was increasing by the minute, and Abe was almost more concerned about the shelters for his little family than he was about these strangers, but he knew he had stay and find out what they were doing at the new house.

"And who might you be visiting?" he said.

"Just wanted to see who the fella is that's building a house on our land."

"Your land? How's that?"

"Well sir," the shorter one said slowly, possibly mimicking Abe's southern accent. "We've got a claim on this whole end of the valley. Filed it last year, just had no time to come back up here and look in on it."

"Far as I know this here is still Indian land and I'm caretaking for them. Kind of a lease, you might say."

"Well, I don't see no Indians around here, don't matter if I did. Claim's a claim."

"Their leader was just here the other day, and they'll be back soon. Lots of them." "Then I guess we'll just have to tell'em they're trespassing when they show up. Or maybe we'll have you tell'em for us. Right Luke? Maybe we'll let you stay on, caretaking for us. Nothing would change except the owners. Nice bunch of cattle you got out there. We might double or triple it here when our grass runs short back home."

"Where you fellows from? If you don't mind me asking."

"Don't mind a bit," the taller one spoke for the first time, "long as you don't expect an answer."

"Now Luke, no need to be rude to this young fella. He might be a veteran as well as an Indian lover. Sorry for my friend's manners. We hail from down Nevada way. Looking to expand our holdings and this place come to our attention. Didn't look like anyone was using it when we first checked. Few tipi fire pits, but hell, Indians don't know how to use land, never did far as I can tell. They can live in a hole in the ground, right Luke?"

Just then a bolt of lightning split the air from cloud to ground, almost immediately followed by its roar of thunder.

"Well young fella, pleased to meet you. We'll check in on you in a month or two. See how this house is coming along." They walked past him, one on either side, nearly brushing against him, and then they quickly mounted their horses.

The one called Luke nodded toward Bird. "Strange-looking horse. Don't look natural with that white leg." And then they galloped off.

Abe watched them go, mumbling, "Don't look natural because she's supernatural." Then he turned to gather up the coil of rope he'd come for, jumped on Bird and took off, wondering what to do about this and whether or not he should tell Sarah Beth about the encounter. Probably not, he decided, not until he had time to check out the records at the county seat.

When he got back to camp, he found the three women huddled in their kitchen area, each holding onto a corner of the covering. He jumped down and began tying the rope to the corners, telling them to hold on while he got some stakes. He came back with sticks of scrap lumber and a maul and pounded them in. For a moment the wind died down completely. The silence was increasingly eerie until Mattie began singing a hymn in her beautiful clear voice. Helga joined in, humming with the chorus as Sarah Beth came over next to Abe and they all waited for the next blast of the wind.

CHAPTER EIGHTEEN

Neighbors Arrive

As soon as the weather cleared and he could get away, Abe rode off to Silver City to check on the two strangers' claim to the land. The courthouse was attached to the jail, one of the newest buildings in town. He thought how the more permanent facilities for government services were the first to be built as a town became more permanent, along with a hotel and a newspaper, both of which Silver City now boasted.

The only person on the so-called courthouse side of the establishment was a napping man leaned back in an office chair with his feet up on the desk. Abe was afraid to wake him suddenly for fear he would fall over backward. So he stepped back to the doorway and knocked softly at first, and then a little more loudly. The man slowly stretched his arms into the air and then quickly awoke to the business at hand.

"Sir," he said in a loud voice, "you have business with the court, or with the deeds and records division?"

"Deeds and records, it would be."

"All right then." The man moved to another desk, straightened some papers and looked up. "Well?"

"I've come to inquire regarding a piece of what I understood to be Indian property."

"Located where exactly?"

"Out past the place owned by a Mike Skinner."

"Yeah, what about it?"

"Well, I'd like to know its legal status. I was given permission to stay there by an Indian named Hawk Man, but the other day, two fellows showed up from Nevada saying it was theirs."

"Well, it isn't. Not yet, unless they want to get killed over it. And that's what I told them when they first showed up asking about it. Now, how do you come to know that Indian?" about that place. I rode on out and ran into this Hawk Man. Turned out we have a friend in common, another Indian, name of Lefty." He paused.

"Heard of him. Works both sides against the middle, they say. Indian with white ways, but who knows? There's so much confusion these days over Indians and us, can't keep none of it straight. Anyways, told those boys they couldn't claim that particular piece of land until the Indians give it up or the government takes it away. But not sure that helps you."

"Oh, but it does. Hawk Man wants to keep the land for him and his folks, but if it's going to get taken away, he wants me to have it because I'm willing to guarantee he can still use it the way he does, camping and so forth, from now on, what I believe is legally called perpetuity."

"Well, that's nice for both of you, but far as I'd say, this little agreement of yours doesn't have any legal standing."

"Is there anything we can do to gain that kind of standing?"

"Well sir, you just might want to sign a piece of paper says you're first in line if the United States does claim that land. Of course those boys from Nevada also signed that piece of paper, but it'd be up to our judge to decide, and he doesn't come out here from Boise hardly ever, unless there's a murder or some such."

"So how would this judge decide?"

"Probably look at the dates of those two pieces of paper kept in this here desk. Now I didn't say anything to those boys from Nevada, but I didn't much like their attitudes, kind of surly and I might say they did actually try to push me around. So, like I say, I didn't tell them that I already had your piece of paper and it was dated prior to theirs. Of course they didn't ask about it either. But next time they may, and I'll have it to show them if you'll just sign it, right here. I'll take care of that date, and the rest of it."

Abe thought hard for a moment and pondered whether what he was doing was really illegal. But in fact, it wasn't him doing it. All he was doing was signing his name. It would be this clerk, or whatever he was, doing the date on the deed paper. "All right, where do I sign?"

After he had signed the paperwork in three copies, the man went on to tell him that he and those other two weren't the only folks wanted that piece of land, but when he told the others it wasn't available, none of them had been either pushy like the Nevada boys, nor had any of them been able to claim to be friends with Mr. Lefty and the Hawk Man. So once again Abe was in the unlikely position of accepting his destiny, or his opportunity, whichever it was.

When he finished shopping for the few items he could pack in Bird's saddlebags, he began the ride back. He knew it was already too late to arrive home before dark and that he might have to sleep out along the way. He was also thinking about the oddness of the arrangement he'd just entered into, and how Dr. Randall was probably smiling at the hair-splitting and subterfuge that it took for God's will to work itself out in their lives. Above all, once again he felt Lefty's smile of approval from wherever he was at this time. And it didn't seem to him like it would hurt any of this that he'd gone out, purchased and then delivered a replacement for the nearly empty bottle of bourbon whiskey he'd noticed in the partially open cabinet in the courthouse office. It was probably best that the clerk wasn't there for this second visit; having stepped out, he was just returning when Abe mounted up, waved and rode away.

As he rode along, it turned into a beautiful, clear night with a half moon, and he was luckily able to make it all the way home. He put Bird out to graze, and crawled into bed beside Sarah Beth, hardly waking her. He was tired, but satisfied that he'd gotten the best results he could expect from his effort. Now it was a matter of waiting for Hawk Man to show up again and they would, hopefully, be able to figure out the situation together. In the meantime, it still made sense for him to continue working on the house, both as a way of making progress on the place, and as an act of faith confirming they were where they were supposed to be.

One morning a few weeks later, summertime was lengthening the days and the air was filled with breeze-blown fuzz from the willows along the creeks. Abe was returning from picking up hardware from Mike Skinner. This batch was mostly hinges, heavy ones for the main doors, front and back, and lighter hinges for the inner doors to the bedrooms. Abe was quite satisfied with the workmanship, and also pleased with the extra work Mike had put into some added decorative elements. As he, Bird, and Ginger with her pack of fixtures, rounded the bend in the road that led to their little settlement, he saw Helga glance up from hanging out laundry and then come running toward him.

"Mr. Abe, Mr. Abe, there's Indians across the creek. They're putting up those tipis, three of them so far." Now she was walking alongside the horse as he reined toward the little shelter where he kept the tack and treats for the horses.

He knew it was Hawk Man and his party, but he couldn't resist having fun with Helga. "Do they seem hostile? Is it a war party?"

"I wouldn't think so," she replied. "They've got children with them and the women are the ones setting up the tipis and the camp."

"You must have good eyes. This is good. It's our neighbors arriving, Hawk Man and his people. How many do you think there are?"

"I couldn't tell. I'd just gone down to the creek to rinse these clothes when I heard the commotion over there, and I climbed a tree so I could see where the noise was coming from."

"I'm glad they're here, I need to talk with him. Don't suppose I'll get much work done on the house today. We may want to prepare some of our best food to take as a welcome gift. Where's Sarah Beth?"

"Mattie wanted to see how the house is coming along, so they took a walk up there."

"That's a pretty long walk. Maybe I should go over to the Indian camp now. Want to come along?"

"Oh yes, yes. I've never been close to real Indians."

"Well, get Ginger. The stream's still high enough we should ride across."

As they went through the creek and neared the growing camp, the was a flurry of motion as children ran and hid and three women they could see, lined up together in front of the largest tent. Two other women and a man were seen moving out of sight behind one of the other structures.

"Hello," Abe said loudly enough to be heard, and was pleased when he recognized Mary Wolf moving toward him. She held out her empty hands in a simple gesture of welcome. He motioned to Helga and they both dismounted. He said quietly, "She's the one who speaks English."

"Mr. Abraham," Mary Wolf said as she approached, "It is good to see you again. We are happy to be here."

"And I am happy to see you. It is good you have returned."

"And this your wife?" she asked.

"Oh no," he said, "more like my niece. She lives with us."

"Oh," the woman gave them a strange look, and then made a quick bow to Helga who returned a curtsy.

"Where's Hawk Man?" Abe asked.

"He is coming. He will be here this night. Bringing horses, many horses." She turned toward the tipis and called out. The young man who was behind one of the tents showed himself. She motioned for him to come closer. "This is son of Hawk Man, he is name of Cloud Catcher, white man name, Carl."

The young man stopped behind her and held up one hand in greeting.

"Well, it looks like you're busy getting set up. Do you need our help?"

"Oh no, but we will see you when our man arrives. I can send Carl to tell you."

"Good. We'll all come back and visit."

She said, "Yes," and then the two of them walked back to their work. She spoke loudly and children reappeared from within the partially set up tipis.

"Come, let's go," Abe said to Helga. They mounted up and rode back.

Abe let Bird go and then retrieved the hinges and took a file to some of the sharper edges. Helga went back to hanging the laundry on a line. He glanced over in that direction and for perhaps the first time realized that the girl was becoming a woman very quickly, and that as she stretched to hang clothing it was made even more obvious. Good, he remarked to himself, we'll have to help her find a man. It would be good to have help around the place. He suddenly thought of this Carl, the young man who'd just arrived. Not likely, and probably not for the best, he mused, but . . . He went back to filing on the new hinges, eager to get them on the doors he'd been building, to see how well everything fit together.

Before long Sarah Beth and Mattie showed up, and Abe told them the news about the arrivals. Mattie appeared to be a little frightened at the idea of Indians nearby, but he assured her they were all going to be good friends. He mentioned to Sarah Beth that they would be going over there later and it would be good to have something, maybe a baked dish to take along. She said that would be easy enough, she'd get started on it right away. Some of her special sweet cornbread. He watched her as she turned away and headed for the kitchen area. Now that Hawk Man would see her for the first time, Abe wondered what the man's reaction would be. She was a beautiful woman and he was proud of her, but he found himself hoping that maybe she wouldn't be so very attractive to Hawk Man. She certainly didn't have an Indian look about her, and he didn't want that issue of wife sharing to come up again.

Carl didn't show up that evening, but finally appeared the next day. Abe was just getting ready to ride out, to check on the cattle and get on with the work at the new house. Carl rode up close to Abe on a black horse with a white head and a few white patches on its rump. The young man gave signs that seemed to mean that it was time to go visit his father. Abe wasn't about to ignore the call, but it was an inconvenient time. He signed that he would come soon and the young Indian rode off.

Mattie stood outside the kitchen watching, and when he walked over near her she said, "First time ever I saw a real Indian up close, my, my." She took off her eyeglasses and wiped them with her apron as if to show that she wasn't sure she'd really seen what she thought she saw. "My, my," she repeated as she went back inside.

Mattie did not want to go to the camp, so that meant they wouldn't need to take the buggy. But Helga was excited and eager to go along with Abe and Sarah Beth. They wrapped up the cornbread in its basket in a blanket Abe had purchased just for this occasion, and the three of them rode over to the new campsite.

Mary Wolf was outside the largest tipi with some youngsters and waved to them as they approached. "Get down, and be welcome" she called, "I tell him."

Almost immediately Hawk Man came out with his arms held wide open, palms up in a sign of friendship. Carl, another young man, and Mary Wolf joined him as Abe and the two women dismounted. Sarah Beth removed the blanket and held out the basket of cornbread wrapped in a checkered cloth. She offered it to Mary Wolf who bowed and then stepped forward to accept it. Abe held the blanket to Hawk Man, who took it, shook it out and wrapped it around himself.

"Good. Ha-Ho. Thank you, friend." He gestured and led the way over to some trees near the stream, and he motioned for his guests to be seated. He remained standing and then offered what seemed to be a prayer in his own language, his hands held up to the sky. "Now, we eat," he said, sitting on the ground with the others.

Mary and another woman brought a kettle of steaming liquid and meat from the tipi, and a young girl came along carrying Sarah Beth's basket. These were set down and the women backed away while Hawk Man motioned for his visitors to take food. Some carved wooden plates appeared from a small pack that Mary had on her back.

When the guests had served themselves, Hawk Man and the two young men joined in, placing the hot pieces of meat in cupped hands and breaking the cornbread into pieces on top of the meat. They ate quickly and replenished their handfuls while Sarah Beth and Helga ate carefully and Abe tried to eat quickly enough to look like he was enjoying the tough pieces of meat. No one spoke until they all had stopped eating and Hawk Man gestured to his women to take the rest of the food away. Mary Wolf invited Sarah Beth and Helga to come with them and they all went over to the tipi. Hawk Man pulled out a short pipe and slowly filled it with rough-cut tobacco leaves.

"So you have two women now," he said. "Two wife and old woman back at camp. Three women now," he said holding up three fingers.

"Well not exactly," Abe said, trying to think how to explain their situation. "Older woman was my wife's father's woman after her mother died . . ."

"Stop," Hawk Man said. "Need Mary Wolf for talk. We smoke now." He called out to one of the boys, who soon came running with a burning stick from inside the tipi. The man took the stick, blew on the flame and then lit his pipe. He smoked deeply, and then passed the pipe to Abe, who took no more than a small puff and passed it back. Hawk Man waved it back to Abe. "Smoke for good life," he said. So Abe smoked a little more and then again handed the pipe back. Hawk Man inhaled deeply and coughed once, smoked again, and emptied the ashes from the small bowl of the pipe. Then he called out in his language, and Mary Wolf came to see what he wanted.

"Now," he said, "talk of women."

"Well, the older one back at our camp married my wife's father after her mother died." He stopped and waited while he watched Mary Wolf try to translate with words and her hand movements pointing back toward the tipi.

Hawk Man spoke, and she said, "The black one, yes?"

Abe nodded his head and wondered if Hawk Man had seen Mattie yet or just heard about her, and if he'd ever seen a Negro before.

"And the young ones?" Mary translated.

"The older one, the taller one, is my wife, Sarah Beth. The other one is like a niece to us. Lives with us now, but is not my wife." He suddenly realized how this arrangement must look to a man with three wives.

Mary Wolf translated. Hawk Man spoke with her for awhile and the woman looked down at the ground, shaking her head in a negative gesture, but Hawk Man used a commanding voice and she turned back to Abe.

"He says that now you are like brothers on this land and he wants you to stay here. He says to become real brothers and for the land to be healthy with everybody and the animals, you must become true brothers . . ." she paused and seemed reluctant to go on, but Hawk Man made a hissing sound and said a sharp sounding word. "He say now he want one of your woman to be with him and he will trade me to you . . . but only for one moon. This will make you brothers forever. He say when this is done if one of you die, the living one will take care of other man's women. Is his way, our way, he say."

Abe just sat still in silence, not knowing any way to respond.

Then Hawk Man broke out in laughter, and said, "Not now, not for this many days," and he held up all ten of his fingers, and jumped to his feet. He grabbed Abe's hand and leaned back to pull him up. He motioned for Mary Wolf to leave them.

"Come," he said. "You must see horses." And with quick strides he moved to the edge of the camp where a pure brown horse with a white mane and tail stood tethered to a sapling. He leaped onto its back and motioned to Abe, "Come."

Abe whistled for Bird, who looked up from the thick grass she was eating, shook her head as if being bothered by flies and then came to him at a slow walk. He cinched up the saddle, took the bridle hanging from its horn, slipped it on, mounted and moved over to join Hawk Man. His mind was still roiling with the confusion of the situation he had just been thrust into, but for now he knew it would be best to go along with his host or landlord or whatever the man was to him, and not to object or agree.

They galloped up the narrow valley to where it opened up at the confluence of the two streams, and they then took the wider of the two canyons to where it spread out into a large, mostly grassy area. Feeding there were seventy or eighty horses of all sizes and colors.

"You take one, and one to tall wife, one to young wife. I pick good ones for you. Not today, ten days," he held up all of his fingers, laughed and then slowly urged his horse to begin circling the herd, many of them raising their heads in curiosity. "Come," he called.

They rode slowly around all of the horses except for a stallion that was standing some distance away on a slight rise. He was shining in the sunlight. His reddish coat rippled with his agitated movements as he turned in circles and stamped his feet. Abe and Bird were both mesmerized by the animal's obvious strength and fearless behavior. He was clearly asserting his ownership of everything and every horse within range, and even Bird was agitated. Abe wasn't sure how long it had been since she'd had a foal, if ever. Hawk Man smiled that same smile again and made a motion with his hands, placing one on top of the other as a semblance of one animal mounting the other. Then he pointed to Bird and to the stallion and rubbed his hands together, gave a loud whoop and took off at a gallop, back toward the camp.

Abe followed a bit more slowly, trying to figure out what day of the week it would be in ten days. He couldn't do it; he realized he no longer kept track of the days of the week out here where they hardly mattered. In any case, he didn't think he would tell Sarah Beth about the arrangement until he'd tried harder to get them out of it, unless there truly was no way to avoid it. He pulled Bird to a stop and said out loud, "What do I mean no way to avoid it? There has to be." Then he gave his horse a slight kick in the ribs and she responded with a short buck and took off running.

When he and the two women had returned to their own camp, he was hoping he still had enough daylight left to get some work done on the house, and he waved to them and rode off. As he left he could tell that Mattie was asking the other two women all kinds of questions about the real Indians, and they seem to be having a great time answering her.

When he got to the new home site, he realized that he could easily see the thin lines of smoke from the tipis. Well, he thought, always good to know when your neighbors are at home. He went straight to work, using the plane on boards that would be fit together for a loft over the sitting room area. The house was coming along. If he didn't get too many more interruptions, it would be ready for them by cold weather. Sarah Beth had been a big help, especially for those jobs that required more than one person to raise or hold, or help secure the boards that made up the walls. They'd had an interesting conversation about the need for individual rooms for all of them, and trying to figure things out regarding Mattie and Helga. Things such as how long they would they each be around, and would they need their own rooms inside the house, or should they be given shed-type additions off two of the sides? After some discussion, they agreed that Mattie would need to be within the house for the heat from the fireplace, and that Helga would probably be happier with her own space being a bit more separate.

Now, as he thought about that conversation, he was surprised at what he remembered but hadn't really noticed at the time. Sarah Beth raised several questions about Helga and her future. What if she just wanted to up and leave someday? Whose responsibility was she, her own or theirs? And would she be able to find anyone to marry if she did stay out here with them? And then, almost as if it was a afterthought, she'd said to him, "Don't you find her becoming quite an attractive young woman?"

He'd said he had never thought about it in that way, she was just Helga. Yes, she was growing up now, but he still thought of her more as the girl that rode into their camp running away from the Bishop than as the young woman she'd become. Sarah Beth's only answer was that maybe he should take more notice of what was going on around him, that Helga really was very pretty and seemed to be making more of an effort to show it off by keeping her hair neat and her clothing a bit more close-fitting.

He stopped his work on the boards for a long moment, and let that memory sink into his mind. Why was she talking about Helga that way anyway? He really hadn't noticed it at the time, but now with the Indians here, and both Carl and Hawk Man seemingly interested in these women, perhaps he needed to pay more attention. And maybe he and Sarah Beth should have some kind of talk with Helga about this responsibility and independence matter, before it became an issue or caused a problem. Then as he went back to his work, he smiled at the thought that he was beginning to act like someone's father, or, rather, like someone who might get a little bit defensive of the young woman if a man came to take her away. As his hands and arms rhythmically pushed the plane back and forth along the edges of the boards, he wondered if Sarah Beth wasn't being a bit suspicious about his feelings.

At dusk, riding back to their place, he realized that he'd neglected to tell Hawk Man about the two men from Nevada and the courthouse business. He would surely need to get together with the Indian about that soon, and hopefully he'd be able to avoid matters regarding the women. He realized he would need to be quite diplomatic because of the delicacy of his role straddling the divide between the Indian ways of having land and the white man's legal system. If he made any serious mistakes in either direction, it could cost them their new home, and he neither wanted nor knew of any alternative at this point. Besides, he thought, they all needed each other to make it work out.

Following their supper, Helga cleaned up and Sarah Beth went out to put away the chickens for the night. Mattie and Abe sat outside together having cups of tea made from a batch of sweet mint the older woman had brought with her from back home in Virginia. It was a bit unusual for the two of them to be alone together, but it was the quiet time of the evening, and Mattie seemed preoccupied with her knitting project until she looked up quickly and asked Abe, "Is it true these Indians have more than one wife?"

Abe had been glancing through the Book of Genesis in his copy of the Bible when she asked. He often read something at this time of day. He closed it and thought about his answer, wondering if she would condemn the Indians or was just interested. "Yes, it's true. They have a hard life and it takes many hands to do all of the work of a family or for a small band of folks like our neighbors here."

"Well," she said, "I was just thinking about that, and I saw you reading your Bible and it seems to me that back in those olden days, it was mostly a common enough thing. Matter of fact, Mister Abe, I can't think of any of those old-time men who didn't have more than one wife, except maybe Adam," she laughed, "and he didn't have much other choice."

"I guess you're right, but that was a long time ago."

"Of course it was, but so was the Creation and the Crucifixion and we still believe in them."

"Mattie, I have to ask you what are you getting at here?"

"Well, my young friend, seems to me that it's only the white people have got themselves all worked up about this business. Negro folks and red Indians and probably even the Chinee people have always had more than one wife so no one woman would have to kill herself trying to raise a family, take care of a man, and still have any time for herself or the things that matter like church and even having a friend or two."

"Mattie, you sound like the Indian over there, Hawk Man. He says he feels sorry for Sarah Beth because she's the only one taking care of me because I don't have any other wives."

"Well, he's wrong, isn't he? What about this Helga girl? Don't see how Sarah Beth could do everything herself, and even with my old bones struggling to help out, there's still so much to do; and we've even got some of these modern things like grinders and all to help us."

Sarah Beth poked her head in through the canvas doorway. "What are you two talking about?" she said. "I wasn't listening, but I thought I heard Mattie say there's too much for me to do around here."

Abe stood and offered her his chair, "Here, sit down, maybe the two of you can keep talking about whatever it's about. I have to go make sure the cattle got to water today." He gave Sarah Beth a hug and moved on past the doorway.

Sarah Beth stood up again and said, "That tea smells good, I think I'll have some. Mattie, do you want more?"

"No thank you, child. I'll probably have to get up in the night as it is."

"Well, what were you and he talking about? First, let me say, I'm glad to see you talking together. Far as I know, you've never done much of that."

"Well, it's not for being strangers. It's just one of those things that has not got its ways always worked out. I mean, Lordy, what do you call what your step-daughter's husband is to yourself? But I think he's a fine young man and I'm glad he's been willing to take me in. He's a little set in his thinking, but that's not always a bad thing."

"And what would it be about at this time, besides me not being able to do all my work alone?" She sat down and slowly stirred the tea in her cup to cool it.

"That wasn't exactly our subject, but it fit in somewhat. I had asked him about these Indians having more than one wife in a family, and isn't that the way it was in the Bible. He said that was a long time ago . . . as if we Negroes and Indians don't live that way nowadays ourselves, at least that's how I hear it is in Africa and out here in the Indian lands."

"Well, you might be right about that, but it's against our religion. Except for the Mormons who say they have the same religion, but do have many wives. But don't remind me about that. I still think about that Bishop too much as it is, and sometimes I can't get him out of my mind. Terrible man. Thank the good Lord Helga got away from him."

"Well, that's all there was to what I was thinking. How Abe's not so different from these friendly savages, if you can call them that. It's like as if he has two wives and an old mother. And it keeps us all busy, living out here this way."

Sarah Beth didn't answer, but did pick up Abe's Bible and turn some of the pages. Then she said, "It does make a person wonder doesn't it? How it could be right in those old days, but wrong now. Not that I would ever stand for another woman with Abe in the ways of a wife. Absolutely not." She finished her cup of tea and lit one of the lamps to set beside Mattie so she could see her work better.

"Oh, thank you, dear, but I think it's time for these old eyes and this old girl to get herself ready for night-time. Seems to take longer and longer all the time." She slowly gathered her project into her arms and stood. She stopped to give Sarah Beth a kiss on the cheek, and she then let the younger woman hold open the door-hanging while she eased her way out.

Almost a week went by, with a lot of work getting done on the house. Sarah Beth was there as much as she could be, and sometimes found it strange the way Abe would just stop working on whatever he was doing and stare out across the land. Then, without a word, he would resume his task. After seeing this several times, she finally felt it was her right to ask him what was on his mind.

He responded with silence at first, but finally spoke, saying, "We have a kind of problem coming soon."

"You mean with the house, if it rains hard before we get the roof on?"

"Well, that could be a problem, but things would dry out sooner or later as long as we get the roof done by the end of the warm weather . . . No, I'm talking about something that has to do with what I guess we have to call our landlord here, with Hawk Man."

"Abe, you didn't have a disagreement did you?"

"Not exactly, or not yet."

"Well, tell me what it is?"

"Here, let's sit down over on those logs. It's hard to find a way of speaking about all this. With you," he said. "Here." He helped to her find a comfortable seat on the rough-barked logs. "I guess you know he has a different way of looking at things, they all do."

"Of course, they're Indians."

He looked at her as if he were going to ask a question, and then said, "Yes, they're Indians, but they're not the only ones who . . ." He paused and stood up, and then sat down again, this time so he could face her. "Many Peoples have had the men having more than one wife, or even taking on another man's wives when that man died."

"Oh my, yes of course. Is that what you and Mattie were talking about the other night?" She reached out and took his hand, "I know this, after all I was married to the Bishop, you remember. At least he thought so."

"Well, then, maybe you won't be so surprised to find out that Hawk Man wants to have you for a month, as his woman."

She pulled her hand back quickly and covered her mouth. She was silent for a long moment, then softly but firmly said, "No! That's impossible. He already has three wives doesn't he? Why? What?"

"Shhh. Let me try to explain." And he told about what had happened the first time the two men met, and how he turned down the offer of the younger wife, but that he wasn't able to tell her about it when he got back to her, because of what she'd been through with the Bishop, and how quickly they had to get away. "Under different circumstances, I would have told you. I know I would have, but then it just slipped away from even seeming important until last week when he brought it up again."

"Brought up what again, you having that Mary Wolf as your woman?" Now she stood up and began pacing back and forth in front of him.

"No, not exactly that. He offered to trade her for you for one month, but I refused and told him we didn't believe in anything like that. It was very difficult because she, this Mary Wolf, was having to translate our words to one another and it made her very uncomfortable, I could see that . . . but he said he was coming for you in ten days, and that was nearly a week ago. And I haven't talked with him since . . ." He put his head in his hands, "I don't know what else to say . . ."

"Well, I hope you told him NO!" she raised her voice and then knelt down beside him. "Abe, you did tell him no, didn't you?"

"Of course I did. But when he first offered the land to us, he made me take a vow and spill some of my blood into the dirt, and the vow was that we would follow the ways of this land if we lived here. And now, I think he's saying that this is something we owe him in order to be here . . . I am so sorry, if I ever had any idea anything like this would happen, we never would have come here, but now we don't have any . . ."

She cut him off. "No choice? Right! Now we have a house and cattle and my stepmother, and so we have to sacrifice me to some heathen set of rules? I don't think so. I'll just go tell him myself that he can't expect us to be like him, and, and . . ."

"And what?"

"I don't know. And you'll shoot him if he lays a hand on me. Or, or, oh I don't know. I just can't believe you'd go along with this."

"Sarah Beth," he stepped up behind her and took her shoulders in a strong grip, then turned her around to face him. "I am not going along with anything, I am just asking for your help. Because I don't know what we can do, and I've been praying and thinking and worrying, and I get no answer, no guidance, no help from God, or from your father, or from anyone. And even Mattie pointed out . . . and we weren't talking about this situation, she doesn't know anything about it, we were just talking about how different people have different customs, and she said what was true of these Indians was also true of most Africans . . . and even the Mormons."

"Well, we know all about the Mormons, don't we? Maybe you should have left me with the Bishop. Now you get another chance. You can just go on and leave me with the Indians." She was crying now and pushed him away. "And that's going to be your way to escape me because I can't have your baby." Then she took off running down the slope toward her horse.

Abe called after her and started to run, but then he realized he would most likely only make things worse if he didn't leave her to herself, for now. But he was worried about where she would go. What if she went straight to Hawk Man and confronted him, what if she just ran away and left them, what if . . . ?

He slowly put away his tools, still mostly looking out across the valley to make sure he could still see her, or at least the dust her horse was making. Then he hurried to throw the saddle on Bird and follow after her. As he headed in that direction, he saw that she veered off back toward their own camp. He was relieved that she hadn't gone directly to Hawk Man. He slowed down and waited to see if she really was going back to their temporary home. Sitting there on Bird, he decided he ought to wait until she settled down a bit. He needed to check on the cattle anyway and there was still plenty of time until darkness.

Sarah Beth arrived back at their camp and unsaddled Morning. He was foamy with sweat from the run, so she wiped him down and turned him out. She went straight into the kitchen, promising herself that she wouldn't be doing any cooking that night. Mattie was standing at the makeshift sink, peeling potatoes. She looked up as Sarah Beth kicked off her boots and threw her jacket on the floor.

"Well, sakes alive, what's got into you?"

"Oh nothing, I just think I've been sold into slavery."

Mattie wiped her hands with her apron and came over to the younger woman."Now what can you possibly mean by saying that?"

"Oh Mattie, this is just the worst thing that's ever happened." She began crying. Mattie held out her arms and embraced her.

"Now, now, easy there. When you can talk I want to hear all about it . . . there, there, my sweet little girl."

Sarah Beth withdrew from the hug, straightened herself up and then used a corner of Mattie's apron to wipe her eyes, shaking her head. "I'm so sorry, it's just that something horrible has happened and I don't know, I don't know . . ."

"Is Abe all right? Is he hurt?"

"Oh no, he seems fine, that's part of it all. Where's Helga?"

"She hasn't come in yet, working on another quilt, I suppose. Never seen anyone such a seamstress. Doesn't want to do anything else."

"Well, pretty soon she'll have plenty to do. I won't be here in a few days."

"Why? Where could you go?"

"I'll be moving across the valley. Part of some deal these men have come up with, something to do with us being here on the land and the Indian ways and Mr. Hawk Man acting like the Bishop. Oh, I can't take this, Mattie, not again."

"All right my little one, sit down and catch your breath. Mattie's going to make us some of that calming tea potion and we'll both just settle down here. Is Abe on his way?"

"I don't know and I don't really know what I'd do if he walked in right this minute."

Mattie stoked up the cook-stove fire and placed a kettle of fresh water on top. "Now, let's get to the bottom of all this."

Sarah Beth cleared her throat and then blew her nose on a clean soft rag. "It seems that the Indian way allows for a man to share his wife with another man under certain circumstances, and this is one of those. We're here as his guests and it must be some kind of trade or something. Abe told me that in three or four days I am supposed to move over to Hawk Man, and that Mary Wolf is supposed to come here. And when I asked him how this happened all he could say was that when he was here the first time, the Indian made him take a vow that if we lived on this land we would follow their ways."

"And what if you refuse?" Mattie spooned the tea leaves into two cups.

"Refuse. I'm only a woman, you know. I guess I don't have anything to say about it. And what happens to us and to our house and to you and Helga if I don't go along with it? We have nowhere else to go."

"Well, honey, I always said you were too pretty for your own good, but I never thought it would come down to this, a Bishop and a Chief all fighting over you and your own husband doesn't know what to do about it at all, does he. Sakes, poor man."

"Poor man! I think he's half happy to get rid of me since I haven't been able to give him his precious child."

"Now, now, you know that's not a fair statement. I think you might want to think about that before you start believing such a thing. From what I can tell, he truly loves you, with or without a baby."

"I can't believe I once said to him that maybe we wouldn't know whose fault it was we couldn't have a child unless we both tried with someone else. And now look what's happened. I almost had to kill that Bishop . . . but this time . . ."

The sound of a horse trotting up silenced them. "Must be him," Sarah Beth said as Mattie handed her the steaming cup of tea. "Mattie, please pretend you don't know anything about this."

"All right, dear. But I don't think I can pretend for very long." She turned and went back to peeling the potatoes.

Sarah Beth peeked out the doorway, holding the canvas aside. "Yes, it's him. I'll just change into something clean; then I can help you."

She was gone long enough that when Abe came cautiously into the kitchen area she still hadn't come out from behind their curtain.

He slowly removed his boots, looking around. "Hello, Mattie, did Sarah Beth come in?"

"Oh yes, she's changing for supper. And how are you?"

"I've been better. But it's all right." He got down on his knees and busied himself chopping some kindling to refill the wood box beside the stove. "How is she?" he asked.

"Oh, she seems all right, maybe a little tired is all."

Right then Sarah Beth came in from their bedroom. She was wearing a dress she only wore to church. Her hair was brushed up on the sides and flowed down her back. She was rolling up the sleeves of the dress, and said, "Guess we better get this meal ready to eat. Us women have a hungry man here to take care of." Then she set to work grinding some grain.

When the two of them were alone after the mostly silent meal, he asked her if she wanted to take a walk with him.

"Why Mr. Saunders," she replied, "it would be my pleasure."

They'd only gone a short ways when Abe spoke softly, "There must be something we can do. I haven't thought of it, but there's got to be something."

Sarah Beth pointed toward the nearly-full rising moon, "Isn't that so beautiful? I don't know I'd ever want to leave here."

"But how can we stay, with what's happening?"

"Oh, well, you can kill Mr. Hawk Man, and then we'll all die, or we can just go through with it."

"Sarah Beth, I can't ask . . ."

"You're right," she turned to face him, "you didn't ask, remember? Now," she tossed her hair and took his arm, the wounded one, "how's this feeling these days?"

"Well, it's doing quite well, but that's clearly beside the point."

"No, I don't think it is. Everything that hurts either heals or gets worse. So let's not spoil our last few nights together."

Early the next morning, Hawk Man and Mary Wolf rode up. Abe and Sarah Beth were finishing their early morning meal and he went out to meet them. Sarah Beth hung back, holding the door canvas open only enough to see out.

"Howah, my friend. You are well," the man spoke as he climbed down from his horse and held out his hand for a white man's customary shake.

Abe shook his hand, and said, "We're all right. And you, and you?" He looked up at Mary Wolf who sat still on her motionless horse. She nodded yes to him.

Hawk Man began speaking in his own tongue, pausing for the woman to translate, "I have come to tell you that this land must be yours by the law of the white man's court in Silver City. A judge has sent me a message that you were fortunate enough to sign for this land before some others, and now you must make good on your claim in the white man's way. That is the first thing . . ."

The woman stopped speaking. Now she also climbed down from her horse's back. "Can you do this, he says? Otherwise there may be a war for this land, and we don't want more war. Had enough."

"Hawk Man, I never had a chance to tell you about the men from Nevada who came and said the land was theirs. I went to the court and signed papers, but I didn't mean to take over your land, only to protect it from those men."

Mary Wolf translated and Hawk Man held both his hands up toward the sky. "It is the way of the Mystery, he says. Now you must only complete your agreement with our people for this land and you can build your house and have your family here as long as the grass grows, under Creator's Law, and also by White Man Law."

"Agreement with your people?"

"He means your vow to follow our ways on this land." She talked quietly with Hawk Man for a long while, shaking her head no several times. "He says he will be here in the second morning from now to take the woman with him." She lowered her eyes and her hands twisted the long shell necklace she wore. "He says I am to come here and be with you."

Abe looked away from her and the man as he said, "Tell him I am not one of your people and that I cannot have you be with me, it is not our way, tell him . . ."

Just then Sarah Beth came up beside her husband, took his arm in her hands and said, "And what about me, don't I have anything to say about any of this? Ask him that," she said to Mary Wolf.

The woman spoke softly. Hawk Man smiled at Sarah Beth as he spoke again. Mary Wolf translated, "He says that you and he will have plenty time to talk together, and he will listen carefully to all that you have to say."

"Tell him I will come with him to fulfill his terrible agreement for this land, for us to live here. Tell him I will come with him, but he will have many regrets for doing this. Tell him I am a Dreaming Woman, and he will wish this was not happening." Then she turned quickly and went back through the canvas door and into their shed.

Once again the woman translated in a very soft voice. Hawk Man laughed and said to Abe, "I like this woman, she is very strong." Then he went on in his own language and it was translated, "Go to Silver City and make it right with the white man. I have sent word that I approve. This will save us more trouble in the future. And in two mornings I will come for her. I am pleased that she will come with me. Ha Ho, thank you, my friend."

He leaped onto his horse's bare back, spun the animal around and took off at a run. Mary Wolf pulled up the bottom of her dress and also jumped lightly onto her horse belly-first, swinging one leg over its back. Abe couldn't help seeing the flash of her bare legs as he closed his eyes too late not to.

When Sarah Beth got back inside she was met by Mattie and Helga's obvious curiosity. "Well, what? What just happened?" Mattie said.

"Mattie, it's happening, I'm being given away to Hawk Man, just like I told you, and that Mary Wolf is supposed to come here for Abe. He says he doesn't want her here, but who knows what a man thinks. She's very pretty, in an Indian kind of way, and he'll be alone, without me I mean. It'll be up to you two to take care of him and help him with his work . . . I just can't believe this, I want to scream and scream . . ."

"Now, now, my girl, we can come up with something, I'm sure we can."

"Yes, I could run away from everybody, both of them, you too, everybody. Go where no one could find me, where no one knows me."

Helga was listening intently, and when no one else spoke, she quietly asked, "Are the Indians followers of the Mormon ways?"

Sarah Beth stepped over to her and put her hands on the sitting girl's shoulders, "No, no, sweet, sweet Helga. They just happen to have these customs in common."

"I didn't think so because from what I heard they don't like each other very much."

Mattie spoke up, "Mormons are still white men, and they don't seem to get along with any other kind of people, and not even with each other, never seen such for fighters and haters. Why back East, I've heard . . ." Then she stopped and apologized and went back to her bread-making.

"It appears it's just what men have to do, Mattie. After all, what was that War we just went through, all hate and killing . . . Helga, I'm going to have to ask you to be especially thoughtful and watch out for both Mattie and Abe. We'll sit down together tomorrow and plan out some of the work . . . Oh, what?" She looked into Helga's eyes, "I know, I'm acting as if it's just a normal thing, like when I left for Father's death . . ."

Just then there was a knock on the board beside the doorway. "May I come in?"

"Of course you may, aren't you the Master of the House?"

Abe eased his way into the space, "I guess Sarah Beth has told you what is happening. I want you to know I would do anything to prevent this, even if we have to move away from here. I'm sure that God would find us a new place to live if we follow His wishes."

Sarah Beth stared at him, then looked at the other two women, and said, "And how do we know what His wishes are? As far as I know, it was His wish that we come to this place, this Jordan Valley. You said so and I believed you."

"But this goes against everything else," Abe said softly.

She looked straight at him this time, and said in a loud whisper. "You should read your Bible more carefully. Don't you remember what happened to the first Abraham and Sarah?" And with that she turned her back on him, poured a pot of hot water into the sink, and began washing the dishes from their morning meal. Abe turned and left.

CHAPTER NINETEEN

Separation

Sarah Beth lay still beside the sleeping Abe waiting for daylight after a restless night. They had tried to be affectionate and loving when they went to bed, but the tension and the awkwardness of the situation prevented them from finding any comfort. He tried to talk with her, but neither of them had much to say. Every time he tried to apologize, she would place her hand over his mouth and say, "It's all right." Finally he drifted off to sleep, having worked himself especially hard that day. The last thing she said to him was "The Indian will never get the chance to touch me in a man's way."

As the light of day began to filter in through the cracks in the makeshift wall, she couldn't help but wonder what she really meant by that. How far would she go to protect herself, to keep herself away from the man and his desires? Oh, dear God, she thought, you've certainly come up with the hardest test of your daughter's faith. I almost don't want to believe in you because of all this, and it'll be a long time before . . . She suddenly realized she was about to threaten God, turned to the edge of the bed and eased out from under the covers. She felt Abe's hand gently take hold of her shoulder as if to pull her back down beside him. She turned from his touch and pulled away, standing and looking down on him. He looked so good to her, but it was too late and he was asleep again. She shrugged, turned away and grabbed the hairbrush from the top of the small chest of drawers they'd brought all the way from Virginia, one of so many things that had been with them as long as they'd been together. She brushed and then braided her hair as tightly as she could, hoping it would somehow make her look more unattractive.

"You don't have to do this," his voice sounded choked off.

She slipped out of her nightdress and into her baggiest pants and shirt, again hoping that her womanliness would be hidden or at least appear less desirable. Her bag was already packed with other clothing, and, yes, her pistol. It wasn't as if she planned to use it, but there might come a moment when it would be needed as a threat. Behind her, Abe finally climbed quickly out of the bed, and into the clothes he'd left lying on the floor. He passed her and went out. Well, she thought, he couldn't expect much more from her on this particular morning. It was enough that she'd spent the night in their bed.

She was heating water for tea when she heard the sound of horses galloping closer and then stopping. It would be time now, because there was no time to avoid or escape this. She removed the damp rags from under the sink and rolled them in a towel, and grabbed a loaf of yesterday's bread to place in a small pack that would ride along with her. She looked around at what she was leaving behind, wondering how and when she would return. The hard part now was not to cry, not to show any weakness.

Hawk Man was waiting on his horse, holding the single nose rope of another animal, a beautiful paint horse with both brown and black patches against a white background. He dropped the rope to the ground and pointed to her, then to the horse. She saw that it had a small saddle of some type, like one for racing or for children. She looked around, but there was no sign of Abe. Was it cowardly or brave of him to disappear at that moment? Perhaps it was the only way he could allow this to happen without some kind of violent reaction, or without seeming to go along with it, either way being worse than not being there.

She pulled her hat down tight and picked up the rope from the ground. The horse stood as still as a statue as she tied her bag behind the little saddle. Hawk Man still had not said a word, soundlessly watching her every move and seemingly ready to help if she needed it. She didn't. She swung her leg up over the horse's back, settled herself in the seat and, for the first time, looked directly at Hawk Man's face. He didn't change his stern expression as he urged his horse to turn and leave the yard. He seemed to know she would follow without him needing to say or do anything. And she did. After all, now she was expected to be like an Indian woman, his woman, and the sickness in her stomach was matched by the attempt to control the angry beating of her heart. This was impossible, and it was happening.

They rode silently toward his camp, and as they moved along she thought back to her last conversation with Mattie, and how the older woman advised her to just take what comes, as it is a woman's role to survive the men in her life rather than to rule on anything for either them or herself. Then it was Mattie who killed a chicken for their supper and collected a small amount of the bird's blood in a medicine bottle, tightly plugging the opening with a cork and handing it to Sarah Beth.

"That should give you a couple of days. Take the damp rags behind the sink and make yourself into an unclean woman. I've heard the Indians won't go near their women when they're in that way. Just like it says in the Bible also."

"Oh Mattie, I don't know if I can do that. What if they find out?"

"It will work, child, been used many times by many women. After a few days you should have learned enough about what's going on and what he intends for you to be able to come up with some other excuse or plan. If it has to happen, and you can't avoid it, God will forgive you, because you have tried everything you could. And Abe will forgive you because he already feels so terrible about it all."

"I don't think I can let that happen, I just don't think I could."

"You have to close your eyes and your mind. And don't let him think you're having any pleasure at all. If it comes to it, God forbid, make him feel like he's useless to you in that way and every way . . ."

"How do you think Abe will behave? Will he stay here? Will he try something foolish and get himself hurt?"

Mattie had quietly gone on plucking the feathers from the chicken, almost as if she hadn't heard the question. Then she spoke in a whisper, "You might remember when we talked about how to find out if you're the one who can't have a baby, or if it's Abe?"

"It's never the man, Mattie."

"Oh yes it is, believe me. I saw enough to know about that. The way we were shuffled around in the quarters, being bred to each other like horses."

Sarah Beth was rolling a pair of skirts tightly so they would fit in her small bag. "I won't wear these unless I have to . . . but what are you trying to say about Abe and I?"

"Let's take a walk. We'll just let this little old chicken soak here for awhile." Mattie wiped her hands and gathered up the feathers in the bucket of what had been scalding water. Then she picked it up and walked out the doorway. Sarah Beth followed.

When Mattie dumped the water and feathers some ways away from their shed, she turned the bucket upside down and sat herself on it. "Sit dear," she said, motioning to Sarah Beth to take a seat on the ground beside her. "It truly is beautiful here. I think I love it more every day. And it would be a shame to have to leave it just because of some foolish men." She seemed to lose herself in the landscape for a long moment. Then she began talking more quietly, "Child, your father always used to talk about how God gives us an opportunity for every need that he sends our way. Right now your need and your opportunity seem to be very much lined up."

"What, you think I need to be carried off by this savage?"

"No, no, not that. But I do think that you and Abe need to have a child before one of you leaves the other, or something worse should happen because of it all."

"I don't understand you Mattie. You'll have to speak more plainly to me."

"The answer to your question about whether Abe and you can't have a child is right here, as they say, right under your nose."

"I still don't have any idea what you're trying to say."

"Helga." Mattie looked away across the shallow valley to the low-lying ridges on the other side.

"Helga? How?"

"Child, you don't want that Indian woman to come and be with your man. And you want to have a baby in your family. Helga is family."

"Oh," Sarah Beth expelled her breath as if she'd been hit in the stomach. "Oh, my God."

"Yes, He is still your God, and He will watch over you while you are gone away. And if it is His will, he could give you and Abe the child that the two of you haven't been able to have."

"Mattie, that's just so horrible. How can you?" She stood up and paced away and then back again. "I can't believe you said that."

"All right then," Mattie stood up as well, "forget I ever said anything."

"Mattie, it's a sin. What would . . . what would Father say?"

Mattie had already started walking away, then she turned back to say, "Depends on how bad he wanted a grandchild."

"Well, it wouldn't be mine, so it wouldn't be his. That's crazy. That's all it is, it's wrong and crazy and I wish you never . . ."

"All right, dear, I'm sorry. We'll forget I ever said anything about all this. I was just trying to help us work through the mess that these men have made of it all." She turned away again and resumed walking back to their shed. "I've got to get that chicken cooking."

Sarah Beth felt herself begin to shake, but no tears came. It was the first time she ever let the thought into her mind that maybe she would never, ever have her own child. And even though it had begun to seem hopeless and wasn't happening no matter how hard they tried, she still never admitted that it could truly be impossible. Now Mattie was trying to tell her that truth. She stifled a scream and found herself kicking at the dirt. It would pass, this would all go away. In one month she would be returned to her husband, they would begin again, everything would be all right, she wouldn't let that Indian touch her, she'd die first . . . And there it was, the only other thought she couldn't allow into her mind, into her heart. Would she have to die, or would she have to kill to save herself?

Mattie!" she called after the woman, "I'll think about it." Then she sat down on the bucket that was left behind and let the tears come, the tears of hopelessness and even anger at everyone, at God, and especially at Abe. Let him have someone else, Mary Wolf, Helga, anyone else. Let him go. He wasn't man enough to hold onto her, he wasn't her man at all. Maybe she wouldn't even come back to him. Let him have Helga, let her have him all to herself. She would find someone else, and not the Indian either. Another wave of shaking passed through her chest and she fought it off, fought to control her body, her mind, and yes, her heart. She started back for their home, their temporary home, whatever it should be called, and she was reminded of the other temporary home, the one in Utah.

Next morning, as she and Hawk Man came in sight of his camp, he stopped his horse and held up his arm to bring her to a halt beside him. "You angry?" he said. "You be with me, I be good to you. I not hurt you. You see I good man. Come." And then he rode off, motioning her to follow.

Sarah Beth had forgotten that he could speak some English. Every time she'd seen him, the Mary Wolf woman was translating, but now she remembered Abe telling her that the man could speak English in a limited way, enough to get some things across. What did he mean that he was a good man? Maybe he meant he wouldn't force her to do anything she didn't want to, but not likely. Maybe he meant that he could take very good care of her, maybe in bed, maybe that's what he meant. More likely. But he wouldn't get the chance, not now, not ever; that much she'd promised herself. She nudged the horse and it went from standing to a gallop almost without a pause. It was some horse.

When they arrived at the camp, he dismounted, waving his arms, sending the other women and the children away from the tipi that was his own. Then he came over to her, held his hand up to help her down. She slid off the other side of the horse and unfastened her bag, dropping the horse's rope to the ground. Hawk Man came around the horse, gently took her bag and motioned for her to follow him into the tent. Once they were inside, he motioned to the two beds, low piles of buffalo hides and white man blankets. He set her bag on one of them and motioned from her to that bed, then he motioned from himself to the other bed, and covered his mouth with his hand, then pointed toward outside and then covered his mouth again. Then he was gone, out the flap, and she was left alone, alone with what seemed to be her own bed and a secret to keep from the others in the camp, at least it seemed that was what he meant with those gestures, but who knew what an Indian meant by anything . . .

She looked around the inside of the tipi, seeing his bags and weapons hanging along the slanted walls, and seeing also the empty places where the cookware had been the last time she's visited. She knelt down beside her bed and opened the bag. She pulled out some necklaces, her mother's, and hung them from the pole that leaned in above the bed, then her Bible, which she placed at the head of the bed, more as a source of protection than as something to read. Then she made a pile of the hides by folding them several times, and she sat on the pile, looking up through the opening at the top.

She could hardly believe what she'd told Helga when she was saying goodbye the night before. The young woman was completely shocked and hardly able to speak. "I want you to try to have a baby with Mr. Abe while I'm gone . . . I don't want him to be with that Indian woman. I haven't been able to give him the child he wants so much, and I'm afraid he will let that woman be with him. You must prevent that."

Helga had looked at her as if she were a ghost or worse, and could only shake her head back and forth, mumbling, "No, no, no."

"Yes," Sarah Beth said, "for me, for my sake. I've made up my mind that we must have a child, and it will be mine as well as yours, and Abe will be the father. I will leave a letter for him, telling him of my desire that he do this, but it will be up to you to make yourself as attractive as possible. Mattie will help you, she knows of this, now do as I say, and in a month, I will see you again . . . leave me now, leave me alone, I must be ready to leave in the morning."

And that was it. She'd been able to say it, say it out loud, and once it had been said, it didn't seem as bad or as unlikely. It just was, and now as she removed her boots and slipped on a light pair of shoes, she realized that perhaps it was God's will that she provide a witness for these people, a witness whose strength in the face of their customs was unwavering and without regret, and who was not afraid of anything they could do to her.

A few minutes passed. She lay back on the pile of hides and felt sleepiness from her restless night begin to overtake her. She had no idea how much time had gone by when she was awakened by a strange sound. And she had no idea where she was, at first thinking perhaps she was somewhere under a wagon on the trail. She pushed herself up on her elbows and saw the Indian standing in front of her. It came back to her in a flash. She was here in a tipi, a captive, of this man . . . She started to stand, but the man gestured for her to stay seated. He was holding out a dress, a dress made of leather. He shook it out and held it toward her. It was beautiful. She could see what looked to be animal teeth and shells hanging in a curved line across the bodice. As he shook the dress, the objects made a rustling and a clicking sound. He reached out for her hand, but she pushed herself to her feet. He held the dress up in front of her, smiling.

"Is good? Is for you. Take," he said as he gave the dress a little toss so it landed on her shoulder. He backed away, saying, "You, on you." It was a command rather than a suggestion, and then he was gone from the tipi.

This was one more way of being expected to accept their ways, she thought. She knew she could refuse, but what good would it do? It might make him angry, and that would not be a good thing. She tried to compare this to the time with the Bishop when he tried to force her to wear a black dress for the wedding, and then had two of his women come in and try to forcibly change her clothing. She'd been able to resist and push them away, but this time no force was being used, at least not yet. And the softness of the leather felt nice in her hands as she stroked the entire length of the gift. It was even softer than the dress Lefty's wife had given her back in Missouri. When she'd taken out that dress the night before and thought about bringing it with her, she'd decided there was no way she could allow herself to look like an Indian woman to the man, and packed it away again. Now the question was whether accepting this one and wearing it would be seen as a sign of her agreement with his and Abe's transaction, and whether he would continue as respectful to her as he'd been so far. Well, she thought, it wouldn't hurt just to try it on and see how it felt. She thought she could count on him having manners enough not to barge in on her while she was changing, to at least announce himself and ask for her permission to enter.

She slipped out of her baggy pants and Abe's shirt, lifted the dress above her head and pulled it down over the length of her body. She brushed one hand across the shells and teeth, supposing they were elk teeth. She made the teeth rattle, then shook herself and twirled about. The rattling sound was soft, but insistent, and the feeling of the dress as it moved and slipped across her body was very special. She'd heard about Indian woman dancers, and now she couldn't help wondering how they danced, as the dress seemed made for dancing. Suddenly she stopped and froze. This would be what the Indian wanted, this was why he gave her the dress, so she would like it, so she would feel more like an Indian herself, so she would be more receptive to him, the one who'd given it to her. No! She wouldn't let it work on her that way. If he wanted to be Abe's friend, that was their business, but she wasn't going to let him buy her friendship, gifts or no gifts.

After Sarah Beth tried on the dress, and was making up her mind whether or not to leave it on, there was a soft knocking at one of the doorway poles of the tipi. She made an answering sound and heard the voice of Mary Wolf asking to come in. Well, at least it would be someone she could talk with, maybe even ask questions of.

"Yes, come in."

The woman slipped in through the door flap. She was carrying a small pot and a bundle. "Food," she said. "We did not forget you."

"Thank you, I'm pleased you are here." Sarah Beth was intent on making someone a friend here, since she really had no idea what to expect. And she was relieved that this woman was still here, in the camp and not with Abe. Mary Wolf set the pot down near the fire pit, and laid the bundle next to it, pointing and saying a word in their language followed by the word bread. She looked up and clasped her hands together, smiling.

"Now you are Indian woman. Only with light in your hair." She kept smiling. "Look good for you. Very good."

"Thank you. It feels nice, so soft."

"Is yours now." She looked around and saw the hides Sarah Beth had used for her nap. "He wants you to know he has good feelings for you. Also kindness. Do not be afraid of him he says. More you must be careful of other two wives. They are sometimes mean to me, and will not like you here, but do not give them your words by talking to them. They are harmless. They make noise but have no teeth," she said, smiling again. "They want me to go to your man, but I think is better this way, for you to have me here when you are here."

Sarah Beth was taken aback by this. She just wasn't used to these kinds of things being talked about. Even with someone as close to her as Mattie it was difficult, and now this woman was speaking about the whole situation as if it were the weather or something. She smiled back.

"Also, he wants me to tell you that he will be taking you with him on journey. Chiefs have meeting and he wants you beside him. I think he is proud about you, but you will be all right with him because he will take the old one, his mother, with you."

"Can she ride?"

"As good as me and you. She is not so old, but is our oldest one."

"What is she called?"

"Red Bird. Her hair is much white. She was Many Ponies, but now Red Bird."

"And you? You will stay here?"

"Yes. To keep the others from fighting." She smiled, "And, he says, if your man still wants me."

Sarah Beth looked straight at her, but said nothing. Of course, they would think there was still a chance Abe would want this woman. This somehow made her more sure of the need for the arrangement she'd left to Helga. And Mattie.

"How far to the Chiefs meeting?" she asked.

"Three days good riding, good weather."

"When do we leave?"

"In the morning. You will sleep here. He will sleep here. Sleeping only, before journey."

Then the woman reached out and handed Sarah Beth another small bundle, wrapped in soft hide.

"For you, a woman's knife. For cooking what he hunts, and for taking care of yourself."

Sarah Beth held the bundle in her hands and could feel the length of the blade and the thickness of the handle through the leather. Mary Wolf took a step closer to her and quickly separated Sarah Beth's dress at one side. Taking Sarah Beth's hand, she guided it inside the dress to a flap of leather, an interior pocket of sorts. Next Mary Wolf pulled Sarah Beth's hand over inside her own dress, where Sarah Beth could feel a similar pocket that also held a knife. The woman backed away and turned to leave.

"Mary Wolf," Sarah Beth said, "Thank you. I will remember you."

The woman held out both of her hands clasped together, "Woman friend," she said, and then she was gone.

As soon as Sarah Beth was out of his sight, Abe returned from the little grove of willows down by the smaller creek. He found himself trying to be angry, but he wasn't sure who he could be angry at. Hawk Man for pushing him into this bad situation and taking advantage of them? Or at Sarah Beth for going with him, even though it was his own responsibility and obviously his fault, or was he just angry at himself for all of it? Now there would be Mattie and Helga to face and to try to explain why he'd let this happen. He grabbed at the ax that leaned against the barn and swung it at a piece of firewood that somehow had survived their needs. The wood split in two and he chopped those halves in half. Then he set the ax back in place. Hitting things wouldn't help. He'd just have to live with his failure to stand up for his wife and himself. But was it the only way to live in this place? Was it his only choice for them to have a home, trading a month of his wife for a permanent home? It had to be wrong, but he hadn't been able to figure any way out. Now there was the matter of the trip to Silver City to take care of the rest of the bargain he'd made for this land, because now there was the white man's law to fulfill, even as he was losing his wife by following the Indian way.

Morning whinnied to him from the shade of the shed he'd made for the horses. "I know, boy. I miss her too. But she'll come back. At least I hope she will."

He went toward the kitchen, feeling his morning hunger and wondering by who would be cooking, not that he couldn't help himself. He pushed aside the door flap and saw Mattie standing over the stove, stirring in a large pot. She looked up and stared at him before turning her eyes away.

"Are you hungry?" she asked.

"Yes, I am. But I can find something. I need to get going to work on the house."

"Well, have a seat. Your food has been waiting." She bent down and opened the oven door, pulling out a plate and some bread. "Here, you'll need this. I'm making broth from that chicken we had last night, but it won't be a lot. I'm hoping you'll be going into that town and can bring back some things I need for us."

"Thank you Mattie. Yes, I'll need to go. There are more details about this land that have to be dealt with. Perhaps tomorrow. Will you two be all right here?"

"Of course. You could even take Helga with you. I'm sure she'd welcome the opportunity."

"Well, we'll see about that. It worries me to think of you here alone."

Mattie sniffed and said, "Well, it doesn't worry me. I've got my charming self, and I can shoot the gun you left me. Besides, I might like a little time to myself."

"What makes you think you can shoot it?"

"Now don't be making fun of me, Mr. Abraham. There was a time before I came to work for Dr. Randall when the only food my family got to eat was what we killed ourselves. And I was pretty good at shooting, if I say so myself. They didn't like us Negroes having a gun to use, but they needed to eat too and we would to hunt for them as well."

"Like I said, we'll see about the trip to town." He ate quickly and left to get to work.

Mattie took down the letter that was hidden behind the stack of towels on the counter. She could almost feel what it said through the envelope, but wasn't sure when to give it to Abe. And now that he might take Helga along with him to town, she couldn't decide if it should be before they left or when they came back. She almost wished Sarah Beth had given it to him herself, but then that might have been unwise. That girl certainly was being brave. Mattie looked up, and could only hope the good reverend would approve or at least try to understand.

That evening after their supper, Abe offered Helga the chance to go to Silver City with him the next day. She was instantly excited. "Oh yes, that would be so good. I'm running out of so many of the things I need for my sewing." Then, just as suddenly, she stopped herself and became quite serious. "Well, I'm not exactly sure I should go. Is Mattie going and who would stay here? Somebody needs to."

Mattie smiled, and said, "Child, I'm staying home, right here, and looking forward to it."

Helga looked over at Abe with a question in her expression.

"Yes, that's right, it'll be fine. Mattie assures met she can take care of herself and anything else that needs looking after. You'll take Morning and we'll make better time than with Ginger. We may be back here even before it's dark, depending on how long my business takes."

Helga looked back at Mattie, trying to read the woman's thoughts. But Mattie just looked away and said softly, "It will all be fine. Besides we've got neighbors now. If I do need help."

That night when Abe was out making sure the saddles and gear were in good shape for a hard ride, Helga had a chance to be alone with Mattie, and to ask, "Does he know?"

"No dear, there's a letter for him from Sarah Beth, but I don't think I'll give it to him until after you return. Just be the way you always are. Be nice to him and don't show any upset. I'm fairly certain he has no idea."

Helga started to leave, but she couldn't help being upset, and suddenly she didn't want to be alone. "I just can't do this. Why would she even think of it? It's so unfair. If God cares about us at all, it's a sin."

"Child," Mattie said, "you have to see it as love. Sarah Beth's love is so strong and she's so afraid of losing him if she can't give him a baby. You must know that. They've not been a bit shy about how much they both want it, and I know from her they've been trying as hard as they can. Besides, if you did this, it would be the family's baby, because you're one of the family."

"Yes, but I've always felt more like a daughter than a . . . what? What would I be?"

"Well, you're a grown woman now, not a little girl. Just don't think about it too much. It's a solution to a problem and you'll all be the better for it. Now here," she reached into the pocket of her apron and pulled out a folded bill. "I never knew when your birthday is, so I'm sure I missed it. Take this and get yourself something pretty to wear, something that shows what a woman you've become, maybe something for nighttime." She smiled and said, "Here take it and run along. Be ready to go early in the morning. And don't worry. I, myself, had it much worse than you, and I lived through it."

Helga took the money, gave Mattie a quick hug and then hurried out the door. A minute later Abe walked in. "Where was she going in such a hurry?"

"Just going to get ready for the morning. Think I'll go now myself, so I'll be well rested for my big day alone tomorrow. Good night, Mr. Abe."

She let herself out quietly and he was left alone. It had been some time since he'd spent the night without Sarah Beth, since her trip back to Virginia. But this was completely different. How was he going to keep from grabbing Bird and racing across the valley to the Indian camp? And what would he do there? Fight Hawk Man, grab her, and ride away? No, this was his doing as much or more than anyone's, and it seemed the only thing he could do now was be patient and keep himself under control, whatever that might mean. As far as sleep, he wasn't sure if he could.

The next morning, they left in the dark. Abe would lead Ginger for packing the load of supplies coming home. Helga would ride Morning. Mattie had prepared food for the journey, and was smiling as they rode away. It was a beautiful daybreak, and she'd already planned most of what she could get done with everyone gone. Her first chore would be to reorganize the kitchen. Sarah Beth was a good cook, but didn't have things arranged for more than one person to work there at a time. After that, she would fix the washstand where they did laundry. By then it would be time to take a nice long walk to look for a place where she might be able to have her own small house someday. In her mind, she was seeing a cabin of her own after the big house was finished. After all, and she laughed at herself with this thought, after all, she wasn't too old to attract some kind of a suitor someday, who knew . . . She laughed out loud, this time thinking, what color would he be?

Abe didn't sleep much that night, thinking of Sarah Beth forced into the Indian's bed, or even fighting back and getting hurt, thoughts that swirled in and out of his mind and his half-asleep dreaming. Never could he have imagined that he would have to use his wife as a payment for a home, never had he imagined God would allow such a thing. In the end, he'd given in to sleep with the thought that he would have to trust her to keep her promise to protect herself by any means. When he woke up it was as if he hadn't slept at all.

They got off to an early start, and stopped for a mid-morning meal, only a few miles from the town. Helga quickly and carefully laid out the contents of the bundle that had been attached to her saddle. Abe had noticed that she and Morning worked well together. Even though Helga was a bit stockier and shorter than Sarah Beth, and they'd had to shorten the stirrup straps, she probably weighed about the same. She was very quiet while they were eating, much quieter than her usual curious and talkative self. He wondered if she too was missing Sarah Beth, or was feeling awkward being alone with him? That didn't really make sense since they'd spent all that time alone together while Sarah Beth was gone back in Missouri.

"You seem quiet today. Are you all right?"

"Yes, Mr. Abe, I'm all right."

"Well, last night you were so excited about coming along, I just . . . And by the way, how about we just drop the Mr. as a part of my name. I'd be much more comfortable if you simply call me Abe."

"Yes, Mr. Abe," she said and then caught herself and laughed. "Yes, Abe." It sounded strange to her and she couldn't help wondering why the change now. Mattie said he didn't know anything yet, about what Sarah Beth was asking her to do, but he seemed to be noticing something. Noticing how she couldn't be the same with him anymore, couldn't just talk and ask questions and go on as if he was her big brother or father or uncle or . . . Now that he was supposed to be something else to her, she found herself afraid.

He said, "Well, all right. That was a good meal. Mattie does an excellent job of taking care of us doesn't she?"

"Yes," she paused, "yes, Abe."

He walked away to go behind a couple of trees for privacy. She looked around for a similar place for herself and went into the bushes nearby. Neither said anything when they reappeared and he caught up the horses while she packed up the things from the meal. They mounted and set off again, soon nearing the town as they trotted along.

He came alongside her and said, "I'll try to get this business finished as quickly as possible. You can take Ginger and this money, and maybe get started on the supplies we need."

He handed her a couple of coins, and she realized that combined with the money from Mattie, she now had more money on her person than she'd ever seen at one time before, well, except for in a bank or on the Bishop's table.

As they entered the town, Abe pointed out the building that held the court offices where he would be, and then made sure she knew where the mercantile was. She didn't ask if there was a women's clothing store; she would have to find that on her own. She knew if she didn't, Mattie would be disappointed, even if she never wore what she bought.

"So I'll meet you there, or in front of that statue," he said, "over there by that grassy spot if you get done before me. And don't you try to load Ginger. Not by yourself. Just have them set it all aside at the store. We'll get it when I'm done."

Abe rode back to the office. He wondered how Helga would do, since as far as he knew she'd never done any real shopping alone before. He hitched Bird to a rail and went into the building, looking for the clerk he'd met. There was a woman sitting at that same desk, but the man wasn't there. The woman seemed busy, and didn't look up when he entered.

He coughed and said, "Pardon me, ma'am. There was a clerk here before, a man whose name I don't remember."

Still not looking up, she said. "He's gone. Promoted to the Boise office. I'm here now. What can I do for you?" Now she looked at him. "Mister . . . ?"

"Abe, Abraham Saunders. It's about a piece of land, out past Mike Skinner's place. It's been Indian land."

"Yes, I know it. What about it?"

"Well, a while back, with that man, the other clerk, I signed what he called a provisional permit to be allowed to settle there if the Indians ever decided to give it up. It's my understanding that one of them, a Mr. Hawk Man, has decided to do so, and I am here to make good on a homestead application."

"Ah yes, I was informed about this matter." She went back to writing for a minute, then looked up. "It's not quite so simple, Mr. Abraham. Your claim has been contested, and the Indians have not signed anything to say it's now available for claim. To complicate matters, the other party has filed suit in civil court to have your permit revoked. So you see, it's not so simple." She went back to writing.

"What do I have to do? Or, more to the point, what can be done?" He was dismayed to hear what she'd said, having assumed it would be an easy matter of a few pieces of paper, signing his name, and getting a receipt for whatever the court costs might be. Now this.

"The nearest Indian agent is at Fort Walla Walla. What you are asking for will require him to cede such land and extinguish the current status, thereby releasing it for homesteading, and then there will be the civil suit proceedings. In the meantime, Mr. Abraham, I would advise you to continue with the construction of a house, which is what I understand is going on anyway, thereby being more likely to fulfill the requirements of proving up on a claim should the other matters be resolved. Any questions?"

"No, no ma'am. But the name is Saunders, Abraham is my first name."

She wrote quickly on another piece of paper, "So noted, Mr. Saunders. Oh, and about the house? You didn't hear that from me. Good day, sir."

Abe backed toward the door, then stopped. "Excuse me again, but is there any sort of paper that I could take with me that has any relevance at all to my claim, to any of these matters?"

"Mr. Saunders. I can give you a receipt for the payment of sixty dollars if you wish to make that payment now. It will state that you have placed a deposit in trust for this claim. However, should you fail to successfully negotiate this claim, your money will not be refunded."

"Please then, please, let's do that."

When that was finished and he walked out the door, he stopped to read over the sheet of paper that she'd given him. It seemed to be in order without making any kind of promissory arrangement, just a receipt for fees paid in connection with said claim, and a description of the property's location by some kind of survey. Better than nothing, he thought, perplexed as to what would be the best next steps concerning the land. But first things first, he should get back to Helga to help her out, then they might get an early start home.

Ginger and Morning were tied to the rail in front of the mercantile, so he looped Bird's reins over the same rail and went into the store. He searched the aisles that were piled high with goods, but he didn't see Helga anywhere. He waved at a clerk and asked if a young woman had been in a short while ago. The young man answered yes, and said she was asking about a store for women's clothing. When Abe asked if she'd done any purchases in this store, the man told him, "Not yet, but she said she'd be back."

Abe figured she'd return soon, so he started shopping for the things that he remembered from the list Mattie and he had prepared: lamp oil, sugar, candles, flour, and for some reason Mattie had insisted on a new kettle for boiling tea water. She'd even given him some money for it. He gathered these items onto a counter near the front of the store, and then heard the bell over the door ring as Helga walked through it.

"There you are," he said. "Have you got the list?"

She was fumbling with a package, almost as if trying to hide it from him. Or maybe she was just having difficulty reaching into her coat pocket for the crumpled list.

They quickly gathered the rest of the items, mostly small things. Abe let Helga pay the bill while he went outside for the canvas saddle bags.

When everything was in place, they mounted and began the ride out of the town. Near the end of the street there was a bakery, and the smell of fresh baked goods wafted out onto the street. Abe pulled up and said to Helga, "Why don't you run in there and get something good for us to eat on the way home? It'll be late by the time we really eat, if we make it home."

Helga jumped down and ran into the bakery. She was back in a couple of minutes with a large bag, saying, "I got something for Mattie as well." She handed the bag up to him and climbed back on Morning. Then she reached out for the bag. He pulled it away.

"Think I'm going to let you have it all to yourself?"

She laughed and then told him to get going, saying she'd ride behind to keep an eye on him if he tried to eat any of it. With that he handed the bag back to her and rode off, leading Ginger.

It was late in the afternoon, with the sun still fairly high when they stopped and let the horses drink and graze for a while. They stood quietly and shared out a couple of small pastries. Then they sat down by the small creek that ran along the trail, and each took another roll from the bag.

"Helga," Abe asked in a quiet voice. "If you don't mind, I'm curious about your parents, your folks. Did you know them?"

"Only my mother," she said quickly, her mouth nearly full.

"And she's where?"

"The Bishop kicked her out of his church and she's probably still back there somewhere. Indiana most likely. I haven't seen her for a long time."

"Do you miss having her?"

She looked at him for a long moment, and he apologized for asking.

"No, it's all right," she said. "I just don't think about if I miss her. I guess I miss having a mother . . . but I don't miss that one. Can you understand that?"

"I suppose so, if she wasn't good to you?"

"You could say that. Want some more of this before I put it away?"

"No, I'm fine."

She stood up. "We should probably get going."

"You're right." He started for the horses. "Still a ways to go."

Mattie had a fine supper waiting late for them and was pleased with the pastries they brought for her. While they were eating, she bustled about unpacking the goods from town, sorting and putting things where they belonged.

"Things look different in here," Abe said.

Mattie stopped for a moment and said, "Needed a bit of rearranging, don't you think?"

"I imagine so. This is good stew."

"Thank you, when we butchered that pig awhile back, I saved the feet, kept them with the other meat in that cellar we made. It worked good."

Abe held the fork with his next bite still halfway to his mouth. "Never ate pig's feet before."

"Now you have, and it's not really hoofs, it's the whole lower bone," she said.

"Guess so." He put the bite in his mouth and chewed slowly.

Helga had stopped eating. Mattie asked her if there was something wrong. "Oh no," she said, making a funny face, "just thinking about where those feet have been."

"Well, I cleaned them good. Lord, you'd think you white people would have starved to death by now, what you won't eat."

"Didn't say I wouldn't eat it Mattie, just thinking about it, that's all."

Mattie muttered something and went on organizing the kitchen shelves and putting away things from their shopping trip.

Helga and Abe exchanged glances and then both of them took another bite of the stew.

"Best pig's feet I've ever had," Abe said through his mouthful of stew. "How about you, Helga?"

Helga smiled and nearly choked before saying, "My goodness, I never knew they could taste this good. Must be Mattie's secret recipe."

Mattie turned around and stared at the both of them and they both filled their mouths again. She smiled and said, "I surely do like to see white folks eatin' real food."

Then she laughed, and they laughed with her as she went back to her work. As soon as her back was turned both Abe and Helga covered their mouths with their hands and chewed their mouthful as fast as they could, swallowing quickly.

"Well, that was great," Abe said, "but I don't think I can eat another bite. We did have quite a little bit to eat on the way home. What about you Helga?"

"I know what you mean, those pastries kind of filled me up. Mattie you didn't eat any of the ones we brought for you?"

"I got them," she said without turning around to look at them. "I'll save mine to have with the leftovers from this meal tomorrow." Then she turned around and smiled, "I'm sure there'll be plenty left for all of us."

Helga excused herself from the table and gathered up their plates and utensils.

"Don't worry about it, young lady. I've got the sink full of these old dishes I'm going to store away so we can use the better ones, and I'll clean up when I'm done. Never made any sense to me to have nice dishes you never use. You can go along now."

Helga said thank you, gathered up her package of new quilting goods and left. On the way back to her little shed she stopped and picked up the package she'd managed to hide from Abe, the nightgown she'd bought with Mattie's money. As soon as she was inside her own space, she stripped off her clothes and pulled it on over her head and shoulders. It felt nice and soft, but she thought it would've been nice to have a mirror to see how it looked on her. Then she took it off again, not wanting to wear it because of what it meant, or because it was too special, she wasn't sure which. Something about this thing she was feeling would never ever happen. Then again, she thought, why not? After all, if Sarah Beth was with the Indian, Abe might as well have some company, and he was the most handsomest man she'd ever seen.

As soon as Helga left, Mattie cleaned up the dinnerware, swept the floor, and said her goodnight to Abe. As she was about to leave, she reached into the stack of towels on the counter and pulled out the letter. Handing it to Abe, she said, "Something Sarah Beth left for you." And then she was out the doorway.

Abe sat back in his chair and turned the folded paper over in his hand. Her script of his name was as careful and well-done as always. He thought back to the first time he'd gone shopping in their town back in Virginia, when Sarah Beth was still a girl, and how he'd been impressed by her handwriting on the shopping list. He tore the little seal she'd used on this letter, unfolded the paper, and began reading.

Dearest Abe,

I don't have any idea what you might be thinking about what is going on. By now I will be in the Indian camp, and neither of us knows what that will lead to. I am sorry for getting angry at you. I know now that this was the only thing you could do and save our chances for the home we have both worked so hard for in this perfect place.

I know how much you want a child, how you must have prayed for that, and yet this prayer we both share has not been answered. From all of my experience with women's medical problems and the ones having babies, I am convinced that I am just one of those women God has chosen to be barren (how I hate to use that word), and to serve others rather than to have our own children. For this reason, and because I love you so much, I am asking you, nay telling you, to take

> *steps to give us the child we both want. I beg you to*
> *do everything you must do to have a child with Helga.*

He stopped reading, staring at the paper in his hands as if it were on fire, as if he had to drop it or otherwise get rid of it immediately. He simply couldn't believe what he'd read. It wasn't true. There had to be some mistake; yet it was unmistakably her handwriting. As if it were a terribly mean joke she was playing on him for letting Hawk Man take her away, as if . . .

> *I know you must be thinking I can't possibly mean this,*
> *but I have thought it through, and Helga is part of our*
> *family now and this would be just the best way I can*
> *think of for us to have the child we both so desire. And*
> *I am certain in my own heart that if my father were still*
> *alive he would want a grandchild of his own and would*
> *make every effort to make this possibility allowable.*
>
> *Dearest, you must do this for me, even as I am doing*
> *everything I can to remain chaste for you only. Please,*
> *please give me this opportunity to be a mother, even if*
> *it is shared.*
>
> *I love you more than ever, and this is how I can show*
> *you just how much, and how you can show how much*
> *you want us to stay together.*
>
> *Your everlasting wife, Sarah Beth*

His head fell against the back of the chair, eyes closed, disbelief turning his mind into a twisted knot of confusion and even fear. His first thought was that this was her way of leaving him, that she was so angry at what was happening, angry at him for letting her go without a fight, that she would put him up to something like this so it would justify her leaving him forever. But that didn't make any more sense than if the letter were true in what it was saying. He folded the paper and stood up, moving over to the alcove and their bed. He slipped the letter under the pillow. Then he hurried out the doorway and into the moonlight.

He suddenly wanted to leap on Bird and ride across the valley, burst into Hawk Man's tipi and tell the man that it was over and never should have happened and he didn't care what it meant for their future, he and his woman were leaving this land and its bedlam. Then, in his mind's eye version, he would demand that Sarah Beth tell him what she really meant by this, what she really wanted, and was he to believe this terrible curse she was trying to lay on him?

He didn't realize how far he walked by the time he looked around to get his bearings. He was beyond Helga's shed, almost to the draw where the creek came off the hillside. He turned back and looked at the young woman's little building, hardly more than enough room for a bed. He wondered if she was awake. Wondered if she knew about this trap of Sarah Beth's. Or if it wasn't a trap? Did the girl know anything about it? If she did, how did she feel? Just then he saw, through the cracks between the boards of her shack, the light of a candle or a small lamp blink out.

The next morning, just as Abe was finishing his coffee and almost ready to head out to the house site, they heard the sound of horses outside the shed. It was Mary Wolf and the young man Carl. Abe walked out, wondering if this was going to be some further attempt to get him to take this woman into his camp, into his life.

"Hello," he said.

"Hello to you," the woman replied. "I see you worry I have come to be forced on you. That is not why we are here. Hawk Man and your woman have gone on a journey and he wanted you to know so you would not be worrying."

"Gone? Gone where?"

"To one of the agencies," she gestured to the north. "There is a meeting of Chiefs and the United States agents. I don't know more than that. But he said not to try to follow him." She looked down and spoke very quietly, "Says he is taking good care of your woman and she is still your woman."

Abe started to ask more questions, but realized that even if she answered, she wouldn't be telling him any more than this. But the agents would be there. His felt like his mind was trying to tell him something he didn't know yet, but should know. He saw the two riders were starting to leave.

"No, wait. There is business we must think about. This land, the courts, it will take an order from the Indian agent up at Fort Walla Walla. Isn't there some way we could get a message to Hawk Man?"

Mary Wolf looked down at him. "Can you put this business in a letter? Carl could ride after them and give it to Hawk Man and he could take it to the agent."

"Yes, yes, that would work." He turned and called out, "Helga, Mattie, something for our guests while they wait." Then he turned back to the woman, "Come down, they will take care of you. I will write the letter, quickly, quickly." He went back into the shed just as Mattie was coming out.

He sat at the table with a pen and an ink block, ground some ink and began writing on a clean sheet of paper. Within minutes, he'd written to the agent about the nature of the problem and the need for official approval as part of the solution. He gave the name of the new clerk in Silver City and the previous clerk, now in Boise. Then he wrote another short note to Hawk Man, to have Carl give to Sarah Beth to read to the Indian. But how could he say what he wanted to say to her? What could he write that she would see and understand? Nothing that wouldn't be terribly odd if someone else ended up with it, ended up translating it for the man. So he wrote briefly, stating the situation and then signing his name with a flourish of loops that he would never usually use. Maybe that would mean something to her, maybe she would know that he simply wasn't himself now.

He went out and explained the two letters to Mary Wolf, who looked quite strange holding a teacup between her hands; at least he thought it looked strange. She handed him the empty cup and he gave her the letters. Once again, he couldn't help noticing the strange quality of her beauty. He wondered if he was somehow wrong about all of this. Then as he looked away from her he caught a glimpse of Helga smiling at Carl and reaching out for his cup, which was still mostly full. Abe thought he remembered the young man having a wife of his own. Still, he couldn't help being startled by the sharp feeling of protectiveness, maybe because he knew having one wife didn't seem to matter to the Indians.

Mary Wolf placed the letters somewhere inside her buckskin dress, mounted, and then the two of them rode off. Mattie took the cups from Abe and Helga and quietly suggested that she would be fine alone for the day if Abe needed Helga's help at the new house. Then she went inside.

CHAPTER TWENTY

Complication

It was late afternoon. By riding hard, Carl caught up with Hawk Man, Sarah Beth, and the older woman who was with them. They were moving slowly along on the banks of a river, looking for a good place to cross. The young man pulled up next to Hawk Man and held out two envelopes. Sarah Beth could see that they looked like the ones she used back home for her own letters. Maybe something had happened to Abe, she thought. The two men talked in rapid sentences with many gestures. Then Hawk Man turned to her and said, "Here, camp." He dismounted and beckoned for her to do the same.

She held on to the reins of the new horse she was still getting to know, and Hawk Man handed the two letters to her. One was addressed to the Indian Affairs Agent of Fort Walla Walla and the other was addressed to her. She opened the one with her name on it and read its explanation of what the other letter was about. There was nothing more, no personal note. Only the strange curls that ended his name and wandered across the page. She'd never seen this in his signature before. If he was trying to say something to her, she had no idea what it was. She realized Hawk Man was waiting for her to explain to him what she was reading.

She held up the other envelope and said, "This is for you give to agent, to government man. Is about the land. Is message from Abe to agent man."

Hawk Man shook his head slowly, as if he was trying to understand her, so she repeated herself. Then he said, "Abe to government for land." He seemed to understand and nodded his head up and down. Then he spoke again to Carl who went to help the older woman to dismount. They busied themselves making a small camp. Carl went for sticks of wood, the woman pulled a circle of long brown grass out of the earth to make a fire pit, and Hawk Man began making a small fire out of dried moss that he produced from somewhere. Sarah Beth stood still, not knowing what to do to help. Hawk Man pointed to the blankets on the horses and tied to her saddle, and he made a gesture with his shoulders that was clearly a sign for her to take the gear off of the horses. As soon as Hawk Man had the small fire going and was able to feed it with some of Carl's sticks, he sat down and began the ritual of lighting and smoking his short pipe. The horses began to move away to some greener grass. The older woman got out some dried meat, and handed Sarah Beth a pot, pointing to the running water of the small river.

After they'd eaten, the sunset made a brilliant display of colors and it was quickly dark. Hawk Man produced a blanket out of the bag he'd carried on his back all day, handed it to Sarah Beth, and showed her where to put it. Then he took his riding blanket and laid it down next to hers. He said softly, "Is good. No fear." When darkness came they all lay down in their places and she heard some rustling about as the man moved himself further away from her place.

They were up and riding in the early dawn. Carl headed back the way they'd come. Sarah Beth had thought she would be unable to sleep with the man so close to her, but when she woke up, she realized it had been a good night's sleep, most likely from being so tired after the long day's ride. After another arduous day of travel, on the second night Hawk Man woke up screaming, leapt up and moved his blanket farther away from Sarah Beth. The few times during the night she awoke, she could see him sitting still, sometimes smoking, sometimes just leaning forward and rocking back and forth, slowly adding sticks to the little fire. In the early morning he was impatient with his mother, snapping at her, as if to hurry her along. He completely ignored Sarah Beth, leaving her to wonder what was wrong with him, and having no idea.

Two days later they arrived at the encampment near the small town of Lewiston. There was already a wide circle of tipis. Many horses were grazing between the circle of lodges and a large creek. The camp was filled with the busyness and movement of many people. Hawk Man was greeted by a tall man with a scar on his bare shoulder who showed him to one of the tipis. It was the one that they would use. Hawk Man gestured to tell Sarah Beth to take their things inside and unpack them. He seemed to be telling the older woman the same thing, but in spoken words. Then he walked off, as if looking for someone, greeting people as he went along.

Sarah Beth and the older woman, whose name was Red Bird, had smiled at one another during the journey and cooperated to some degree in the duties of their camping, but there had been no other communication between them and no introduction from Hawk Man. Now, they took everything they'd brought with them inside the tipi and Red Bird began unpacking and arranging things around the tipi's circle, and making to piles of robes and bedding on opposite sides..

A few minutes later, she heard voices approaching their tipi, and was surprised to hear a man's voice calling her name. "Sarah Beth, Sarah Beth, can you come out and see me."

She ducked out through the small doorway, looking up into the sun. Then she found the source of the voice. It was Lefty. "Oh my goodness," she said, gasping and covering her mouth with her hand. "Oh my, oh my."

The man smiled and held out his hand to her. "How are you? And how is Big Bear Man, my friend, Abe?"

She could hardly talk, but soon answered his many questions, as well as she could. Finally Lefty smiled approvingly and said, "I knew you would find your way to the right place." Then he looked at her more seriously, "My cousin here, told me why you are here. And he told me Abe refused to take his woman. He says your husband has bad manners, but is a good man anyway." Lefty laughed, and then got serious again, "He also said that the other night he have terrible dream. In the dream, you gave him sickness, a bad sickness that was eating him there," he pointed down at his own crotch. "When he described who you were, I told him you are a Dreamer Woman. You have power to make strong dreams, have power to make them be true. He says he was leaving you alone at first, but now he will stay away from you from now on."

Sarah Beth glanced at Hawk Man who had been listening, but she knew he wasn't able to understand much, if anything, of what they were saying. In spite of her still burning anger, she realized she felt sorry for him, felt sorry for the differences in their ways of living that led them into this situation.

After some silence, she said to Lefty, "Your woman, your women, are they with you?"

Lefty said, "Let's sit." And then he spoke to Hawk Man in their own language. Hawk Man quickly set out Sarah Beth's saddle as a chair for her and sat down on the ground cross-legged. Again Lefty spoke to Hawk Man, and they both laughed. "I said to him, he forgot to bring a woman to cook for us, to make coffee now."

"Oh, I can do that, I'm sorry," she started to get up.

"No, no, we will soon go to my mother's camp. Moon Fish, she is here and my woman Patsy also. They will be happy to see you."

"And I, them," she said, suddenly remembering that Abe once told her this adopted mother was a white woman, the one who taught Lefty his English.

The man went on, "Hawk Man tells me about you and Abe and the land. He says someone else tried to take it away from him and Abe stopped it. He says now he needs help from Indian Agent. He has showed me letter from Abe to the Agent. I do not understand all of it. What do you know?"

"Very little," she said. "He must have gone to the town, to the people at the courthouse right after we left, after I, after . . ."

"Yes, I know, after you came on this journey with your friend here. He has told me about all of that. You are being well taken care of?"

"Yes, yes I am. Thank you. I'm not sure how I can help out or what I am supposed to do here, but it will surely be interesting for me, and I'm thinking I don't have to be afraid now that you are here."

"I call you Dream Woman in our words? I told your man that you have that power and now it has been shown to Hawk Man. He was given this dream to warn him of what would happen if he took you into his bed. You have no worries about that now. He is afraid of you, afraid of your power and of your God protecting you. He has told me this. He will be good to you, but for him it would be good if, in this camp, when you are outside of your tipi, if you be like you are with him, as a woman. It is important for him to look strong at this gathering, not weak, not as if he was your child, or you maybe only a captive." Then he took out a pouch and rolling papers, made a smoke for Hawk Man, handed it to him, then rolled one for himself. He took the feather from his hat and handed it to Sarah Beth. "We will smoke," he said, "and you will bless us by waving the feather to brush the smoke on us. HaHo, Thank you." Then he struck a flame with something like a match in his hands, and motioned for Sarah Beth to stand up.

She stood and waited until the two men exhaled a cloud of their smoke and then she waved the feather to sweep the smoke back at them. They both cupped their hands, cigarettes in their mouths, and made as if they were washing their faces, heads, and chest with the smoke. Then Lefty reached for the feather and the two of them finished the cigarettes.

"If you would like," Lefty said, "now I will take you to my camp for some coffee."

As Abe and Helga were riding out to the house site, Helga suddenly remembered that she'd forgotten to bring her own gloves. "My gloves," she called out to Abe who was riding ahead of her, "will I need them?"

"I think so," he said, "better get them."

"Go on then, I'll be right along."

When she got back to their camp, she slid off Ginger and quickly retrieved the gloves from her shed. Mattie came out into the yard and beckoned to her. When she got close the woman spoke, "He knows. I gave him a letter from Sarah Beth last night. He hasn't spoken to me since then. But he knows what she says she wants to happen. Now, it will be up to you to make him comfortable."

"Mattie, I can't do this. I know I can't. I had a dream of meeting someone, someone who would love me. Not this."

"Do you like him? Have you ever imagined, in your own heart, having him like you? Tell me the God's truth."

"Yes, well, yes, but he is the only man around us. There will be others. I want to wait."

Mattie turned away from her as if to go back inside, then turned her head and looked straight at the young woman, and said, "Think what they have done for you. Is it nothing? Now you have the chance, no the duty, to do this for them. Otherwise, I promise you, they will go their own separate ways, and you will have nothing. This is what I believe will happen. Now go, and see what happens." Then she disappeared into the kitchen.

Helga mounted and rode slowly back the way she'd just come. There were too many thoughts in her mind for her to be able to think clearly about any of them. She couldn't believe this was happening to her, yet she knew it would have been much worse if she'd stayed with the Bishop. He would have taken her himself and she would have been treated worse than Grace. And this strange thing was what Sarah Beth wanted, she said so. She wondered what Mr. Abe wanted. She knew he wanted a child more than anything, she'd heard them talking about it several times, but she also knew that he said he was willing to wait forever with Sarah Beth as his wife, and if it didn't happen . . . She hadn't heard any more than that. She stopped the horse and looked out across the valley to where she could see a thread of smoke rising out of the trees, over at the Indian camp, and it seemed to her that almost everyone around her had always had more than one wife, even if it was against the white people's law, even if it was a sin.

She slid off the horse and led her to the small creek that was still running with snow that melted in the faraway mountains. She let the horse drink; Ginger noisily fluttered her lips when she finished. Helga knelt down to wipe the fresh cold water across her face. She was kneeling beside a small pool and could see her own reflection. She removed her hat and brushed her hand through her hair, straightening it as best she could. She undid two buttons and pulled the collar of her shirt open a bit. She'd always thought he was the best looking man she ever met, but she never thought about it in this way. He had always belonged to Sarah Beth, but now she was giving him up to her, giving him to this Helga reflected in the water, their adopted serving girl. She smiled to think of herself as a serving girl, but that's really what it was. Suddenly she knew that if this happened, she would make them call her his wife and be the same to him as Sarah Beth. She would not allow herself to just be "that girl" to anyone. She stood, pulled herself back up on Ginger and galloped toward the house site.

When he heard the hoof beats of Helga's arrival, Abe was just finishing the plane-work on a board to frame one of the window openings. He'd been imagining that even small squares of glass, formed into a large rectangle, would give them the view of the valley and the far mountains that made this such a special place. He smiled to himself as he thought of the possibility of inserting some stained glass somewhere in the house. But did he always want to be reminded of that incident? He moved the finished board off to the side and went to the pile to choose the next board.

She was dismounting when he got to the lumber pile. He greeted her and said he only had a couple of boards left to prepare and then he'd need her help attaching them to make the perimeter of the larger windows at the front of the house.

"I'm looking for a certain kind of board," he explained, as he started shifting the pile.

Helga pulled on one of her gloves and bent over to help him with the heaviest pieces.

"Should use both gloves," he said.

"I would, but stupid me. I went all the way back for them and I must have left one when we stopped for Ginger and me to get drinks of water, at the little stream. Must have taken it off and left it."

"We'll get it on the way back, but be careful. This wood is rough."

They worked together, unstacking and restacking. Abe picked out two more boards that he wanted and they rebuilt the pile. Just as they were almost finished Helga made a small cry and gripped her bare hand with the gloved hand.

"What," Abe said, "what is it?"

"Splinter. I wasn't being careful like you said to be."

He could see that the pain was starting in her hand and he came around and reached for it.

"It's all right. It's my fault; I'll get it out." She turned away from him; he could see her whole body flinch and he heard her make another sharp sound.

"Let me see," he said, gently taking her by the shoulders and turning her around to face him. He held her hand and carefully unclenched her fist. A large splinter stuck out from between her fingers. There was no way to tell how deep it went. He said, "I've got to get it out. Let's go down to the creek, the water's cold enough to numb your hand. That will help." He took her by the elbow and led her down the slope to the water.

They knelt down beside a shallow pool and he dipped her hand into the water.

"Oww, it's so cold."

"Good," he said, and he couldn't help remembering the day that Sarah Beth had bruised her fingers working on the house, and he'd carried cold water for her hand.

"Now, let me see it. You don't look. Think about something beautiful or funny." He spread her fingers apart and then pinched the tip of the piece of wood. He knew the worst thing would be to have it break off, so he was very careful as he twisted it slightly to get a better grip with his fingers. Then he twisted again and pulled at the same time. Her hand jerked back, but now he was holding the splinter tightly between his fingers and it looked like it was all there. All the boards were new and clean, so now the wound only needed to bleed a bit to cleanse itself.

"You did good. Now you have to pinch it to make it bleed. If you don't get it to bleed, it could close up and have something trapped inside and that wouldn't be good."

"All right," she said now looking at him. "Thank you. I wouldn't have been able to do that to myself." She squeezed on the skin between her fingers, making a small amount of blood drip into the small pool of water and dissolve slowly until it disappeared.

"Can you get anymore?" She nodded a "no" and he said, "I think that's enough. Now hold it in the water and move it around a little."

She smiled, "Are you a doctor?"

"No," he said, "But I've been in a war."

"Sarah Beth told me you were wounded. I could always tell from the way you moved your arm that something was wrong, so I finally asked her. I hope it's all right she told me."

"Of course. Here let me see it now. It needs pressure to stop the bleeding."

He took her hand in his and tightly pinched the area of the small wound.

"Thank you. I'm sorry. First I left my glove, and then I was careless. I'm not much good to you, am I?" She made eye contact with him for a moment, and then looked down.

"You've been wonderful for us. And I'm very happy you came." He reached out and touched her chin with his other hand, tipping her head back. "I just don't know how I should feel about you now that you've grown up."

She pulled her hurt hand out of his grasp and said, "I can do that now." And she closed her eyes as she pinched herself where the pain was. Then Abe found himself leaning forward slightly, looking at her hands until he could feel her breathing on his cheek. His only thought was whether this was how it was supposed to be, how it was supposed to happen. And then, unexpectedly, they were kissing. He reached up and held the back of her head, pressing his mouth to hers, wanting this and not wanting it, but above all not wanting to think about it, not wanting to know it was real.

Helga pulled her face away and his hand slid slowly down her back through her long hair. He realized he was now sitting beside her with his boots in the water, not knowing how he got that way. Helga wiped her mouth, leaving a slight smear of blood from one of the fingers that had been pressing the wound. Then she looked up and straight into his eyes. "Is this what we're supposed to do . . . is it?"

Abe swung his feet out of the water and twisted himself up into a kneeling position, taking her in his arms and softly holding her head against his chest. "I don't know," he said. "I'm not sure. And I'm not sure I can do this even if it is what we're supposed to do."

She mumbled something and he asked her what she said. She leaned her head away from him and said, "Do you like me, do you like me at all?"

He was silent for a long moment, looking down into her eyes, at her lips, at her face, "Yes. I like you very much. I just never thought about it this way before."

Helga pushed back and stood up, looking down at him. "It's her, isn't it? She wants a baby so badly, for you, for herself, but what about me?" As he stood, she turned and started walking up the slope toward the house. Then she came back to where he was now standing motionless, looked up into his eyes, put both arms around him and lifted herself on her toes, tipping back her head. "Kiss me again," she said. "Right now I don't care about her and what she wants. This is for me. Except for that horrible Bishop's boy, I've never been kissed before." Then she reached up and slipped the fingers of the hand that wasn't hurt into his hair and pulled his face toward hers. She pressed against him and let her lips find his and they kissed again, this time for a long time, the kind of kiss when everything else is finally forgotten. Then she broke it off, leaned back and reached up to cradle his face in both of her hands, looking into his eyes.

When he looked away, she pushed herself away from him. "It's bleeding again. I got blood on your face."

"It's all right. It will wash off. But we should wrap your hand, something tight that will soak up any more blood." He turned and knelt back to the water, splashing some of it onto his face, then turning and asking, "Is it gone?"

"Yes, it's gone, and so am I." And with that she ran up and away to the half-built house, leaving him to follow after.

They barely talked the rest of the afternoon. Abe finished planing, cutting and preparing the boards for the window space frames. Helga spent the time straightening up, doing one-handed sweeping of the sawdust and shavings into neat little piles. She gathered all the tools into one area. On the way back to camp at the end of their workday, they paused at the little stream and he retrieved her glove. When they'd returned, Helga went straight into the kitchen, saying she wanted to have Mattie put a proper salve and dressing on her hand. Abe went riding off to check the cattle before dark.

As soon as Sarah Beth saw Patsy outside the tipi in Lefty's camp, she could tell that the woman was well into pregnancy. They hadn't seen one another since the wedding back in Missouri, but the smiles they exchanged were genuine. Patsy said some words of welcome, and commented on Sarah Beth's new dress, "Now you have two good dress." She went inside the tipi and came back with a pot of hot water and some cups.

"I remember you like tea," she said.

"Yes, thank you."

Hawk Man and Lefty sat a short distance away, engaged in a rapid-fire conversation that, from the sound of it, could have been either argument or excited agreement. An older woman with gray hair and light skin, dressed in the Indian way, came slowly out of the tipi.

"This Lefty mother, Moon Fish," Patsy said. "And this Sarah Beth, woman of Lefty's friend."

The woman nodded in greeting, and then sat on a piece of log that seemed to be there for that purpose. Sarah Beth sank to her knees and took the cup that was held out to her. Patsy poured hot water into it, releasing a mint aroma.

The older woman also took a cupful, and then said quietly. "You're a white woman, but wearing Indian dress. You are his woman now?" She gestured toward Hawk Man.

"No," she said as she wondered if the woman didn't hear Patsy mention Abe. "Only traveling with him." How else should she explain it? It sounded awkward, but she didn't want the woman to think otherwise.

"I see." They sipped their tea in silence, and Patsy disappeared back inside the tipi.

The woman stood up, set her cup by the tipi's door and said, "Let's walk."

Sarah Beth did likewise and followed her. There was a field near the encampment and it was filled with some kind of daisies and countless insects. Their humming made a background sound to the noise of the camp where there was much activity, and camps and tipis still being set up. Those sounds diminished as the two of them got further away. Finally they came to a stream that wandered alongside the far edge of the field, gurgling its way through small boulders and sticks.

The older woman found a seat on a half-buried log and motioned for Sarah Beth to sit. "It's good for me to talk English. I think I am forgetting most of it after all these years."

"Moon Fish, is that it?"

"You can call me Kate, I'd like that."

Sarah Beth picked up a small stick and began picking its bark away. She didn't know what to say to this woman who had been living like this for so long. She wanted to ask about everything, but didn't want to appear rude.

Finally, to break the silence, she asked, "How long have you been living this way?"

"Probably thirty-five years, or more. And you, how long have you been out here?"

"Oh, we just arrived. It's over a year now, though."

"And Lefty tells me you had a husband."

"Yes. I still do. His name is Abe."

"Lefty's friend, the one he gave the Hummingbird to?" Sarah Beth nodded yes, and began scratching in the sandy soil with the stick. "Don't be anxious, young woman, I am happy to see you, happy to be with a white woman who is not married to a government man. They're the only ones I've been around all these years. You have children?"

"Me? No, not yet. You see . . ." she said and then stopped. For some reason she wanted to talk to this woman, confide in her, but she couldn't do that. It would be bad manners.

"I can guess," the woman said. "You've tried. But what about this Hawk Man, why are you with him? Pardon my inquisition. Isn't that a lovely English word? Inquisition . . . Pardon my questions if it makes you uncomfortable."

"No, no. He, Hawk Man offered for us to settle on his land. Abe, that's my husband, had to promise to follow Indian ways if we accepted. But we didn't know that meant sharing wives. This man wanted my husband to take his woman and I would come with him for one month. I guess you could call it a payment for the land."

"A lease payment, you could say," Kate said. Sarah Beth looked down at the tip of the stick. The woman went on, "Well, you're not the first one of us to be used in some kind of a bargain."

"In what way? What bargains?"

"Has happened to other white women. Mostly to Indian women, but a few of us whites. When I first met Lefty's father he was passing through the country of the tribe that had captured me. I was what we used to call "smitten" by his greatness, and I got a message to him that I would run away from the Indian man who thought he owned me. I didn't want to go back to the whites; my people were hard and cruel. But I was not happy with the Indians in that desert down there, or with some of the ways they treated their women. He replied to me that if I ran away with him it might start a war, so he had better just buy me. I guess I was kind of flattered that I cost him three fine horses."

"And you've been with him ever since?" The woman nodded yes. "Any other children, besides Lefty?" Sarah Beth asked.

She looked at the young woman for what seemed like a long time. "He was already with the man who took me, a very young son. The mother died before I came, in her next child's birth. He knows of this. What I'm going to say, I don't tell to anyone, but you seem to need to know and I'd ask you not to speak of it . . . I have never been able to have any children of my own. I was shot through the belly in the battle when I was captured. It tore up my insides, and I was fortunate to survive. One of their medicine women saved me, but I haven't even had a moon time since that . . ." She paused for awhile. "But I have raised many of these children, as if they were my own."

"Abe and I are almost desperate for a child, at least he is. I feel so useless for him." She wasn't going to talk about what was going on with Helga, but she wanted something from this woman, she could feel the strength of this person and was feeling almost a physical hunger to have something from her that she couldn't describe.

"Tell me," Kate said, "has Hawk Man used you, in the way of a man and a woman? You don't have to answer if you don't want to."

"No, he has actually been quite considerate. He had a very bad dream our second night on this journey. He has stayed away from me at night, in a separate bed, but he wants it to look like we are together. For his reputation, I suppose."

"Of course." Kate took out a small pipe and filled it slowly. She pulled a match from somewhere in her dress. "Do you smoke?" She asked.

"No, I don't. Neither does Abe."

"Well, I do. They don't like it. It's not for a woman, some say, but it is for me. Here, kneel down in front of me." Sarah did as she was asked and the woman began puffing on her pipe and exhaling smoke across the top of Sarah Beth's head and hair, waving her hand to spread the smoke down and around her body. "When Lefty came home from the East, he told me about you, and about your husband. He said you may be a Dreamer. What you tell me says so as well. There are very few women who can protect themselves with Dreams. But you must cleanse yourself whenever you use this power or you, yourself, will begin to dream of bad things. That is why I am washing you with this smoke. Whenever you have a powerful dream or someone close to you or even threatening to you has one, you must cleanse yourself in the smoke. I will give you some of this mixture for your use."

She stopped smoking and emptied the ashes out of the bowl of the pipe. From far away they heard the notes of a bugle. Sarah Beth shifted her weight and said, "I don't have a pipe."

"You won't need a pipe. You can place herbs on a stone, light them, and use your hands to pull the smoke toward yourself." She put the pipe away inside her dress. "Now about your children. We'll talk about it tomorrow. That bugle means a meeting will begin this evening. I must help prepare the meal."

"May I help?"

"Of course." She stood and stretched, and said, "Gets harder to get up all the time, always moving about, sleeping on the ground, riding horseback. But I'm all right, just getting older."

As they were walking back toward the camp, Kate asked Sarah Beth if she would give her the peeled stick she was still carrying.

"Oh, I didn't even notice I still had it."

"Good. I'll need something of yours, something that you've handled."

Sarah Beth started to ask why, but stopped when she remembered something Mary Wolf told her about not asking too many questions. And about waiting for the answers. "If you're supposed to know something, it will come to you," she'd said.

Abe and Helga were silent at their supper, but Mattie was cheerful and talkative, reminiscing about the old days when the South was both the best and the worst of places to live. She talked about the endless fields of cotton and corn, and the hundreds of folks who would gather together for food and dancing, and celebrations of their own design. All Negroes at events only allowed by the plantation owners because to try to stop it would have provoked some kind of dangerous and unpredictable reaction among the slaves. She talked about all of the romances that were begun at those events, and about the ones that ended at the same occasions. Then she served them pie. An older woman at the Hawk Man camp had shown her a kind of berry that grew wild and was now ripening, and she'd made a pie for their dessert pleasure.

Abe and Helga still hardly spoke or even looked at one another, seeming to pay close attention to Mattie's stories, and eating with little or no appetite. When they finished, Mattie cleared the table and started heating water for cleaning up. Helga stopped her and said that she would take care of it.

"And how are you going to wash these plates and pans with only one hand?"

"I'll wash," Abe said quickly.

"And I can dry," Helga responded.

"Well, all right. All these memories have put me in a mind to write some letters, so I think I'll just run along." She quickly took off her apron and hung it on its hook. "You two have a nice evening, now," she said as she ducked out the doorway.

The two of them began the chore of cleaning up, still holding onto their silence. Helga was trying to think of a way to apologize for her abruptness that afternoon, but the words wouldn't come to her. Most likely, she thought, because she didn't feel she'd done anything wrong. Abe seemed lost in his own thoughts, even though he wanted, above all, to tell Helga that she couldn't expect anything further between them. It just wasn't possible.

When the last dish was put away, Helga hung the dish-towel and then straightened her hair. Abe suddenly asked, "Are you working on any quilting projects these days?" He reached down into a cupboard and pulled out a small package, and said, "Because last time I was in town I saw these and thought you might be able to use them." He handed the package to her and she pulled the paper apart and opened it.

"A new pair of scissors." She worked them open and shut in her good hand. "They're perfect. Thank you . . . And yes, I am working on a new project. I don't suppose you'd like to see it?"

He didn't respond at first, but then slowly crossed his arms across his chest and nodded yes.

"But I can't bring it over here. It's all still in pieces. Come. Just for a minute." She led the way out of the kitchen. They walked somewhat separately across the open area toward her little shelter. Overhead the stars created a brilliant multitude, and although there was no moon, the starlight was good enough to see their way by.

As they neared Helga's place, she stopped him and said she needed to straighten up a bit before she could have a visitor. Then she hurried forward and ducked inside past the heavy canvas door. Abe turned around and faced out across the valley. He could see a dim glow of light from the Indian camp, and couldn't stop himself from wondering where Sarah Beth was this night. Was she alone or with the Hawk Man? He knew these thoughts would do him no good, and there wasn't anything he could change now. If he'd been wrong to allow it, so be it.

"You can come in now."

He'd never been inside the small space since she'd moved into it. There were small objects hanging and placed on the board walls, many more than he would have expected. Where did they all come from? There were glass animals and miniature paintings of country scenes, as well as little mottos embroidered and framed to hang on walls. The overall look made it feel like someone had been there for a long time and decorated every possible nook or cranny.

"Where did you get all of these little things?"

"Sarah Beth brought most of them back from her trip east. Some were hers when she was young, but many she got from the church, where they were stored away. She said no one seemed to want them anymore. She said people were so kind to her there because her father had died and she probably could have asked for anything, but she said she wasn't thinking of herself at that time. Do you like it here?"

"It's, how you say, quaint. I would never have imagined."

"And then some of these, the little toys, came from the Bishop's camp. I thought those people owed me something for all the time I spent taking care of their children when they were too busy."

"Now I'll know what to get you when I go to town. Instead of scissors."

"Oh no, Mister-um, Abe, the scissors are wonderful, just the size I don't have. Here, let me show you this." She began laying out small squares of cloth, each made up of smaller squares. He tried to stand back out of her way, but there was no room to move away. "Here," she said, pushing some bags under the bed, "you'll just have to kneel down here. I don't have any chairs, do I?"

"Where would you put one?"

She laughed, and then pointed at the square in the center. "It's kind of a story quilt, about some people who have come a very long way to get to this place in the center. See the green? It's supposed to be the grass, and those purple triangles are mountains. That whole square of different colored blues is the big sky. On one side of the quilt will be mostly desert country they pass through, but there will be rivers. On the other side will be where they came from with its forests and fields. What do you think?"

"I never knew you could tell that kind of a story in a quilt."

"Me either. I just decided to try it. Maybe it won't work out, or maybe it won't look good. I don't know." She knelt down beside him and picked up one square. It was blue and gray and there was a tiny red patch off to one side of it. "This is where the man gets wounded in that War back there. See the two armies are the two colors, gray and blue."

"And who is this man?"

Helga seemed to blush, looked away, and then her eyes found his. "Oh, just someone."

Then they were kissing, once and again. Helga pushed him away and began grabbing the quilt squares and stuffing them back into their bag. When she'd finished, she turned and sat on the edge of the bed, with Abe still kneeling, now in front of her. She took his hands and placed them around her back.

"Hold me," she said as she leaned back so her head touched the bed. Abe leaned forward, his knees still on the hard dirt floor. His body was between her legs and his elbows on either side of her. There was still the stiffness in his one elbow, but he was able to place both of his hands on her shoulders and reach forward with his face to nuzzle into her neck with his lips. There was a soft fragrance coming from her skin, and then he was trying to push away, back away from her, but her hands found the back of his head and pulled his face down onto her breasts, her young and fully-formed breasts, now rapidly rising and falling with her breathing.

"Be careful," she mumbled.

"I'm sorry," he said, trying once again to push himself away.

He felt the strength in her arms as she held him to herself, "No, be careful how nice you are to me because I might love you." She blew out one of the candles and quickly pulled her loose-fit shirt up and over her head. Her eyes were closed, but her back was arched to him. He touched one of her nipples with his tongue and both of their bodies shuddered, in unison. A wolf howled from somewhere nearby.

"I don't," she said, "I never . . ."

"All right. It's all right. I understand."

"No, no, that's not what I mean. You don't understand. I can't believe it, because I dreamed it, I dreamed this, this, weeks ago, us, now, except she was watching from the doorway."

Abe lifted himself so that he was above her, supported by his own arms. She was pushing up against his shoulders with her hands. "You dreamed about this?" he said softly.

"Yes, yes, only I didn't feel anything . . . Not like now, now I'm shaking all over and I'm crying inside."

"I'm sorry." He started to pull away and she caught him and pulled his face back down against her chest.

"Don't be sorry. I'm crying because I'm happy. I don't care about her, or anything, anything else. Here," she began unfastening the buttons on his shirt, twisting her body so she could pull him down next to her. "Let me . . ." And then she had his shirt half off. They lay there pressed against one another, skin touching skin, breathing heavily, not moving, except for her lips wandering across his face and seeking his lips. "Show me," she said.

He pushed off his boots and slipped off her shoes. They lay back, nearly falling off the narrow bed that was hardly wide enough for her when alone. She pulled him on top of herself to keep him from rolling onto the floor. Then they were very still, not moving, just trembling along the full length of their bodies. Waiting . . .

Abe was careful as he continued slowly undressing her. She pulled a covering from under the bed up and over them. He slipped off more of his own clothing, saying, "We don't have to do this."

She laughed once sharply, and then some more, as she was saying, "We might as well since we're this far." Now they were both laughing, and their hands were everywhere, stroking and kneading and scratching and touching, touching . . . And almost without knowing, he slipped inside of her.

She gasped, and thrust herself against him, and then she let a small cry escape her throat.

"Did I hurt you?"

"No," she said, "only a little."

They fell asleep locked in each other's arms and awakened only enough so he could move off of her and try to fit between the wall and her warm body. The next time he awoke he saw just the slightest hint of light coming into the space. He propped his head up on his good elbow and watched as a few minutes passed and her face became more visible. Its softness gave him renewed desire. But he didn't move, not wanting to awaken her, wondering what it would be like to be with her from now on, to see her again in the daytime, from now on.

He slowly eased himself down the short bed and up and over her legs. His hands searched the floor for his clothing. She stirred and moaned. He found his boots and pants, gathered them up, and was quickly gone out into dawn's early light. He dressed as best he could and walked to the barn, whistled for Bird, saddled up, and told himself he needed to go check the cattle. He rode off, fighting to keep his mind empty of thoughts, of memories, and new desires.

The meetings between the chiefs and with the government people took most of a week. During that time Sarah Beth found herself being more and more accepted by Lefty's woman and mother, and by some of the other women. No one asked her any direct questions, and she assumed that Kate was explaining to them some story about why she was there. She was taught how to make a kind of greasy bread, fried in fat, and how to peel and cook some of the roots that were kept in the packs of food.

One day, Kate again asked her if they could walk together. They returned to the same place by the small stream. When they were seated, Kate pulled out the stick she'd taken from Sarah Beth after their first visit.

"My son tells me you will be going back soon. So, I want to tell you some things."

"Yes?"

"We will come and visit you this summertime. If you want, I can help you find your body's truth. Find your emptiness, and we will make a way for you to fill it with a child. It is what we can do with certain herbs and prayers. But only if you want this."

They were quiet for awhile. Sarah Beth waited to see if the woman was going to say more, or if she was supposed to say something, to respond.

"I will try anything," she said softly.

"It is not easy. You will go without food and water for a time. You will be alone. I will take care of you, but you will become sick from the medicine." Then she looked up with a smile, "But I promise, you will not die from doing this."

The woman pulled her leather dress up to her thighs and slipped down the grassy bank until she could put her legs into the water. Then she glanced back at Sarah Beth. "You remind me of my sister. She was older than me when I was taken, and I never saw her again, but you look like my memory of her. Her name was Doris. I wonder where she is?"

Sarah Beth removed her new moccasins and lifted her dress so she could sit beside the woman and push her feet into the sand at the water's edge. "I never had a sister, but I always wanted one."

"Well, I'm old enough to be your mother," Kate said, "but I think I'll call you Little Sister just the same." They were quiet for awhile. Kate stirred the water with the stick. "Do you want to talk about Hawk Man? Has he still not tried for you?"

"No, not at all. Inside the tipi we are like strangers. Each under our own robes. He comes in late and leaves early. Sometimes he brings me a small candy from the trading post store, but he hardly speaks to me. Then when we are outside the tipi, he always wants me beside him, serving him. I don't mind, but he's very different from anyone I've ever known, very stern with everyone, and then he will suddenly laugh like a crazy man."

"He is a Changer. He is like that, just how you say different, but it is his place in the tribe that he must be like that. And I think he is very much afraid of you. He wants it to appear that he is taking care of you and being taken care of in every way, but he is afraid of you, just the same."

"The dream?"

"Yes, afraid of the dream, and of you. You are a very strong woman, maybe like Mary Wolf."

They were quiet. The soft bubbling of the stream was like a quiet melody, and Kate began to sing in a low voice, too soft for Sarah Beth to hear any words, just sounds. The song made her feel lonely, made her think about Abe, Abe and Mattie, and of course, Helga.

"Yes, Little Sister, you are sad now, I feel that in you."

"I am lonely."

"I know how that feels. I have been lonely all these years, but there are some things worse than being lonely."

Sarah Beth didn't say anything for awhile, then she spoke up, and said, "I did something maybe very foolish before I left home . . . Can I tell you?"

"Yes, certainly."

"There has been a young girl living with us since we left Utah, all the time we've been living where we are now. She's a good girl. She ran away from the Mormons, the same ones we had to get away from ourselves. And then we were taken care of by other good people of that church. This girl, this young woman, when she escaped she came to us, and she has been my friend . . . like my Little Sister."

"That must be nice for you."

"It was. But now I don't know. When I left I told her to be with my husband so maybe they could . . . and I left a letter for my husband saying the same thing. Now I am crying inside all the time because of this, because of what this might mean for us, for all three of us. But I was so upset, I'd given up, nothing was working for us. I couldn't go on and I knew inside that it was because of me, and now I've done this and it's just terribly wrong," she was crying.

"There's nothing wrong with that," Kate said putting her arm around her new Little Sister's shoulders, pulling her close. "You will always be his first woman, I can see that. I know that. I think it will bring you even closer to one another. Besides she's in your family now and that's better than him having Hawk Man's woman."

For the whole next week after their night together, Abe and Helga avoided one another except for the necessary exchanges having to do with work and at meals. Mattie acted as though this was all just normal and kept herself busy, continuing to unpack her things. She was making the shed and kitchen as home-like as possible. Abe spent a couple of nights out at the home-site, going back out there after having supper with the two women. He claimed he needed to work as much as possible and get started early during the longer, warmer days.

One evening, he didn't show up for supper. After waiting quite awhile, Helga packed up his portion of the meal and rode out to make sure he was all right. She found him sitting by a small fire, roasting a rabbit over it, and carving on a long piece of wood. She dismounted carefully to keep the food from spilling out of the container in her bag. She let Morning go loose.

She sat down across the fire from him, removed the food she'd brought and set it between them where he could reach it. "Thought you might be hungry," she said.

"I am," he pointed at the rabbit and fire.

"I guess I thought you might be having some trouble or something," she said looking away across the valley. "Or maybe you'd gone over to the Indian camp."

"No, just using my time to get some things done I don't get to do during the daytime."

"What is that?"

"It's a kind of a railing. Thought I'd make it for the stairway to the loft in the back there. This," he said, twisting the piece of wood he was working on. "Kind of a knobby thing for getting a good grip climbing up there."

She pushed the food toward him. "While you're waiting for the rabbit to cook," she said.

"Thank you . . . Helga, I have to say something, but I don't know how.'

"Then don't," she said. "I probably know what it is anyway."

"How would you know?"

"Because I think you feel bad, that's all."

"Feel bad?"

"For Sarah Beth, even though it was her idea."

"No, that's not it." He took a piece of bread and then said through the mouthful, "That's good, you make it?"

"No, Mattie."

He swallowed the bread and said, "I guess I feel bad for you."

"Why for me? I'm not a little girl, you know. And now I'm certainly a woman."

"But I shouldn't have, I mean . . . Maybe I spoiled your life, even if it was because of her."

They were quiet for awhile. She pushed the jar of stew she'd brought toward him. He opened it and began eating. "I wouldn't expect you to know that it made me happy," she said. "Only sad too, because it can't last, can't go on for us. But I don't want you to feel sorry for me. I'm my own woman. I mean, I'm thankful for you and her and for what you've done for me, but I could leave anytime I want to, and maybe I will so I don't have to . . ."

He waited for her to go on. When she didn't, he asked, "Don't have to what?"

She turned away from him, and said quietly, "So I don't have to see the two of you being happy again when she comes back, and I'm . . . ." Then she got up quickly and started walking down the slope toward the small creek where Morning was grazing.

He caught up with her, placed his hand on her shoulder and turned her around. "I see you brought her horse."

"More fun. Besides she has a new one, doesn't she?"

"Helga, I really care for you."

"What does that mean? I love you, but it won't make any difference." She tried to walk away, but he held on to her.

"We're on Indian land now. And I promised to follow their ways. I can . . ." He didn't go on, but kept holding on to her. She looked up at him, and then touched his lips with her fingertips.

"Be good to me, that's all I ask. Don't turn against me." Then she kissed him.

He returned the kiss and knelt down on the grassy slope. She stood next to him, holding his head to her waist. The sun was gone, behind the far western ridges, and a bird sang in the willows on the other side of the creek. Then she knelt and they kissed again and pulled each other down, their hands and mouths moving quickly as this became more familiar.

The next morning, they rode together back to the camp and tried to act as if nothing had happened and nothing had changed. Mattie fixed a breakfast for them and once they'd eaten, she told them she was going over to the Skinner place to learn about drying meat and making jerky. She said she'd expect Abe to get her an antelope, or preferably a deer. Then she asked him to hook up the buggy.

"Are things going well?" she asked him as she settled herself into the buggy's seat and prepared to leave. "You don't have to say a word, just an old woman's curiosity."

"Things are all right," he said. "Have a good day."

About an hour later, when he was about to leave for work at the home site, Mary Wolf and Carl came galloping up.

The woman was yelling at him, "Hurry, come. Two men, bad men."

He ran into the shed and grabbed his pistol. The rifle was already on the saddle. Helga came running as he was asking Mary Wolf, "Where?"

"They came to our camp, told us we better leave. They rode toward your house. Hurry."

"I'm coming, too" Helga yelled and ran off to get Morning.

"Can't wait," Abe yelled after her.

"I'll catch up."

He jumped on Bird and the three riders took off at a run to the home site.

Bird was the fastest and freshest of the horses and Abe was in the lead when he saw a thin line of smoke rising from behind the low hill where the house was. He urged the horse to even greater speed and came around some trees just in time to see two riders mounting up and leaving the site. A fire was just taking off in a pile of brush right near the half-built house. He pulled up, spun Bird around and waited a few seconds for Mary Wolf and Carl to come close enough to hear him yelling.

"Try to keep the fire from the house. I'm going after them."

He kicked Bird around and took off, cutting across rough ground to save distance. The two riders caught sight of him and began to race their horses. His only hope of catching up to them was trusting Bird to find her way through the tangle of brush and boulders at top speed. He knew this was what the animal had been bred for, ever since Lefty called her a "war pony" and told stories of her ability to speed across open ground and difficult trails. He was closing ground on the riders ahead of him when one of their horses stumbled. The rider nearly pitched off, regained his seat, but had been slowed down and was now closer to Abe. The horse was limping. The man pulled it to a stop, leaped off and took cover behind a fallen log. Two shots rang out from his gun, both missing Abe. He slowed and circled away from the shooter, debating with himself whether to go after the other one or stay and deal with the one behind the log.

The shooter's horse was trotting away, probably startled by the shots, and Abe decided to leave this man behind and try to catch the still-mounted rider. He gained ground as they raced across the valley floor. The larger creek was just ahead, and he saw the man's horse slow slightly and hesitate at the water's edge. They were downstream a ways and Abe asked Bird for more, urging her down through the brush. She took the width of the creek in four jumps and they were up and out on the other bank. Now Abe could hear the other horse splashing through the water. He quickly leaped to the ground and hunched down behind a large rock.

The other rider came slowly up out of the creek, looking behind himself. He pulled out his rifle and held it across the saddle as he moved forward, nearing Abe's hiding place. Then his horse neighed loudly, likely sensing Bird's presence. The man put his gun up to his shoulder and scanned the area in front of himself and his horse. Abe stepped out with own rifle pointed straight at the man.

"Stop right there," he said.

The man slid off the far side of his horse, firing in Abe's direction from behind the animal. On the second shot Abe felt a sudden flash of pain in his shoulder just as the man's horse reared away, leaving him exposed. Abe fired once and the man crumpled forward. Leaning on his gun and fighting to remain conscious, Abe moved slowly toward the man on the ground. There was a loud scream, and then the man on the ground fired again. A small clod of dirt burst from the ground a few feet from Abe, who then circled behind the shaking form on the ground. He waited, moved closer, and pushed the barrel of his rifle into the man's back.

"Turn over." He pushed at the form with the toe of his boot. There was no response other than a single spasm twisting the body. He grabbed the man's gun, jerked it loose and used his wounded arm to throw it away from them. He'd forgotten about his wound in the horrible commotion of the other man's agony, and he nearly passed out from the pain of using that arm. He looked down at the man's face and recognized him as one of the men from Nevada, the ones who promised to take the place away from Abe and the Indians.

He'd seen enough death on the battlefields to know this one was gone. He'd killed him, killed a man, he thought, but only to save himself. No doubt it was him or the other. Now he ripped the torn sleeve off where the blood was seeping from his wounded shoulder. Same arm, that was the good luck. But a serious wound, that was the bad luck. He suddenly realized he didn't know if Carl or Mary Wolf were armed, and this man's partner was still out there. He wrapped the torn-off sleeve around his armpit and used his teeth and his good hand to tie a knot and cinch it tight. He whistled for Bird and, using a boulder as a step, managed to get into the saddle. They crossed back over the creek. He urged her into a slow gallop, even as the jerky motion caused him more excruciating pain. After a short distance, he had to slow the horse to the gentlest gait he could, a slow, loping canter, and he found that by leaning forward against Bird's mane and neck he could still hold on, but not feel as much of the jarring. It wasn't far to go, and he hoped it wasn't too far for him to hold on, to stay on.

He heard shots, one from a rifle, and the others from a smaller gun. He again kicked Bird into a run and felt himself screaming in pain and anger as they closed in on the scene ahead. The other stranger was kneeling on the ground with one leg bent out at a strange angle. Helga stood a few feet away with her pistol pointed at the man. Carl was sitting up on his horse, a hatchet held at the ready. There was the smell of smoke. The last clear thought Abe had was that there was no smoke in the air, just its smell.

Helga handed the gun up to Carl and moved to Bird's side, where she could help lower Abe to the ground. She grabbed the rope from his saddle, and went quickly back to Carl, trading him the rope for her gun. She gestured the motions of tying up the man on the ground, hoping Carl would know what she was saying. He seemed to understand, got off his horse and went toward the man, who struggled to stand and move away. Carl simply hit him on the head with the flat of the hatchet and he fell over on his face. The Indian hurried to tie the man's hands behind his back and then made a loop around the man's uninjured leg and tied that to a nearby bush. Then he turned back in the direction of the house and made a loud animal call. It was answered by the same call, but in a woman's voice.

Helga was now on the ground beside Abe, holding his head in one hand and looking for the source of the blood with the other. She let his head down and pulled a folding knife from her skirt pocket, removing the blood-soaked material from Abe's shoulder, then cutting off her own shirt-sleeve. Mary Wolf arrived just at that moment and immediately got down beside Helga. She grabbed and ripped a clump of grass from the ground, shook off the dirt around its roots, and pushed it against the wound. Abe screamed and tried to sit up, but his head fell back again, held by Helga's hands.

"This stop bleeding," Mary Wolf said. "Is not so bad."

"But it is bad, isn't it?"

"He will live to be old," the Indian woman said. "He is protected by Lefty's spirits. Can you bring me water?"

Helga gently laid Abe's head down on the ground, and said, "But I have nothing to carry it in." She was standing, waiting.

"Just soak some clothing, anything." Helga ran to the creek. She stripped off her skirt as she was running, thankful she wore an underskirt as well. She soaked the cloth in a small pool, partially wrung it out, then ran back as fast as she could.

Mary Wolf shouted something to Carl, and he rode off. She said she'd told him to go and make sure if the other man was dead. When he was gone, she told Helga to keep the pistol pointed at this one.

"How is he, Abe?" Helga asked, relieved that the Indian woman was taking charge.

"He's alive. Is good he sleeps. We cannot move him without wagon. Where is?"

"Oh, Mattie took it over to the Skinners' place. The buggy is there."

"We have to get back to fire too, see it is stopped."

"How did you stop it?" Helga had forgotten about the fire.

Mary Wolf looked up from the wound. "Log of tree. Tie ropes to both end. Carl one rope, me other. Pull through fire, spread out to stop burning. But maybe still some fire."

"I don't see any smoke."

"Good."

They heard the sound of Carl's horse coming back. "You stay with him here. Shoot that one if need to. We go stop any fire and return with little wagon."

Carl shouted something in their language. Mary Wolf turned to Helga, "He say that one dead. You be all right?"

"Yes, I'm all right. Is there anything more I can do for Mr. Abe?"

"Only be with him. If he wakes, he will not know where he is. Help him know. We hurry. Keep him not moving." She caught up her horse, mounted and waved at Carl to follow. As soon as they were gone, the man who was tied up started screaming and swearing at Helga. She pointed the gun at him and ordered him to be still. He didn't stop shouting, so she fired a shot that made leaves fall from the bush Carl had tied him to. He crawled around behind it and was quiet.

"You try anything, and you'll be as dead as your partner. Hear me?" There was no answer and she knelt beside Abe and once again cradled his head in one arm, still holding the pistol in the other. After some time had passed, Abe's eyes opened and he struggled to raise himself off the ground. Helga gently held him down and made soothing sounds to calm him.

"What . . . ?"

"You've been hurt. But it's going to be all right."

"I've been shot . . . haven't I?"

"Yes, but it's not bad."

"Feels kind of like last time," he said, trying to smile up at her. "Same arm."

She heard a sound from behind the small tree and remembered her other task. She checked the pistol and found only two shots remaining. No more warning shots, she thought to herself. Then she leaned closer to Abe's face, trying to hear what he was trying to say. He was quiet and his eyes looked up at her, seeming to be asking something, but not speaking.

She bent herself over close to his face, and kissed him carefully. They stayed like that until she pulled away to look toward her prisoner. The man was quiet. Abe reached up and pulled her close again. She heard him say, "Thank you."

She replied, "I love you."

Epilogue

After three weeks of traveling to and from and at the gathering where the meetings were held, Sarah Beth and Hawk Man returned to his camp. As soon as they heard what had happened with the shootings, she raced across the valley to their own area. She slid off and ran from her horse to the kitchen's door-flap, throwing it aside. Mattie and Helga were standing at the sink and counter, and turned to her as if they'd been waiting.

"Where is he?"

Mattie gestured into the small alcove where the bed was. Abe was napping when she reached the side of the bed and leaned over him, saying his name over and over again. He woke up and saw her leaning above him. Mattie and Helga went outside and let the door-flap close.

"You've come back," he said. "How are you?"

"Me? How are you? Oh my God, I've missed you terribly, and now this. No, don't move. Can I get you anything?'

"No, I have everything. I don't need much just lying here."

"I can't believe it. I had to go away and then this happened. Is it over? Will they be back? Is the house all right? But really, how is the pain for you? You must need something."

He turned his head and nodded toward the kitchen. "Get a chair and sit here with me. Tell me all about your travels, all about it."

She pulled up the chair and sat down. "And then you'll tell me everything?"

He hesitated, and then said, "Of course."

During the month that followed, Abe healed quickly. The stitches that held the skin of his shoulder together had been removed by the doctor from Silver City, who was pleased there was no infection. When he'd first seen this patient, coming all the way out from the town at Helga's insistence, he was quite put off by the dirt from Mary Wolf's grass-root dressing that he found inside the wound. He'd cleaned, sewn, and wrapped it, and said he'd be back. The Indian woman continued visiting almost every day to see that Abe was beginning to move his arm so it wouldn't, as she said, "freeze up."

Sarah Beth moved back home the day after their return, and there was some awkwardness when the Indian woman visited. The only time they'd had much talk, they each assured the other that nothing had happened between themselves and the men.

The situation between Sarah Beth and Helga was not so easy, and they tended to stay out of each other's way. When Helga wanted to visit with Abe for anything, and it was fairly often since she'd taken over monitoring the cattle, Sarah Beth always found reasons to be nearby. As soon as Abe was able to sit outside in the sunshine and even to take short walks, that changed somewhat, but there was still mostly silence between the two women. Mattie tried to keep things from breaking down, and was after both of them to get along like they used to; if not for their own sakes, then at least for Abe, who needed peace and quiet in order to heal properly.

Lefty, Moon Fish, Patsy, and a few others arrived in time for some early summer ceremonies and there was a great reunion among all the parties. Although Helga had never met the new arrivals before, she'd heard the stories and had long known all about Bird and how she was a gift from Lefty.

By the time two months had passed since the incident with the fire and Abe's wounding, he was riding and even able to practice shooting one-armed with a lightweight rifle Mike Skinner loaned him. He was amazed at the difference in recovery time between this wound and the previous one. As he said, "Second time's much better."

He and Sarah Beth had reconciled once he told her he tried to do what she asked of him, but that it had been difficult. His arm provided an excuse for the two of them not to have full relations in bed, but they held on to one another as best they could during those nights. She didn't press him to know what exactly went on between him and Helga, and, for his part, he was relieved when she told him that Hawk Man's fear of his terrible dream had prevented him from ever touching her. Some tensions did arise when Kate called on Sarah Beth and told her she should prepare for her week of 'medicine.' She told Sarah Beth she would need to be alone for a few days of fasting and medicine treatment.

Sarah Beth once again felt she was at a crossroads concerning her desire for her own child, and for Abe to have what he so clearly desired. Now here she was going away again, leaving him alone. She couldn't help being afraid he would use the time of her absence to spend more time with Helga. She still didn't think she truly knew where things were between the two of them, but she was too proud to ask. Mattie was noncommittal, and Helga wouldn't talk with her about anything except ranching and household affairs. Sarah Beth wanted to press Abe about the issue, but felt that it wouldn't be satisfying unless he told her on his own. When she mentioned it to Kate, the woman simply replied, "What is most important?"

Sarah Beth was given a sweat bath in a small lodge. Water was poured on red-hot rocks, and herbs were added to fill the small space with smoke and steam. She coughed at first, but then lay down to breathe the air closest to the ground as she'd been told to do. Afterward, she was dressed in a simple cloth-sack dress and her face was painted, although she couldn't see what it looked like. Then Kate led her away from the camp area and up an animal trail to the top of a low hillside where one could look down on the open land below. From up there she could see smoke from the two camps, but not the camps themselves. The woman told her that sometime in the future she would be given a more intensive ceremony to help her make a baby, that this was just a purification from their journey. She was given a blanket and a feather. Kate hugged her and said she was to eat the roots she'd been given and then to pray for what she wanted most. Also to pray for her man, and her family. Kate promised she would return at dawn on the second day and take her back down to their camp to share water and food. Then she left.

Sarah Beth had explained to Abe what she was about to do, and was careful not to make it seem that it was in anyway related to whatever had happened between him and Helga. She told him, "This was a plan from Kate, Lefty's mother, before I returned home. She wants to help me and I agreed."

On the second night that she was gone, Abe took a bedroll and some bread and walked slowly to the house site. He wanted to go further to see where they'd buried the man he'd killed, but he'd been almost too weak to even get as far as the house. He set about making a bed for himself, ate the bread, had some water from the small creek, and as darkness came, he lay down to try to sleep. The stars seemed especially bright and as the minutes slipped away and darkness deepened, he listened to the cries of coyotes that seemed to be split into two groups, the one behind him and the other across the shallow valley. He wondered how Sarah Beth was doing, what she was doing. They'd never spent any time apart during the past weeks. Although it was still somewhat strange, he felt himself getting used to having her back. Most of the time when they were together now they were quiet, and though there was still affection between them, neither had tried to find a way for any kind of lovemaking.

He heard a sound, and then another, the sounds of brush being moved. Then he saw a small light, a candle in the kind of lantern he'd made from a sheet of metal when they first arrived in this place. Helga called out his name, and though he was tempted not to answer, he knew she would easily find him, and he had to admit to himself that he had missed her.

"Over here,' he called back.

She was quickly by his side, kneeling and blowing out the candle. "I had to see you. Well, I can't see in this darkness, but be with you, talk to you . . . if only for a few minutes."

"All right. It's good to hear you again, talk to me."

"Abe, something has to change. I'm so unhappy."

"I know it must be hard for you."

"Well, you don't seem so happy anymore either."

They were quiet until she lightly placed her hand on his wound. "Does this still hurt?"

"Only when I move it." He winced slightly as he twisted toward her and spoke.

"Abe, I'll go away from here if I have to."

"I don't think that's . . ."

"She can make me leave. I know she can."

He tried to sit up, gave another small groan and then lay back. "I won't allow that."

"I won't stay if she doesn't accept me. It's too hard for me the way it is."

"I guess I hadn't noticed it much," he said.

Helga felt his face with her hand, then leaned down and kissed his forehead. He touched her cheek with his fingers and then turned his head away.

She stood up quickly, saying, "Something's got to change," and then she was gone. He could hear the brush rustling as she stumbled through it without her light.

Sarah Beth returned on the night she finished her small ceremony. Lefty brought her back to the compound and spent some time with Abe. At first they discussed the things that were being worked out about the land. The government office in Boise was following the Indian agent's advice to place two sections of land in a kind of trust for Hawk Man, with Abe having the rights of administration over the trust agreement. It was going to require that all of them meet together at some point, but the most important thing was that there wasn't going to be any trial or attempt at prosecution over the shooting of the one stranger, and the other one was being held in a prison in Utah, pending a trial.

"You done good,' Lefty said, getting up to leave. "I gave that horse to the right man."

"Thanks, friend. Your horse has done a lot for me."

"Maybe we change your name. Maybe change from Big Bear Man to Happy Horse."

"I think I'd like that," Abe said, holding out his good hand to shake with his friend.

Later that night, Abe was in the bed and Sarah Beth was brushing her hair. "The thing I missed most out there was my hair brush," she said. "Oh I mean besides you."

"I missed you to," he said softly.

"That woman told me to call her Kate, her white woman's name, and she's been like a mother to me, even though she calls me Little Sister. She said now that I'm home again, home with you, we will have to be very good to one another, and to everyone else in order for her medicine to work."

"Good idea," he said.

It was almost two weeks later that Helga brought her newest, just-completed quilt into the dining area. She moved directly to Sarah Beth and placed the quilt on her lap. "For you," she said. "It's your story." And then she left as quickly as she'd come.

Two days later Sarah Beth found Abe down at the stable, brushing Bird, using both hands, but still being very careful with the injured arm.

"Good for you," she said. "Keep moving it."

"I know. It's getting better, soon be almost good as new." He turned back to the horse.

She stood behind him, watching his shoulders work, and then said softly, "Abe, Helga's going to have a baby."

He turned around and faced her. She was looking down. He put one hand on her arm, but she pulled away.

"What are you going to do now?" she asked. Then she hurried away before he could think of anything to say.

End of Book I

To the Reader

First of all, thank you for reading this book. I also want to apologize to those of you who are disappointed by the abruptness of its ending and lack of a conclusion. My only excuse is that the story of Abe, Sarah Beth, and Helga seems too big for only one volume of manageable length - both for the readers to hold in their hands, and for this writer to sustain its development without some kind of a break.

The reason for this has to do with the nature of its sources and my commitment to them. I don't want to take any short-cuts with this material, and I want to pay full attention and homage to its origins and evolution. The original, scriptural story of these three individuals stands at the beginning and foundation of the three largest monotheistic religions in the world today. In the Jewish Torah, the Christian Bible,* and the Islamic Quran, the record of these three lives stands as the source of religious faith and as the essential explanation of their religious beginnings. For this and for other reasons, this story is regarded as both sacred and historically significant, and has attained a unique influence and timelessness all its own.

In this version, the narrative is transposed from ancient times to the period just following the Civil War between the States of America, and is based on the migratory journeys of multitudes of people crossing this continent, both before and after that wrenching conflict in search of improved lives for themselves and their descendants. The challenge in borrowing from this ancient story and its migratory themes has been to find ways to echo not only its resonance over time, but to attempt to demonstrate its plausibility as an essentially human saga in, perhaps, any period of time. If I have fallen short in this endeavor I am not embarrassed at having tried. If in your estimation I have either failed or succeeded, you are welcome to let me know. At this time, I am embarking on Book II of this project, and your comments would be very helpful.

Thank you, Johnny Sundstrom
<siwash@pioneer.net>

---

*   Reference: I have used the King James version of Genesis 12:1-25:10 as a guide.